ROYAL
BRIDES
LUCY MONROE

M&B™ and M&B™ with the Rose Device
are trademarks of the publisher.
Harlequin Mills & Boon Limited, Eton House,
18-24 Paradise Road, Richmond, Surrey TW9 1SR

ISBN: 978 0 263 87535 5

010-1009

Harlequin Mills & Boon policy is to use papers that are
natural, renewable and recyclable products and made from
wood grown in sustainable forests. The logging and
manufacturing processes conform to the legal environmental
regulations of the country of origin.

Printed and bound in Spain
by Litografia Rosés S.A., Barcelona

The Prince's Virgin Wife

LUCY MONROE

A collection of bestselling novels
from some of our favourite writers,
brought to you

With Love

August 2008
BOUGHT BRIDES HELEN BIANCHIN

September 2008
VIRGIN BRIDES LYNNE GRAHAM

October 2008
ROYAL BRIDES LUCY MONROE

November 2008
PASSIONATE BRIDES PENNY JORDAN

Lucy Monroe started reading at age four. After she'd gone through the children's books at home, her mother caught her reading adult novels pilfered from the higher shelves on the book case…alas, it was nine years before she got her hands on a Mills & Boon® romance her older sister had brought home. She loves to create the strong alpha males and independent women that people Mills & Boon® books. When she's not immersed in a romance novel (whether reading or writing it) she enjoys travel with her family, having tea with the neighbours, gardening and visits from her numerous nieces and nephews. Lucy loves to hear from readers: e-mail Lucymonroe@Lucymonroe.com or visit www.LucyMonroe.com

For Elizabeth Eakin, otherwise known as
Lady B…a fabulous reader and one of my dear
LFBJ pals. Thanks so much for your help with
naming the country Isole dei Re for this trilogy.
Hugs, Lucy

CHAPTER ONE

"So, WERE you able to hire her?"

Principe Tomasso Scorsolini paced the Hong Kong hotel suite, his cell phone pressed against his ear and waited with barely concealed impatience to discover if his prey had taken the bait.

"She came to the palace for the interview as agreed and she impressed me very much." Therese's voice rang with approval across the phone lines. "I don't know how you heard about her, but she's a sweet woman and will be good with the children. She really is ideal, but I was not certain at first that she would accept the position."

"Why?" He'd made sure Maggie Thomson had no conflicting loyalties, arranging for her current employers to dispense with her services while at the same time suggesting she consider the position in his household.

"She was concerned about the impact her leaving in a couple of years would have on Annamaria and Gianfranco, particularly in light of Liana's death."

"A couple of years? She assumes she will leave?"

"She has plans to open her own day care center after she has saved enough money. It is why she has taken positions with older children up to this point."

Ah, so she still held onto her dreams. He should not be surprised. Maggie Thomson had a stubborn streak almost as wide as his own. "What did you tell her?"

"I took your advice and introduced her to Gianni and Anna. They liked Miss Thomson immediately and she fell completely under their spell. You know how shy little Annamaria is and yet by the end of the interview, she was sitting in Miss Thomson's lap. I've never seen anything like it." Therese paused as if collecting her thoughts. "I know this is going to sound strange, Tomasso, but it was as if she was their long-lost mother...the connection between the three of them was that strong."

She didn't need to say what they both knew. The connection between the children and their real mother had never been that significant. Liana had not been a nurturer.

"That is good to hear." Very good.

"Yes, well. I told her that if she would commit to a two-year contract, we would provide her with a generous bonus at the end of it to help her with her business."

"Did that sway her?"

"Not at first. She was still concerned about the children, but I explained that when hiring domestic help, a two-year contract *was* a long-term commitment and really better than we might expect to do with someone else."

He had no plans to let Maggie Thomson go in two years, or anytime thereafter, but Therese did not need to know that. "Brilliant. And she accepted?"

"Yes."

"Good." Satisfaction filled him. "Thank you, Therese."

"It was my pleasure, Tomasso."

"Tell Claudio I will see him when I return to Isole dei Re."

"You may well see him before I do." There was something in his sister-in-law's voice that bothered him.

"Are you all right, Therese?"

"Yes, of course. Miss Thomson agreed to begin her duties immediately as you suggested."

"Very good."

"Yes, but I shall miss having the children with me."

He hadn't considered that. "I am sorry, Therese."

"Don't be silly. I enjoy their company, but it is important for them to have a more consistent caretaker in their lives. If you lived here in the palace, it would be different, but since you make your home on another island entirely, I cannot make up for their lack of a mother."

"It sounds like Maggie Thomson will do that nicely."

"For the next two years anyway."

For a lifetime if it all worked out the way he planned. "I thank you again, Therese."

She dismissed her role as unimportant and rang off.

Tomasso flipped his phone shut and smiled to the empty room. It was all coming together.

Better than even he could have anticipated, and projecting a plan's outcome was something he had perfected during his years running Mining and Jewelers.

Apparently his children and Maggie had adored one another on sight and, equally important, she was the same sweet-natured woman she had been in college. He hadn't really expected anything different since reading the report Hawk's agency had compiled on her. It also said she retained other characteristics he remembered from his college days.

According to her past employers, she was efficient, content in the domestic environment and peaceful to be around. Traits he hadn't appreciated nearly enough at the time. He'd been too interested in outward beauty to understand how much her presence meant to him…until it was gone.

He'd taken for granted how smoothly his life had run

when Maggie was his housekeeper. Four years in a volatile marriage with Liana had cured him of that complacency.

The first year after her death, Tomasso had refused to even consider taking another wife, having no desire to repeat his first foray into marital disharmony. But neither did he wish to end up like his father and for the past few months, he'd begun to crave the peaceful ease his older brother had in his marriage to the kind and even-tempered Therese.

Every time Tomasso fantasized about that kind of harmony, he could only picture it with one woman. Maggie Thomson. He could hear her gentle voice reminding him to eat breakfast before leaving the house, could remember her busy hands making sure his life ran smoothly.

He wanted that harmony again, but this time he would not make the mistake of giving her an out.

She'd walked away from him once, saying they had nothing more than a working relationship and one that had no place in her life once he was no longer her boss. He'd accepted that blatant untruth for two reasons. The first was because he knew he had hurt her and even though he'd meant to do anything but, he had felt he owed her the honor of respecting her desire to cut him from her life.

The second was that Liana had been jealous of his relationship with Maggie and quite vocal in her desire for him to sever ties completely with the other woman. The unreasonable jealousy had flattered him at the time. He'd taken it as proof of Liana's passionate love for him. The idiocy of that belief still rankled.

Liana had loved only one person…herself.

He had been the means to her having the lifestyle she wanted. Nothing more. Marry a prince, become a princess. He wondered if knowledge that he was a prince would change Maggie's attitude toward him.

It did with everyone else. Which was why he had attended college under the assumed identity of Tom Prince.

He'd wanted to make relationships based on who he was, not what he was. He'd wanted to prove that he could succeed on his own, not the strength of his family name. He'd proven that, at least. He'd graduated with honors solely on his own merits, but the relationships had been another story.

Unbeknownst to him, Liana had known his royal status all along, and Maggie had walked away from the simple man Tom Prince too easily.

Would she want him as Liana had, once she knew he was of royal blood?

He conceded that it did not matter. She was exactly what *he* wanted in a wife and mother for his children. Why she chose to marry him wouldn't matter because she would still be herself, a woman eminently suitable to make his life more peaceful and to give his children the nurturing they so desperately needed.

He wasn't a fool, though.

He would not base a lifetime commitment on memories six years old. By hiring her to care for his children, he would have a chance to observe Maggie and be certain she was all that he remembered before informing her of his desire to make her his wife. He also wanted to be sure the latent passion that had existed between them had not disappeared and that it was as intense as the one scorching encounter of his memories.

He was not a man who would be comfortable with a wife who did not appeal to that side of his nature.

He refused to be like his father, finding sexual solace outside the marriage bed. He considered that behavior reprehensible and so in fact, did his father, which was why the king had never remarried after one failed attempt following the death of his first wife.

His father had called it the Scorsolini curse. According to King Vincente, Scorsolini men were fated to have one true love. Claudio and Tomasso's mother had been his. After her death, no other woman could hold his interest completely enough to ensure fidelity. He'd married Marcello's mother only months after the death of his queen because he'd got her pregnant.

He had an affair and the usually mild-mannered Flavia had gone ballistic. She had refused to be cuckolded and moved back to Italy with the young Marcello, doing the unthinkable and filing for divorce in the process. Since then, his father had had a string of mistresses.

Tomasso didn't care about his supposed fate. He *never* wanted to love like his father had and end up a widower, always searching to fill an empty void that could never be satisfied.

He knew that he was different from his father. Even a superficial passion would be enough for him to remain faithful. It had been with Liana. Though he'd believed when they married she was his one true love, he'd soon discovered differently.

Yet he had remained faithful to her despite the troubles in their marriage and his discovery that what he had thought was love was nothing more than being blitzed by her outward beauty.

How much easier would it be to maintain fidelity in marriage to a woman he respected, even if he did not love her?

"Papa will be home soon, won't he?"

Maggie smiled and tucked Annamaria into the child-size bed. "Yes, sweetie. Just two more days."

"I miss him."

"I know you do." Maggie brushed the little girl's dark curls away from her face, leaned down and kissed her forehead. "Good night, Anna."

"Good night, Maggie. I'm glad you came."

"Thank you, I am, too."

She turned off the overhead light and left the small night-light glowing before making her way to her own suite of rooms in the opulent home after checking in on Gianfranco one more time. He was asleep…finally, a small lump in the race car bed that was the same diminutive size as Anna's.

Tall for his five years, he would need a big boy bed soon. Maggie wondered if that would fall under her jurisdiction. There were so many questions she wanted to ask her absent employer, not the least of which was why it seemed the entire domestic staff looked to her for direction as if she was the housekeeper, not the nanny?

There was a housekeeper-slash-cook already, two maids and a groundskeeper besides, but they all seemed to turn to her for major decisions and she found that odd.

It was certainly different than in her last two positions, but then she was working for royalty now. They obviously had their own unique way of dealing with the domestic side of life. It felt odd, but she liked the sense of respect she got from her fellow employees and the obvious importance the prince placed on her role in caring for his children.

She closed the door to Gianfranco's room, hoping he and his little sister slept well tonight. Their father had not called as was his norm and it had been difficult settling them both into their beds. Her small charges needed her, even more than the family she had left behind.

Which was not surprising considering the fact that Gianni

and Anna's mother had died and they were both so very young, but it was shocking how much she cared already.

She loved them, truly loved them.

It should be too soon to have such deep feelings for children that she had not given birth to, but she felt an elemental connection to and had from the moment of meeting. She'd been all set to turn down the prince's offer of employment tendered through his sister-in-law, and then she'd met the children and found she simply could not walk away from the need she sensed in them.

She'd agreed to the two-year contract, but her heart was already asking how she thought she could walk away from her small charges when her time was up. She'd been their nanny for only ten days, but in some ways it felt like a lifetime.

She'd lived in more than one foster home growing up, had had different roommates her last couple of years of college, and then been nanny to two different families, but she had never connected to anyone as quickly as she had to these two.

Except Tom Prince.

And that relationship had ended in pain for her, just as this job was going to.

From what she could tell, both Anna and her older brother spent a great deal of time missing their workaholic father. They needed her on so many levels, she was powerless to turn her back on them. Workaholic, or not, the prince couldn't be all bad, not and have such two sweet children and such a caring and obviously approving sister-in-law.

He wasn't exactly neglectful, either. He called the children daily, sometimes twice a day, and spoke to them on a level that showed he understood they were children. She didn't mean to eavesdrop, but Maggie couldn't help but overhear the children's side of the conversations.

She thought he must be a really decent father despite his preoccupation with work.

Her former employer had been much the same. It seemed to be a common enough condition among the world's truly wealthy. She'd been in her last position for two years and could count on one hand the number of major holidays her employers had spent with their children. It wasn't a lifestyle she envied, even if it meant living in luxury and extensive travel.

She'd never been interested in connecting with any of the men she'd met in the world in which she had moved since graduating from college. If she ever married, it would be to a man who knew how to be part of a family, not just provide for one.

She wanted something real, something lasting and warm…the kind of family she'd spent her childhood dreaming about.

She sighed and plopped down on the small, elegant Victorian-style sofa in her sitting room. She was twenty-six and beginning to doubt she'd ever meet a man she wanted to share her life with. That thought didn't hurt nearly as much as the prospect that because of it, she might never have children.

She grabbed the remote and flipped on the television.

She certainly wouldn't meet one in this crowd, that was for sure. She liked Princess Therese, but her husband, the Crown Prince, was every bit as focused on his work as his younger brother. Maggie doubted that would change when the couple had children and wondered if that was why they had not yet had any.

She flipped through the stations until she came across one of her all-time favorite movies—a romance made in the 1940s. She adored it and knew she'd be up until the wee hours watching it. The hero always reminded her of the one man who had made her heart rate soar into the heavens and her body feel like it was on fire.

Unfortunately, just like the man on the screen, Tom Prince had married another woman. A beautiful, sophisticated, sexy woman. The kind of woman that drew every male eye when she walked into a room. The kind of woman Maggie knew she would never be.

Tom had been her employer and housemate in college and in many ways, no matter what she'd said to the contrary when they parted, the closest friend she ever had. She'd been thinking about him a lot lately. Something about Gianni and Anna brought back memories of him and the feelings he sparked inside her.

She'd been having more of the dreams, too…the erotic ones where she relived the sensations she'd known in his arms that fateful night six years ago. She didn't understand the connection and liked it even less.

It had been hard enough losing him to Liana and learning to live without his daily presence in her life *once*. But now she felt like she was going through the withdrawal all over again and she didn't even understand why.

Determined not to think about the past and its pain, she focused on the movie, but for once, her favorite love story could not hold her attention and soon she was lost to memories she couldn't stifle no matter how hard she tried…

Maggie nervously smoothed her hands down her skirt. The letter had said casual attire for the interview, but she had wanted to make a good impression.

So, she'd pulled her long, kinky blond curls into a ponytail and pinned it into a bun, hoping she looked just a little older than her eighteen years. She was wearing a longish twill skirt, the color of wheat, and a classic white button-up blouse she'd bought at the secondhand store the year before to wear to her part-time job as a waitress.

And she'd washed all the scuff marks from her single pair of white sandals, the ones her foster mom had bought her in exchange for mowing the lawn two summers previously. Her nails were clean, but unpainted. Her lightly freckled and very ordinary features were without makeup. Which was a good thing because if she'd been wearing lipstick, she would have chewed it off her bottom lip in nervousness by now.

She needed this job. The salary listed wasn't huge, but the live-in position would make it possible for her to pursue her studies without getting another low-paying job to cover living expenses.

She rang the doorbell and took a hasty step backward when it opened almost immediately to reveal a man who was way younger than she'd expected. In fact, he wasn't much older than her. With curly black hair, a face that could have been chiseled by Michelangelo, blue eyes that would have graced an angel and a body that towered over her with finely honed muscle, he was also drop dead gorgeous.

"There must be… I think I made a mistake." She looked away from his to-die-for body and surveyed the other homes on the tree-lined street.

Had she gotten the number wrong? She pulled the paper from her purse and looked down at the highlighted address. The number was the same as the one beside the open door.

"Are you here about the housekeeping position?" Tall, Dark and Gorgeous asked in a voice that made her stomach flip.

"Um…yes."

He looked her up and down, his expression weighing. "I expected you to be older."

"Me, too."

"You thought you were older?" he asked with a gleam of amusement in his cobalt-blue eyes.

"I thought *you* would be older," she corrected, blushing.

He stepped back and indicated she should enter. "Then we were both destined for a surprise, were we not?"

"I suppose so."

"I'm Tom Prince and you must be Maggie Thomson."

"Yes. It's a pleasure to meet you, Mr. Prince."

"Tom, please."

"All right." She followed him into the living room.

"You have experience keeping house?" he asked as they took seats on opposite sides of a glass coffee table.

Remembering her years taking care of her foster siblings and ailing foster mom, she nodded with vehemence. "Lots."

Then realizing that probably wasn't as specific of an answer as he would like, she proceeded to outline her household duties for the past few years.

His expression was odd. "You took care of the house, the children and your foster mother while working a part-time job?"

"I'm good at multitasking." Hopefully that would be in her favor.

"But now that you are eighteen, you have moved out?"

"Once I turned eighteen I was no longer eligible to be part of the system. Helen couldn't get help for my living expenses, and needed me to leave so she could take another child in."

Knowing that, with all she'd given to her foster mom, Maggie still hadn't meant any more to the older woman than the money she brought in from the state had hurt. She didn't share that bit with Tom though.

His too observant and surprisingly compassionate eyes

said he'd read between the lines anyway. However all he asked was, "The small salary is not a deterrent for you?"

"No. It would be a godsend to tell the truth. My scholarship doesn't stretch to living expenses."

"You are attending university on scholarship?"

"Yes. An academic one." As if there would be any possibility that her average build would somehow have managed to enable her to attain an athletic scholarship. She smiled self-deprecatingly.

"You must be very bright."

That made her shrug. Her intelligence was something she'd always taken for granted. If she hadn't been smarter than the average student, she would have flunked out of high school for lack of time to study between her part-time job and caring for her foster family. "I like school."

"What is your major?"

"Early childhood development."

He didn't laugh like a lot of people did when she told them. For some reason, the idea of going to college to earn a degree so she could care for children seemed amusing to most people.

"What do you want to do?"

"One day, I want to have my own day care center."

"You should take some business courses as well then," he said rather bossily.

But she didn't mind. "I plan to."

He nodded his approval at this and the interview went on from there. Surprisingly they had a lot in common. Neither liked to watch television very much, they both liked the same authors and they shared a similar sense of humor. It was nice.

She would have thought she would be tongue-tied around him, but she wasn't because although he was the

most beautiful man she'd ever met, he didn't act at all conceited or cocky about his looks.

She was getting ready to go when he said, "I have one
last thing I need to discuss with you before I can make
my decision."

"Yes?"

For the first time in forty-five minutes he looked less
than totally self-composed. "I think we could be friends."

She nodded eagerly.

"I like you, Maggie."

"I like you, too," she said breathlessly.

He got very serious. "The position is a live-in one."

"Yes, I know. That's perfect for me."

He nodded. "If I hire you, you have to promise you'll
never attempt to take our friendship beyond that. From
your letter of application, I thought you would be older…
I didn't think this would be an issue I would have to bring
up, but I see that I must and there is no benefit in putting
it off. I don't date people who work for me. Ever."

She stared at him and didn't know what to say. He
seemed awfully young to have such a policy, but she certainly didn't expect him to break it with her.

When she said nothing, his expression turned even
grimmer. "If I wake up to find you naked in my bed, I will
fire you on the spot."

She couldn't help it, she burst out laughing. The very
thought of her doing something so bold…so absurd…was
more than she could take. She laughed so hard, she fell against
the wall, her head shaking in negation to his comment.

Realizing that he was frowning, she forced herself to
stop chortling. "I'm sorry. I shouldn't have laughed."

"I am quite serious."

That was weird, the way his speech patterns got so

formal sometimes, like the informal speak of a college student wasn't natural for him.

"You've had that happen before?" she asked with disbelief.

"Yes," he said shortly.

Wow. Bummer.

"I promise on both of my parents' graves that I will never climb into your bed, naked or otherwise."

"Both of your parents are dead?"

"Yes."

"I am sorry."

"Me, too, but thank you."

"You'll never try to seduce me?" he asked, as if there was still some doubt in his mind.

It took every bit of her self-control not to laugh again, but she managed it. "When you know me better, you'll realize what a ridiculous thought that is, but please believe me when I say that you don't ever have to worry about that kind of thing from me."

"Why, are you gay?"

She gasped and then closed her eyes, trying hard to stay collected. She opened them again. "No. I'm not gay. I'm not the type to try to seduce *anybody,* male or female," she said for good measure.

He still looked worried and she sighed.

"Look, you said you thought I must be pretty intelligent. Well, I am. Definitely smart enough to realize you are way out of my league. I don't know where you come from that you have women falling all over themselves to have sex with you, but I was raised to keep out of men's beds until I got married and that's exactly what I intend to do. Even if you were a reincarnation of John Wayne, I would not climb into your bed and beg you to have sex with me. Okay?"

"John Wayne? You lust after the Duke?"

She rolled her eyes. "Never mind who I fantasize about…just don't worry about it being you."

Suddenly a smile lit his face and she just about fell against the wall again, this time from the sheer animal impact, but managed to stay upright. Barely.

"You're hired."

CHAPTER TWO

SHE moved in a week later.

The job was an easy one. Tom was not a slob and although he was clearly used to money, he didn't require Cordon Bleu meals. She had plenty of time to pursue her studies and take care of his domestic needs. On top of that, he made her feel like his house was her home.

All she had to do was perform her job to his satisfaction and she had the run of the place. He was adamant she didn't limit her time at home to cleaning and then staying in her room. It was very similar to living in the foster care system, where she'd figured out early that if she performed well and made herself indispensable, she'd always have a home.

Mostly it had worked for her.

The only drawback to the perfection of her arrangement with Tom was the fact that she fell totally, hopelessly, forever-after in love with him. And he'd made it clear he wanted nothing more than friendship with her…ever.

His girlfriends were beautiful, sophisticated women that made Maggie feel worse than ordinary. Every single one of them underscored a truth she could not deny: even if she didn't work for him, Tom Prince would *never* look at her as anything but a friend.

Then halfway through his last year of graduate school and her sophomore year at the university, he broke up with his latest girlfriend. Instead of starting to date another drop-dead beauty, he took Maggie with him when he wanted companionship…out to dinner, to a movie, to a sports event, or even to a party.

The feelings she'd had during that month were still vivid after six long years of trying to forget.

It had been a cross between Heaven and Hell. She loved the extra time they spent together and her susceptible heart reveled in having his attention all to herself. But she never forgot his warning that he'd fire her on the spot if she tried to pursue anything more than friendship with him. Not that she would. She wasn't such a fool as to think that the change in his dating pattern meant anything special for her.

One night all of that changed, though.

She was curled up on the plush leather sofa in the living room, studying for her midterms, when he came home.

Looking totally yummy in a pair of dark jeans and Ralph Lauren sweater over a navy-blue T-shirt, he made her feel things that turned her virginal ideals on their head.

She just hoped the sensual hunger did not show on her face. "Hi. You eating in tonight?"

He dropped his books on the table by the doorway. "I thought we could both eat out."

"I wish I could," she said sincerely. "I have to study." She indicated her books and notes surrounding her on the sofa. "Midterms."

"You work too hard. You need a break."

"No, I don't." Life was easier for her now than it had been in a very long time. "You're just spoiled."

"And you are the one who spoils me." He moved closer to her, his rich, masculine scent tantalizing senses always on edge when he was near. "Let me spoil *you* and take you to dinner."

"I can't. Really, Tom. I have three tests tomorrow."

He shook his head, his expression disapproving. "You would not have so many tests if you did not take extra classes."

"I take the maximum the scholarship allows for. I want to be done early. It's better for me that way. I can start working sooner."

"If you would let me pay for your living expenses until graduation, you would not have this worry."

"No can do. What you do for me now is enough. Too much sometimes."

"You are too stubborn, you mean. And I do nothing for you that you have not earned."

"Well, since you won't be living here next year, you can't say I would be earning my keep if you provided it, could you?"

"Can you not consider it another scholarship?"

She wasn't the only stubborn one. "No."

"What are you going to do next year?"

"Get a job, or two, and find an apartment. I think one of the girls in my economics class wants to be my roommate." She hated talking about the next year, when Tom would be gone.

It hurt to know that for all intents and purposes he would be walking out of her life as easily as he had walked in. While she had a horrible suspicion she would miss him forever.

"There is no reason why you cannot stay here."

"There is every reason. It's not my house."

"It is mine and I want a caretaker."

"No, you don't. You want to give me charity and I won't accept. Please stop pushing it." She hated arguing with him as much as she hated thinking about never seeing him again.

He grinned, his expression flashing from annoyed dominant male to smiling confidence. "I am very good at getting my way."

"I noticed. I *have* lived with you for a while now."

He plucked her book out of her hand and tossed it to the end of the couch and then grabbed her wrists and tugged her up. "Then you should accept that if I want you to have dinner out with me tonight, that is the most likely scenario for our evening."

She landed with a thud against his hard male body and gasped before scrambling as far back as his hold would allow. She tried to break it, but though he wasn't hurting her in the slightest, there was no chance. "I need to study."

"You need to eat. What can that hurt?"

"We'll be gone too long. You never just go eat somewhere."

"So, maybe there is a movie playing that I want to see…you need a break. I said so."

"And because you said so it must be true?"

"Yes, this is true."

She rolled her eyes. "You're awfully arrogant for a man who isn't even twenty-five."

"I was bred to it."

"I guess." She never asked about his background because he made it clear it was not a subject he wished to discuss, but it didn't take a rocket scientist to know he came from major wealth.

"Why don't you ask one of your friends to go to the movie with you?"

"I am. I am asking you."

"I'm your housekeeper."

"You are also my friend."

Maybe…but somehow she didn't see them exchanging

phone calls and Christmas cards after he finished graduate school and moved on. And that was what decided her. She had only a finite amount of time left in Tom Prince's life. She needed to take advantage of it.

"All right. I'll study when we get home. Please tell me the movie is an early showing."

"Your wish is my command, little Maggie." He sealed his promise with a kiss.

On her lips.

He'd never done that before.

The logical part of her brain told her that kind of salute was common for him, even if she'd always been adept at avoiding any sort of touching between them.

But her body had other ideas, and lips that had kissed only one other boy before him went instantly soft against his, parting in an invitation that was as old as time and equally unmistakable. Being the natural predator that he was, he accepted the deepening of the kiss with alacrity.

His tongue slipped between her lips and slid along hers. She'd dreamed of tasting him, but no dream could compare to the rich ambrosia of his mouth. His lips and tongue explored her with such effective mastery, she moaned in pure pleasure. He made a feral sound low in his throat that sent shivers throughout her body, and pulled her forward, tugging her hands around his hips.

Her fingers convulsed in his sweater, gripping it so tightly it would have ripped if it hadn't been so well made.

His hands came around her and pressed against her tailbone, bringing her into intimate contact with his lower body. She felt his rigid length hard against her belly, but couldn't quite work out in her brain what it meant. She was too busy being devoured by an expert kisser. And loving it.

Some small part of her sanity remained and the muffled

voice of reason asked her what she thought she was doing, but she had no answer. A far more strident voice, that of unrequited love, told her she would never have such a chance again. It urged her to experience all of him that she could.

Her heart and her clamoring body demanded compliance to that voice.

Tom did something with his hand against her back and her knees buckled.

Suddenly she was tumbling backward and he was going with her. She landed with one hip on the sofa and one hip off. Her equilibrium wasn't up to keeping the balance and she and Tom tumbled to the floor. She landed on top of him, but amazingly he'd kept their lips locked together. He growled and flipped her under him, his hard thigh settled between her legs. She went utterly still, feelings rushing along her nerve endings that made her tremble and yank her head away from his.

It was too much.

She clamped her lips shut on a tiny whimper, but it escaped anyway.

He looked down at her, the angles of his face drawn with an emotion she did not recognize. "Did I hurt you?"

She shook her head, unable to speak.

"You whimpered."

She stared up at him, mute, her legs separating just a tiny bit in an involuntary gesture that she immediately tried to rectify, but could not. He had settled more firmly between her legs and pressing her own back together only had the effect of hugging his masculine thigh tighter to her.

She gasped and closed her eyes against the disgust she knew would be in his. She'd promised never to do this, but it was as if her brain had lost control of her body and it had a definite will of its own.

The fact that it was following her heart did not help her self-control.

"Open your eyes, Maggie," he demanded in a tone she doubted many people would have the strength to disobey. "Look at me."

She steeled herself to deal with his anger and opened them. "I'm sorry," she managed to whisper.

Far from being angry, his eyes were heated with a look he'd never directed her way before. "Why?"

Her gaze slid to his lips before returning to his eyes. "For kissing you."

"I kissed you."

But she had invited more. She'd been the one to open her mouth. She simply shook her head, unwilling to put her culpability into words.

"You want me." He sounded as if the thought had never once occurred to him, but she could still see no evidence of anger that she had broken their agreement. "Since when?"

She turned her head away, her pride refusing to give him an answer. The sofa was so close she could see the grain of the leather, but as a distraction from his presence it failed miserably.

He tugged her chin with implacable fingers until she was once again looking at him. "I want you, too."

"You do?" she asked in utter shock. "That's not possible."

He laughed and moved against her, making her aware of more than just the hardness of his thigh. "I'd say it's very possible."

As the implication of what she felt sank in, she blushed hot crimson.

He laughed again and then his mouth lowered over hers. This time, it was he that demanded entry to her mouth with his tongue. The kiss was incendiary, burning her sense of reality to ashes around her.

All she could do was feel. Every touch was new for her, every caress a step into an unknown but amazing world. One where passion ruled and desire was a tangible presence surrounding her.

He traced the curves of her face and neck with barely there fingertips. But when he reached her breast, his touch changed, growing more insistent and he cupped her soft curves possessively through the thin fabric of her worn flannel shirt. It was so intimate, she shuddered from the impact while he growled his approval of her braless state.

He began to knead her with a knowing finesse that made her ache in her most private place.

She needed to touch him, too, wanted to feel his skin with no barriers between them. She yanked his T-shirt out of his jeans so she could get her hands under it and his sweater. His skin was hotter than she expected, emanating warmth that made her fingertips burn deliciously.

And the hair on his chest was silky smooth. She touched everywhere she could reach, exploring his tight body with hungry innocence. When she found the nubs of his hard nipples, she stopped and circled them with her thumbs, then brushed over them, primal delight shimmering through her at his passionate response.

She was only vaguely aware of him unbuttoning the front of her shirt and peeling it back.

She noticed when his hand touched her bare skin though. Her whole awareness was consumed with the feel of his hands on her bare flesh, as her nipples hardened almost painfully and small goose bumps broke out on her flesh.

He kissed along her jaw and down her neck. "You're so soft, Maggie, so delicious."

Her only response was another soulful whimper as his mouth found her breast and then a scream as he began to suckle the nipple. Her hands fell to her sides, thudding against the carpet. She twisted her head back and forth as a mewling sound came from her throat that she could barely recognize as herself.

Then speech burst forth from her, words she did not plan on uttering tumbling from her lips in a breathless cascade. "Oh, wow! I knew it would be wonderful, but this beats anything. I feel so much, like my whole body is buzzing from a beesting."

He laughed, pulling his mouth from her nipple. "I will gladly sting your petals and drink your nectar with my tongue."

The erotic words shivered through her and she moaned.

He smiled darkly and went back to sucking her tenderized flesh. She tried to arch off the floor, but his body held her down.

"Tom…that's so good, oh, it feels so *good*…" The word drew out long and low on a moan she didn't even try to stifle.

She wasn't sure how it happened, but he lost his T-shirt and sweater and then she felt his bare skin against hers. It was amazing and things were happening inside her she'd never experienced before…a feeling of spiraling tension she didn't know how to handle. It just grew tighter and tighter and then he unzipped her jeans and slipped his hand inside.

His fingertips trespassed the top of her panties, touching her mons and then slipping between her swollen lips to caress her sweetest spot. Something happened inside her. It was like a rocket exploding and she screamed as her body bowed with unbearable pleasure.

"That's right, *bella*. Let me feel your pleasure."

She stared at him, her body convulsing as his fingers continued their ministrations. Who was Bella? Her thoughts splintered as one fingertip barely slipped inside her and he pressed the heel of his hand against her clitoris, prolonging the bliss.

He pushed further inside and she felt a stab of pain at the same time as he said, "Maggie!" his voice laced with stunned disbelief.

"You are a virgin?" he demanded as he withdrew his hand from her body, but his hand remained in possession of her most private flesh.

"Yes."

Something strange flashed in his eyes and he started whispering in a language she didn't understand and pressing kisses all over her face and throat. Overwhelmed by sensation, she didn't realize what was happening until he started pulling her jeans off.

"Tom?"

"What, *bella?*"

His use of the other woman's name again brought her back to herself with a jarring thump. Of course he was thinking she was another woman. He wouldn't want *her* otherwise, but she couldn't give him her virginity on such a pretext. *Could she?*

"What are you doing?" she asked stupidly.

He laughed, the sound husky and strained. "Making love to you."

But it wasn't love. It was sex and she didn't know if she could go through with it. "I'm a virgin."

"I know."

"I mean I'm not on the Pill, or anything."

He had her jeans down to her knees and he tugged them to her ankles. "I have condoms."

"But…" She put her hand down to shield herself even though she was still wearing panties. "Please, Tom. Wait."

He stopped and looked at her, his expression frightening in its intensity. "You do not want to go all the way?"

"You called me Bella."

Uncomfortable chagrin flashed in the depths of his cobalt blue eyes, confirming her fears she was a substitute for another woman. "Well…yes. You need me to explain?"

"No!" The very thought of hearing about some other woman he had loved while she lay practically naked below him was repugnant. "Absolutely not."

Now he looked confused. "Then what is the problem?"

Was he really that dense? "I don't want to make love with you while you're thinking of one of your girlfriends."

"I would never do such a thing," he said, his whole body going stiff with affront.

She wished with all her might she could believe him, but what had he just been doing if not that very thing?

Driven by fear of playing substitute and what making love would ultimately entail physically, she said with pure honesty, "I'm not ready."

"I think you are."

"You said you'd fire me if I ever tried to seduce you. What would happen if we had sex right now?" she asked.

His expression turned grim, disappointment flashing in his blue eyes. "It would no doubt ruin a good friendship," he said cynically.

Despite her protests, that was not what she had wanted to hear. Pain lanced through her. "I guess you're right. It would be stupid to make love, then. I can't afford to lose my job over a single night of lust."

She hated saying the words, no matter how true they were.

He jerked back from her, an impenetrable emotionless

mantle settling over him. "I will not push you into doing something you believe would be damaging to you," he said stiffly.

"I know that."

He did not reply, but moved to sit on the sofa. She could not see his expression because his head was down and his big body shuddered with several heavy breaths.

Without the passion to lose herself in, she became embarrassed and quickly redressed. She stood up, awkward and unsure what to say.

After a few seconds, even his breathing was under control. When he looked at her, there was nothing in his gaze to tell her what he might be thinking. He simply sat there in silence with his hands dangling between his jean-clad legs.

"Tom, I, uh…"

"If I found you naked in my bed, I would not fire you." That was all he said and then he got up and walked out of the room without another word.

A second later, the front door opened and shut and she was completely alone in a house that seemed to echo with all that had not been said.

Had he really wanted her?

Who was Bella?

She took his place on the couch, tears burning her eyes. Had she just avoided a monumental mistake or made the worst one of her life?

Those questions along with his words played inside Maggie's head throughout the following week.

They popped into her consciousness first thing in the morning when she woke up in the morning and bedeviled her throughout the day and then made it hard to sleep each night. When she did sleep, she dreamed of him and the pleasure he'd given her.

She would wake up aching between her legs and craving

him. Her desire for him grew to unbearable heights. Two things held her back from jumping into his bed: the memory of him calling her by another woman's name and the fact that he was rarely around. Being honest with herself, she had to admit that if the latter were not the case, the former probably wouldn't even matter.

He hadn't dated a Bella that she'd known of, but when Maggie had stayed on as caretaker of his house the past summer, he had gone home. He could have dated anyone then. Had he fallen in love with Bella and she dropped him?

It would explain why he hadn't been as focused on his relationships with women this year, why he'd only had one girlfriend and he'd broken up with her when she started getting serious. Maggie hated the thought of being a substitute for another woman. However, the temptation to try to capture his affection for herself through passion became more irresistible with every passing day. Particularly as Tom grew more distant and spent less and less time around her.

He wanted her and he'd practically invited her to his bed. Those were two facts she simply could not dismiss from her mind.

Finally the fear of losing what she did have of him decided for her. It was after eleven already and Tom wasn't home. He'd called and said not to worry about dinner, that he had a study group he was going to. On a Friday night. Like he had ever attended one of those before. He was avoiding her and she couldn't take it any longer.

She'd known it would be hard to watch him walk away at the end of spring, she hadn't known it would be impossible to live in the same house and lose what she had of him anyway. Right or wrong, she was going to sleep with him and she just hoped it would regain the closeness they'd shared before the encounter in the living room. It was worth any risk to have a future with the man she loved…even knowing that future might be extremely short-lived.

She donned her nightgown, nowhere near bold enough to actually climb naked into his bed, and turned out the house lights except one in the hall. Then she walked into his dark, empty bedroom with her heart pounding a mile a minute. She had no idea how she would have survived doing this if he'd actually been home.

The prospect of him finding her in his bed seemed much less daunting than to have to go to him and explain what she wanted. He was smart. He'd figure it out.

Even so, she got beneath the covers gingerly, feeling like a thief or something. But he had told her he would not fire her if he found her naked in his bed. She clung to that thought as she snuggled into his pillow, inhaling his scent. They would be intimate tonight and then this awful, empty void inside her chest would be gone.

As she lay there waiting for him, her week of sleepless nights caught up with her and unbelievably, her eyes grew heavy. Her last memory was looking at his digital clock to see that it was now after midnight.

She woke up to whispered voices on the other side of the bed. The mattress dipped at the same time as the small bedside lamp was clicked on and she gasped at what the light revealed.

Tom had his hand on a woman's shoulder. A gorgeous brunette with deep brown eyes, her blouse unbuttoned to reveal perfect curves encased in black lace.

"Maggie, what are you doing here?" Tom demanded, his blue eyes wide with shock, his hair obviously mussed from what they'd been doing before coming into the room.

"Sleeping," she blurted out blankly.

An explanation for her motives in being there was totally beyond her and Maggie's heart shattered while the beautiful brunette looked at her like a particularly nasty bug caught under her shoe.

The light of understanding dawned in Tom's blue gaze and along with it a wary chagrin that hurt as much as his new girlfriend's sneering regard.

"Maggie, I…" For the first time in eighteen months she saw Tom Prince at a total loss for words, but his girlfriend wasn't.

"Why is your housekeeper sleeping in your bed?" she asked Tom, her voice laced with suspicion.

"I forgot to tell her I was coming home tonight. It's wash day. Her bedding must have been unavailable." As excuses thought off the top of the head and given without the least advanced warning, it was a pretty good one.

However, the knowledge he didn't want the other woman to know Maggie might have another reason for being in his bed burned through her like acid.

The beautiful woman's lips pursed in disapproval. "I should think she'd sleep on the sofa, then."

"Yes. I should have," Maggie said with quiet dignity. She stared at Tom, her eyes accusing. "It was a big mistake to come in here."

"The timing was unfortunate," he replied, a wealth of meaning in his words.

"Most unfortunate," the brunette agreed. "However, the problem can now be rectified, can't it?"

"Of course." Maggie climbed from the bed, glad she'd worn her white cotton gown.

If she'd been naked, she wasn't sure she could have survived the humiliation. As it was, she felt angry and mortified, tears burning the back of her throat. She'd been such an idiot not to realize a man like Tom Prince wanting her could only be a temporary aberration.

Refusing to justify herself, and frankly incapable of saying another word, she spun on her heel and rushed from the room. She sprinted down the hall to her own room and rushed inside, slamming the door and locking it before collapsing on the floor and giving into the pain mushrooming inside her.

She'd been so stupid to think he really wanted her. She'd thought he was avoiding her because he couldn't handle the fact she'd said no, when in fact he'd simply found another woman and had been spending time with her. Her foolish dreams mocked her with painful indictment.

But he hadn't bothered to tell her he'd found someone else. Probably because in his mind it wasn't someone "else" but merely someone. What he'd said hadn't meant anything more to him than a reassurance about her job after the embarrassing debacle the week before. His comment hadn't been an invitation at all. It couldn't have been, not with him going out with another woman immediately after.

It had all been a product of her overactive imagination. Nothing more. But he shouldn't have said it if he didn't mean it. It wasn't fair. Maggie felt like she was going to be sick, but she swallowed down her bile. Instead, for the first time in years, she let the silent tears flow.

In that moment, she hated Tom Prince as much as she loved him.

CHAPTER THREE

THE next morning, Maggie woke feeling like she had an empty hole in her chest. Her relationship with Tom was irrevocably altered and she knew now without the shadow of a doubt that her feelings for him could never be returned. There would always be another beautiful woman waiting around the corner for men like Tom Prince.

She would have to find a roommate sooner than she had expected…and another job. It wouldn't be easy, most of the part-time jobs that worked around student hours had been filled at the beginning of the year, but she had no choice.

She walked on silent feet into the kitchen, not wanting to wake the other occupants of the house. Unfortunately, Tom was standing near the coffeepot waiting for it to finish brewing when she entered.

He eyed her warily. "Good morning."

"Is it?" she asked in a flat tone. She supposed for him, a highly sexed male whose sexual fast had ended the night before, it was.

He winced. "I am sorry about last night."

"Are you?"

"Yes. It was unfortunate."

"That's one way of putting it."

"I did not mean for you to be embarrassed that way."

Was that all he thought had happened? That she'd been embarrassed? She wished. He'd broken her heart and, like Humpty Dumpty, not all the king's horses and all the king's men could put it back together again.

"Liana doesn't know you came to my bed to make love. She believed my excuse last night."

"It was a clever story. You think fast on your feet in these situations. Are you sure you haven't had a little practice at it?" she asked with unusual cynicism.

And did he really think that it would make her feel better to know the other woman saw her as such a noncompetitor that she'd swallowed the story whole?

"Do not be sarcastic. Please. It is not like you and I have said I am sorry."

"And that is supposed to make it all better?"

"Yes," he informed her with breathtaking arrogance. "We did not have a relationship. I broke no promises. You should not be so upset."

Pain that should not be possible considering how numb she felt in her misery sliced through her. "No. We didn't...don't have a relationship, but you told me you wouldn't fire me if I came to your bed."

His face cleared as if finally he understood what was upsetting her. "And I will not," he said as if he deserved a medal or something. "It was a simple misunderstanding."

She shook her head at his misreading of the situation. "I'm going to be looking for another job today."

He frowned in irritation. "You cannot."

"I can."

"Not over this. There is no reason. It was a foolish mistake we would both be better off forgetting."

"There is every reason. *I* can't forget it. I'm sorry."

"I do not want your apology. I want you to stay on as my housekeeper."

"How can I?"

"You are being unreasonable. You have no reason to be embarrassed or want to leave. As far as I'm concerned, last night never happened."

"Does Liana know that?"

"I did not mean—"

"I know what you meant."

"It is inappropriate for you to comment on my private life in that way."

"Pardon me. I guess it's a good thing I'll be looking for other employment, then, isn't it? I'm obviously not as discreet as you need me to be."

"This morning is an aberration. One I intend to forget."

Just like she had been forgotten when a beautiful woman had come along to usurp her in his sexual desires.

"Have you considered it will not be so easy to find another job?"

"Yes."

"At least agree to stay until you find something else."

"Fine."

She'd ended up staying until the end of the semester as she'd originally planned, because finding another job to work with her tight school schedule had been impossible. But things changed between them.

She still took care of the domestic side of his life, but she spent a lot more time on campus, at the library and with the few friends she'd made. She now prepared most of his meals ahead of time and left instructions for heating. When he wanted Liana to dine with him, she made the extra portions without complaint, but never shared another meal with him herself. Not even breakfast.

Thankfully Liana was not a local college student, so she wasn't there often, but her presence could be felt in the daily constraint between Tom and Maggie.

When he asked the other woman to marry him, Maggie was not surprised, but being prepared for it did not soften the blow, and her heart bled.

He invited her to the wedding and she told him they didn't have that kind of relationship, that she didn't plan to see him again after school ended for the summer. He was her boss, not her friend and when school got out, he would no longer be even that.

For once, he had not stubbornly insisted on getting his own way, which said all she needed to know about how he really saw her.

She'd worked out a job and living arrangements by the end of the semester and moved out a week before he did. She did not bother giving him her new address and did not ask for information on where he planned to live after graduation.

She would not be able to handle seeing him married to the other woman, but she hoped he was happy. She loved him too much to ever wish otherwise.

She attended the graduation ceremony though, sitting high in the bleachers where he would not see her watching him receive his master's degree with honors. He'd worked hard to be at the top of his class.

She clapped enthusiastically when his name was called, but was gone from the stands by the time the graduates left their designated seating to join the crowd.

She'd never seen Tom Prince again, but she'd never been able to forget him, either.

Some women only fell in love once, or so she'd been told, and she figured she was one of them. He'd married a woman worthy of his incredible looks and dynamic personality, but there was a part of Maggie's heart that would always belong to him.

Maggie had only been asleep for about forty-five minutes when the feel of a small body climbing into either side of her bed woke her. She opened her eyes. "Gianni?"

"Anna got scared, Maggie. She wants to sleep with you."

The little girl snuggled up to Maggie's back, giving credence to her brother's words.

"And you do, too?"

Gianni nodded in the shadowy dark of the room. "I had a bad dream."

"I miss Papa," Anna said from behind Maggie.

Maggie was too tired herself after staying up with her memories and the movie to argue. She merely cuddled them both close and slipped back into sleep herself.

However, two hours later, after the third small and pointy elbow poked a sensitive body part, she carefully climbed out of her bed and went in search of somewhere else to sleep.

Both children were sleeping too soundly for her to willingly wake them and put them back in their own bed, but she wasn't sure what to do with herself.

Their beds were much too short for a grown person, even a woman of her no more than average height. The Victorian-style sofa in her sitting room was no longer than a love seat and no better a proposition. To her knowledge, the only other bed made up was in the master suite.

She stumbled sleepily down the hall to Anna and Gianni's father's room. He would never know she'd slept there. She'd get up in the morning and wash the sheets and replace them and when he returned the next day, he would be none the wiser.

She tossed the extra decorative pillows from the bed onto the floor and slid between the sheets. There was something vaguely familiar about the scent on the pillow where she laid her head, but she was too tired to work out what it was.

Tomasso let himself into his home quietly, forcing a brain muddled by lack of sleep and other things to remember the alarm codes to allow his entry without setting off sirens. He'd pushed himself mercilessly for the last five days so he could finish his business early and come home. He missed his children and he was impatient to see Maggie again, to find out if she was all that he remembered.

He'd gone totally without sleep for the last thirty-six hours, catching only a catnap on the plane between bouts of work. He didn't want to go into his office for a couple of days and that meant getting ahead on everything. He'd taken meds for the motion sickness he got flying when he was too tired, and then forgotten he'd taken them and had a glass of wine with his dinner and a neat Scotch whiskey an hour later.

He'd never been drunk in his entire thirty years, but he thought this graceless fumbling was as close as he had come to doing so.

Nevertheless, he scaled the stairs with a sense of anticipation and relief he had not felt in a very long time. Tomorrow Maggie would learn she was working for him. He had no idea how she would react to that news, but now that she was bonded with the children, he did not believe her first reaction would be to quit her job.

He had planned it that way of course, doing his best to stack the odds in his favor, like he did with any business deal. Unlike his first marriage, where he had allowed lust and foolish emotion to cloud his judgment, he planned to approach the situation with Maggie from the same perspective he did business. With cool, calculated reason and an intent to win.

Regardless of how she reacted to learning she was working for Tom Prince again, or that he was really Principe Tomasso Scorsolini of Isole dei Re, he had no intention of letting her walk away from him a second time.

He dropped his briefcase in the study connected to his bedroom and his carryall in the room beyond. He pressed a small button on the panel beside the door and low-level recessed lighting came on. Even so, it felt glaring to his bloodshot eyes. He was never taking that antinausea medication again.

He was loosening his tie as his gaze landed on the pile of pillows on the floor. His foggy brain could not work out why they would be there. His staff was impeccable and his children far too respectful to have had a pillow fight in his bedroom, even assuming the new nanny would let them.

Frowning over that mystery, he peeled off his jacket and hung it over the suit valet while his gaze skimmed the rest of his room. As it landed on his bed, he stopped still in his tracks.

The bed was occupied.

Who would have the temerity to invade his sanctuary? No woman he knew could make it past his security and his staff were too loyal to help any woman intent on snagging a royal lover and/or husband.

And no one, man or woman, would have been expecting him to sleep in his bed tonight. As far as anyone but his personal security team and pilot was concerned, Tomasso was still out of the country on business.

He moved closer to the bed to get a closer look. He had to brush back the mass of curling blond hair to reveal the woman's features. He did it carefully, so as not to wake her.

Disbelief warred with a feral sense of purpose as his brain identified the intruder.

Maggie.

What was she doing in his bed?

Memories of another bed, another time washed over him.

They'd shared a scorching kiss and he had come very close to making love to her. But she'd been a virgin and she'd hesitated at the last step. He'd wanted her so badly, he was shaking with it, but she had chosen her job over him.

His ego had taken a blow and he'd been both disappointed and angry, but he'd told her he wouldn't fire her if she changed her mind. Then he'd spent the next week avoiding her and trying to get his libido back under control.

He'd seen their passion as a mistake and was acutely grateful she'd refused to go all the way once he cooled down. Maggie hadn't been his type back then. She was too ordinary, too innocent and sweet. He went for gorgeous women with sophisticated tastes and a similar outlook on life. He'd thought that was what he wanted, but he'd learned that kind of woman came with a cost.

It was one he would not pay again.

He wanted the simplicity and kindness the woman in his bed had once represented in his life.

One night, six years ago, she had climbed into his bed by way of invitation, but he'd brought Liana home with him and in doing so lost any chance he'd ever had with Maggie.

She was in his bed again. A wholly unlooked-for second chance to rectify the mistakes of the past.

His brain told him there was something wrong with that scenario, that she didn't even know she was working for him, so she could not be extending any kind of invitation here. Her presence in his bed was no doubt explained by something as prosaic as the excuse he had made up to tell Liana six years ago.

But he didn't like that logical conclusion.

Okay, so his brain was a bit fuzzy, but even he could see that Maggie Thomson's presence in his bed was fate. She belonged to him. He should have seen it before. She even bore his name, or a derivative of it, but it meant she was his. Of course it did.

No. Wait. He was supposed to test her out…to see if she fit his life as well as she had before.

But how better to test her than to share her bed? That was important. It was key, even. He already knew from Therese that Maggie and his children were a good fit.

His mind worked sluggishly with arguments for and against sharing the bed with his new nanny while he finished undressing, but in the end it was physical exhaustion that decided him. He was too tired and muddled to worry about finding another place to sleep. She'd opted to use his bed. She could share it.

He slid naked between the sheets. He'd never worn pajamas. He wasn't about to start tonight. Yet as tired as he was, he did not immediately go to sleep, but turned to watch Maggie's soft features in repose. Her lips were slightly parted, perfect for kissing.

Would she mind if he kissed her good night? He was a prince. Of course she wouldn't mind. He'd never had a woman deny him a kiss, not once.

He slid toward her, his tired body reacting to her sweet feminine fragrance with surprising strength. By the time he was close enough to kiss her sleep-relaxed mouth, he was hard and aching, his body taut with need.

He pressed his lips to hers in a chaste kiss.

Her eyes opened and she looked at him as if he were an apparition. "Tom?"

"Yes, little Maggie." Tomorrow would be soon enough to explain who he was.

She relaxed again, as if his presence did not bother her at all. Her eyes slid shut. "That was nice," she whispered.

So he kissed her again, and this time she responded with drowsy generosity, parting her lips further so he could find his way inside.

He kissed her with his tongue, tasting the mouth that had haunted his dreams for far too long. She moaned softly against his lips and her small hands began exploring his body the way they had that night six years ago. He deepened the kiss with passion he hadn't felt for too damn long. She tasted perfect, she felt perfect, and he craved her like he'd never craved culmination with a woman before.

But even as confused as his brain was with exhaustion and the combined effects of the alcohol and the meds, he knew there was something not right about this.

Calling on the last vestiges of his sanity and self-control, he broke the kiss. She made a sound of protest and pressed kisses along his jaw, searching for reconnection to his mouth. His body jerked with need as her hand drifted down his stomach and brushed the hair above his sex.

"Maggie, *bella*….do you know what you are doing?"

Her eyes stayed closed, but her lips curved in a sensuous smile. "Oh, yes. I'm kissing you." And she did it again, this time right on his mouth with unerring accuracy.

He forced himself to break contact again. "Who am I, *bella?*"

"Tom." Her brows drew together in a frown. "Don't call me Bella. I don't like it."

"All right."

Her eyes opened, only a slit, but he could see the gray of her irises. "Kiss me again, Tom. I like it when you kiss me…and do other things."

The woman was a minx. Even though she talked like a wanton, she had an air of innocence that tantalized him. Her touches were not those of a woman who had pleased many men and knew how to do it. That knowledge excited him more than if she'd wrapped her fingers around him and brought him to climax.

"Is it safe?" he made himself ask, not sure if he could stop if she said *no.*

"It's always safe with you. Only you," she whispered against his lips and kissed him again, sending her tongue to mate with his in untutored enthusiasm.

Satisfaction surged through Tomasso.

Like him, she remembered how good it had been and she wanted it again too.

This time though, she was no frightened virgin. He had no regret at the thought. He wasn't sufficiently in control of himself tonight to initiate an innocent and had, in fact, never done so before. He had no desire to improvise with his brain at best in marginal control of his body.

She ran the tip of her tongue along his bottom lip and he lost it, flipping her beneath him and devouring her mouth with a need that had gone unmet for too long. Maggie went stiff as if unsure what to do, but soon she was kissing him back with a passion that undermined any desire he might have to take it slow.

He touched her everywhere, stoking her arousal and reveling in the feel of her soft feminine flesh under his fingertips. Impatient with the impediment of her pajamas, he yanked them from her body with an economy of movement.

She shuddered against him as their completely naked flesh met for the first time.

He rubbed his rigid sex against the silky curls at the apex of her thighs. "I want you so much, *tesoro mio.*"

She gasped against his lips, her body going still. "This isn't a dream."

Tomasso laughed low in his throat. "Oh, yes, it is. A dream it has taken too long to see reality."

"But…"

He kissed her again, but her body was stiff and unyielding against him. Was she going to turn him down again? Memories of his frustrated desire six years ago haunted him. No. She could not. She wanted him, her response had been too headlong and he would have her. It was meant to be.

He leaned up on one arm and cupped her breast. The nipple beaded instantly and he brushed it with the palm of his hand. She arched into his touch, while he smiled inwardly in triumph. He set about arousing her with all the skill he had at his disposal, which was considerably more than he had had at the age of twenty-four.

Liana had made love only when seduced, withholding her passion until he coaxed it from her body every single time. If there was one thing he knew about making love, it was how to tempt a woman to desire.

Maggie came to full consciousness as Tom touched her breasts with knowing caresses that drew forth the passionate need she'd kept locked deep in her soul for six years. She didn't understand what Tom was doing in her bed, where he had come from or how he had gotten there. But none of that mattered right then.

This was the man she loved and he was touching her in the way she'd dreamed about for so long. It was unreal, and yet she knew it was real. It didn't matter if it made sense, it was happening and she was glad it was happening. Her trip down memory lane earlier had left her vulnerable and aching emotionally. Only this man could fill that emotional need.

And for whatever reason he seemed to want to fill it. He wanted her. Every touch on her body told her so. Every caress that drew forth desires she'd denied so long, proved that he felt the same things. She didn't understand how it could be so. He had married Liana.

He had married Liana.

Maggie tore her mouth from his, this time her entire body writhing to be freed.

"No. We can't. You're married."

He groaned. "Yes, move like that. It's so good."

"No!" She smacked his shoulder with her fist. "You have a wife."

He stilled and then he said in a voice she could not doubt. "No, I do not."

Before she could ask what had happened, or anything else, his mouth again covered hers.

Liana was gone. No one stood between her and her six-year-old dream. The need to be loved, to belong to someone, was so strong in Maggie in that moment, it was a screaming ache inside her. She hadn't felt this needy since her parents' deaths. Was it the realization that she wanted a family and might never have one, or the acceptance that she never had…not since death had taken them away?

She didn't know what, but she wanted the hollow lone-liness to be filled. Just this once and only with this man. When his fingers slid between her legs, she didn't fight the intimacy. She remembered too well the pleasure he was capable of giving her and let her legs fall open to his touch.

He made a sound of approval against her lips as his fingers encountered the slick and swollen wetness there. Her dreams often left her like this, but tonight was not a dream. No matter how it had come to be, Tom Prince was in her bed and he was making love to her with even more effective caresses than her memories or her dreams had ever been able to conjure.

His mouth moved down to her breasts and he tortured the rigid peaks until she was shuddering with the intensity of her feelings. She didn't know what to do, so she did nothing…but he didn't seem to mind. His body was quite obviously excited and his enthusiasm made her feel beau-tiful even when she knew she wasn't.

She arched under him, needing something for which she had no name.

He lifted his head from her breasts. "Do you want me, Maggie?"

"Yes, yes, I want you so much…"

His expression glowed with victorious light and he parted her legs with a deliberate move that she could not mistake. She did not fight him. She did not want to. Soon, he would be inside her and they would be one and she would not be alone anymore.

He poised above her for a short breath and then surged inside her with one swift thrust.

Pain tore through her feminine center and she cried out, instinctively trying to buck him off.

"Yes!" he shouted as he thrust against her again, stretching tissues unused to penetration and holding her hips with hard hands.

Once again his mouth came down over hers, the quality of the kiss as out of control as his body surging over hers. Tiny zings of pleasure radiated from her core, but they could not compensate for the pain, and she felt tears sliding down her temples even as her lips returned his kiss.

That part at least was good.

He bucked and shuddered above her, a primal groan tearing from his throat and erupting against her mouth. His body went completely rigid and then relaxed, falling over her like a huge, heavy blanket.

It didn't hurt quite so much anymore, but a sense of incompletion gnawed at her. It was horrible, as if a huge crystal promise of pleasure had shattered into jagged edges that were cutting at her nerve endings. She couldn't believe she'd waited twenty-six years to experience *this*.

And she was having a hard time breathing under his weight.

She pushed against his chest. "Tom…"

He lifted his head, his expression dazed. "Are you done?"

Done? Yes, she was definitely done. "Yes," she said in a choked voice she could not hide. "I'm done. Please, *move*." She pushed against him again.

He rolled onto his back. "I am too heavy." His words were slurred, as if he'd had too much to drink.

He reached for her and she flinched, but he didn't seem to notice. He was strong and simply pulled her body into his side before his breathing pattern slid into one that indicated he'd fallen asleep. Just like that.

He'd made love to her, brought her into full womanhood and gone to sleep without so much as explaining how the heck he'd come to be in her bed.

CHAPTER FOUR

MAGGIE lay next to him for what could have been minutes or hours…she was too enervated to gauge the passage of time with any accuracy. Her entire being was in complete and utter shock.

She had just made love with Tom Prince and she could not believe it. Could not believe he was here, in her bed…or that she had allowed him to touch her and welcomed him into her body when she had never permitted another man to take such liberties.

She'd woken up fully aroused, shivering with a need she'd had no idea how to assuage. And apparently he didn't either…because it wasn't. The hollow ache she had believed would leave her when they made love was a deeper, darker pit than ever before.

How long had he touched her while she'd thought she was dreaming…thought it was just another erotic nighttime fantasy like the hundreds she'd had over the past six years? She couldn't believe she'd been so stupid.

But in her defense, although she had only one truly passionate encounter with him for her imagination to draw from, the dreams were always so real, she often woke up blood pulsing from an orgasm. The only waking one she'd had in her whole life, he'd given her.

He was also the *only* lover of her unconscious fantasies. No other man would have made it past her subconscious defenses. The touch of anyone else in her sleep would have sent her waking up and screaming in shock.

But not Tom Prince.

Only tonight had been no dream and at the last she had known it. She'd made a conscious decision to make love to him, even if it had been under the influence of pleasure so intense she'd been melting from it. The stinging ache between her thighs was proof it hadn't been pure pleasure, though.

In the end, making love to him had turned out to be as much of an untouchable chimera as her hungry desire for her own family…for a place that was uniquely hers and people she belonged to, and who belonged to her, in a way no job could ever give her. The pain between her thighs was nothing compared to the one in her chest where her heart was. She hurt so badly, she wanted to cry.

The warm wetness on her cheeks told her she already was.

Questions her pleasure drugged mind had dismissed came back full force to torment her now.

How had Tom Prince come to be in her bed? No, not her bed, but her employer's bed. Her mind could not wrap around that reality. It was too fantastic…way beyond the realm of the believable.

Were the two men friends? How had he gotten into the house? More importantly, was he still married? He'd said he wasn't and she'd believed him, but should she have? Could he be trusted? She hadn't seen him in years. Maybe he'd changed, but could a man change that much?

Tom Prince had been too honorable for that kind of behavior. Was he still?

Oh, gosh…had he even known who she was when he made love to her? Had he thought she was Liana?

No…he'd called her *little Maggie,* just like he used to. He'd told her he wasn't married, but was that the truth?

Nausea rolled in her stomach at the thought of having sex with a married man, while her body throbbed with the pain of her lost virginity.

She climbed from the bed, needing to get away from the setting of her downfall.

The prince was going to fire her for sure when he found out she'd slept with one of his friends. She would have to leave the children. More anguish tore through her. She didn't want to leave them. They needed her and she needed them. She could not believe what she had just done.

She had put her job at risk for a chance at nothing but more pain.

She stumbled into the en suite where she ran a bath and soaked until the water cooled, trying to come to terms with what had happened.

She could not believe that on the one night she'd decided to sleep in her employer's bed, he had invited a friend to come and use it. Even less comprehensible to her was that the friend would be the one man in the world she would allow to touch her in any intimate way.

She remembered him asking in her dream if she was safe and she had said always with him. Only him. Because in that moment, she'd believed he was her fantasy lover, a man who visited her only in her dreams. A man she *was* safe with.

How could Tom Prince be friends with her prince? Her employer, that was…just a second.

Cold chills raced down her spine in spite of the heat of the water surrounding her. What if Tom Prince was not a friend of Tomasso Scorsolini, but was in fact the man himself?

It all made a crazy kind of sense. Principe Tomasso…Tom

Prince. What man would dare sleep in a prince's bed but the prince himself?

Surely Tom...Prince Tomasso...had known who she was when his sister-in-law hired her. Only Therese had said nothing about the past employer-employee relationship. Or had Tomasso even cared enough to ask her last name? Yes, he had cared. She'd already decided he had to be a fairly decent dad, which meant he had to have known he'd hired her.

Or did he?

There was more than one Maggie Thomson in the world. She wasn't all that remarkable in any way.

Another thought entered her mind and shoved every other one aside. Gianni and Anna's mother had died two years ago. Relief flooded Maggie in a wave that brought tears to her eyes. *Tom* was not married. He had not lied.

But why had he made love to her?

She had been dreaming at first...or thought she was, but he had been fully awake from the beginning. Or at least she assumed he had been. What if he'd been dreaming, too?

Had he gotten into the bed, not noticing someone else was there? Had he gone to sleep and then woken to her next to him and thought she was Liana, or a girlfriend? Then he had done what men like him did with their women in the middle of the night...he'd made love to her. It was all too likely a scenario, if a painful one.

He'd called her by name, but had the times he'd called her Maggie been her dream or reality?

At some point he had to have realized she wasn't the other woman, didn't he? If so, then why had he kept going? But maybe he'd thought he was dreaming the whole time. No, that didn't make sense. Nothing made sense right now.

All she knew was that he hadn't wanted her as Tom

Prince and she knew she had no chance with a royal prince. Whatever had prompted him to make love to her, he couldn't have meant it to lead to anything important. Not with her.

She couldn't think straight. She needed to calm her racing thoughts and heart and the no longer very hot bath was definitely not doing the trick. Though the ache between her legs was a little better.

She got out of the bath and dried off and then faced the door back into the bedroom with the same feeling she would have had if it led to an arena full of hungry lions. She pulled it open slowly, hoping against hope he was still asleep as she'd left him. The room was still dark, which was a good sign, and all she could hear over the pounding of her own heart was the sound of even breathing. Good.

She tiptoed into the room, the big bath towel wrapped around her, and went in search of her pajamas. Thankfully she found them in a pile on the floor near the bed where she'd been sleeping. She would have made a mad dash back to her own room then, but remembered the security cameras in the hall and didn't want to be caught by one traipsing around in a bath sheet.

She went back to the bathroom and hurriedly dressed, then she snuck out of the room, closing the door silently behind her. She turned and had to jerk to a stop or run smack into Gianni.

He rubbed his eyes sleepily. "Why were you sleeping in Papa's bedroom?"

Her stomach dropped to her toes and wanted to stay there. "You and Anna took up all the room in my bed."

"Oh. I'll go to my own bed now. I'm not scared anymore."

"All right, sweetie. But why were you up?"

"I had to use the bathroom."

"There's one off my suite."

He rubbed his eyes again, his head drooping. "I forgot."

"I see. Come on." She walked him to his bedroom, her mind racing with ways to get out of having to face Tomasso in the morning.

If he had thought he was dreaming, maybe he'd thought she was Liana…maybe he wouldn't even realize she'd been in his bed the night before. It was a long shot, but sounded good to a sleep-deprived brain still reeling in shock after her propulsion into full womanhood.

Tomasso woke with a strange sense of well-being and anticipation.

He instinctively reached out for human warmth before reminding himself that he did not have a wife or lover who slept with him any longer. Strange that he should forget when it had been two years. Then fragments of memory began to surface from the night before and his actions began to make sense.

Maggie was in his home…in his bed. He had made love to her the night before. His eyes shot open and he looked for her, but the room was empty.

Was she being discreet for the children's sake or had she even been there? Everything that happened the night before had a dreamlike quality anyway. Even his flight home, but that had not been a dream and neither had been arriving home to find Maggie in his bed.

But what had she been doing there? And what the hell had he been thinking to kiss her and seduce her like that?

He could not believe he had made love to her the first time he'd seen her in six years…or that she had let him. The Maggie he had known would never have submitted to a man's advances that quickly. And it was only because he'd been out of his head with exhaustion combined with the effect of those damn antinausea pills mixed with alcohol that he'd made any advances at all. He had not been thinking straight.

The plan had been to test how well she fit into his life, to discover if she was the woman he remembered and then find out if the passion was still a factor between them. He had that answer at least. The chemistry between them was not a problem…she'd excited him more than any other woman he'd made love to, but he didn't feel good about that.

How could he when the evidence pointed to a promiscuity he would never have suspected of her? Damn it, could the investigative reports be wrong? What woman turned over in bed and invited a man she hadn't seen in six years into her arms? *A promiscuous one,* the logical albeit cynical side of his brain insisted. She'd climbed into his bed six years ago, too…she'd said she was a virgin then, but what if that had been a lie?

Liana had lied to him, had used her sexuality to trick him into believing her emotions were more involved than her mercenary tendencies. He couldn't afford to make the same mistake twice.

But perhaps Maggie was not promiscuous so much as opportunistic, as Liana had been. Did she now know who he was and had she decided to take advantage of her new circumstances? Unless the investigative report on her was riddled with error, that scenario was the more likely one. According to it, she rarely dated and had not had a sexual liaison in the last year or was discreet to the point of hiding it completely.

Which did not explain how she had discovered his identity before his return. He'd made sure all the portraits with his image were put away but she might have stumbled upon family photos of him with the children. Had she been waiting in his bed on purpose, hoping to take advantage?

No. That theory was illogical in the face of the fact that she had not expected him home for two more nights. No one had.

But whatever her reasons had been for sleeping in his bed, she wasn't there now. And he wanted to know why. He also wanted to know why she had let him make love to her. She had not protested once. It was completely out of character, or at least it would have been six years ago. He had changed a lot in the intervening time, perhaps she had too.

And not for the better.

His superior brain spun with the possibilities but came to a screeching halt as he pulled back the covers to climb from the bed.

There was dried blood, not his, on him and on the sheet. Not a lot, but some. Had she started her monthly? Was that why she had left?

"Papa!"

The ear-piercing squeal jolted Maggie out of a sound sleep and she sat straight up in bed, her eyes popping open to the sight of her small bedmate launching herself at the tall, gorgeous male standing beside the bed.

"Hello, *stellina*, did you miss me?"

Anna threw her thin, child's arms around his neck and hugged him tight. "Yes!"

"I missed you too, *piccola mia*."

"He missed me too," Gianni announced importantly.

"I certainly did." Tomasso bent down and swung the little boy up in his arm so he was holding both of his children, his expression filled with a fierce kind of tenderness that made Maggie's heart squeeze in her chest.

Then his gaze met hers and went blank. Her heart started pounding wildly as memories from the night before bombarded her before she had a chance to erect her defenses. And they hurt. She still had no idea why he'd made love to her, but she knew one thing for sure…he was even further out of her league than Tom Prince had been.

He could never be hers.

"Hello, Maggie."

"Good morning…" Oh, gosh, what was she supposed to call him? He wasn't Tom Prince, not really. "Um…Your Highness."

"Tomasso is fine," he said sardonically.

"Papa isn't Maggie lovely?" Anna demanded.

"She's perfect, Papa…the best nanny ever." Gianni grinned at Maggie with adoration.

She smiled back even though she wanted nothing more than to dive back under her covers and hide. She'd made love with that man last night and she could barely breathe for the memories. "It's easy to be a good nanny when you have such wonderful children to look after."

"They are wonderful children, the best," Tomasso declared.

Both children beamed at their father's praise and Maggie felt the strangest sensation near her heart. A yearning she'd never experienced when caring for her other charges. She'd always wanted her own family, but never wished that the children she cared for belonged to her. Never before, anyway.

With Gianni and Anna, it was different. She felt possessive and protective toward them. It wasn't professional and she hated how vulnerable it made her feel, but seeing them with their father and knowing she was outside that family circle hurt in a way that it should not.

"I'm sure you want to spend lots of time with just them," she said by way of a hint to get him out of her room.

The bedroom had seemed huge the first time she'd walked into it, the queen-size canopied bed in rich mahogany almost lost in the spaciousness of the bedroom area. Even a full bedroom set to match the bed, a pair of reading chairs and a marble fireplace could not make the room feel crowded, but Tomasso seemed to fill the space entirely.

And for once, the room felt overwhelmingly small to her.

He kissed Anna's cheek. "I thought we could *all* have breakfast and then go to the beach for a couple of hours."

That plan was met with screeches of delight while Maggie's heart stuttered in her chest. He wanted to spend the day together? All of them? After last night? Wasn't he going to fire her? Was it possible he didn't remember?

He had sounded slurred there toward the end. He could have been really, really tired…but maybe he'd been a little drunk. If so, it increased the possibility that he had forgotten.

Hope blossomed in her heart. Maybe it wouldn't be so terrible after all.

"Oh, Papa, really?" Anna asked with delight.

He smiled down at her. "Yes. I have cleared my desk and will not be going to the office for a few days."

Gianni whooped with glee, not a bit like a proper prince, but very much like a small boy who was thrilled at the prospect of spending time with his father.

Maggie had suspected the children's relationship with their workaholic father was a good one, but watching the evidence filled her with bittersweet joy in the man Tom Prince had become.

Both children squirmed from their father's arms to rush from the room, Gianni saying he wanted to get his new kite and Anna proclaiming she wanted to wear her favorite shorts.

Tomasso, however, did not leave.

He stood beside the bed giving Maggie an impenetrable look.

Tomasso gritted his teeth against desire he should not feel slamming through him. It was even stronger than the regret that filled his mind to the exclusion of almost everything else. He'd come a long way from the feeling of repleteness upon waking this morning. He was ashamed now for that weakness.

He was not a stupid man. In fact, he was smart enough to successfully run a multinational company and expand it to the level of being a true world competitor, but he seemed destined to make the same mistake where women were concerned. And he hated that.

Maggie Thomson had played him just as Liana had done because no matter what his plans had been before, he had little choice but than to pursue the marriage objective now. She could very well be pregnant with his child, though the fact her menses had just started did give him a better chance at avoiding another bout of emotional blackmail with his baby as the weapon.

The knowledge did not make him feel better because even the remotest possibility that she was pregnant made him vulnerable, and that made him furious. Both with himself and with her.

"If you want my help with the children at the beach, I will have to dress," she said when the silence had stretched to uncomfortable levels.

"By all means." He put his hand out to pull her from the bed, but she scooted away from him.

"I'm in my pajamas." And in a move he considered total overkill, she drew the covers to her chin.

His brows lifted sardonically, while irritation warred with the sexual desire one bout of lovemaking had not quenched. Not after a two-year drought. "You were not so shy last night," he said with some derision, not at all impressed by her belated play at modesty.

"Last night?" she asked, striving to look confused.

His anger and derision went up another notch. She was almost as good a liar as Liana, but why she should be pretending ignorance now, he did not understand. "In my bed."

"I don't know what you're talking about. You must have been dreaming." Maggie never lied and she wasn't very good at it, she acknowledged, as the words came out sounding high and uncertain rather than convincing.

Tomasso looked totally offended and absolutely unconvinced. "I was *not* dreaming."

She winced. He sounded dangerously angry as well. "Are you sure?"

"Yes," he bit out. "We had sex last night."

She flinched at the baldness of his words, at the certainty in them. Her heart contracted at another certainty…he *had* been awake and therefore, there was no excuse for what he had done. He had seduced her from the vulnerability of sleep. She could not believe it of him, but she had no choice.

Why had he done it?

"I—"

"Do not attempt to hide your behavior by pretending it did not happen. I am not such a fool." His eyes and voice were filled with chilling contempt.

"*My* behavior?"

"Perhaps you are concerned I will fire you for the blatant promiscuity you exhibited last night, but my children are much too attached to you for me to take such a drastic measure before I assess the situation completely."

"Assess it how?" she demanded in shock at his gall, while she couldn't help the relief that surged through her that she wasn't about to be fired.

"I must determine what prompted your behavior and whether or not such behavior is likely to influence Annamaria and Gianfranco in the future. I do not wish my daughter to learn such…free and easy ways."

"Such—You think I'm *promiscuous?*"

"Please lower your voice. I do not want the children or the other servants to overhear this conversation."

Other servants? So, she was nothing to him but a servant whom he'd had sex with. How convenient. And how telling. The man saw her as totally unimportant in his life. Not only that, but she'd never been more than a servant to him. Once she'd been his housekeeper, now she was his nanny. Sex aside, she was nothing to him but another well-paid domestic.

The knowledge hurt when it shouldn't, but it also made her angry. He wasn't putting last night all on her because he was some snobby prince and she was a nobody and therefore a convenient scapegoat. "I am *not* promiscuous!"

"Perhaps you do not see your actions in that light. But you came into my arms after a six-year separation without a murmur of protest."

"If that's all you're going on, what does that make you? The promiscuous prince?"

"We are not discussing my behavior. We are discussing yours and the possible detrimental effect it could have on my children."

"There will be no detrimental effect!" He had to believe her. She couldn't leave Gianni and Anna. Hadn't she lost enough in her life?

Part of her rebelled at giving him any sort of an explanation, but her fear at having to leave the two children she'd grown to love so helplessly in such a short time overrode it. "I thought I was dreaming, or it never would have happened."

"I am disappointed in you, Maggie. You never used to lie. You were undoubtedly awake last night. I was there. I know."

"Barely. I was *barely* awake," she stressed. "I *thought* I was asleep. At first I *was* asleep and by the time I was full awake, you'd done things to me that undermined my natural defenses. You seduced me!" She glared up at him, her knuckles curling whitely around the sheet, anger heaving through her in waves that drowned her fear.

"And I wasn't the only one in that bed having sex with someone they hadn't seen in six years, but *I* didn't initiate it, did I? I wasn't the one doing the seducing," she said scathingly. "How dare you accuse me of promiscuous behavior after the way you took advantage of me last night? That is just so low I don't even have words to describe it."

His eyes flashed outrage that easily matched her own. "I did *not* take advantage."

"What would you call invading a sleeping woman's bed and seducing her before she was even awake? I call it contemptible, but perhaps you've got another word for it."

"You were awake," he ground out, his anger making the emotionless façade slip another notch.

"I was not! Not at first, anyway."

"You spoke to me when I kissed you. You knew who I was. You kissed me!"

"I thought you were Tom Prince…a man in a dream."

"I am Tom Prince."

"No, you are not. You are Principe Tomasso Scorsolini

and if I'd been aware of what I was doing, I would never have let *you* touch me intimately."

"That is a lie. You did let me touch you. You asked for it…begged for my possession."

Memories of her wanton display did not improve her temper, nor did thinking how much it had hurt when she'd gotten her wish, or how empty she'd felt afterward. "You believe what you like. *I don't care.* Do you hear me? I can't believe I let you touch me, even in my dreams." She was out of control and tears burned her eyes, but she wasn't going to let them fall. She'd cried twice for this man…once six years ago and once last night. Never again. "Only a real sexual predator would take advantage of a sleeping woman. I can't believe that's what you've become."

"I am no predator." The outrage practically vibrated off him now.

"Call it what you like. I'm not interested."

"You are being entirely irrational and perhaps that is understandable considering your condition, but I will not tolerate these insults, Maggie."

"You think I care?"

"I am your employer. It is in your best interests to care."

"What are you going to do, fire me? You can't. I quit!" She couldn't believe she'd said the words.

She sucked in air around the pain they brought, but she knew she couldn't keep working for him…even if it meant staying with Gianni and Anna.

"You tried to quit on me once before and it did not work."

"It will this time."

"Not unless you want to be taken to court for breach of contract. You signed on for two years," he said with grim implacability.

CHAPTER FIVE

THE threat sent Maggie's rage to new levels.

She hopped out of the bed and stormed over to him and poked him right in the chest. "Then sue me, or send me to jail—I don't care. I couldn't live in this house with you for another two days, much less two years!"

He stared at her in shock, like she'd grown two heads or something. "You are being extremely unreasonable. I don't remember you getting like this before."

"Before what? Before you became such a sleazebag, you mean?"

He flinched as if she'd struck him. "I realize PMS is an accepted excuse for unwarranted annoyance, but you are going too far and I warn you, my patience is not limitless. Do not call me another name."

"You think I'm angry because I'm in PMS?" she asked in disbelief.

"It is the most logical explanation."

"As opposed to the fact that I find your behavior and subsequent sanctimonious attitude abhorrent? You're like a rapist who blames his victim for enticing him." Okay, maybe *that* was going a bit too far, but she was mad enough now to spit nails. "For your information, I am not in my period and I am not in PMS. I'm not even due for two weeks."

He looked dubious. "You are not?"

"No! And I can't believe you're asking about something so personal."

"What we did last night was far more personal."

"I doubt it, not for a man like you." And knowing how impersonal it really had to have been for him to react this way was like having a razor taken to the most tender spot of her heart.

His blue gaze glittered dangerously and she watched as the patience he'd said wasn't limitless snapped.

He grabbed her shoulders and asked in a voice that made her shiver, "What is that supposed to mean?"

"What do you think it means?" she asked painfully.

"Tell me, Maggie. I am very interested in your interpretation."

Something about his quiet words made her swallow her first retort—something truly nasty—and say, "I'd say it's pretty obvious. I'm not the one with all the experience."

"If that is true, then I am glad. I am not in the habit of having unprotected sex like we did last night."

"What do you mean, *if?*" she asked, newly incensed and feeling another slashing chunk ripped from her heart. If she had imagined a thousand morning-after scenarios, not one of them would have even remotely resembled this one. "I don't make a habit of lying."

"You lied when you said you didn't remember last night."

He had her there, but she wasn't backing down. She'd lied to avoid an embarrassing confrontation he had obviously been intent on having. She hadn't lied to hurt or manipulate someone else. "I only wish I could forget."

"Do you? I wonder. You lied when you said you had not started your monthly."

"I didn't! Okay, so I lied about not knowing what you were talking about. I hoped you didn't remember. Like I said, I wanted to forget it. But it's just plain dumb to think I'm lying about having my period. Why would I?" And how could he keep accusing her of it?

Maybe they hadn't been as good friends as she'd thought six years ago, because he'd never told her he was a prince. But he had to have known her pretty well after living with her for almost two years. She'd never hidden *her* real self from *him*.

"I don't know why you would lie, but I do know you are doing so. There was blood. You *must* have started."

Blood? There had been blood? She hadn't noticed in the bath, but then she'd been too busy dealing with the shock of having sex for the first time with a man she had thought forever lost to her and had never expected to even see again. "I didn't start."

"Then what was the blood from?"

She refused to answer, staring at him in stony silence.

Something about her expression must have gotten to him because his dark complexion paled. "I did not hurt you?"

"Yes, as a matter of fact, you did," she slotted in, feeling vindicated, but not one whit less devastated by the emotional pain shredding her insides.

He went positively pasty and her soft heart refused to allow her to continue the torment, no matter how much he might deserve it.

"It wasn't your fault…at least, not in the sense that you were rough with me or something. Apparently pain and some blood is inevitable."

He wasn't looking appreciably better. "Why inevitable?"

"First times hurt, or so I've been told," she mumbled, looking away.

He made such a strange sound that her gaze flew back to him. "You were a *virgin?*" He looked well and truly horrified by that prospect.

"Yes. Not that it matters. It's not an experience I plan to repeat anytime soon."

He stared at her in total shock. "No. That is not possible. You are twenty-six."

"I don't know what my age has to do with it. Women don't have an expiration date on their virginity, you know. *I am not promiscuous,*" she repeated for good measure.

He moved over to sit on the edge of her bed, almost as if his legs were not quite supporting him. Though she dismissed that thought as fanciful. Prince Tomasso was much too strong for such infirmity.

Suddenly she remembered she was standing there in her pajamas and nothing else. They weren't racy by any stretch, but the thin cotton wasn't exactly disguising, either. Her nipples were erect…she must be cold. It could not be his presence that was doing it, but it didn't matter. She didn't want him noticing.

She walked around the bed, giving him a wide birth, and climbed back under the covers. She wanted some answers and she wanted them before the children came back.

He frowned. "If you were untouched, then why did you ask me to kiss you…and do other things?"

"I told you, I thought I was *dreaming.*"

"About Tom Prince." Some of his color returned and with it a measure of his natural arrogance.

"If you must know, yes."

"But you were awake."

She shrugged. They'd already been over this.

"You are saying I took advantage of you in the basest way."

"Well, if the shoe fits…"

His jaw set as if hewn from granite and his eyes blazed at her. "I am not a sexual predator. I believed you were awake. I would not have touched you otherwise. You must know this."

She shrugged, but deep in her heart she suspected that was the truth. As real as her dreams seemed to her, she could very well have responded to him in a way that would have deceived him about her level of awareness before she ever came awake.

"You wanted me…your body was very receptive," he said confirming her thoughts.

"Not receptive enough," she muttered however, remembering the pain of his penetration.

"I did not know of your innocence. I took you too quickly."

"You shouldn't have *taken* me at all."

He contemplated her in unnerving silence for several seconds. "For you to be so receptive you must have frequent dreams of this nature with me in them."

If only he knew. "That's none of your business."

He smiled, for a moment looking so much like the man she remembered, the man she had loved, her heart ached. "You never forgot me."

"It wouldn't say much for my brain if I had. It's only been six years, not sixty, since I saw you last."

"But I think it is more than mere clinical memory…you did not want our friendship to end."

"Then why did I end it?"

His eyes narrowed and then he smiled again, this time the expression too smug for her liking. "Because of Liana."

"I suppose it boosts your ego to think so."

He considered her in silence for several seconds, all lightness draining from his expression, and a man she did not know—the prince—took over his countenance. "Or maybe this whole 'it was a dream' story is a ruse and you exchanged your virginity for the hope of a crown? You thought to trade on the guilt you knew I would feel when you told such a story? It was a good gambit, and may yet work."

She gasped, so shocked by the level of his cynicism coupled with the implication he would allow himself to be manipulated, she forgot to be angry. "Do you really believe that?"

His gaze shuttered, he stood again as if her nearness was no longer acceptable. "It is a possibility."

"My goodness, technically, so is the end to worldwide hunger, but it's the realm of *probability* that we're discussing here."

"Women throughout history have gambled their innocence on the chance of wearing a crown."

"Not in the last century, I'm sure."

"You would be surprised."

Maybe she would. This was a rarified world she knew very little about. "Nevertheless, I assume I would have to marry you to do that."

"Yes."

"Then you have nothing to worry about, do you? I can hardly force you to the altar."

"Can you not?"

"Of course not."

"If you are pregnant with my child…" He let his voice trail off, the implication of what he was saying obvious.

Maggie choked on what she wanted to say next as the prospect of pregnancy filled her consciousness to the exclusion of all else. A baby? Tom Prince's baby? No, Prince Tomasso's, but still…a baby. A family. Her own family that no one could take away from her.

Her hand slid to her stomach and she pressed against it, her heart beating much too fast as the blood drained from her head.

She couldn't be pregnant. Not after just the one time, but even as she thought the words, her knowledge of the sexual reproductive system mocked them. One time at this particular time of the month was more likely than if they made love over and over again a few days later. She could feel the horror of fearful certainty stamping itself on her features.

"I see the idea had not yet occurred to you." But a strange look of speculation on his face made her wonder if he thought it had and she was faking her shock.

Where the thought came from, she didn't know, but she couldn't shake the impression that he thought she might have done the whole thing on purpose.

She shook her head mutely, the movement making her dizzy.

"Why look so dismayed? As bargaining chips go, it's a very strong one indeed."

"Babies are not bargaining chips," she whispered, unable to believe she was having this conversation, much less what had led up to it.

She'd had sex with a prince and he thought it had been entirely consensual…which, if she was honest with herself at least, she'd have to admit it had been. She might have thought she was dreaming at first, but even after she realized she wasn't, her desire for this man had been too strong to deny.

She should probably apologize for the predator comment.

"For some women they are."

It took her a moment to remember what they were talking about…oh, yes, babies as bargaining chips. He'd made it sound like he had personal experience in that arena.

"I'm not one of them."

Too caught up in the ramifications of the night before on her own life for her to wonder what had prompted the bitter tone in his voice, she got up from the bed.

She pulled the covers with her, not caring if he thought her modesty ridiculous after last night. "Please get out of my room. I would like to dress."

"We have more to discuss."

"You're right. I have a lot of questions for you." Like how she'd come to be working for Tom Prince again. "But not right now." She didn't have the ability.

His eyes narrowed. "Very well. Carlotta will be serving breakfast in fifteen minutes."

"Eat without me. I'm not hungry."

"If you are pregnant, skipping meals is not good for the baby."

"Please don't mention that. Not…not right this second." She needed time to cope with the possibility.

"You've got the shocked and dismayed bit down pat. I have to give you that."

She stared at him. "Are you accusing me of trying to get pregnant on purpose?" she asked baldly, refusing to banter about it.

"Not accusing you, no."

But he didn't trust her. She was sure of it. Pain splintered through her. Bad enough to know she was so far from the kind of woman he would want to marry she might as well be a nun, and an alien one at that, but to have him doubt her integrity on top of that just hurt, a lot.

Without another word, she turned away, heading toward

the sanctuary of her bathroom, the sheet trailing behind her, her heart and mind in pain-filled turmoil.

"Maggie."

"Go away, Tomasso, *please*."

"I will have Carlotta hold breakfast until you arrive."

That made her turn. "Please don't."

But he was already headed out of the room and made no indication he had heard her.

Maggie would like to have spent the day hiding in her room, but one thing that had clearly not changed about Tomasso from six years ago was his stubbornness. The man liked to get his own way and considering the fact he had been raised a prince, she understood why he was so used to it.

To think that she'd lived two years in the same household as a prince and not even known it.

Tomasso looked up when she entered the dining room, his gaze going over her with tactile strength, and her skin heated with feelings she would rather forget. He stood politely and pulled the chair out from the table beside Anna.

He smiled at her as she took her seat, nothing in his expression giving away the fact that he'd dropped the biggest bombshell of her life on her. "You look lovely."

She barely refrained from rolling her eyes as she said, "Thank you."

She'd pulled her long, corkscrew curls away from her face with a clip at the back of her head and donned a pair of slim-fitting jeans and a yellow T-shirt with matching yellow flip-flops for the beach. She was hardly dressed like one of his normal companions, being as far from haute couture as a woman could get without wearing a burlap sack.

"But I think you will be too warm in those jeans on the beach."

"I'll be fine. I'm used to the heat on the island. My last job was in Houston, Texas." Besides, she felt protected in the jeans.

The thought of prancing around in front of him in a pair of shorts—or worse, a swimsuit—after what had happened the night before made her shudder inwardly.

"That's a long way from where we went to college. How did you end up there?"

"A job. I'm sure all of that information is in my employment file."

"But perhaps I would rather hear it from you."

"And there is quite a bit I'd like to hear from you."

His eyes said he could guess at what those things were. "Perhaps that can wait until later?" he asked with a pointed look at the children.

"Yes."

"Tell me how you ended up in Houston."

"My first job out of college was with a family in Seattle. They knew the family I went to in Texas and recommended me to them." She'd hoped the move across country would help her forget Tom Prince once and for all.

It hadn't worked. Her dreams traveled with her.

"Why did you leave the first job?"

"Their youngest started high school and they felt my position had become redundant."

"You sound like you did not agree."

"High school can be a really difficult time and both parents were too busy to spend much time with their children. I felt taking away the steadying influence of the only adult in their lives that had time to be there for them was a mistake."

"Did you tell the parents this?"

"No. I'd only been with the family two years and it wasn't my place, but it's not a decision I would have made."

"You would be the mother who made sure she was available after school for her children, no matter the ages, would you not?"

Considering their conversation earlier, that question had more than passing significance. However, he might as well know from the beginning that she had no desire to be a glorified single parent. "Yes, but I would expect my husband to be just as committed to their emotional welfare."

"That isn't always possible."

"It should be."

"A man's commitments—"

"Should begin and end with his family. Everything else is filler, not the other way around."

"That's a simplistic view of life."

"Maybe," she conceded. "But it's the way I feel."

"You have very strong opinions on family for a woman who was raised in the foster care system."

"You don't have to be raised with two loving parents to know that is what is best for a child."

"Perhaps not."

"I grew up knowing my place in the family was dependent on what I did for the family. I wasn't loved. My children, if I have any, are going to know a different kind of life. They will always know they come first, that they are loved and that I don't expect them to earn my affection through work or perfect behavior. I won't marry a man who won't give them the same sense of emotional security."

There. He could put that in his pipe and smoke it. His concept of family was vastly different from hers, from what she could tell.

"What's foster care?" Anna asked.

"It's when you live with someone besides your parents as a child."

"Like we live with you?"

Maggie laughed. "No, darling. You still live with your papa. I am your nanny. I work for him. I'm not a foster mom."

"But I want you to be my mom. You would be the best." She turned to her father. "Can Maggie be my foster mom, Papa?"

"No, silly. Maggie can't be our mom unless she married Papa, and he is a prince," Gianni said. "He can't marry a servant."

The arrogant words spilling from such young lips made Maggie wince, but Tomasso merely laughed.

"You are wrong, my son. This is the twenty-first century. A man, even a prince, can marry who he likes. Your mother was not a princess and I married her."

Gianni looked at his father with eyes that reflected the same cobalt-blue. "But she was beautiful like a princess."

Pain slammed through Maggie. Pregnant or not, she could never belong to Tomasso and he would never belong to her. Because Gianni was right. She wasn't beautiful enough to be the woman in Tomasso's life. She was too ordinary for a man of his extraordinary status and personality. She could never live up to the type of woman that he was used to being around. No way could she hold his interest for a lifetime.

She'd learned six years ago that she could not even hold it for a couple of weeks.

The thought of marriage to a man who might find a more beautiful, exciting partner around any corner filled her with dread. She hadn't been enough for him six years ago and she knew she wasn't enough for him now. She was not and never would be one of the Lianas of this world.

"So is Maggie pretty," Anna staunchly defended. "Don't you *want* Maggie for a mama?"

Gianni's expression went stoic, so like his father's that Maggie sucked in a breath as her heart constricted. "Maggie is only staying for two years. She told *Zia* Therese. I heard her. A mama has to stay your whole life unless she dies like our mama did. Besides nannies are better than mamas. We get to see Maggie every day. We don't need a mama."

Guilt flayed Maggie as she realized one of the reasons for the distance Gianni sometimes kept between them.

He was a small child who had already faced the tragic loss of his mother. He knew Maggie did not intend to stay around forever and so he was trying to protect his emotions. She should never have agreed to take the job in the first place, but looking back she did not know how she could have walked away from the children after meeting them.

She also found it terribly sad, not to mention revealing, that Gianni thought having a nanny was better than having a mother.

"I don't care what you say. I want Maggie for my mama!" Anna's voice carried the conviction of a three-year-old on the verge of major meltdown.

"Perhaps you will get your wish, *stellina,*" Tomasso said soothingly and then turned and ruffled Gianni's hair. "And perhaps you will learn to like the idea of having Maggie for your mother, my proud little son."

Gianni's lip quivered. "But what if she goes away?"

"If she married me, I would not let her go away."

Both children looked at their father with the kind of hope that broke Maggie's heart and filled her with anger. Didn't he realize how hurt they were going to be when that hope was disappointed?

No matter what he had said that morning, he could not

seriously be considering marriage with her. She wasn't his type and she never could be. And that knowledge had the power to wound in a way nothing else did. Not his distrust, not even his stupid male posturing about the night before.

She didn't fit in his world. She was too ordinary and that wasn't something a fairy godmother could change with a magic wand.

They went down to the beach and helped the children fly kites and then Tomasso waded in the surf with them while Maggie arranged a blanket under the large pavilion set up for the family's use on their private beach. She lay down on her stomach and watched the three play in the surf while her mind spun with the possibility of being pregnant by Tomasso.

Even if she was, he couldn't be serious about marriage. Could he? But he was a prince…maybe the thought of his child being born out of wedlock carried more weight than it did for the average modern man. Why hadn't he used protection then? Even if he had believed she was experienced, there was no reason for him to assume she was on the Pill…or even physically safe.

Far from answering any of her questions, their discussion that morning had only added more to the morass of thoughts in her head.

But overriding it all was an insidious thought that would not leave her alone. If she married him, she would be mother to his other two children as well and she would never have to tell them goodbye. She would have the family she had always longed for.

Eventually the three got tired of playing in the water and joined Maggie in the pavilion, where they built an amazing sandcastle and Maggie got to see first hand how caring Tomasso was with his two small children. For an alpha male who could cynically accuse her of using her virginity to try to trap him into marriage, he had a surprisingly tender side.

He also flirted outrageously with her, as if he was really glad to be in her company as well. In light of his accusations, it made no sense and she was careful not to let herself fall under his spell. But it grew increasingly difficult as the day wore on and she saw more glimpses of the man she'd known and loved six years ago.

He insisted on putting the children to bed together, and she felt a treacherous sense of family growing on her. But she wasn't his wife. She was his nanny…his *servant*. But then, when had she ever been anything else?

Afterward, he stopped her in the hall before she could make good an escape to her suite. "Come for a walk with me."

There were questions she wanted to ask him and the children were nowhere around to overhear the answers. "All right."

He led her out the sliding glass doors on the south side of the house and down to the path that led to the beach.

It was a beautiful night, lit by a full moon. The island breeze lifted her hair and sent it swirling gently around her face despite the clip. "I love it out here."

"According to Therese, you have been very happy here on Diamante."

"Your home is beautiful."

"It was my parent's vacation home."

"A vacation home?" While it wasn't on the level of grandeur of the palace filled with Italian marble and artwork that rivaled that of the Vatican on Scorsolini Island, Tomasso's eight-bedroom house was hardly what she would have considered a vacation cottage.

"They escaped the pressures of state here. At least that is what my father told me."

"Your mother died many years ago, didn't she?"

"There were complications with my birth." And the knowledge of that hurt him, she could hear it in his voice.

"I'm sorry. That must have been hard to know growing up."

"No harder than knowing both your parents were gone."

"They didn't die until I was eight years old. I had enough years with them to know what I want to give to my children by way of a home."

"Yes, I suppose you did. Was there an accident?"

"Yes. I survived. They didn't."

"We have that in common." She knew he meant he had survived his birth while his mother had not.

"Yes."

He looked back over his shoulder and flashed her a smile.

Her heart contracted and she tripped, barely catching herself before pitching forward into him. Thankfully the path to the beach was well lit and lined with a curling wrought-iron railing. She grabbed it and held on as she continued walking. "The children said that there are diamond mines on this island."

"Yes. The island is named for them."

"Does that mean there are ruby and sapphires on Rubino and Zaffiro?"

"No. Those islands were named with some poetic license. However, we have discovered lithium on Zaffiro. Soon, the mining operations and jewelry stores will rival the shipping company for contribution to Isole dei Re's GNP."

"You should be very proud of yourself."

"I am not the operations."

"But you drive them."

"Therese said something?"

"Your children love to talk about their wonderful papa."

"And you feel I spend too little time with them?" he correctly guessed.

"Since you are asking…yes."

"And the fact that a whole country's GNP is impacted by what I do away from them—?"

"Means that your job is important, not that it is more important than them."

"You and the children share a strong rapport."

"Maybe it's too strong."

"Why do you say that?"

"They will be hurt when I leave. You heard Gianni this morning."

"As I told my son, perhaps I will not let you leave."

"You can't marry me just because of one lustful mistake."

They had reached the beach and he stopped and turned to face her, his determined expression all too easy to read in the light of the full moon. "If you are pregnant with my child, you will marry me."

CHAPTER SIX

"DON'T be stupid, Tomasso."

He cupped her shoulders, coming so close their bodies practically touched. "I like the way you say my name... your American accent is cute."

She didn't feel cute. She felt hot and bothered and suspected he knew he had this immediate impact on her.

"Your accent only shows when you are agitated...or rather, I should say, the way you speak changes."

"How?" he asked, sounding genuinely interested while his thumbs drew lazy circles on her shoulders.

"You get more formal in your speech patterns, though you seem to speak more that way now, regardless," she mused, trying for a casual attitude she did not feel.

"Ah. I made a concentrated effort to blend in with the other college students six years ago, but Italian is the primary language of Isole dei Re. The speech patterns of my native tongue are slightly different than your American English."

"But everyone here speaks English." At least everyone had to her. Even the children.

"Our small country is close to the United States...there are many American influences."

"I didn't notice any on Scorsolini Island. The palace is incredible. The frescos in the formal rooms rival the Sistine Chapel."

"The Scorsolinis are from Sicily, not Rome."

"They're both Italian."

"A Sicilian is a Sicilian first, Italian second. It is the way they are made."

"That explains it."

"What?"

"The arrogance."

He laughed and the sound shivered through her.

"I used to love your laugh."

"I think you used to love me."

She turned her head away, looking out over the dark, dark sea. "What an ego you have."

"No. Merely a logical brain. There is only one man whom you would have allowed into your arms last night. Tom Prince. Why is that? Because you dreamed of me so frequently, an erotic encounter in the night could be dismissed by your subconscious as one more fantasy. That says much for how deeply you felt for me."

"I thought you'd convinced yourself I was lying about the dreams."

"I only considered the possibility you were lying to me; I was not convinced of it and now I am certain you were not."

"Why?"

"The way you responded to me last night…it was too much like a woman touching and allowing the touch of a longtime lover, not a woman making love for the first time to a man she had not seen in six years."

"And you would know the difference?"

"Yes," he said with all the arrogance she had accused him of having earlier.

"I see."

"I doubt it. You are much too innocent to do so."

"Not anymore."

"Very much innocent still. You did not experience completion, did you?"

"That's not something I want to discuss."

His thumbs moved to either side of her face, gently forcing her to look at him. "Next time it will be much better."

"There will not be a next time."

"Yes. Maggie, there will." His expression was incredibly possessive. "You belong to me now."

"No, I don't."

His lips cut off any further protest.

It was a claim-staking kiss pure and simple, but it didn't matter to her treacherous body. At the first touch of his lips, she melted into him and when he broke his mouth from hers, her fingers were clutched in the hair at his nape and her body was molded to his.

"You are mine."

She always had been, but she wasn't about to admit it to him. He was too darn confident as it was.

"I'm not the only one breathing heavily here," she pointed out.

"And your point is?"

"That if I belong to you, then you belong to me." Which wasn't something she was sure of at all, but he needed to know that she intended their relationship to be equal...even if inside she knew it never could be.

"Naturally."

She stared at him in shock. "You don't mean that."

"Why would I not? Marriage is no small step. It requires effort and commitment from both parties."

"We aren't talking about marriage here."

"Are we not?"

"You're so stubborn. That hasn't changed."

"I know my own mind."

"And think everyone else should share its leanings."

"That is not true."

She tugged out of his arms, surprised that he easily let her go. "Right."

"Maggie, you will discover that we want the same things."

"You want to give up your mining and jewelry operations to run a day care center?"

He laughed and started walking again, his body betraying none of the tension she felt.

"Did you know who I was when Therese hired me?" she asked. It was time to get some answers.

"Yes."

"Did she know you used to know me? She didn't say anything."

"I did not tell her."

"Why not?"

"I wanted you. I was not sure you would come if you knew."

"Why was it so important I accept the position of nanny to your children?"

"I had a plan."

"What do you mean, a plan?"

"A plan to find an acceptable mother for my children. An acceptable wife. When I met Liana, I was swept away. I married her because she was a beautiful, glamorous woman, but she was not a natural mother, nor did she take on the responsibilities of her position. I could not risk another such mistake by setting out to 'marry for love' again." There was scorn in his tone. "I require a wife who understands what duty is and who will fulfil her duty—to me, my children, my country. I remembered your dedication when you worked for me before…and I realized that, if you had not changed, you might well be the wife I needed. And I decided to bring you here in order to ascertain that."

As she listened to him, her mind numbed with shock. He wanted to marry her, but he did not want to love her and he made it clear that what he wanted her for most was her Girl Scout loyalty and willingness to serve. She could not imagine a more mundane, less romantic beginning to a relationship. A less successful one.

"You've got to be kidding."

"I do not joke about things this important."

"But you can't choose a wife based on a woman's performance as a housekeeper."

She stopped and he followed suit, turning to face her again. "I am certain I could, but in this case, I planned to watch you in action with my children. The position of nanny was eminently suited to offer me a chance to test the waters and see if you were the woman I remembered and if you would have the same harmonious effect on my children's lives that you had at one time had on mine."

"I wondered why your staff seemed to come to me for decisions I would not expect a nanny to make."

"It is true that I gave instructions to place you in this role." He sounded extremely proud of his forethought.

"So, you were testing my suitability?" she said flatly.

"Yes."

"That would make your talk of marriage now a bit premature, wouldn't it? I mean, don't you need to do more tests?"

"Things changed last night."

"Because we had sex?"

"Yes. I had planned to wait for that, to make sure everything else was as it should be before we tested the passion between us."

Passion, not love. He'd loved the beautiful Liana, now he wanted a marriage of convenience with the ordinary Maggie. "Then why didn't you?"

"I was not thinking straight."

"Why not?"

"I'd had no sleep for a day and a half. I'd taken motion sickness pills and then had a couple of drinks. They didn't mix well. My mind was clouded."

His explanation was no less unbelievable than his plan to test her out as a possible wife material.

"So, you were drunk?" She'd been right about the word-slurring thing. Only now it didn't feel like nearly such a hopeful prospect as it had that morning, because the connotations were far more detrimental to her sense of feminine value.

He'd only made love to her because he was out of his mind on meds that should not have been mixed with alcohol.

"Not exactly."

She wrapped her arms around her middle, but she did not feel comforted. She just felt alone. Again. "Close enough to it."

"*Sì.*"

"Did you know I was in the bed before you got into it?"

"*Sì.*"

"Then why did you?"

"The truth? I was too tired to go elsewhere."

"You weren't too tired to seduce me."

"I kissed you good night. You responded."

Even that didn't make any sense to her. "Why did you kiss me?"

"I cannot explain it. It made sense to me at the time," he said with a self-deprecatory gesture that was at odds with his usual arrogance. "You must accept that our coming together was meant to be."

"How can you say that?"

"It happened, did it not?"

"That's hardly proof that Providence was behind it. I'm not your type, Tomasso. I never could be." He had to see that. "I'm nothing like Liana."

"And I am glad of that. She brought more discord to my life than joy."

"What do you mean?"

"Marriage to Liana was not the equivalent of domestic bliss. She did not like the strictures of our duty to the crown or our people. Nor was she enamored with motherhood, and spent little time with our children. She accused me of working too much but she was never here when I was home. The most domestic peace I'd ever known was when you were my housekeeper. Six years ago, Liana's beauty and charm dazzled me, but I am not so easily swayed by a pretty face now."

He might as well have said flat out that Maggie was far from beautiful. Which she'd known, but having it reiterated so baldly was shattering. "But what about passion?" she asked in a whisper.

"We share that…in abundance."

She wasn't so sure about that. They'd had sex because he had been drunk, for all intents and purposes, and she was there, convenient and in his bed. How real, or focused, was that kind of passion? It certainly wasn't enough to sustain a marriage to a man of his sexual appetites and stunning appeal to the opposite sex.

"Let me make sure I have this straight. You had me

brought here to the island so you could *try me out* as wife material?" Just saying the words offended her.

Tomasso had not believed she was worth courting through the usual channels. He'd had no plans to court her at all if she didn't pass his tests.

"Yes, but my behavior last night circumvented the time for any such assessment. It is lucky for me that you are so obviously well matched with my children."

"In other words, you really wanted a nanny who was willing to sign a longer contract than two years."

"Don't be foolish. Being my wife constitutes much more than merely caring for my children."

"Yes, I suppose it does. You'd expect me to warm your bed as well."

"A situation we will both enjoy."

"You couldn't tell that by me."

Instead of being piqued by her insult, he smiled with supreme male confidence. "The next time I will make you scream in ecstasy."

"Yes, well…that's not something *I* want to test right now."

He moved in closer, his scent and his presence causing a reaction inside of her she tried desperately to stifle. "I could make you want it."

"I would rather you didn't."

"Why?"

She stepped back. "Because while you are apparently convinced you've found your answer to domestic peace, I'm not nearly so certain. I signed on as your nanny and as far as I'm concerned that's all I am at the moment."

"That is not possible after last night."

"On the contrary, today showed how very possible it is."

"And if you are pregnant with my child?"

"I don't want to discuss that."

"I do. You told me you were not due for your monthly for two weeks. That makes conception a strong possibility."

"But it still isn't certain."

"It can be."

"How?"

"Tomorrow, I can take you to the doctor."

"Don't even think about it. I have no desire to be the center of a media frenzy."

"Then a pregnancy test. They are very accurate now."

"You know this from experience?"

"Liana tested her second pregnancy before consenting to see a doctor."

"Oh. Where did she get the test?" She couldn't see a princess going to the local grocery store and buying one.

"I do not know, but I will procure one for you."

She opened her mouth to argue that it would be little improvement over her going to the doctor for a pregnancy test.

He pressed his forefinger against her lips to silence her. "In secrecy."

She closed her mouth and he pulled his hand away, tracing her bottom lip with his fingertip in the process. "All right?"

"Yes. Thank you."

She turned to walk back to the house.

"Maggie."

She didn't stop walking, but looked back over her shoulder. "What?"

"If you are pregnant with my child, I won't let you go."

The next morning, Tomasso announced at breakfast that he wanted to take the children and Maggie snorkeling.

"Are you sure you need me along?" Maggie asked, even

as the prospect of snorkeling the crystal blue waters of the nearby lagoon tempted her.

She would have to be with Tomasso and his presence was much more detrimental to her peace of mind than it had been six years ago.

"But, Maggie, you said you'd love for Papa to take us snorkeling, don't you remember?" Gianni asked.

She had said that, when the children were talking about going with their father…before she'd known who their father was. "I didn't say I didn't want to go, sweetie. I just wanted to be sure your papa doesn't mind having an extra person along. After all, he's been away from you two for over a week. He might want to spend time with you alone."

"But it will be more fun if you are there, too," Anna said plaintively.

"I want you along," Tomasso affirmed in a voice that brooked no argument.

"Papa knows the best places to go. And there's nothing to be scared of in the water," Gianni said with an endearingly earnest expression. "Papa said so."

And since Papa said it, it must be true. Maggie smiled. "All right then, but you must promise not to abandon me to my own devices."

"I'll stay with you," Gianni promised.

"I as well," Tomasso said with a timbre to his voice that sent awareness arcing through her.

And he knew, the fiend. One thing she was beginning to realize. This man was more merciless than the one she had known six years ago. If she couldn't be swayed by logic, he wasn't averse to using seduction. Both were toward the result he wanted…a wife who would cause him no trouble and would care for his children.

Being thought of in those terms was not exactly flattering, but she got the impression that her opinion wouldn't carry much weight with him, either.

"Me, too," Anna piped in, so obviously not wanting to be left out that Maggie ruffled her hair and thanked her.

At least the children would be around to act as a buffer between her and Tomasso.

Forty-five minutes later, the protection she'd expected to feel in their presence was sadly lacking.

Tomasso had been giving her swimsuited body hot looks for the past ten minutes…ever since she'd taken off the shorts and T-shirt she'd been wearing over her modest one-piece. It didn't feel modest, with him watching her as if he could see right through the skin-hugging lime green Spandex.

Darn him anyway. None of it was real…this pseudopassion he insisted on projecting at her. It was just his way of getting what he wanted. Something he was really good at, but her body didn't know the difference. Her stupid, susceptible heart insisted on being affected. No matter how many times she told herself it was just his way of convincing her to his way of thinking, she still reacted as if all that hot passion was real.

She helped Anna get her last fin on with fumbling fingers and hot cheeks.

"Do you need a hand?" But his expression said he knew exactly why she was all thumbs.

"No, thank you. I've got it."

He nodded and then thankfully, climbed off the end of the boat and jumped into the water to wait for the rest of them to join him. Maggie helped the children into the water before sliding in herself to land against Tomasso's hard muscled body.

She gasped as his arm snaked around her waist and his lower body tangled with hers. *"Tomasso."*

"Yes?"

"The children."

He grinned. "They swim like fishes and are waiting right here."

"But…"

His hand brushed down her body, curving possessively over her rear before he pulled away. The man was a master seducer. "Are you ready?"

"Yes, of course." But really, she was breathless from his brief touching, and tingling in places she didn't want to mention.

"Okay, then."

They all pulled their masks down, the children doing so with such competence it was obvious they'd done this many times before. Tomasso made sure they all stayed together and Gianni had been right. His papa did know the best places to snorkel.

The water below them teemed with the vibrantly colored life of the ocean. It wasn't long before Maggie was totally lost to awareness of time or anything else. She was shocked into screaming when her body was suddenly flipped over by a pair of strong arms.

She sank and then bobbed back up, tearing her mask from her face as she did so and spitting out her mouthpiece. "You *fiend!*" she shrieked at Tomasso.

He widened his eyes with feigned innocence. "What? I was only trying to get your attention."

The children chortled where they trod water nearby, their laughter as obvious as the amusement lurking in his blue eyes.

"You could have tapped me."

"I did. Twice."

"Oh." She hadn't noticed.

"I even tickled your foot," Anna said.

"My feet aren't ticklish."

"Apparently," Tomasso said with a wicked gleam. "I wonder if that is true of the rest of you?"

"Don't try finding out," she warned, though not at all sure what she would do if he did try.

"We're hungry for lunch," Gianni informed her before his papa could say anything else provoking.

"But it can hardly be time."

Tomasso pointed to his diver's watch. "Thirty minutes past actually."

She stared at him in shock and then quickly examined each child's back for sunburn. Luckily, there was no evidence of redness, but she still felt terrible. "It's a good thing we used such strong sunblock, but I'm so sorry I kept you all in the water so long."

Gianni squirmed away from her in the water, giving her the look a child gives his mother when she's fussing. "We were having fun, too, but we got hungry."

"Yes, we were and are…for many things." The innuendo in Tomasso's words no doubt went right over the children's heads, but Maggie got it and had to fight hard not to blush at the implication.

"Daddy went swimming underwater without his snorkel. He pretended to be a shark. It was funny, but you didn't notice him under you, did you?" Anna asked.

"Uh…no."

Tomasso gave her a look that singed her to her tiptoes. "The view from down there was even better than from the surface."

She knew the seduction was just that, but this time she

wasn't even sort of buying it. She didn't believe for a minute that looking at her average figure had put that look in his eyes. "Shall we go back to the boat?"

"Sure."

Tomasso helped the children back into the boat before turning to help her, but she peddled backward. "I can get in fine by myself."

"But a gentleman always assists a lady. Isn't that right, Gianni and Anna?"

"Yes, Papa," they chorused.

"You wouldn't want me to set a poor example for my children, would you?"

Right now she didn't particularly care what kind of example he set. Only, the bigger a deal she made out of it, the more likely she was to spark awkward questions from the two small chaperones she'd been a fool to believe would make a significant difference in the way Tomasso treated her. The man had subtle seduction down to an art form.

She didn't answer, but swam forward and allowed him to lift her onto the wide step.

He kept his hands on her waist. "I do not want you wearing this swimsuit in front of other men."

"What?" The comment was so unexpected, shock coursed through her. "Why not?"

"Have you looked at yourself when it is wet?"

She didn't make a habit of looking at herself when she swam, no. She did now, peeking downward, unsure what could be putting that territorial tone in his voice and gasping in shock when she saw.

The suit was unlined, but dry it was perfectly opaque. Wet, the lime green Spandex looked painted on and see-through. Her nipples showed dark and hard against the clinging fabric, while the curve of her breasts was perfectly molded as well, and she could only be eternally grateful God had made the curls between her thighs even lighter than the blond hair on her head because there was just the vaguest shadow alluding to her feminine place.

She wrapped her arms around herself and glared. "You could have said something."

"Why? I enjoyed the view, but I do not want to share."

"I'm not yours to share, or otherwise," she hissed too low for the children playing in the boat to hear.

His dark brow rose in questioning mockery. "That is a matter of interpretation."

"No, it isn't."

"Would you like me to remove your fins for you?"

What could she say but yes, considering that to insist on doing so herself would mean moving her protective arms from her exposed body? She nodded.

He took his time, caressing his way down her calf, one hand gently massaging her ankle as the other removed the fin from her foot. His hand moved from her ankle to her foot, still massaging in a way that made even her bones tingle. "Feel better?"

"Y-yes…"

He smiled knowingly and tossed the fin into the boat before repeating the entire process with her other foot. It took far longer than she would have taken herself, but she couldn't make her mouth form words of complaint. By the time he was done, she was panting in little gasps that gave away her reaction to his touch.

He might be seducing her into accepting his marriage of convenience, but her body was more than willing to react and she couldn't seem to do a thing about it.

He winked as his hands fell away. "All done."

Swallowing, she nodded. He certainly was all done, but

if his primary objective had been to remove her gear, then she'd eat the fin he'd just tossed in the boat. The man was a walking—make that swimming—menace.

Using one hand, while her other arm remained across her breasts, she climbed into the boat. She could feel his gaze on her backside and she didn't even want to know what her wet suit revealed to him. With a sense of desperation she didn't attempt to hide, she literally dove for one of the brightly colored beach towels stacked on one of the empty seats.

She didn't even bother to dry off before wrapping the large terry sheet around her sarong style. She was never wearing this swimsuit again.

CHAPTER SEVEN

TOMASSO climbed into the boat with a grace she envied and then started the small outboard motor. He lifted anchor and then guided them to the shallows, cut the engine and dropped anchor again an easy paddle from the shore.

This time when he went to help her out of the boat, she gritted her teeth, determined to bear it in silence. She'd given him far too much reaction already today, but she couldn't stop her heart from racing.

Her initiation into intimacy had been painful, but her body chose to remember the pleasure before penetration as well as the mind-numbing completion he'd given her six years ago. She craved closeness with him, both physically and mentally. It was as if the last six years had never happened and her emotions were as tightly wound up in him as they'd ever been before. How could something so devastating happen overnight?

Her desire-befuddled brain had no answers, but nor could it deny that a profound change had occurred inside of her. Her heart had once again made a place for Tom Prince…or Prince Tomasso. It didn't matter what she called him, her heart knew he was the one man who would ever reside there.

It wasn't fair that he should have such an impact on her and she have no defenses against it, except to pretend indifference when she felt anything but. But life was not fair, and she'd learned that long before she'd met him the first time.

With the children's help, she spread out a blanket under the shade of the dense island foliage further up the beach and then laid out the lunch. Once they'd eaten, Anna and Gianni cajoled Tomasso and Maggie into a game of tag. Afterward, she was only too happy to lay down on the blanket in the shade with the little ones and take a lazy nap.

She woke to the feeling of something soft brushing across her stomach. Her eyes slid open and she saw that Tomasso was seated on the blanket beside her, sweeping a palm frond across her sensitive flesh. Her now dry, but still thin bathing suit was no barrier to the riotous sensations he seemed intent on evoking.

She realized the towel was no longer wrapped around her at the same time as the palm frond took a dangerous sweep upward, trespassing the valley between her breasts. "What happened—"

His fingertip pressed against her mouth. "Shh…the children are still sleeping."

And they were, looking so angelic, it made her heart ache.

The palm frond continued its tantalizing touching and she put her hand on his wrist to stop him, but part of her didn't want to.

His fingertip slid from her lips to the rapidly beating pulse in her neck. "I want you, Maggie."

"No."

"Yes. And you want me, too."

She wanted to say no again, but her mouth refused to utter the lie. Though a certain amount of fear mixed with that desire. Would it hurt again?

"No."

"I didn't ask a question," she whispered.

"Your eyes did."

"What question was that?"

"You are afraid it will hurt again, but I promise you, it will not. Had I known of your untouched state the first time we made love, I would have done all that I could to avoid giving you pain then."

She couldn't help noticing he had not said he regretted touching her, though. "It has to hurt, doesn't it…the first time?"

"Perhaps, a little. But there are ways of making the pleasure so great, any pain is barely noticeable."

"There was a lot of pleasure…before."

"I took you too quickly. I should have eased you into it."

"Would that have helped?"

"Yes."

"Have lots of experience do you, in deflowering virgins?"

He moved so he was lying beside her, propped up on his elbow. "No, actually. I had never bedded a virgin before."

"Then how would you know?"

The look he gave her made her squirm inside.

"I am so not in your league, Tomasso," she whispered sadly.

He traced the lines of her face with one gentle fingertip. "In this you are wrong."

"I'm not."

"You are the woman I want to be the mother of my children…that puts you in my league." Then, before she could utter another protest, his mouth covered hers in a tender kiss.

She'd been expecting more claim-staking aggression when their lips met, but had no desire to halt this gentle onslaught. His lips moved over hers, teasing her to a response her body was only too happy to give. Within seconds she was all hot and quivery inside, her inner core pulsing with a desire that overwhelmed her.

His hands were everywhere, touching her, stroking her, exploring every inch of her exposed flesh and then trespassing the lines of her swimsuit to shock her with intimacies that made her moan.

"Shh…" he whispered in her ear. "The children."

Remembering, she tightened her throat on another moan and buried her fingers in his longish hair, gripping it tightly. He didn't complain, but kept up the kissing and touching until her body felt on fire with needs and desires only he had ever been able to create in her.

"Papa, why are you kissing Maggie?"

The sleepy child's voice barely dented her passionate stupor, but Tomasso pulled back with a cool ease that shamed her. He smiled at Anna, who had sat up and was rubbing her eyes. "I like to kiss Maggie."

Did his daughter believe that because he was her papa and a prince, that excuse was sufficient? If Tomasso Scorsolini liked doing something, he automatically got to do it, Maggie thought wildly. But she had liked it, too.

Much too much.

"Will you make her our mama then?" Anna asked.

"Perhaps."

Maggie was amazed that he did not come right out and say yes, considering his arrogant belief that she would fall in with his plans despite her protests.

She asked him about it later that night, after the children were in bed. She'd come into the lounge to read a book and he had been making phone calls in his study, but had joined her moments before.

He swirled the Scotch in his glass and looked at her.

"I will not make promises to my children I am not positive I can keep."

"I thought you were convinced you would get your own way."

"I cannot force you to marry me."

"But you are sure you can seduce me into it."

"It is only a matter of time before I have you in my bed again," he said without bothering to deny it.

"Has anyone ever told you that you're so primitive you belong in an exhibit on prehistoric man?"

"No. I am fairly certain I would remember such a comment."

"Well, I'm saying it."

"Wanting you does not make me a Neanderthal."

"Your belief you can drag me off by my hair does." And she didn't believe for a minute he wanted her. Not really. Men could manufacture desire, couldn't they?

All he had to do was think of someone else, someone more exciting, as he had the first time they'd almost made love. She was his answer to domestic harmony, not a woman he could love and passionately desire on her own merits.

"I have no desire to drag you anywhere. I wish for you to come to me willingly."

"You want me to engineer my own downfall?"

"Marriage to me is not a pit to fall into," he said with an expression she didn't understand. "I have no desire to jail you."

"I never said you did."

He visibly shook off whatever was bothering him. "Of course not."

"Did Liana accuse you of that?"

"The joys of living the life of royalty palled very quickly under the strictures it imposed."

"But surely she did not blame you for that."

"Yes, she did. Just as she blamed me when she became pregnant a second time."

"Didn't she want more children?"

"No."

"But…"

"She agreed to carry the baby to term if I would agree to allow her total personal freedom after Anna's birth."

"Oh, my gosh. I can't believe she did that."

He shrugged as if he had long ago come to terms with his wife's mercenary attitude toward her children. "She knew it was her best chance at getting what she wanted."

"Which was what?"

"The life of a princess without any of the responsibilities."

"But that's horribly selfish."

"Yes. And in the end, her selfishness killed her. She was parasailing in Mexico with a company that did not even have proper licensing when she was killed. She chose to go on the trip without me, without her children—she chose to dismiss her bodyguard's fervent request she not sail with that company. She had the freedom to do so, you see. I'd given it to her. And she died."

"You can't feel responsible!"

"Can't I? She was my wife and I did not protect her."

"She didn't want to be protected and from what I can tell, she didn't want to be a wife…not really."

"You are right. I will not make that mistake in marriage again."

"But not all beautiful women are that self-absorbed and spoiled."

"It does not matter. We are not talking about other women when it comes to marriage. We are talking about you only. For you alone are possibly pregnant with my child."

But once again, he had not denied that he did not find her beautiful. Oh, sure…he was attracted to her, but that wasn't the same thing as looking at her and being bowled over by her beauty. She'd seen him looking at Liana that way, and she would never forget it. He could never love an ordinary woman like Maggie and that was the most painful truth of all.

The next day, he informed her that she and the children would be accompanying him to Scorsolini Island for his father's birthday celebration the week after next.

"I'd prefer to take those two days as my days off."

"I want your help with the children."

"But you don't need me there, not with your sister-in-law on site. She's wonderful with the children."

"She's also in charge of the celebration events. She does not have the time to devote to my family, and why should she when I have you to help me care for Anna and Gianni?"

"You don't *have* me. I'm your nanny, and my contract stipulates at least one day off per week and all evenings when you are not away on business."

"You begrudge eating dinner with the children and me?"

She rolled her eyes at his obtuseness. "No."

"You do not wish to tuck them into bed at night?"

"That isn't the point."

"What is the point, Maggie?"

"I don't want to go to Scorsolini Island with you."

"Why not?"

Because she didn't want to see him around the beautiful women of his set, didn't want to witness him flirting with women who were far more suited to the role of princess than she was. "It's just not my scene."

"Are you telling me you never socialized with your employers and their children in your previous two positions?"

"Well, no…" In fact, they had always assumed she

would attend social functions to care for their children's needs so they could concentrate on the socializing aspect.

"Then this is no different."

"What day do you plan to give me off then?" she asked, stubbornly determined to gain some ground here.

He tensed as if he was really bothered by the question. "When you worked as my housekeeper you were content to be with me every day."

"That was then, this is now."

Looking inexplicably offended and definitely irritated, he said, "If you must have a day off, then make it the day before we leave for the other island."

"Thank you. And this week?"

"Do not thank me for merely doing my duty to fulfill our *business* contract. As for this week, take whatever day you like. You can inform my secretary of your decision so arrangements can be made for the children."

"Do you have business meetings over the weekend?"

"Not on Sunday. Do you want one of those days off?"

"Sunday would be fine."

"So be it," he said and turned to address Gianni about something.

She felt chilled by the dismissal, but she also wondered at it. Tomasso was a businessman to his toenails and yet he resented adherence to the business contract between them. It was another confusing puzzle in a long line of them where he was concerned.

He was still responding with cold politeness toward her two hours later when he received a phone call that made him frown and mutter something in Italian that got him a scolding from Anna.

"What is the matter?" she asked as he flipped his phone shut.

"You will get your wish to be rid of my presence earlier than anticipated. There is a problem with one of our lithium customers in China. Negotiations have hit a wall because of government requirements related to imported raw materials. I have to leave for Beijing tonight."

"But you just got back from a trip abroad. You told the children you would be home with them for at least another day."

He looked driven. "This cannot be helped."

"It's okay, Papa," Gianni said, his face set in stoic lines Maggie hated to see on a five-year-old.

"Why can't you take them with you?"

"That is not practical."

"Why not? If you're going to travel so much, you need to be prepared to take your family with you. It's not as if you can't afford the extra tickets."

"It is not a matter of tickets. I travel by private jet, but taking them would require taking you."

"Naturally."

"You do not mind this?"

"Why should I? As their nanny, my primary concern is the children's welfare."

"And you think it is best served by traveling with their papa?"

"Sometimes, yes."

"Do you like to travel?"

"Yes. I did quite a bit of it with the first family I worked for. I can have the children and myself packed within the hour."

"That was not in your file."

"My file?" she asked delicately.

"What's a file?" Gianni asked, when the silence between the adults had stretched uncomfortably.

"In this case, I believe it refers to a report compiled about a person. Me. Is that right?" she asked Tomasso.

"Yes. It is so."

"What kind of report?" Anna asked.

"An investigative report," Tomasso answered flatly.

"You had me investigated?" She should have known he didn't trust her—he'd doubted her after that first night—but it still hurt.

"Naturally. All Scorsolini employees have background checks run on them."

And that said everything about how he saw her position as his wife if she were to marry him.

"I see."

The provoking little witch, Tomasso thought.

He didn't know what it was she thought she saw, but from the expression in her usually warm gray eyes, it wasn't something that put him in a complimentary light. The last two days had shown him that she was a perfect fit with him and his children. However, she stubbornly refused to acknowledge it.

But she wanted him. No matter how she tried to disguise it, her face and trembling body gave her away. However, she was adept at escaping to her suite or hiding behind the children's presence to keep him at bay. He allowed it because he wanted her to come to him of her own free will, but perhaps he was playing the game the wrong way.

He wanted her to be his wife. His instincts had been right from the beginning. She was everything he remembered and their shared passion was perfect. He would have no problem maintaining fidelity in the marriage bed, but he would not make the mistake this time of confusing lust with love.

He liked Maggie and that was more than he had felt for Liana at the end.

Though he had to admit, to himself only, that it would not bother him if she fancied herself in love with him again. It would make her happier because she wanted to marry for love, and he wanted her to be happy. He however, did not need to believe himself in love to be content with the prospect of marriage to her…particularly if she were pregnant with his child.

This trip to China could turn out to be a smart tactical move on his part, as well as a welcome opportunity to keep his children with him. Sharing a single hotel suite, even one with three bedrooms, would force them into a proximity she had avoided.

True to her word, Maggie and the children were ready to leave for Tomasso's private airstrip exactly one hour later.

She carried a large duffle bag onto the plane with her and when he asked about it, she smiled. "It's filled with their favorite games, art supplies and snacks. I wasn't at all sure your private jet would be stocked with the kind of snacks children like to eat while traveling."

"No doubt you are right. We usually take the yacht when we travel to one of the other islands."

"They never travel with you anywhere else?"

"To Italy to visit my stepmother, but then my staff know to prepare the plane for the children's presence and we usually do our journeying at night so they sleep for most of the trip."

"Your stepmother?"

For some reason it surprised him that she did not know about Flavia. "My father remarried within a year of my mother's death."

"The Queen of Isole dei Re lives in Italy?"

"She is no longer the queen. She divorced him when Marcello was small."

Maggie's face registered almost comical shock. "Why?"

"My father had an affair. She refused to forgive him."

"How horrible for her, but I'm surprised she divorced him for such a thing. I thought royal marriages lasted no matter what."

"She preferred life without a crown if it meant separation from a philandering husband." And he had respected her for it.

"Wow."

"You sound as if you admire her."

"I do. That must have taken a lot of courage. Did your father fight for custody?"

"Not that I am aware of. He even allowed Claudio and me to stay with her weeks at a time on several occasions each year."

"How unusual."

"Not really. He was hardly in a position to raise three sons without the help of a wife, and she had become our mother for all intents and purposes."

"I guess as king, he was too busy to be a single parent."

"Yes. I have never envied my brother his claim to the throne."

"I can understand that, but I always had the impression you were trying to prove something."

"That I could make it in life without my position? I used to feel that way." He'd given up worrying about it after learning Liana had known he was royalty when they met.

"You succeeded."

"To an extent."

"Your father never married again."

"No. He chose a string of mistresses over compromising his own sense of honor by speaking vows he did not think he would keep."

"Why wouldn't he keep them?"

"The Scorsolini Curse…or so he says."

"What in the world is that?"

"According to my father, the men in the Scorsolini family are fated to love once and to love so deeply that if the true love is lost then there is no chance another woman could ever take her place."

"That's an ingenious excuse for serial adultery."

"Not adultery. I told you, he did not remarry."

"But he assumed he would commit adultery if he did."

"Yes."

Maggie eyed him askance, her gray depths speaking messages he had not trouble interpreting. "Are you similarly inclined?"

"No. I do not break my promises."

"So you don't buy your dad's excuse?"

"No. Actually I don't."

"I would like to meet your stepmother, I think."

"I will arrange it. You will like her. She is very down to earth and warm. She gave my brothers and I a sense of family and normalcy in our childhood despite the fact we were princes. She is the only person who dares to scold Claudio, even now."

"She sounds wonderful."

"She is. You remind me of her in many ways." Suddenly he realized that one of his main reasons for seeking Maggie out was how similar she was to Flavia.

He knew he could trust Flavia and felt the same way about Maggie. He'd doubted her at first, but now that he understood how she'd come to allow him to make love to her, he accepted she was the same woman of integrity he had known six years ago.

CHAPTER EIGHT

THE first leg of the flight went surprisingly well. While Gianni and Anna were younger than her previous charges, Maggie had a lot of experience keeping children occupied on long journeys. Besides, it was much more comfortable on Tomasso's private jet than it ever had been on a commercial flight, even in first class. He had to work for several hours of the first leg, but put his papers aside to eat lunch with her and the children.

He turned his focus entirely on them—and her—while they ate, making the children beam and unnerving her.

For a workaholic, he had a surprising ability to set his work aside.

When they stopped to refuel, he surprised Maggie by leading them off the plane. He took them all to eat at a local restaurant for dinner and then arranged to go to an outdoor play area for the children he'd had his staff locate.

"Don't we have to get back in the air?" she asked as Gianni and Anna ran toward the merry-go-round.

"We will have a much more pleasant second half of our journey if we allow the children to use up their excess energy so they will sleep."

"The first half wasn't so bad."

"It was not bad at all. You did an excellent job with them. I was very impressed, but it is late and if we do not give them time to play, they will spend the rest of the flight fretting instead of sleeping."

"You know your children very well, don't you?"

"Naturally."

"You're a good father. I'm sorry Liana wasn't more interested in family life. If she had been, you would have made an excellent team."

"I am counting on that team being you and I, Maggie."

"It's not the same."

"Are you saying it would bother you to be the mother for two children to whom you had not given birth?"

Anna sat on the merry-go-round while Gianni pushed it and then jumped on, both of them shrieking with laughter as it whirled. They were both so precious…so loveable.

"That's not the problem. How could it be?"

"Liana did not wish to be a mother to her own children. Many women would hesitate to take on that role with children that are not their own."

"I'm not those other women, nor am I Liana." In more ways than one, she thought. But in this instance, she certainly didn't mind. "And I don't believe you would have any trouble finding a stadium full of women who would willingly be stepmother to your children if it meant a chance to marry you and wear that princess crown you were so sure I wanted to trade my virginity for."

His gaze settled on her, all serious and intent. "I have admitted I was wrong, have I not?"

"Yes, but you never said you were sorry for thinking it in the first place." Which bothered her. She'd never give him reason to believe badly of her.

"And you believe I should?"

"Absolutely." She turned to face him, leaving the children's safety to the security team hovering at a discreet distance. "Your cynicism is no excuse for insulting my honor."

His blue eyes sparkled with latent humor. "I am deeply remorseful and beg your pardon most humbly."

"You're laughing at me."

He smiled and it was like an arrow straight to her heart. "Perhaps a little but I am sincerely sorry for offending you. You are much too innocent to have hatched such a scheme."

"Honest. I'm much too *honest.*"

"That, too."

She nodded with satisfaction, though his belief she was so innocent rankled a little. It was akin to him thinking she was too dumb to have hatched such a plan. She wasn't, she simply had too much integrity to allow her mind to go sailing in such murky waters.

He brushed a curling strand of hair from her face, leaving a path of aroused nerve endings in the wake of his touch. "So, what is the problem?"

"Problem?" What was he talking about?

"You said the children were not the reason you are balking at marriage to me. That still leaves some obstacle in your mind to be overcome."

"There is the little matter of love between us, or lack thereof." And the fact that no matter how much she might come to love him, he could never, ever love her.

She wasn't princess material and never would be. She wasn't beautiful, she wasn't sophisticated and a regal bearing would really be beyond her. Wouldn't he always be comparing her to that kind of woman and finding her wanting? Part of her wished she could be those things for him. That she could somehow earn his love like she'd earned her place in the foster homes she'd lived in.

But an even bigger part of her wished she didn't have to, wished that his proposal had been sparked by love and not convenience, and that he wanted her heart for the future, not just a glorified nanny and bed warmer.

She'd spent her whole life earning her place through work and the thought of being married for the same reason was really painful. Millions of women just as ordinary as she was were loved by the men that had captured their hearts...why did she have to have gotten involved with a blasted prince?

"Did you know that a socially accepted view of love as the basis of marriage did not come into being until 1200 AD?"

It was not a welcome question on the heels of her thoughts. "Well, it's in existence now."

"Even then, not every culture adopted it," he continued as if she had said nothing. "And among the ruling class it took much, much longer to take root, even in the Western world. My own family did not have their first marriage for love until 1809 and it was 1866 before the first Scorsolini king married a woman of his choice rather than arranging an advantageous political match."

"I don't know what you think that has to do with me."

"Family history is filled with accounts of successful and by all accounts, happy marriages."

"And some not so happy. I don't want to play out the scenario your father played with Flavia."

"I have told you, I do not break my promises. I was faithful to Liana for the entire four years of our marriage, never even looking at another woman with intent."

"I believe you."

"So why are you so worried?"

"Liana was gorgeous and sophisticated. While she obviously failed in the mothering stakes, she was the ideal companion for you."

"You think so?"

"Obviously. She was everything any prince could want. She was beautiful and sexy. You used to watch her with a look of total enthrallment. She was passionately full of life and that charmed you. I remember."

"She was filled with passion for the pleasures of life. That is not the same thing, as I learned too late. And none of the other things you mention made up for her selfish disregard of our children's feelings and needs. Believe me. Beauty that is only skin deep pales quickly."

So he said, but that beauty had been enough to catch his attention completely, enough to make him forget the paltry attraction he had had toward Maggie. And no matter what he said, it must have kept his interest because he'd remained with her despite her incredible shortcomings as a mother. Family was obviously important to him, so to her mind it was very telling he had stayed with Liana even after she blackmailed him with her pregnancy.

"You stayed married to her," Maggie said almost accusingly.

"And remained faithful," he replied grimly.

"Why?"

"She was my wife. I made the mistake, I would not divorce her and hurt the children further. At least as my wife, she saw them more frequently than she would have as my ex."

"The fact you were very attracted to her had to have helped."

"The passion I felt toward Liana had burned out by the third year of our marriage."

Far from making Maggie feel more confident, that knowledge seared her to her soul. If he had stopped wanting a woman like Liana, how could she hope to maintain his sexual interest for a lifetime?

"I notice you do not ask why."

"I would say it was obvious. She no longer appealed to you."

"No, she did not, but not for the reason you seem to believe. I did not turn my eye to another woman."

"Then what?"

"I could not feel strong desire for a woman who used her pregnancy as a bargaining chip and then later pursued her own pleasures while ignoring our children."

"Yet you continued to make love to her."

"I am a man. I have needs and they had to be met in the marriage bed."

The picture he painted of his marriage was a chilling one.

"I could not stand being married to a man who did not want me."

"That will not happen."

"How can you say that after what you just told me?"

He sighed in exasperation. "Don't you hear anything I say? What draws me to you is not something that can ever change."

"What do you mean?"

"I desire your delectable body, but it is the character inside you that acts like a continuous aphrodisiac to my senses."

"Yeah, right," she said indelicately…though *her* senses were busy trying to deal with the arousing nature of his nearness. But delectable body? Could he really think that?

"I am not making a joke here. Your generous spirit is not only a total sexual turn-on, but it is addictive. I want you, Maggie."

"You keep saying that."

"Because it is true. And I will have you."

He'd said that more than once, too. "Not here. Not now," she couldn't resist saying.

"Soon."

The promise in his voice and eyes made her shiver and in self-defense, she turned away to watch the children again.

She couldn't turn away from his claim that it was her character he found so inspiring, though. She found it inconceivable and wasn't sure she believed him, but as cynical as he was, she'd never known him to lie. Was it possible that, despite the fact she wasn't beautiful and he most likely would never love her, she could hold his sexual interest in marriage and friendship? Just by being herself?

And if she did enter such a one-sided marriage, loving him and not being truly loved in return...would that really be enough for her?

By the time they left the play area, Gianni and Anna were so tired, they were both drooping. When they got back to the plane, Maggie went to pull back the covers on the bed in the small bedroom when Tomasso stopped her. "The children can sleep comfortably on the reclined seats because they are so small. You will use the bed."

"But—"

"Do not argue with me. Do you not realize I'm the prince around here?"

"You're bossy, is what you are." She smiled. "At least I understand how you got that way now."

"And how is that?"

"You got used to giving orders, being royalty and all. I can't believe I never knew you were a prince six years ago. You were always uncannily regal in your bearing."

He laughed, but sobered when she did not smile or laugh in response. "What is it?"

"You said you thought you were my friend back then."

"We were friends, though you tried to deny it once."

It hadn't done her any good. Walking away from him had not meant forgetting. She had missed him, both his friendship and what might have been. Her dreams had kept the feelings alive and no other man had ever impinged on that part of her heart.

"I admit it now."

"Good."

"But if we *were* friends, why didn't you ever tell me of your true identity? You didn't trust me," she added, answering her own question.

He sighed. "I wanted to be accepted for who I was, not what I was."

"But I'd already accepted you."

"Did you? You walked away from me and our so-called friendship. Would you find that so easy to do now?"

"What do you mean *now?* Because we, um…" She let her voice trail off, not wanting to say what she was thinking with two sleepy children as witnesses.

"Because now you know I am a prince."

She rolled her eyes. "Don't be stupid. Your being a prince has nothing to do with it."

"Perhaps." But she could tell he didn't believe her.

That bothered her the whole time she and Tomasso readied the children for bed and got them snuggled into their reclined seats with blankets and comfy down pillows.

He was vulnerable to his position. The thought shocked her, but when she considered some things he had said and how hard he had worked to prove himself not only in college, but since, building a new industry for Isole dei Re, she realized it was true. And she hated knowing that he believed she was like so many others in valuing him because of his position and not who he was.

If she told him the truth about six years ago, she could dispel those beliefs, but it would mean admitting to feelings that had not been returned.

She'd protected herself once. For the sake of her pride and emotions, she had abandoned their friendship. She had hurt him and unwittingly fed his belief he could not be cared for simply as a man, as opposed to the man who wore the crown.

For reasons she did not want to analyze too closely, she could not stand for him to continue to labor under that misapprehension on her account.

"Your whole life has been both blessed and marked by your status as a prince, hasn't it?" she asked as he pulled her into a seat beside where he had been working before they'd landed for refueling.

He shrugged and that shrug did things to her heart that she didn't want to acknowledge in this lifetime. It said that as cool as he appeared, she had touched something raw inside him.

"I walked away from our friendship six years ago because it hurt too much to see you and Liana together. I loved you and it devastated me that you were so obviously in love with her. It had nothing to do with your status, or lack thereof. I can guarantee you that knowing you were a prince would only have solidified my decision. Being around the two of you made me realize how hopeless my feelings for you were. It would only have been worse, knowing you were royalty."

He frowned. "I hurt you very much that night I came home with Liana, didn't I?"

She didn't want to talk about that night. The memories were too sharp no matter how much she'd tried to forget. "You came home with Liana on lots of nights, and yes…it hurt. I didn't want to walk away from you—that hurt, too, but not as much as it would have watching the two of you together."

"I am sorry about that night."

"You said so at the time, and I didn't bring this up to dredge another apology out of you. I just wanted you to know it wasn't about you being a prince."

"I find it curious that, though I hurt you six years ago and you've made it clear you find my current proposal more an insult, you still care enough to try to protect my feelings. Most people would say I don't have any feelings to protect."

"They would be wrong."

His expression mocked her and she let out an exasperated breath. "Just call me a pushover then. I care too much about other people's feelings for my own good."

"You are not a pushover, but a rarity in this world: a woman who cares deeply for others."

"I'm not so rare. You just move in the wrong circles."

"Perhaps." His gaze snagged hers and held on. "I have regretted many times my timing in meeting Liana."

She never had. If he'd met the beautiful woman after they had slept together, Maggie's pain would have been multiplied tenfold because she had absolutely no doubt the outcome would have been the same. He would have ended up with Liana and she would have ended up alone.

"It was for the best," was all she said now as she broke eye contact and grabbed a magazine to skim.

Tomasso watched Maggie close the door on the bedroom, frustration roiling through him.

Didn't all the pop psychologists say that talking was supposed to bring two people closer together? But every time he and Maggie talked, she pulled further away from him. He had thought admitting that he had regretted falling for Liana and leaving Maggie untouched six years ago would make her see that she belonged with him.

Instead she'd made it clear that she did not think him turning to Liana instead of her was that great a tragedy.

Was that because she had found it so easy to dismiss her love for him? He had very little confidence in the emotion. His father said he had loved Tomasso's mother, but had certainly never loved any of the women who had shared his life since, including Flavia.

Claudio and Therese had a peaceful marriage, the kind Tomasso desired, but he had seen no evidence that his brother was crazily in love. Marcello had loved his wife, but she had died too soon for that emotion to be tested by time or adverse circumstance.

Tomasso personally believed that the emotion was an excuse strong men employed to justify weakness and to follow the impulses of passion rather than duty.

He had seen it too many times amidst the people of his world who used love as an excuse for infidelity and even the abandonment of responsibility to one's children or country. So why did the thought that Maggie no longer loved him annoy him?

Because there was no denying it did. Every time she said it, or implied that was the case, he was filled with an inexplicable anger and desire to make her recant her words.

No doubt it was for the sake of his children and his own peace of mind. He wanted her tied to him with unbreakable bonds. He did not have to trust in the emotion to know that if Maggie thought herself in love, she would be committed to him, body and soul. In a way Liana had never been.

Maggie would be his.

As she was meant to be.

Maggie snuggled into the heat surrounding her, a familiar scent from her dreams filling her with a sense of blissful peace. A warm weight that did not feel like a blanket shifted on her hip, sliding down her thigh. Her sense of drowsiness dissipated as her mind grew cognizant of the fact she was not alone.

Her eyes flicked open and in the dim blue glow given off by the emergency lighting beside the door she saw Tomasso. He faced her, his eyes closed, his breathing even and shallow.

He was asleep.

In her bed.

He was also dressed, or at least sort of. He wore a pair of shorts and a T-shirt, not an outfit she'd ever seen him in. Even on the beach, where he wore swim trunks that showed off his sculpted body to perfection or a polo shirt and tailored shorts. A curl of midnight-black hair fell over his forehead endearingly and she had to stifle the urge to reach up and smooth it back. She did not want to wake him.

No doubt he'd decided that sharing the bed made more sense than him trying to sleep in a reclining seat, but he had not gotten beneath the covers with her. She appreciated that. It showed that no matter how possessively he spoke to her, he respected her right to choose how far she was willing to go in this relationship.

It also indicated that, regardless of the fiasco of his first night home, he did not consider he had the right to climb naked into a bed with her in it. Not when he was in full possession of his reasoning anyway. In retrospect, if the consequences of that night had not been so serious, the fact he'd talked himself into doing so because of his inebriated (or close to it) state was almost kind of funny.

It was just so out of character. He'd blown his own plan because he'd been thinking fuzzy, and for some strange reason she couldn't begin to decipher, she found that endearing.

That thought made her smile.

In more ways than one, he'd tempered his arrogance for her. Though he certainly had not relinquished it completely. He *was* still in her bed, after all.

"You are smiling," he rumbled in a sleep-husky voice. His eyes, which she had not appreciated were now slit, opened fully. "You like waking beside me?"

She shook her head in disbelief at her own naiveté. "And I thought your arrogance was tempered."

"Why would you want it tempered?" he asked lazily. "You like me as I am."

"Do you always wake with these conceited delusions?"

"Is it conceited to believe it is not only my children's company you find pleasant?" The question sounded serious rather than teasing.

"I decline to answer that question on the grounds it could incriminate me."

"Aha!" He rolled in a swift move that took her by surprise and ended with her under him. "All of this nonsense about you having your days off was on principle, not desire, was it not?"

The blanket pinned her so she could not move, which worried her less than the fact her body was reacting to his position over her in a predictable and very uncomfortable fashion.

CHAPTER NINE

"HAVING regular days off is not nonsense," she argued in an attempt to hide the uncontrollable response from him.

But she was afraid it was a losing battle. Desire was part of love and she loved this man more than anything or anyone else in the world. She'd finally admitted that to herself when she'd come to bed. She'd known he still had a special place in her heart, but after talking to him and admitting her love from six years ago and seeing how affected he was by being wanted only for his status…well, her heart had just cracked wide-open.

She'd gone to sleep with the knowledge that she would love this man to her grave pumping in her heart.

"In our case, it is."

"You don't own me, Tomasso. Even royalty aren't allowed to keep slaves anymore."

He looked seriously offended. "Slavery has never been legal in Isole dei Re and I have no wish to make you my slave."

"Then why begrudge me time off?"

"I do not begrudge it. Surely you know that if you need time to do things for yourself, I will make certain you have it."

"Then why complain about my regular time off?"

"Because you would spend unnecessary time away from me and the children." He wanted to marry her to make his life easier, not harder. Somehow, he knew things would be harder when she wasn't there.

She sighed. "And if one of the things I want to do for myself is something as simple as taking a long bath and reading a book? How necessary would you see that being?"

"As imperative as you want me to. I would make certain you have the time to do so, though I can think of things much more interesting to do in the bath than to read."

"I'm sure you could, but as we've already discussed, I'm not up to your speed."

"In what way?"

"Too many to count, but I'm not exactly princess material, Tomasso."

"According to who?"

"Me."

"You have no experience in such matters and will therefore have to trust me when I tell you that you are wrong. You would make an ideal Scorsolini princess."

"You've got to be kidding."

"I am not. It comes back to character again—you have both the character and integrity for the job."

"I never considered getting married as a job." But then, for most children, being the daughter in a household wasn't a job, either. It had been for her, though.

She'd had to work to earn her place, and now he wanted her to work to earn her place as his wife.

"In many ways, that is exactly what it is." He put his hand over her mouth when she opened it to speak. "And that is not a bad thing. Marriage comes with a defined set of expectations that when fulfilled benefit both parties."

She turned her head so his hand no longer covered her

mouth. "You make it sound just like a business proposition when it should be so much more."

"It is more."

And she knew exactly what he was talking about. Sex. That wasn't enough, but it was all he was offering. Why did it have to hurt so much? If she were mercenary, she'd take his offer and run with it all the way to a really beneficial prenuptial contract. "I told you, I'm not up to your speed in that way."

"In what way?"

"The sex thing." As if he really didn't know.

"I could take you there," he said with a sensual smile.

And end up breaking her heart in the process...not that it felt all that whole anymore regardless. Loving another person hurt. For her, that was all it seemed to do. She'd loved her parents and losing them had shattered her child's heart. She'd loved a foster mom who saw her as nothing more than a source of income and free labor, and she'd loved him.

Her feelings six years ago had given her no joy and a lot of pain. Now she loved both him and his children and knew that to stay would hurt, but so would walking away. Much more than she had hurt six years ago.

Life wasn't fair and she knew that, but sometimes it felt like she was destined for more pain than she could deal with.

"No thank you." And even as she said the words, she wasn't sure she meant them.

She did love him and she wanted him desperately. It didn't seem to matter that she'd been hurt by him the two times she'd thought to make love with him...her heart wanted to try one more time to find an emotional connection through a physical conduit. Her brain screamed that it hadn't worked before and it wouldn't work this time, but her heart wasn't listening.

It beat with incessant hope that she didn't understand, but could not ignore, either.

That foolish organ insisted that things were different now. That Tomasso wanted more from her than he'd wanted before, that if all she could have from him was physical love, it was better than no love at all. It reminded her that she was tired of being alone and he was promising her a future of togetherness, no matter how pragmatic his reasons for doing so.

"I think it is time I showed you how truly well we fit together," he said, showing he wasn't convinced by her denial either.

"I don't want to be used." Where the words came from, she wasn't sure. They hadn't been in her brain, or her heart, that she knew about, but they expressed her feelings very well.

He frowned down at her. "I have made my intentions clear. I want to marry you, Maggie. That is not using you."

"You think I'm pregnant. If you didn't, you'd still be deciding if I was suitable wife material or not." And her susceptible heart would be smart to remember that.

"Even if we had not made love that first night, I would have realized very quickly how well you fit with my children and myself."

She shook her head, not wanting to believe him because if she did, her defenses were going to crumble.

"Yes. You are the woman we need to make our family complete."

"You don't love me, Tomasso."

"So?" he asked as if the single word, confirming his lack of feelings was not like a knife slashing right through her heart.

"So?" she repeated in a near whisper.

"Love is not a requirement for a happy marriage. I will be faithful. I will take care of you. You will have my respect, my consideration and God willing, we will have more children together. What more could a man who loves you give you?"

"His heart."

"You will have my loyalty, my commitment and my honor. It is enough."

"Your arrogance is showing again."

"Because I know what is right for me?"

"Because you are so sure you know what is right for *me*."

"But I do know this."

"You're only thinking about what is best for you and trying to convince me that it is what is best for me too."

"You are wrong. I care very much about what is best for you, but consider, Maggie…you are twenty-six years old. Until three nights ago, you were a virgin. You had not had a single serious relationship with a man."

"Did your report tell you that?"

"Yes. It also told me that you are a loner, but your heart is too generous to be comfortable in a lonely existence."

"Being a loner does not mean I was lonely."

"But you were. Admit it, for it is the truth."

He was right. There was a kind of loneliness that came from not having any family that people with a family could never understand. She had no one, and had had no one since she was eight years old. "So what?" she said, despite his perception of her pain. "We can't all have big families and oodles of friends. My job dictated that most of my time was spent with children, not adults."

"If you married me, you would become part of my family. My papa would be your papa, Flavia would care for you like a beloved daughter just as she does Therese, my children would be your children, my friends would be your friends. You would have *me*."

"Conceited." But, oh gosh…his words were more seductive than his body, and that was saying something.

"Practical. We were friends once. There is no reason we cannot share that friendship again. I know I would enjoy it, but just as important, you need it. You need *me*…even if you are too stubborn to admit it."

"It's not stubbornness."

"What is it then?"

"Fear," she answered baldly with more honesty than she had planned, and immediately wished the single word unsaid.

"What do you fear?"

"Having a family and then losing it again." The words came from a place inside her she thought she'd dealt with a long time ago.

"Like you lost your parents."

"And my foster care families. Permanent ties just don't work in my life."

"I will make them work."

"How can you?"

"I have told you. I will never let you go…and I will never leave you."

"That's easy to say now, but even you can't promise that."

"You mean death, do you not?"

"Yes."

"Everyone dies, Maggie, but to pull away from committing to the living because of it is to live a very lonely existence."

"Maybe lonely is better than hurting." Only it hurt, too, always being alone. It hurt so much.

"It is not."

"You're always so darn sure of yourself."

"It is my job to be sure."

"For your companies maybe, but not for other people."

"For you. Maggie, you are mine and one day soon you will realize it."

She glared at him. "Stop saying that."

"Stop denying it."

The whole time they'd been talking, he'd been on top of her, his body calling to hers, his nearness causing all sorts of reactions in her. The biggest one in her heart, but she felt an empty ache in her most feminine place, too. And her nipples stung against the soft cotton of her nightie. He hadn't touched her, but her breasts were swollen and craving the feel of his fingers and her thighs shifted in an invitation as old as time, as natural as it was risky.

She wanted to kiss him, to taste his mouth on hers and the salty maleness of his skin. She wanted to be naked with him and he with her like they had been that night. But this time she would touch him and concentrate intently on how it felt to be touched....not like in a dream, but for real. Because despite the discomfort of losing her virginity, the other night still had a dreamlike quality for her.

She wanted a taste of reality. Tonight she didn't want to worry about the future, or whether or not a relationship would work between them. For right now, she wanted to be exactly what he claimed she was...his woman.

And she wanted to try this one last time to fill the void in her heart with physical love. Emotional love was not on offer in her life, but this was, and the debacle of the other night could not obliterate the hope that burned too deeply to be quenched by mere logic or her brain's warnings.

"Maggie?"

"What?" she forced out of a throat dry with desire.

"Tell me what you want."

"I thought you knew."

"I need to hear the words."

"You're so sure of what they'll be?"

"I am."

But still he wanted the words. Maybe he wasn't as certain as he wanted her to believe. Or he simply wanted her to be aware of her choice. She'd accused him of taking advantage before, but he hadn't. Not on purpose. He shouldn't have gotten into bed with her that first time, but she believed he had done it without the intent to seduce. Her reaction to his kiss had been the downfall for both of them…something he could never have predicted and neither could she.

But now he wanted her cognizant agreement and she was ready to give it. She didn't want to hold back any longer. Not tonight. She was feeling much too vulnerable in her rediscovered love. She needed this. She needed him. "I want you, Tomasso."

His big body shuddered and he was silent for a long moment. "Are you sure?"

"Yes."

He kissed her then, a soft claiming of her lips that left her wanting more when he broke his lips from hers and stood. He pulled off his clothes in the dim blue light as naturally as if he'd been stripping naked for her every day for the past six years. His gaze caught hers as he skimmed his shorts down his hair-roughened masculine thighs. She couldn't help looking at what he had revealed, her gaze drawn as powerfully as if controlled by an outside force. And it was…his overt sexiness. He was so incredibly attractive. Every part of him.

Daunting, too. He was so very much a man.

Her eyes felt like they were bugging out of her head as she fixed them on his arousal. "Is that normal?" she croaked. "No wonder it hurt."

But did she want to change her mind? No. Which said a lot for the power of desire.

He choked on a laugh and shook his head. "I assure you, I am no monster, but you are very innocent." His eyes burned with satisfaction, their blue depths so dark they looked like a reflection of the night sky. "I find that much more exciting than I should. I am, after all, a liberated man."

It was her turn to laugh despite her nervousness. "Liberated for the Stone Age, maybe."

"You think I am a throwback?"

"You believe you have to marry me because I was a virgin the first time we made love and I might be pregnant. You think I *belong* to you for those same reasons. Yes, I would say that puts you in the running for Neanderthal Man of the Year."

He stilled, his regard intent. "And this bothers you?"

Remembering what he had shared about Liana's accusations that living with him was like being in a prison, Maggie stifled her inclination to give him a flippant retort. "Honestly?" she asked.

"*Sì.* Always, I want honesty from you."

"And will you give it?"

"Always. No lies. Ever."

That was pretty conclusive and the promise sent a sense of warm pleasure deep into her heart. "Neanderthal Man has his charms."

He smiled, white teeth flashing. "I'm glad to hear it."

He walked toward her, his hard flesh not the only thing that drew her attention. Naked, this man was magnificent. Every muscle in his body was defined without making him look like a Mr Atlas wannabe and his tanned skin glowed even in the dim light.

"You're yummy, you know that?"

"The feeling is entirely mutual."

She bit her lip, knowing that it had to be his libido talking. She was too unremarkable to be considered delicious by this man, but she knew he meant the compliment when he said it, however unlikely. He did want her. The evidence was staring her in the face.

"Will you allow me to make love to you without the blankets, or do you wish to hide beneath them?"

She *was* hiding, her body covered from neck to toe by the light cotton blankets and sheet. She didn't want to hide from him. For her answer, she pushed the blankets aside to reveal a short gown of pale pink. There was nothing overtly sexy about it, but it stopped mid thigh and its thin material did nothing to hide the turgid state of her nipples. The flare of his eyes told her he noticed, too.

He ran a fingertip from the rapid pulse in her neck down over the curve of her breast and then circled one hard tip before brushing directly over it. She gasped, her hands clenching at her sides.

"You are so responsive." He traced his fingertip across her chest to her other breast, giving the same tortuous caresses to it. "You excite me until I ache."

"I ache, too," she whispered.

"Then I must assuage that ache."

"Yes…"

He came down beside her, his sex touching her thigh and she sucked in a shocked breath. The intimacy was so new. His member was warm and hard, but felt smooth against her, too. So different than what she would have expected and yet so wonderful too.

He laid his hand on her shoulder, brushing her collarbone with his thumb, his eyes devouring her like a hungry lion. "You have nothing to fear. I will not hurt you again."

Despite the voracious look, she believed him. She was hungry for him, too. "I'm not afraid."

"You are very tense."

She smiled, her heart beat going a mile a minute. "This is all new to me."

"I could tell."

She turned her head away, stung at what she took as a reminder of the disparity in their experience. "Don't make fun of me."

"I am not. I told you…" He kissed along her jaw. "Your innocence excites me." His lips played with the corner of hers, his tongue darting out to taste her in a way that made her shiver. "Very much."

Forcing away her fears of inadequacy, she turned and gave him her mouth. She held nothing back and the kiss turned carnal, its heat scorching her nerve endings into blazing life.

He touched her while their lips were locked in the sensual battle toward pleasure. His hands laid claim to every inch of her flesh, showing her that she had eroge-nous zones she would never have suspected existed. She touched him, too, exploring every part of his nakedness she could reach. He thrust against her when she touched his backside, but when her fingers curled tentatively around his member, he went completely and utterly still, breaking the kiss.

"Yes, touch me there, Maggie."

She caressed him up and down and he groaned against her lips, kissing her again with rapacious desire.

He let her explore, guiding her hand when she grew shy and showing her what he liked touched and how to do it in a way that made his body rigid with vibrating tension.

He pulled her hand away. "That is enough," he growled.

"But I like touching you."

"I like it, too, *tesoro mio,* but if you wish me to leave you insensate with pleasure, you must not push me too hard this first time."

"It isn't our first time."

"Thank the good God. We have no virgin barrier to deal with."

He gave her no chance to respond, but started touching her again, first through her nightgown and then removing it so he could caress her naked body. He knew exactly how and where to concentrate his caresses and soon, she was quivering with need. But he was far from done. He used his mouth to cover the same ground he had recently traversed with his hands.

She shook with pleasure upon pleasure as his lips and tongue made love to her in a way she had never dreamed.

When he kissed her inner thigh, using his teeth to bite gently and then snaking his tongue out to lick her sensitized flesh, she cried out.

His head came up. "You must not be noisy, sweet Maggie. We do not want the children to hear. This room is semisoundproofed, but I would not like to test its boundaries with them in the outer cabin."

"You mean you haven't had noisy lovers in here before?"

"I have never made love in here."

"Oh." She liked knowing that, though why it should matter she had no idea.

After all, she knew he was experienced, but she had a deep inner need she did not understand for this time to be unique and special...for both of them.

His head lowered between her legs again, the sight unbearably erotic to her. This time his tongue touched a spot far more sensitive than her inner thigh and she had to bite her lip to keep from screaming. She whimpered as he made love to her with his tongue, using his fingers to press inside her, stretching her tight and swollen tissues.

Then he took her sweet spot between his teeth and thrashed the hard little nub with the tip of his tongue over and over again.

She came apart, biting her hand to stop a shout of agonized pleasure from escaping as she repeatedly convulsed under his ministering tongue. She was trembling with the edgy aftershocks of pleasure when he swarmed up her body. He pressed the tip of his erection to her quivering entrance.

"You are ready?" he asked in a strained voice.

"Yes." She needed to feel him inside of her.

He entered her in a slow glide that teased her with what would come while he filled her completely. Unbelievably, as exhausted as she was, she began to move under him, needing more than the tantalizing slowness of this tender possession.

He was not slow to take the hint, and with a dark chuckle of triumph, he set a pace that soon had her writhing in renewed preorgasmic bliss.

"That's right, *tesoro*….move with me. Give me your passion, *bella*."

"Bella?" The humiliation crashed down on her. Not now, please, he couldn't be thinking of another woman now…

"Beautiful," he was saying. "You are so beautiful in your passion."

Beautiful? It was Italian. *Of course.*

The realization that all those years ago he hadn't been thinking of another woman got lost in her second climax. His mouth slammed over hers and he swallowed the scream she could not stifle. He went rigid above her, his arms tightening around her with passionate force as he found his completion inside her.

He collapsed. The weight of his big body should have been uncomfortable, but instead it felt right. Wonderful, in fact.

He nuzzled her neck. "You are an incredible lover."

"You're not so bad yourself."

"Naturally not."

She laughed at his arrogance, too sated with pleasure to take issue with his egotistical statement.

He lifted his head and shoulders, balancing on his forearms. "What we have here is very special. You have no other experience to compare it to, but you must believe me when I tell you few lovers reach such heights."

"What about you and Liana?" she asked before thinking and then wished she could bite out her own tongue.

But he did not look offended by her question, more thoughtful. "She always wanted to be seduced. She never gave of her passion freely, like you do. You are so generous with your womanly desire. You cannot know what a treasure that is." He kissed her. "Making love to you is unique and very, very *good*."

The lavish praise filled her with pleasure.

"It was better this time," she felt she should tell him.

The whispered confession made him laugh out loud. "I am glad. I did not like you thinking my lovemaking was not all that it should be."

It was her turn to giggle. "Don't tell me you were bothered by such a little thing."

"It is not little for a man to appear deficient in the eyes of his woman."

"You could never seem less in my eyes," she admitted to him, too thrown by what she'd just been through to protect her words. "You are everything I ever thought a man should be, Tomasso."

He smiled, looking really pleased. "Then you will agree to marry me."

"I—" But her words were cut off by lips making new and passionate demands upon her.

When Maggie woke, she was alone in the bed and wearing the T-shirt Tomasso had worn the night before. He must have slipped it on her while she slept because she didn't remember putting it on. She remembered making love… more than once. She remembered getting every bit as insensate with pleasure as he'd promised her she would. And she remembered his certainty that she would now marry him after the first time.

She wasn't nearly as sure, but she was getting there. It was hard to believe she wasn't enough woman for him after a night like the one they had spent. It *had* been special.

But she was still uncertain. No matter how good the sex was, they wouldn't be spending their lives in bed. And how long would it last if love wasn't what made it so special to begin with? But she did love him…was that enough?

She took a shower, dressed in a fresh pair of jeans and neon-pink T-shirt, clothes appropriate for a nanny to wear. Children liked bright colors and so did she…but she didn't think Princess Therese would be caught dead in the bargain rack jeans and neon colored shirt. How could Tomasso believe she would fit into his life?

There was no doubting he did, but how could he? Was she wrong to be so unsure of herself and her place by his side?

Those two questions played a nonstop litany in her mind as she went to join him and the now awake children in the main cabin. They were eating breakfast at the table Tomasso had been working on before. Gianni was beside Tomasso. Anna sat across from them, an open spot beside her.

Maggie slid into it. "Good morning, everyone…or is it afternoon already in Beijing?"

"More like the wee hours of the morning, but it is the next day," Tomasso said.

Anna reached up and gave Maggie a childish kiss on her cheek in greeting. "You slept a long time. We got ready and everything and you didn't even notice."

"I must have been very tired."

"You need to eat your breakfast, Maggie," Gianni said. "Papa says we're going to land soon."

The flight attendant must have had the same thought because she put a plate of fruit with a bagel in front of Maggie.

Maggie thanked her and then returned the children's smiles without looking at Tomasso. "How exciting. I wonder if it will take long to get out of the airport. I've never been to China."

Anna squirmed as if she wanted to jump up and rush around the cabin. "Papa's been lots of times, huh, Papa?"

"Yes. I have. I will enjoy showing all of you around."

Maggie looked at him then, blushing under his quizzical stare.

"Did you sleep well?" he asked.

"Uh…yes. Very well. Thank you."

"Very soundly, too, I think."

Because she hadn't noticed him leaving the bed? He had her there. It felt strange to know that he had watched her sleeping, almost as intimate as what they had shared the night before. Had she mumbled his name in her sleep?

She'd been known to do so before, according to her former roommates and charges.

"Yes, Maggie…you didn't hear us come in and wake

you and Papa up." Gianni gave her a considering look. "Papa said he had to share your bed because he's too long to sleep in a chair. But you're not too long, are you?"

"But we didn't wake Maggie up," Anna pointed out. "Only Papa. How come you didn't wake up, Maggie?"

Maggie didn't know which child to respond to first, much less what to say. She looked to Tomasso for help, but the expression of intimate humor in his eyes only added to her embarrassed confusion.

"She told you, she was tired," Gianni said, saving Maggie from having to answer that question at least. "I bet she had jet lag."

Maggie wasn't about to explain to the child that jet lag came after travel, not during it, because Anna said, "Oh. I don't have jet lag."

"Me, neither, but how come you were in Papa's bed?" Gianni asked again.

She hadn't been in Tomasso's bed. She'd been in her own and he'd decided to share it, but she doubted Gianni would appreciate the nuances of the situation. "I…uh…it was more comfortable, and it's a big enough bed for two people to share."

"I thought only mommies and daddies shared beds," Anna said ingenuously.

"That's not right," Gianni said with a puckered frown on his forehead. "Zia Therese and Zio Claudio have the same bedroom, but they don't have any kids."

"But they're married," Anna pronounced. "It's the same as them being a mommy and a daddy."

"And so shall Maggie and I be just as soon as it can be arranged."

"You're getting married?" Anna breathed in awe.

"Yes," he said firmly, his blue gaze confident.

"Tomasso!" Maggie squeaked, unprepared for the frontal attack, though why it should surprise her, she didn't know.

This Scorsolini prince had already shown he could be ruthless when pursuing an objective, and that was exactly what she had become to him.

CHAPTER TEN

HER protest was drowned out by the delighted shouts from Anna and Gianni.

"So, you do not mind having Maggie for a mother now?" Tomasso asked his son.

Gianni's eyes so like his papa's were glowing. "No, Papa. You told me that if *Maggie* were our mama, she would be even better than a nanny because she would still watch over us and play with us, but she would stay with us forever."

He'd been talking to the children about her…about what kind of mom she would be?

"It's true, isn't it, Maggie?" Gianni asked, the worry evident in his voice.

For once, he had not accepted his papa's words as gospel, but she could tell he wanted to.

"If I were your mother, I would want to be with you just as I am now and no, I would not go away."

"What about what you told Zia Therese…about leaving in two years?"

"What I told Her Highness would not apply if I married your father instead of being your nanny," she said carefully, making no promises and yet feeling the inevitability of her future wash over her despite her caution.

Anna's eyes filled with tears and she threw herself at Maggie, hugging her around her neck so tight Maggie could barely breathe. "I wanted you to be my mama so bad. I love you, Maggie."

Maggie felt moisture burn her own eyes and she hugged Anna back with fierce affection. "I love you, too, sprite, both you and Gianfranco."

She didn't know how it happened, but Gianni ended up squeezed up next to her in her seat hugging her and Tomasso looked on with a smug benevolence that made Maggie want to scream. She'd never said she would marry him. They'd made love, but that wasn't a serious, full-on commitment in today's world. Was it?

Only, how could she disappoint these two precious children?

She couldn't deny that his preemptive action was getting her what she wanted most in the world, Tomasso and his children…a family of her own. And as scary as that was, as much as she knew this unequal relationship was setting herself up for pain, the joy unfurling in her heart said it was also a dream come true.

Even so, he had no business making that sort of decision on her behalf.

Which was exactly what she planned to tell him now that they were settled into their hotel suite, conspicuous in its design because it only had two bedrooms and a sitting room. The small contingent of personal security that had traveled to China with them had an adjoining suite and Tomasso's pilot and flight attendant were in rooms on another floor.

She left the children playing a game of Snakes and Ladders in the main room and followed Tomasso into his bedroom where he was unloading his briefcase onto the bed.

"Where exactly am I supposed to sleep? Anna's bed is hardly big enough to share."

He looked up, his expression neutral. "It does not seem to matter how luxurious the accommodation in China, it is difficult to find anything with a lot of space or large beds."

"I notice your bed is oversized."

"And it is a good thing, or we would not both fit in it comfortably."

"I am not sharing the bed with you."

He stopped what he was doing and faced her, his blue gaze probing hers. "Of course you will. Where else would you sleep?" His lips tilted in a mocking half smile. "As you pointed out, Anna's bed is too narrow to share."

"In my own room."

"There is not another bedroom in the suite."

"Then rent me my own quarters like you did the flight attendant. Surely I deserve at least her consideration."

"This is not about consideration, Maggie. You belong in my bed. We settled this last night."

"We didn't settle anything of the kind. And we certainly didn't *talk* about where you expected me to sleep once we got here. I would have remembered that conversation."

"After what transpired between us, there was no need to discuss it, surely?"

"You planned this all along, didn't you?" she accused. "You can't even use last night as an excuse because you had the rooms booked before we ever got onto the plane."

"What crime exactly are you charging me with?" he asked in an all too reasonable voice.

Which only made her angrier. She didn't feel reasonable. She felt maneuvered. "Trying to force my hand. I did not agree to come along on this trip as your bit on the side."

"We are going to be married. Do not ever speak of yourself in such disparaging terms again."

"Who says we're getting married?"

"I do."

"Here's a newsflash for you—it takes two cooperative parties to enter into a marriage in this day and age."

"You agreed to our marriage last night with your body and you did not deny it with your mouth this morning."

"I knew it!"

"Knew what?"

"You were using the children as a lever to force me into agreeing to marry you. You knew I couldn't say no to them. That's sneaky, not to mention cruel to them if you are wrong. What happened to you not making promises you weren't sure you could keep?"

"I am not wrong." He looked thoroughly offended she could accuse him of such a thing. "You gave yourself to me last night...you sealed your fate and my own."

"We had sex! I did not make a lifelong vow!"

"In giving yourself to me, you did that very thing. It is the way you are made."

She stared at him, poleaxed by what he had said and how well he knew her. He was right, darn it. She did feel committed to him now, in a way she hadn't after the dream-to-reality incident. But it wasn't just because they'd made love. Although that was a big part of it. She'd also admitted to herself that she loved him.

His calculating blue gaze said he'd known her agreement to make love with him had meant more than only that before she had. That he had in fact known before touching her last night that once she gave her body to him, she would feel fully committed.

He'd seduced her into wanting to accept his offer of a

marriage of convenience and it was only her stubborn pride that held her back from verbal agreement.

Furious at being maneuvered so neatly, she spun on her heel. "I'm not sleeping in here with you."

She never got her hand on the doorknob.

He grabbed her shoulders and pulled her back around to face him with implacable hands. "What is the matter with you? Why are you so angry? I am not such a bad catch, am I?"

She ignored that last bit of conceit. "You mean besides the fact that you obviously intended to seduce me once we got here?"

That really rankled on top of everything else because it said that, despite what she'd believed the night before, he'd never intended to honor her choices.

He sighed, the sound harsh and his expression austere. "Let us take care of that misconception. I changed the room arrangements when we arrived at the hotel. I am a very wealthy man—I do not have problems doing things like that. The hotel was happy to adjust our reservations to my new requirements. However, prior to our arrival, they had us booked for a suite with a room connected for you to stay in and a suite across the hall for the security team. After last night, I assumed—perhaps arrogantly—that you would willingly share my bed. It is precisely where I want you to be, so I arranged our sleeping accommodations accordingly."

"Oh."

"Better?"

"A little." A lot, actually, but she wasn't about to tell him so. "That doesn't alter the fact that you told the children we are getting married without my consent. I don't like being railroaded."

"I did not. You gave your consent."

She gasped. "I *never* said I'd marry you."

"As we both know and I have already stated…you said it loud and clear with your body, *tesoro mio*."

"But—"

"There are no buts, Maggie. Your body speaks more honestly than your lips."

"I don't lie."

"Then tell me you do not want to be my wife…my lover…my woman. Say these words with your lips and I *will* believe you."

She stared at him. She opened her mouth, but no sound came out. She couldn't say the words, not and tell the truth. She settled for a truth that was every bit as important, at least to her. "I don't want you to hurt me again."

"I did not intend to hurt you six years ago, and will not do so again."

She didn't believe him. How could he avoid hurting her when he'd been so oblivious the first time around? Wasn't it inevitable, given she loved him and he didn't love her?

"What happens when another Liana comes along, someone more suited to being a princess?" She looked down at her T-shirt and jean-clad self. "Look at me. I don't fit the mold."

He squeezed her shoulders, his face hard. "What you look like does not dictate who you are."

"This from a man who dated more beautiful women during his college years than most men do in a lifetime?"

"I have grown up since then."

"It's not just a matter of maturity." She wished it was, because no one would accuse this man of being childish.

"I assure you, it is."

"But look at the woman your brother married. I'm nothing like Princess Therese. She grew up around royalty, she's sophisticated and classy to her toenails. For goodness sake, she looks like a poster child for haute couture, not to mention she should be on the list of the Hundred Most Beautiful Women in the world. She's exactly what a princess should be."

"So, let her take you shopping for a new wardrobe if it will make you feel more confident, but it is the woman under your delectable skin I wish to marry."

"How can you?"

He bent down until their lips almost met. "We are great together, Maggie. You are fantastic for my children, good for me. How can I not?"

Then he kissed her and she melted into him with disturbing ease. If she didn't marry the man, she was going to end up being his clandestine lover and probably a pregnant one at that. She had no self-restraint where he was concerned. And no sense of self-preservation, either.

Like the first time, they had forgotten to use a condom last night…during any of the multiple times they had made love.

"You didn't use anything," she whispered as his mouth slid from her lips to explore along her jaw line.

"What?" he asked, his voice satisfyingly husky.

She forced herself to focus on her thoughts, not the sensations shivering through her body. "Was it on purpose?"

"Was what on purpose?"

"Not using any protection again last night when we made love."

He stopped kissing her and reared back, glaring down at her. "What did you say?"

"I want to know if you purposefully made love to me without protection because you thought if I got pregnant, it would be easier to get your way."

His blue gaze narrowed consideringly and then an

expression that looked like guilt flitted across his gorgeous features.

"You did," she said, outraged. "You made love to me on purpose with the intent to increase the risk of pregnancy."

"I did not."

"You looked guilty."

He glared down at her, his gaze hard as granite now. "I do not lie."

"But just now—that look—"

"Was me feeling damn guilty for being so irresponsible with your body, but that alone is a strong indicator we need to marry."

"How do you figure that?"

"I have no control when I am touching you. You have none, either, or you would have thought of it. Sooner or later, I *would* make you pregnant. I would prefer that be within the bonds of marriage."

"If I married you, it wouldn't be like it was with Liana."

"I am aware of that."

"I mean, I wouldn't tolerate the workaholic habits. I would expect you to put me and the children first at least ninety percent of the time and you'd spend a lot of time making up for the other ten percent."

"And would you make that easier for me by traveling on occasion with me as you have done this time?"

"If it means spending more time together as a family, yes. But I'm not the only one who will be doing the compromising. You will be around for important events like birthdays and school plays, which means if a business emergency arises, you consider your children and my feelings of more importance than making another million."

He smiled and she glared. "I mean it. You would have to promise me before I agreed to marriage."

"I believe I can do that."

"You'd have to do more than believe…you would have to follow through. I would also expect you to take normal weekends off as well as at least two family vacations a year, and we spend all major holidays like Christmas and Easter together as a family."

"That is a Scorsolini family tradition, but I'm confident most families only take one vacation per year."

"You're a prince, you can do as you like. You have a high-pressure job and the requirements of your station. At least twice a year, I would expect you to retreat from the world and let the children and I know that we are the most important people in your life." She couldn't believe she was demanding all these things, but she knew what made a strong family and she also knew that if he gave it, their marriage actually had a chance at survival.

"Very well. Two family vacations a year and you in my bed every night."

"Bed is fairly important to you, isn't it?"

"This is true, but I think you enjoy yourself when you are there, too."

"I do now."

He grinned. "So, we are agreed?"

She thought of the alternative. Life without him…again. Life without Anna and Gianni.

"Yes. I will marry you."

Their kiss was interrupted by two childish voices wanting to know why the people on the television didn't speak either English or Italian.

The next two days were hectic for Tomasso, who had back to back meetings late into the evening both days, but on the third one, he took the morning off to take her and the children shopping in marketplace.

She was awed by the way he interacted with the Chinese shop keepers, using his fluent Mandarin to bargain with them for toys that caught the children's eyes and a yellow silk kimono that caught his. It was beautiful, with pink and white flowers embroidered all over it. He asked her if she liked it and she nodded. That was when the bargaining began in earnest.

It went back and forth and at one point the shopkeeper slapped his arm, saying something sharply in Mandarin. Tomasso merely smiled and held his hand out with some money in it.

She cracked a smile herself, shook her head, but took the money and gave him the kimono.

He presented it to Maggie with a flourish that made the shopkeeper laugh and say something to the others around her that had them offering up several items obviously meant for women.

"What did she say?" Maggie asked.

"A fair flower like you deserved many gifts and that I should not stop at a mere kimono, especially one I got for such a good price."

"I really don't need presents at all. You have given me so much more that really matters."

"Yes?" he asked in an obvious bid for a compliment. She grinned, liking that his temperament expressed such a need. It showed a tiny bit of vulnerability. "You've given me two incredible children that will bless me all my life."

"And a lifetime with me, do not forget."

"I'm not likely to," she said dryly, but she reached up and kissed his cheek to show she really did appreciate him.

He went still, his blue gaze going dark.

"What's the matter?"

"That is the first time you have kissed me of your own accord."

She shrugged. "I'm shy."

"Not with the children. You hug and kiss them all the time."

But she was shy with him. Even in bed, only responding when he orchestrated lovemaking, never initiating herself. She was still having a hard time believing he wanted her for his wife, for his lifelong mate. She hadn't thought he'd notice her behavior, but he had.

"I'll hug and kiss you more freely after we are married."

"You promise, as I promised to put the family first?"

"Yes."

"It is a deal then."

"That is really important to you, isn't it?"

"Yes." He didn't say anything else, but she didn't expect him to. Not in front of the children.

But she couldn't help wondering if Liana had not been an affectionate woman. Maybe there were things she could give Tomasso that a more beautiful woman would not.

They were looking at traditional Chinese wedding finery in a shop that ended up being next to a tea house he'd taken them to for some traditional Chinese tea when he asked, "How big a wedding do you want?"

"I get to choose? I thought all royal weddings had to be huge and very, very traditional."

He fingered a headpiece made of gold, while the shop owner's gray-haired wife helped a giggling Anna try one on. "Do you want the pageantry of a royal wedding?"

"You mean I really have a choice?"

Gianni made a war cry and sliced through the air with a sword he'd found on the far wall. Maggie gasped and would have lunged for him, but the elderly owner of the shop was already there, showing Gianni how to hold the traditional sword and speaking to the little boy in broken English that seemed to mesmerize him.

Tomasso cupped her neck, his thumb brushing along her jaw. "Yes. You always have a choice, Maggie. I will not force you to do things that make you uncomfortable."

"Says the man who insisted I attend his father's birthday celebration as part of my job."

"I did not wish to be away from you for two days."

"That's sweet." And comforting.

"I am far from sweet."

Why did men always take issue with that word when applied to themselves? "What are you? Sour as a lemon?"

He leaned down and whispered into her ear, "I'm hot like lava and all I want to do right now is burn you."

She shuddered. He could do things with his voice that she was sure other men would never achieve with even a nighttime of touching. "Let's…um…get back to the small wedding idea."

He smiled, his expression knowing. He was obviously taking no chances on her backing out of his marriage of convenience and planned to keep her sexually enthralled until then. Besides, she had a sneaking suspicion that the man knew exactly how he affected her and he just plain liked knowing it, too.

"So, you would prefer something small?" he asked.

"Yes."

"I am glad."

"Don't you like big crowds?" She couldn't imagine that being the case, but why else would it matter?

"A small wedding means we can marry sooner."

"You aren't seriously afraid I'll change my mind, are you?"

"I will not let you."

"Papa said you're staying with us forever," Gianni piped up, making her aware that he had crossed the small shop to stand near them, the sword strapped to his waist and dragging on the floor.

"I am," she quickly affirmed having heard a tremulous doubt in the little boy's voice that broke her heart.

"Papa, Maggie, look at that," Anna cried and pointed to a man walking by the open doorway to the shop wearing a digital billboard on his head advertising a local restaurant.

They all cracked up while the old shopkeeper shook his head. China had changed since his days as a boy. Technology was everywhere, but he still had family in the country who had never ridden in a car.

Beijing was such a different place to any she'd ever visited before. The dull roar of copious voices was everywhere…the only sense of solitude to be found in their hotel suite. Even there, the sense of being surrounded by humanity remained in the knowledge the hotel was hemmed in on all sides by buildings of steel and glass, filled with people going about their business.

They ate a late lunch at The Emperor's Daughter's House, a restaurant that catered to executives and wealthy tourists. It was housed in the home of the last emperor's daughter, its historic flavor and ambience impressive even to the children. Young women dressed in the formal apparel of an earlier century danced for the patrons of the restaurant while more food than any family could eat in a week was repeatedly replenished on the round table at which they sat.

Tomasso had to leave them at the hotel while he went to yet another meeting, but both she and the children were content to be left behind, more than ready for a break from the constant noise and crowds.

She was sleeping when he finally made it back to the

hotel that night, but she woke when he climbed into the bed and gave a husky growl of appreciation upon finding her naked. For the past two nights, she'd worn her nightie only to have him strip it off of her in the heat of passion.

Remembering his desire for her to show him more affection, she'd decided to leave it off as an open invitation.

Apparently it was one he appreciated. She turned to him and initiated a hot, openmouthed kiss that led to other things that lasted into the wee hours of the morning.

The next day he surprised her and the children by taking them to the Forbidden City, where they toured the many temples, including the Temple of Heaven. He told her it was reputed the last Emperor had worshipped the Christian God, Yahweh, there.

As they walked from temple to temple women of every nationality watched Tomasso with hungry eyes, but he noticed none of them. His gaze never even paused to rest for a few seconds on the most beautiful and exotic.

Would it be the same back in Isole dei Re?

She could only hope.

They stayed in Beijing for two more days before returning to Diamante. Once there, Tomasso called his family to tell them the news of his impending second marriage. She and Tomasso agreed to go to Scorsolini Island before the birthday festivities began so the family could get to know Maggie better.

From what she could tell, none of them had expressed dismay at the prospect of Principe Tomasso Scorsolini marrying his nanny. But that didn't mean they accepted it without question. They could be waiting to express their disapproval until she and Tomasso arrived in Lo Paradiso, the capital city of Isole dei Re.

She wouldn't be surprised. What king wanted his son to marry his children's nanny—a woman who had been his own part-time housekeeper in the past?

CHAPTER ELEVEN

MAGGIE entered the palace in Lo Paradiso for the second time. Located smack in the center of Isole dei Re's capital city, its grandeur was every bit as awe inspiring as it had been on her first visit.

The cavernous marble entryway echoed with the sounds of the children's joyous laughter as they hurtled toward the private reception rooms. The Scorsolini family was very close. The kind of family Maggie had longed for since her parents' deaths. Here, uncles, aunt and grandfather all doted on Gianfranco and Annamaria.

She had yet to meet the youngest brother, Marcello, but the children spoke glowingly of him and with obvious affection.

Tomasso led her into the family reception room where he introduced her to his father. King Vincente had the same cobalt-blue eyes as Tomasso, but he looked at Maggie with an expression that seared her soul and tested her for worthiness. Her smile of greeting slipped from her lips.

His eldest son, Prince Claudio, was equally intimidating, his dark eyes fixed on her with an unfathomable expression as Maggie and Tomasso sat down on a small sofa covered in rich brocade. The children flanked their grandfather on the other sofa and Prince Claudio and Princess Therese were seated in Queen Anne style arm chairs upholstered in a complementary brocade to the one on the sofas.

The room was obviously meant to feel warm and cozy, but its size and the uncertain emotions of the occupants made Maggie feel like she was in a judge's chamber rather than the family reception room.

Only Princess Therese smiled at her, reaching out to squeeze Maggie's hand as if they were old friends. "I am so glad you and Tomasso are to be married. Your connection with the children was uncanny from the moment you all met. I remember telling Tomasso so on the phone when he asked if you'd taken the position. But now I understand."

"And what do you understand, Therese?" King Vincente asked.

"They knew each other before. Maggie saw bits of Tomasso in the children and was naturally drawn to them because of it."

"You think so?" Prince Claudio asked, sounding unconvinced himself.

Feeling like she should stand up for her obvious ally, Maggie said, "You're right, you know. Tomasso is the only other person in my life I connected to as quickly and as completely as I have with Anna and Gianni."

"If this is true, then why have we never met you before? This friendship my son told me about did not extend to introducing you to his family and for six years, you have been completely out of his life."

"I did not want Maggie to know I was a prince," Tomasso interrupted before she could reply. "It was important to me to go through college and graduate school on my own merits, not the cachet associated with my family's name."

"But if she was your friend…" Claudio's voice trailed off, the implication plain.

She had not been the close friend Tomasso claimed if he had kept his true identity from her.

"Sometimes we keep things from even the dearest people in our lives for reasons others might not understand." Princess Therese spoke up again. "Tomasso made his choice about that six years ago, but it is hardly Maggie's fault, nor should you and Vincente expect her to explain it."

"How many times have I told you to call me Papa?" the king scolded his daughter-in-law.

She merely smiled, a sadness flickering in her eyes. Maggie wondered if the others saw it.

"I told Maggie you would welcome her. Was I mistaken?" Tomasso asked in a voice that chilled the room.

"Nonno, don't you like Maggie?" Anna asked, her lower lip quivering. "I love her. She's going to be my mama."

"She promised, Nonno. You can't make her go away," Gianni said in childish desperation, his small face going red with anger. "I won't let you and neither will my papa!"

He jumped up and dashed around the large square coffee table in the center of the sitting arrangement to throw himself at his father. "You won't let Nonno send Maggie away, will you?"

Tomasso hugged his son, his eyes flinty hard and fixed on his father. "No. Now calm yourself, Gianfranco. You have nothing to fear from this family who loves you."

Anna must have moved when Gianni did because she climbed into Maggie's lap and hugged her neck. "I do love you, Maggie. I want you for my mama."

Maggie hugged the small body close and had to bite back a sigh. The situation had gone far enough and was helping no one. "It's all right, Anna. No one is trying to make me go away."

"But Papa got mad. I could tell."

Maggie did sigh then. "Yes, I think everyone could, but there was no reason for him to be mad. Your grandfather and uncle are only asking questions because they don't know me."

"When they do know you, they will love you like I do," Anna said with confidence.

"I am sure you are right, little one," Princess Therese added. "I like Maggie very much, and I am an excellent judge of character."

Her words were obviously directed at her husband and his father and both men frowned in receipt of the subtle criticism.

"Perhaps you can tell us something about yourself," King Vincente said to Maggie in an obvious bid to smooth the troubled waters around him.

Prince Claudio gave her a considering look. "Actually, Tomasso mentioned you many times to me when you worked for him six years ago. You kept his life peaceful."

"Yes, he mentioned that," Maggie said wryly. "Good domestic help is hard to come by." She'd learned that much while working as a nanny for two wealthy families. "It was worth mentioning he had some, I suppose."

"I was under the impression he enjoyed more than the fact you kept the house clean and fed him."

"We were good friends," Tomasso inserted. "I told you this."

"But it was not a friendship that lasted after the working relationship." Though it was a statement, Prince Claudio made it sound like a question.

"College friendships are often like that. How many friends from your days at University do you keep in contact with?" she asked him.

"Very few," Prince Claudio admitted.

"There, you see," Princess Therese said. "You are looking for anomalies that do not exist."

Prince Claudio shrugged and then focused his dark-eyed gaze on his younger brother. "If you knew who Maggie was when you asked Therese to hire her, it stands to reason that you planned to marry her all along."

"Yes."

"Not quite," Maggie said.

"What then?" the king asked.

"You know your son...he had a plan."

"What kind of plan," Princess Therese asked, her eyes lit with curiosity.

"He planned to test me out for suitability first," Maggie said with a straight face.

"You cannot be serious!" Princess Therese exclaimed.

"But I am."

King Vincente nodded his approval. "That was wise."

Typical Scorsolini male reaction. Maggie choked on a sound of amused resignation and winked at Princess Therese who looked ready to burst out laughing.

"Your test was short-lived," Prince Claudio pointed out.

Tomasso shrugged with the same casual arrogance his brother had shown seconds earlier. "It did not take me long to determine that Maggie was all that I remembered."

"I see."

Tomasso went into an embarrassing litany of her praises, aided and abetted by Anna and Gianni. If his family didn't see that her Girl Scout-like qualities were her biggest appeal to a man looking for a *peaceful marriage*, she did. He even mentioned a desire she'd voiced to establish a preschool system in Isole dei Re.

"That is an interesting idea, but will you not be too busy caring for my son and grandchildren to see to such a task?"

"It isn't something that has to happen all at once, Your Highness. I would probably start with a preschool near Tomasso's home on Diamante."

"Even so, that sort of endeavor would most certainly conflict with you looking after Tomasso and the children."

"Your son is an adult," retorted Maggie. "He doesn't need me looking after him as if he wasn't, and I would never neglect Anna and Gianni in order to see to the needs of other children. They are now and will continue to be my top priority, but that does not preclude me taking an interest in anything else." It seemed to her that for all the times Tomasso had told her this was the twenty-first century, someone needed to remind his father of that fact.

The king surprised her by smiling with obvious approval. "Thank you. It is my belief that you could not have engendered such strong devotion in my grandchildren without just cause, but I wanted to make sure. Forgive me if you felt under the gauntlet. Some women do not share your priorities. Both a husband and children can be very hurt by such neglect."

It suddenly occurred to Maggie that Tomasso's marriage to Liana had probably been painful for the other Scorsolinis to deal with. She had been a selfish woman who put her own pleasure at the forefront of her priorities and hurt many people because of it.

"I would never let that happen. Please believe me."

"I do believe you. Therese tells me that you took no days off while Tomasso was away on business, even though the staff at the villa stood ready to care for the children if you wished to do so."

Tomasso gave her a pointed look as if to say, "See, you didn't really want days off anyway."

She shrugged, but had to stifle a smile. The man really liked being right. "I enjoy their company."

"And that of my son?" the king asked.

"Father," Tomasso said sternly, but his father wasn't intimidated.

"Do you love my son?"

Tomasso's frown was now hard enough to crush diamonds. "That is not a question that needs asking. I am content with this marriage. Therefore, you should be, too."

King Vincente shook his head. "You do not think the question relevant? I disagree." He turned to face her again. "I ask you once more…do you love my son?"

Maggie had a choice. She could lie and save her pride, or she could tell the truth. She'd never been any good at lying, so really, she had no choice at all.

"Yes, I do," she said quietly, refusing to be humiliated by the one-sided nature of their relationship, but there was no denying the slice of pain that went through her. "I also love the children."

He hadn't asked, but she thought it was important to say so, for Gianni and Anna's sake if nothing else.

Tomasso went still beside her and she avoided meeting his eyes by smoothing Anna's hair though it hardly needed it.

"You loved him six years ago." It was the king again, continuing to probe the incision he had just made in the protective membrane around her heart.

It hurt and she sucked in a pain-filled breath no one else in that room would understand. "I…that isn't any of your business."

"I agree." Therese stood. "Not only are you poking into things that do not concern you, you are doing it in a venue that is entirely inappropriate." She gave a pointed look to the two children who were listening with rapt attention to the conversation of the adults.

"You have already upset your grandchildren, you have offended your second son, and you have embarrassed a woman you should be calling daughter. I always knew the Scorsolini men were efficient, but that is taking overachievement to the extreme in my opinion. Maggie, would you like to go to your room now?"

Before Maggie could nod, the king said, "I beg your pardon. It was not my intention to upset the children, or embarrass you."

"But you don't mind offending your son?" Maggie asked with no doubt misplaced humor, but she couldn't seem to stop herself.

The king's lips twitched and then he gave her a full-blown smile every bit as devastating as his son's. "I am used to offending my sons. They are strong men."

"I'm a strong woman, but I don't like being grilled on my feelings and I agree with Princess Therese that the children have been unnecessarily upset."

"I am sorry, little ones. You will forgive your *nonno*, will you not?" he asked with his arms outstretched.

Anna rushed to her grandfather to give him a hug and assure that all had been forgiven, but Gianni held back.

"Gianfranco?"

"Maggie is to be my mama."

"Yes."

"I love her, too."

"I can see that you do and it is commendable, *piccolo mio*."

"You aren't going to try to send her away?"

"No. She belongs with your family…with the Scorsolini family. Besides, as you pointed out, your father would hardly allow such a thing. He is easily as stubborn as your *nonno*."

Gianni nodded and then crossed to sit beside his grandfather again, taking the older man's hand in an affectionate gesture that moved Maggie. The Italian influence on this family was obvious and she liked it.

Princess Therese sat down again without looking at her husband who was watching her with a strange expression in his eyes.

She then gave her father-in-law a look that made him shift in his seat and turn to Maggie to say, "Tell me more about these preschools you think we need in Isole dei Re."

That signaled the end of her interrogation, and conversation flowed along less antagonistic lines after that. Now that he wasn't looking at her like she'd climbed out from under a rock or asking embarrassing questions, Maggie found Tomasso's father very charming and even likable. Prince Claudio was quiet, but apparently his concerns regarding the marriage had also been laid to rest.

However, Maggie was still relieved when Therese suggested she might like some time to relax and freshen up before dinner.

CHAPTER TWELVE

"WE'LL fly to Nassau tomorrow morning so we can do our shopping," Princess Therese said as she led Maggie from the reception room.

"That sounds wonderful. Thank you. I don't want to embarrass Tomasso at his father's birthday party by looking like the hired help, but my clothes budget has never run to designer originals."

Princess Therese laughed softly. "Most women's don't and you have nothing to fear in that regard. With the right connections, clothing is an easy matter to see to. The outer appearance of a woman can be manipulated to fit any occasion, but your inner character is irreplaceable."

"I have told her this, but perhaps she will listen to you."

Therese turned to face Tomasso who had followed them out of the reception room. "Perhaps those are not the words she needs to hear from you."

Tomasso frowned and Maggie felt a sudden and horrible urge to cry. The words Therese was talking about were no more likely to pass his lips today than they had six years ago.

"What time are you two flying out tomorrow?" he asked, ignoring the princess's comment.

"Seven in the morning, but I had considered flying out

tonight. Only I thought it might be too much for Maggie after the journey here."

"The helicopter trip was less than an hour. I'm hardly jetlagged," Maggie said with a smile, the thought of getting away from Tomasso for a short while appealing in the extreme.

"Perhaps we could fly out after dinner then," Princess Therese said. "It will give us a full day of shopping tomorrow and the next day before I have to return to attend to my duties for the party."

"That sounds perfect."

"You can't need two days of shopping to come up with one outfit," Tomasso said with an obvious displeasure she could not understand.

"Don't be silly, Tomasso," Therese said. "We will be outfitting Maggie for more than one occasion. As your fiancé, soon to be your wife, she will need an extensive wardrobe. We can add to it later, but we must fit her with the basics immediately so that she will not feel conspicuous or uncomfortable moving within your social and business circles."

Maggie appreciated Princess Therese's understanding and her smile told the other woman so.

"Perhaps I should come with you then."

"No, thank you. Men, particularly those with strong opinions and the certainty they are always right, are not a welcome addition on a shopping trip of this nature."

Before Tomasso could argue, Claudio came into the hall and said he wanted his brother's opinion on a business matter.

"He does not want you out of his sight for two days," Therese said with interest as she led Maggie up the marble staircase.

"I don't know why."

"He is possessive."

"It seems to be a family trait."

"Yes, but you will not hear Claudio offering to come to the States with us to go shopping in order to remain in my company."

"I suppose that in your positions you are used to being separated for the sake of your duties."

Therese stopped in front of a large, ornately carved door that matched the other dozen or so lining the long marble hallway. "Yes."

Maggie sensed a sadness in the other woman she was too sensitive to address. "I really appreciate you taking me under your wing like this, Princess Therese."

"It is my pleasure. We are family, Maggie. And please, you must stop calling me Princess. Therese will do nicely."

She nodded, but said, "I don't think I'll ever call King Vincente anything else."

Therese's soft laughter followed Maggie into the huge suite she was apparently supposed to share with Tomasso.

In some ways, the family had moved very much into the twenty-first century. Her mother, had she lived, would never have allowed Maggie and a soon-to-be son-in-law to sleep together under her roof before the wedding. Maggie wasn't sure she felt comfortable with doing so now. At least at Tomasso's home, she had her own suite…even if he came to her bed the nights he did not carry her to his.

She took a long bath in the en suite, soaking and thinking for so long she had to rush to get ready for dinner. She pulled her hair up in a mass of curls on top of her head that she didn't have time to tame. It didn't look too bad, but she would have preferred a smoother, more conservative do.

Tomasso arrived to change into a suit as she was pulling on one of the dresses she'd bought to wear while attending social functions with her previous employers. It was simple, elegant and black. A far cry from the bright colors she usually wore, it made her feel like she blended into her surroundings, which is exactly what she had wanted to do on those occasions.

She didn't feel appreciably different tonight.

"Did you have a nice rest?" he asked as he peeled off his dress shirt and slacks to don a fresh pair of trousers and new, crisply ironed shirt.

"I took a long soak."

His eyes heated to indigo. "I would like to have joined you. I spent the afternoon in business meetings with my brother while our father played *nonno* to the hilt with the children."

"I'm sure you enjoyed yourself. You thrive on the stress of your job."

"As does Claudio, but I would still have rather been making love to you in the bath."

She rolled her eyes, her cheeks going cherry pink. "Don't you think of anything else?"

Maybe the seduction thing wasn't all for her benefit. The man was definitely oversexed.

He knotted his tie. "You know I do, but I cannot help it if your passion is so addictive that I struggle to get thoughts of you out of my mind."

She turned away, the words too close to real emotion when she knew there was none behind them for her to handle. "Therese changed our flight to nine this evening."

Suddenly his hands were on her waist and his lips pressed against her exposed nape. "I will miss you, Maggie. Will you miss me?"

"You know I will."

"Because you love me?"

She'd wondered when that would come up. There was

no use denying it when she had already admitted her feelings in front of his family. "Yes."

"I am glad."

She wanted to ask why it mattered, but he'd turned her to kiss her and when he was done, she was in no condition to ask anything.

He finished dressing. Then he crossed the room and opened a safe in the wall from which he pulled out a narrow black velvet case. He handed it to her.

"What is this?"

"Open it and find out."

She did, revealing a long strand of perfectly shaped pearls each one an exact color match. "They're beautiful," she gasped.

"They will go nicely with your dress."

She pressed the box back into his hand. "I won't wear Liana's jewelry," she said as she backed away from him, her stomach tightening.

"They were not Liana's. Her tastes were far more flashy. These were my mother's."

"Why aren't they Therese's then?"

"My father gave pieces to both Claudio and myself when we came of age."

"You're sure Liana never wore it?"

"Quite sure."

"Okay." Realizing how ungracious that sounded she added, "I mean thank you very much. They really are beautiful. I'll take good care of them for you."

"They are yours now," he said in a voice that did not invite argument.

"Thank you."

"Would it matter so much if Liana had worn them?"

"Yes."

He nodded, his expression grave. "Then, be assured I will never give you anything that belonged to her before."

Including his heart. He'd already made that clear.

The trip to Nassau was a revelation for Maggie. Therese knew exactly where to go to get haute couture and she had an incredible eye for what would look good on Maggie. They shopped all morning and broke for lunch before starting again.

Tomasso called three times during the day. Once in the morning, once around lunch time and again a couple of hours later. The phone calls were brief and not at all romantic, but she liked getting them and smiled for a long time after each one. She and Therese got the bulk of their shopping done and left accessorizing for Day Two. When they returned to the hotel, Maggie had clothes for every occasion and a killer dress for the king's birthday bash.

She and Therese found out that despite the differences in their backgrounds, they had tons in common and spent a lot of time laughing. Which helped Maggie feel like maybe she would fit in with Tomasso's life. She certainly planned to try her best.

They used the pool's Jacuzzi to soak their aching muscles after the marathon shopping excursion.

Therese leaned against the wall of the hot tub, the water bubbling around her. "This feels so good."

Maggie nodded, groaning as the water jet hit her lower back. "Too good. I'm afraid I'll fall asleep down here."

"Better not. They'd catch you on the security cameras and sell the pictures to some sleazy tabloid with a story about boozing it up, or something equally vulgar."

"It isn't easy living life in the constant public eye, is it?"

"Luckily we don't get the press attention that Buckingham Palace does, but yes, you always have to be aware of the probability that you are being watched. Claudio would not be pleased if he knew we were relaxing here, even." She said it like the knowledge gave her some satisfaction and not for the first time Maggie wondered at the undercurrents in the royal couple's marriage.

"I thought the security team looked a little disgruntled when you said we were coming down here."

Therese shrugged. "You cannot live every moment pleasing everyone else."

"But you try, don't you?"

A look of sadness passed over the other woman's exotic features. "I have tried less lately."

"I think that's a good thing. It's too easy to be taken for granted when you're always trying to make life easier for everyone around you."

"Is that what happened six years ago with Tomasso? He took you for granted?"

"In a way, but I was his housekeeper…it came with my job description."

"But falling in love with him did not."

"No."

"It is hard to love a man who sees you as a convenience. It hurts."

Maggie agreed but the cell phone Tomasso had given her rang before she could say so. She smiled apologetically at Therese and then answered it. "Good evening, Tomasso."

"Hello, *bella mia*. Did you get your shopping finished?"

"The clothes. We are shopping for accessories tomorrow."

"You think it will take the full day?"

"I have no doubt about it."

He sighed. "I had hoped you would return early."

"It's nice to know I'm missed."

"I told you that you would be."

"It's still nice." Even if it was just that he missed having her in his bed.

"The children miss you as well. They wish to say good night."

"Of course, put them on." Anna wanted to know how soon Maggie would be returning and Gianni wanted to tell her all about their afternoon riding horses with their *nonno*.

Tomasso came back on the line. "I hear bubbling water."

"Therese and I are in the hot tub soaking our aching muscles."

"The public hot tub?"

"It's hardly public. It's the hotel hot tub."

"You are parading around the hotel in your swimsuits?" he asked as if women in his world didn't sunbathe regularly wearing nothing but a thong and some sunscreen.

"Hardly parading. We changed when we got to the pool area."

"I am surprised Therese encouraged you to do this."

"Does it really bother you?"

"Do you have security with you?"

"Yes."

"In that case, no. I would of course prefer to be there, but that is more for my own sake than my concern for yours."

"Therese thought Claudio might be upset."

"He is sometimes too aware of propriety."

"Because one day he will be king?"

"Probably. I have never asked." There were a few moments of silence and then he said, "My bed will be very lonely without you in it tonight."

"I assume the children are no longer in hearing distance."

"You are right. I have promised to come tuck them in when I finish speaking with you."

She sighed, holding the phone closer to her ear as if that could bring him closer to her as well. "I do miss you."

"Good."

She laughed softly. "Therese thinks we can arrange a small wedding in a week, two at the most. Is that too soon?"

"It is not soon enough, but it will do."

Warmth spread through her at the evidence he was eager for the marriage…whatever his reasons. "I suppose I had better go."

"What? Oh, yes…but first Claudio has just come in and would like to speak to Therese. Will you put her on?"

"Of course."

She handed the phone to Therese. "Prince Claudio wants to talk to you."

Therese looked at the phone with an odd expression and then took it. "Hello?"

She frowned. "I left my cell phone in the room." She paused. "I am in the hotel's hot tub on the pool level."

Maggie tried not to listen in on the rest of the conversation and concentrated on the relaxing feel of the bubbling water. She was almost dozing when Therese handed her back her phone.

"He is such a Neanderthal sometimes."

"That must run in the family, too."

They both laughed, Therese's green eyes filling with genuine mirth. "Yes, I believe it does."

They flew back to Lo Paradiso the next afternoon, the cargo hold full of Maggie and Therese's purchases.

She saw her family the minute the plane's outer door was opened. Tomasso waited with Anna in one arm and his other hand holding Gianni's. She fairly flew down the stairs to land against him. Within seconds, she was in the middle of a family hug that made her wonder if she might find true joy in her marriage despite the fact her fiancé did not love her.

She was almost positive of it late that night in the depths of his bed after he made such exquisite love to her that she lost touch with herself completely.

He grumbled the next morning when he found out that she had appointments with Therese's personal hair stylist, manicurist and a makeup artist. "Only promise me you will not let them cut your hair."

"The whole point is to get it cut."

"But I like it long."

"I'll ask them to keep the length and then style it, all right?"

He frowned, but nodded. "And not too much makeup. I do not wish to escort a Barbie doll to the party this evening."

"No wonder Therese insisted you not accompany us shopping. You would have been impossible."

"Perhaps, but I would not now be biting my nails in worry over what you chose to buy to wear tonight."

"You don't bite your nails."

"But I do worry."

"You're afraid I will embarrass you?" she asked.

He shook his head decisively. "Do not be stupid. I am concerned you will have bought a gown that shows the delectable figure I like to ogle in private to its best advantage. I am a possessive man."

"You're worried I'm going to look too sexy?" she asked in disbelief.

"I worry it cannot be helped, but with Therese's eye for style, it may be much worse than even I envision."

Her mind boggled that he could really be concerned about such a thing. "I guess you'll just have to wait and see, won't you?"

But several hours later, when she had been combed and

curried into a woman she almost didn't recognize, she was the nervous one. The stylist hadn't taken off much length, but he had styled her hair so that the natural curls fell around her face in sexy ringlets. The makeup artist had not used a lot of color, but enough to accentuate Maggie's eyes, making them seem almost silver rather than their true dull gray.

And the dress did show her figure off to perfection. It was off the shoulder and the burnt-orange of a sunset. It cupped her breasts and clung to her curves down her hips to her knees where it flared out to sweep the floor. Her heels gave her over two inches of height, but she still had to tilt her head to look Tomasso in the eye.

"What do you think?" She pirouetted for him.

"I think I would rather stay in this room and make love to you than introduce you to two hundred people who will insist on making me share your attention."

"Do you like it?"

"You look incredible. You will be the most beautiful woman present." He sounded like he really meant the words and the expression in his cobalt blue eyes said he believed what he was saying.

Her heart stuttered in her chest. "It isn't too bright?"

"I like you in bright colors."

"That's good. Therese insisted I buy lots of the colors I like to wear in the latest styles." She had said that it was important for Maggie to simply be a more put together version of herself, not try to emulate anyone else.

Maggie had liked that idea a lot.

"I am glad. I do not want you to change to fit what you believe my world to be." He pulled her close, taking care not to muss her appearance. "You are the woman I want. You are *real*, Maggie, and that is the way I want you to stay."

"I don't know how to be anything else."

"I am glad to know that."

They shared a smile that warmed her to her toes. And then he kissed her and she didn't mind in the least that she had to reapply her lipstick afterward.

She was very proud to enter the ballroom at his side a few minutes later.

He looked eye-catchingly yummy in his white formal suit, so much so that most of the female guests gave him at least one long glance. It was the same for his brothers though. Claudio and Marcello both received a great deal of female interest. Where Claudio seemed to ignore it, Marcello smiled and flirted with European charm, but still managed to hold the women swarming around him at a distance.

He had arrived from Italy earlier in the day and was as stunningly good-looking as his two older brothers. He shared the blue eyes of his father and Tomasso, but his complexion was darker and his hair was a lighter brown. Maggie wondered if his mother was a blonde. Some Italian women were.

Regardless, he took after his father in one unmistakable way…he shared the Scorsolini male pride and confidence. Which, Maggie realized, was every bit as attractive to women as the men's looks. There was no doubting that he and Tomasso received the lion's share of feminine attention in the room.

They were considered fair game: Marcello because he was, and Tomasso because the official announcement had not yet been made of his upcoming marriage. Maggie didn't know when it would be. No one had said anything to her about it, but she didn't really care it hadn't been made yet.

Watching the way some of the women were with Claudio, she knew even a wedding ring would not deter a certain type of female.

But as the night progressed and one gorgeous woman after another flirted with Tomasso, trying to prise him from Maggie's side, the urge to stake an unmistakable claim grew stronger. Tomasso wasn't shy about doing so, making it clear in subtle and not so subtle ways that they were a couple. Especially when other men asked her to dance, or spoke to her.

It was the fifth time the former had happened when Maggie had a revelation. She was not a princess, but that didn't stop other men in the room from noticing her. She was not as beautiful as Liana, but no one treated her as if she did not belong by Tomasso's side.

It was not merely the clothes, or the makeup, or the jewelry Tomasso had insisted she wear (more pieces passed down from his mother), nor was it her new haircut, though she loved it. It was that she *did* belong beside this man and somehow, most people realized that on an instinctive level. Women flirted, some gave her looks of envy, some even looked puzzled by his choice, but no one had implied by word or expression that she didn't belong.

She loved him. That was her claim on him. He might not love her, but he had made a commitment to her and his loyalty could not be questioned. His passion was as real as her love and his friendship was as precious to her as the passion.

This man was hers and he would be hers for the rest of both of their lives. And that would be enough. She would make it enough.

She turned to look at him, giving him a brilliant smile that made him stop speaking in midword and forget what he was going to say altogether.

The man he'd been talking to, a king from the Middle East no older than Tomasso, laughed. "There is no use in trying to hold a man's attention for a discussion of business when there is such a lovely woman close by to steal it."

Burnished red scorched along Tomasso's cheekbones, but he laughed and agreed.

The Middle Eastern king walked away and Tomasso turned to her. "What is it, Maggie?"

"What is what?"

"You are smiling."

"I like to smile."

"It is a special smile."

"Yes, it is. I love you, Tomasso."

The arm he had slung with casual possession around her waist tightened. "I know, and I am more pleased by that than I can say, but that still does not explain the smile, does it? You look so happy it is bursting out of you and yet I have had the impression from the moment you said yes, you had grave reservations about marrying me."

"I love you and that makes me so happy, I *am* bursting with it. Maybe I was a little worried about marrying you, but I'm not any more. I know you don't love me, not like that, and I thought that meant I would have to keep earning my place with you—no, please let me finish. I see now that unlike my years in foster care, I am not a temporary stop in your life. I'm going to be your wife until I die and I don't have to work at keeping that title, just love you and the children and we'll all be content. I don't know why it took so long, but I've just realized you are going to be a wonderful husband and I'm going to be Gianni and Anna's mom and have more children with you—and I'm very, very, very happy about all that."

His lips creased upward until his smile was as blinding as hers. "I am glad."

It was close to midnight when King Vincente called for everyone's attention. The room grew as quiet as one filled with over two hundred guests could.

"Tonight you celebrate my birthday with me and I thank you, but I have more to celebrate than another year of good health." He paused with the gift of a showman before beckoning Maggie and Tomasso over to him. When they stopped beside him, he smiled. "This lovely and very sweet woman has agreed to marry my son and our family rejoices in welcoming another Scorsolini princess."

Claudio handed him a velvet box, much like the one that had held the pearls Tomasso had given her. King Vincente opened it and revealed a small tiara which he placed on her head with gentle care before kissing both her cheeks. "Welcome to the family, daughter."

Applause broke out and it seemed like every person present wanted to know when the wedding was to take place, but that was one piece of information no one shared. Many guests said they'd been expecting an announcement after they'd seen the way Maggie and Tomasso looked at one another.

Maggie just grinned and accepted the congratulations with a peace she had not felt ever before in her life.

Tomasso had shown in too many ways to count that she really mattered to him. From the elaborate plan to get her back into his life to the way he acquiesced to her demands about his work hours so she would marry him to the way he made love to her so perfectly, he proved that she was special to him.

He might not love her, but he cared for her and he would be faithful and, when all was said and done, that was a lot more than a lot of men who said they loved their wives gave them.

Tomasso finally got Maggie alone and in his bed in the wee hours of the morning. He looked down at the beauty that shone from her rainwater eyes and was grateful she'd washed off her makeup.

"You looked beautiful tonight, but I prefer you without any artifice." His voice came out husky, which made sense because his throat felt like it was crowded with emotions he could not name.

"Thank you." There was that smile again. A sleepier version, but no less devastating to his heart.

"You are so perfect to me."

"You're perfect for me, too," she sighed.

She deserved all the words and somehow he was going to give them to her. He hadn't realized they were beating inside his heart, begging for expression until he'd looked down at her and seen the look of pure love glowing back at him earlier tonight. The love she gave him without asking for anything in return, and which made him see how much she deserved from him.

He'd thought love some kind of illusion, a weakness he did not want to give into.

But he understood now: it was not weak to love. It took strength, the kind that Maggie possessed. It took courage and he was not a man who would willingly fear anything.

"Six years ago, I loved you, but I was too stupid to realize it."

Her eyes opened wide and she sat up, clutching the sheet to her chest. "What?"

"You made my life perfect and I took that for granted. When I met Liana, I was smarting from your rejection, but I was also determined to keep our friendship, to have the best of both worlds. My head was turned by her outward beauty, I will not deny it, but I was devastated when you threatened to quit, and something inside me knew that if I did not allow you to walk away from our friendship later, my promises to Liana were in jeopardy. I was not mature enough to realize that should have clued me into the fact that what I felt for Liana was not love."

"It wasn't?"

"No. I loved you. How could I love another woman? Maybe Liana sensed that my feelings for her did not run as deep as they should have. Maybe that is why she spent so much time away from our family, but all I know is that I did not miss her when I worked. I miss you. Even a simple day in the office is enough to make me wish I were home, with you and the children."

"I..." Her voice trailed off as if she didn't know what to say.

"That first night, when I climbed into the bed with you...it was like a dream from my subconscious coming true. I cannot understand my own actions that night except that I finally had you where you were always meant to be and I think I was willing to do anything to keep you there."

"You said you didn't love me... I don't understand."

"I was being stupid again. Six years did not teach me that much, I guess."

"When did you realize?"

"I think I became aware that my feelings for you were far stronger than simple physical passion mixed with friendship when you were in Nassau shopping with Therese. I missed you so much and I craved talking to you on the phone. Claudio asked me if I was marrying you for the children's sake and I told him I was doing it for my own sake and understood at once how true that was, but I did not put the right words to the emotion until tonight...you smiled at me and all I wanted to do was carry you up here and make love to you until you screamed your pleasure."

Her eyes probed his. "That's lust, not love."

"Lust…or passion…it is a part of love, an easy part for a man to understand. The emotions, they are not so easy."

"And you feel the emotions?"

"So much that I would die if I were ever to lose you."

Her beautiful eyes filled with tears, but she smiled. "You will never lose me."

"And you will always have me," he vowed.

"Til death us do part."

"Until death…" He could not hold back and kissed her.

She melted against him like she always did, yielding to his body, giving herself so completely that an unfamiliar moisture burned his own eyes.

"I love you," he whispered against her lips as he entered her body minutes later.

"I love you," she said back to him with such conviction his soul stirred.

This woman was the true other half to himself and he would spend a lifetime thanking God for bringing her to him and showing her how very much he loved her.

His Royal
Love-Child

LUCY MONROE

For Lidia Chernichenko, a dear friend and a valued reader. I enjoy our friendship so much and thank you for helping me name the Scorsolini family. And for Theresa Brookins, a wonderful reviewer and another special LFBJ pal. Your presence at my chats always blesses me and thank you for managing my "claim list".
Thank you also for having the idea to name the country after the family which gave the main island in Isole dei Re its name.
You're both the best!
Hugs, Lucy

CHAPTER ONE

DANETTE MICHAELS closed the tabloid and put it down on the coffee table with careful precision.

Her hands were steady. It amazed her. A hurricane of pain was shaking her insides. She made no sound, though she wanted to scream. She wanted to rip the offending magazine to shreds, too. But she couldn't do either. If she so much as touched the tabloid again…if she gave vent to even a tiny bit of the storm tearing apart her soul, she was going to lose it completely.

She refused to do that. She'd spent years controlling her emotions, hiding both physical and mental pain while denying her tears. Ray's betrayal had made her cry and she'd sworn she wasn't going to let another man do that again. Not even Principe Marcello Scorsolini.

"He's just delish, isn't he?" Lizzy breathed, oblivious to the devastation her visit had wrought in Danette. She leaned forward and flipped the magazine open again, and pointed to the picture that was the source of Danette's current mental agony. "Can you imagine being that woman?"

Danette looked down at the picture. She didn't want to. It hurt, but she couldn't help herself. Her eyes were drawn by an emotion as powerful as the love that lay bleeding at the bottom of her heart. The *need to know*, and a desperate hope that her vision had deceived her the first time.

It had not.

The picture was exactly what she thought it was. It showed the drop-dead gorgeous president of the Italian arm of Scorsolini Shipping dancing with an equally attractive woman at his father's birthday bash on Scorsolini Island. They were practically molded to one another's bodies. Prince Marcello was smiling and the woman looked like a beautiful, sleek cat who had just copped a whole bowl of the richest cream.

How could Danette have been so stupid that she'd allowed herself to get involved with *this* man…to actually believe that they had enough in common where it counted?

She'd fallen into his arms with about as much self-preservation as a lemming following the pack leader off the side of a cliff. She'd given him her virginity and asked for nothing in return but his overwhelming passion. He'd offered her his fidelity, but that picture made her doubt the sincerity of the gift.

Contrary to what he had told her, her prince was the king of the playboys. Was she terminally stupid where men were concerned, or simply unlucky?

"Earth to Danette. Hello, is anyone in there?" Lizzy's voice penetrated Danette's crushing thoughts.

"What?"

"Where were you at, *chica*? Don't tell me you were thinking about work."

"Something like that," Danette said in a strained voice. In her mind, her job and her lover were inexorably linked.

"I *said,* can you imagine being her?"

Only too well, except when Marcello held Danette close like that, she was never wearing a designer original ball gown. Most of the time, she wasn't wearing anything at all. "Yes."

Lizzy laughed. "You've got a better imagination than me then."

"Not really."

"Are you okay?" Lizzy asked, her face creased with concern. "You seem out of it, and more than just your normal preoccupation with being the original Wonder Woman at work."

Danette forced herself to look away from the picture and at her small, blond friend. They were both Americans, but that was where the similarity ended. Lizzy was five feet even with the body of a pocket Venus and short blond hair that fell in wild ringlets around her heart-shaped face. She also had an infectious smile that had drawn Danette to her immediately.

Danette, on the other hand, had slight curves, a very slender build, a neck that Marcello said looked like a graceful swan's, but which she felt was too long, average looks he called refreshingly natural, and average height that felt very tiny beside his six-foot-two-inch frame. Her chin-length mouse-brown hair was straight and even when she tried to curl it, it never held. So she'd given up trying.

Marcello said it felt like silk against his fingertips and he loved the fact she didn't starch it with lots of product, but the blonde he was holding so closely in the picture certainly looked made up to the nines. So much for Marcello's evinced preference for the *unadorned lily.* It was obvious he liked hothouse orchids just fine.

That picture made her wonder if she hadn't fooled herself about Marcello just as badly as she had with Ray.

She tried for a smile, but failed. She settled for a sigh. "I'm fine. Just tired. I've been working hard on the Cordoba project."

"With the hours you put in, it's no wonder you don't have a social life."

But Danette did have a social life…a secret one that gave her more pleasure than she'd ever dreamed was possible. At least it had until this moment.

She managed to force the smile this time, though she wasn't sure it was a very convincing one. "You know how it is."

Lizzy's smile was genuine, if tinged with worry. "What I know is that you work too hard."

"Not really. I love my job."

"I love my job, too, *chica*, but you don't see me spending every waking moment dedicated to it." Lizzy winked. "I've got better things to do with my off hours. Speaking of, I've got to get going…you sure you don't want to come down to the taverna with the rest of us?"

Danette shook her head. "Sorry, but I think I'll go for an early night."

Lizzy sighed and shook her head, her blond curls bouncing. "You need to get out more."

"I do get out." With Marcello, and nowhere anyone from Scorsolini Shipping was likely to run into her.

Lizzy just snorted, then her expression turned calculating. "If you aren't there, Ramon from sales is going to be disappointed."

"I doubt it."

"The guy has the hots for you, he's good-looking,

great at his job, and he's single. Why not come down, spend some time with him? See where it goes."

"Ramon has had four different girlfriends in the last six months…he's a bad risk." But she had to swallow a burble of hysterical laughter as she realized what she'd just said.

No worse risk existed in the relationship stakes than Marcello Scorsolini.

"All of life is a gamble, or haven't you learned that yet?" Lizzy asked as she got up to go.

"Some chances are more worth taking than others."

"And you don't think Ramon is one of them?"

Danette sighed. "I don't know, but not tonight. I'm sure about that much, all right?"

"Okay." Lizzy smiled again and reached out to hug her. "Get some sleep. I'll see you at work tomorrow."

Danette hugged her back. As she stepped away, she remembered all the times she'd encouraged her friend, Tara, to go for it with Angelo Gordon, but this was different. No one could compete with Marcello…not even the sexy, charming Ramon from sales. "Have fun tonight."

"We will." Lizzy turned to leave.

"You forgot your magazine."

"Keep it," Lizzy tossed over her shoulder on her way out the door. "It'll give you something to read before bed."

The door shut behind the other woman before Danette could respond.

She didn't want to read the tabloid. She didn't want to look at it. She didn't want it in her apartment, but when she picked it up to throw away, she found herself rereading every single word of the article about King Vincente's birthday party. It was a four-page spread with tons of pictures, a few quotes and enough innuendo to sink an oil tanker.

She was staring at the picture of Tomasso and the woman dancing when a peremptory knock sounded on her door.

She lived in what had once been the groundskeeper's cottage on a large estate on the outskirts of Palermo. The family still occupied the main house and the security system was top-notch. Angelo and Tara had helped her find the place and she was really grateful. Even though Angelo had arranged for her job, she'd wanted to make it on her own in Italy from that point forward. So, she had refused her parents' offer to help her buy another condo like the one she'd had in Portland, or in procuring what they considered an acceptable place of habitat for their one and only child.

The groundskeeper's cottage with security services provided by the main house had been a compromise they could live with.

Because her home was far from the main road and the security was so good, she didn't worry about getting unwanted guests. However, Marcello had drilled into her enough times never to open the door without checking first to be sure she knew her visitor, that she automatically did so now.

It was him.

She didn't know why that should shock her, but it did. After seeing the article, her mind had told her he no longer belonged to her…if he ever had. Therefore, why would he bother showing up on her doorstep?

Yet, there he stood on the other side of her door looking like the epitome of Sicilian male perfection. From his golden-brown hair styled casually to enhance his sculpted features, to the tips of his Gucci leather shoes, he exuded delectable masculine appeal. He also looked tired, the skin around his cobalt-blue eyes lined with fatigue.

He'd probably been too busy partying to sleep. Even as the unpleasant thought surfaced, she was forced to dismiss it. She knew better.

He'd been gone on a business trip for more than a week before his father's birthday party. They'd spoken on the phone every night and he'd made it clear he was pushing himself and everyone around him to finish.

Only seeing the picture had made her think that he wouldn't come straight to her from the airport. Why would he when he had beautiful, sophisticated women like the one in the photo to spend his time with?

Perhaps it was an irrational line of reasoning, but she wasn't at her logical best at the moment. He knocked a second time, the staccato rap and his scowl communicating his impatience at being kept on the doorstep.

She opened the door and then stood staring mutely at his large frame as it filled her doorway.

His sensual lips transformed from a frown to an enticing smile. "Good evening, *tesoro mio*. Are you going to let me in?"

"What are you doing here?"

His eyes narrowed, the smile disappearing as quickly as it had come. "What kind of question is that? I have not seen you for more than a week. My plane landed not an hour ago…where else would I be?"

Six months ago, when they'd begun their affair, the question would have been ludicrous. He had made it a point of seeing her only a couple of nights a week, but as the weeks progressed the number of nights they spent together increased until they were practically living together…albeit in secret.

"Maybe spending time with your new girlfriend?"

He stepped into the small cottage, forcing her to move backward if she didn't want him touching her. And she didn't. Not right now. Maybe never again.

She tripped backward with speed, not stopping until she was several feet away.

"What other girlfriend?" he asked, enunciating each word with quiet precision as he pushed the door shut behind him and then followed her across the room.

She lifted the gossip rag toward him. "This one."

He stared down at the magazine and then took it from her hand to look more closely. His eyes skimmed the pages, his expression turning to one of disdain before he tossed it to the coffee table behind her. "That is nothing more than a scandal sheet. Why were you reading it?"

"Lizzy brought it over. She thought it was a hoot to read an article about the big boss. What difference does it make how it came into my possession? Dismissing it as a low form of journalism isn't going to make the pictures go away or the behavior that got caught in the camera lens for that matter."

"Nothing untoward was caught on film."

"You don't think so?"

"I danced with a few women at my father's birthday party, smiled at some, talked. There is no crime in that."

"Not if you weren't attached, no."

His frown intensified, eyes that usually looked on her with indulgent affection going wintry. "You know I will not tolerate a possessive scene, Danette."

She almost laughed. He sounded so darn arrogant it wasn't hard to believe he was a prince, only that he was the youngest son. That kind of egotism should be reserved for the heir to the throne.

"Fine. Leave and we won't have one."

He jolted as if she'd slapped him. "You want me to leave? I've just arrived."

"Well, since apparently the only thing you want me for is sex and I'm definitely not in the mood after seeing those pictures, you might as well."

"I have never said that." He cursed volubly in Italian. "Where did that come from? Why would you say such a thing? I do not see you as a body without a brain."

"Good, because I have one, and it's telling me that if I was more than a body in your bed, I would have been by your side at your father's party, not reading about it in a gossip rag two days later and having to see pictures of you flirting with other women."

"You know why you were not at my side."

"Because you don't want anyone to know about me! You're ashamed of me, aren't you?" she asked, slipping one more notch into pain-induced irrationality and unable to do a thing to prevent it. Which terrified her more than the pain itself. She had always been able to control her emotions, no matter how devastating, but what she felt for him was too big.

Apparently he thought she'd gone over the edge, too, because he stared at her as if she'd lost her mind. "You are insane tonight. First you accuse me of having another woman, then you say I see you as nothing but a sex toy…or as good as." He shook his head as if to clear it. "This is crazy. *I am not ashamed of you.*"

"But you don't want anyone to know about me."

"For your own sake." He swore again and tunneled his long brown fingers through his hair. "You know how invasive the paparazzi can be. The minute they got wind of my relationship with you, you would be watched your every waking moment. You would not be able to go to a public restroom without having a reporter ready to take your picture from under the stall next to your own."

"It wouldn't be that bad. I'm not big news."

"But I am. I have lived my whole life the son of one of the relatively few royal couples in history to have divorced. I had no privacy in my marriage. Bianca had to travel everywhere with bodyguards not only for her personal security, but to protect her from the intrusive press. I have told you this."

Danette said nothing. The logical part of her brain knew he spoke the truth, but she could not make herself admit it. Even if her mind told her that he was determined to keep their relationship private because he valued it so much, her heart said that a relationship that had to be hidden wasn't valuable enough.

The way he'd been dancing with the blonde certainly made it look like he valued *her*.

He sighed. "I developed a playboy facade after Bianca's death to protect myself and the woman I truly wanted to be with. You know this. We have discussed it before."

She did know it. She had even seen it as something deeply personal they had in common. After all, hadn't she developed an outgoing, flirtatious image to hide the very private person she was beneath the facade? She'd seen his playboy reputation the same way once he explained it to her. Only that photo implied the persona was the man.

It made a mockery of the love she'd discovered she felt for him. Love wasn't supposed to be like this. It wasn't supposed to hurt so much. It was supposed to make life beautiful, to empower the lover…but all she ever got from it was pain and a horrible sense of insecurity.

"How many women have you *truly wanted to be with* since Bianca?" she demanded, feeling waspish and hurt and unable to hold back the ugly question.

"That is none of your business."

"Apparently most of your life is none of my business."

"That is not true."

"You don't share it with me."

"That is a lie." He looked like he wanted to shake her. "You get more of my time than anyone else. Did I not work twenty-hour days while I was gone so that I could fly back to you after the birthday party rather than returning to our shipping office in Hong Kong?"

He rubbed his eyes, his face drawn with exhaustion and reflecting disappointment. "We spend practically every evening together doing more than sharing our bodies and you know this, *tesoro mio*. We have been to the theater, out to dinner many times…we have put puzzles together because it is something you enjoy doing and you have taught me to play odd American card games. The only part of myself I do not share with you is the public spotlight. I understood that was not something you craved. Was I wrong? Do you wish to be known as the latest lover for a Scorsolini prince?"

His sarcasm didn't even faze her. "If it means I don't have to see pictures of you plastered against another woman, yes."

He shook his head. "We were dancing. That is all. It meant nothing. You must know this."

"All I know is that you two looked like you were getting ready to make a hasty exit from the party and find someplace private to continue dancing."

"You are jealous." He shook his head. "There is no need."

"I'm hurt!"

"Only because you do not trust me."

"How can I?"

"I told you that for as long as we are together, our relationship would be exclusive. I gave you my word. You have known me for a year, intimately for half as long. When have you ever known me to break it?"

"I don't like being your dirty little secret."

"What we share is not dirty, and you are a secret because our relationship is so special to me that I do not want to lose it," he gritted out between clenched teeth.

She averted her face, refusing to answer, and the silence stretched between them. She sensed his movement, but was still shocked when one of his hands brushed the hair back from her temple and then slipped down to cup her chin. He gently turned her face until their gazes met.

"I am very sorry if the pictures hurt you."

She knew he considered this a major climb-down, and to give him credit, for him it *was*. He had started the conversation off with a refusal to have a scene and was now apologizing. He was too darn perfect to have to apologize much and too powerful to be forced into giving one even when he was wrong in most cases, but it didn't make her feel any better.

What difference did an apology make when it wasn't accompanied by the assurance the offense would not happen again?

Seeing the picture had hurt her. A lot. She felt like her heart was being ripped into shreds even now.

"Just tell me one thing," she said. "How would you feel if our positions were reversed? What if you were the one looking on at me flirting with other men?"

His jaw clenched as if the thought was not a pleasant one, but then he visibly relaxed his tense facial muscles. "In order to keep our relationship private, I must act naturally at public social functions. It would be entirely *unnatural* for me to ignore a roomful of women. Speculation would be rife if I was to do so and the paparazzi would soon begin looking for my secret liaison or making assumptions about my masculine urges, or worse."

"That's not an answer to my question."

He was a master at redirection, which made him a force to reckon with in the business world and not much more user-friendly in a relationship. But she'd been with him six months and worked for him six months before that. She knew most of his techniques by now and wasn't about to be swayed by them.

"It is all the answer you need. This is not about tit for tat. My behavior was necessary."

"And if I behaved similarly *out of necessity* it would not bother you?"

"The occasion does not arise."

"Are you sure about that?" She paused, giving him a moment to let the question prick at his arrogant certainty. "Just because I'm not gossip-column worthy doesn't mean I never flirt with other men."

"And do you?" he asked with an indulgence that said more clearly than anything else could how little he worried about the possibility.

"I haven't, because I considered myself taken, but I realize now that I shouldn't have."

CHAPTER TWO

"YOU *are* taken," Marcello said forcefully, no indulgence in evidence any longer.

"Not if you aren't, I'm not."

He let out a breath of obvious frustration. "It is not a matter of not considering myself in a relationship…it is merely that were I to ignore the overtures of other women completely, it would lead to too much speculation."

"Whereas my loyalty does not?"

"It is not a matter of loyalty," he denied, anger starting to curl around the edges of his forced patience.

"Yes, it is."

"I told you, it is a matter of expediency."

"And if me turning down invitations led to the same speculation that worries you, would that be reason for me to respond similarly? To go out with other men, to flirt with them?"

"I did not go out with anyone! I danced…I talked…I flirted as Italian men do, but I did not touch anyone as I touch you. *I did not want to.*"

"You had that woman's body as close to yours as you could get with your clothes on."

"It did nothing for me."

"Is that supposed to matter?"

"It should."

"Why?"

"It tells you that despite your insecurities, you are special to me."

"So special I'm a big, dark secret no one in your life knows about."

"So special that only the thought of seeing you turns me on. Holding another woman with her body pressed to mine does not because she is not you."

She didn't want to be moved by his description, but her susceptible heart told her that *was* unique…particularly for a man like Marcello Scorsolini.

He put his hands on her shoulders, his thumbs brushing her collarbone in a way he knew made her shiver. "The only woman I want, the only woman I crave to touch and be touched by right now, is you."

If he hadn't tacked the *right now* on, his statement would have been perfect.

He crowded close to her until their bodies brushed. "You are the only woman I *want* to hold this close. Everything at the party was window dressing…it meant nothing. Believe me, *tesoro*. Please."

The *please* did it. This man was not accustomed to begging. For anything. She had to be special to him, or he would have walked out when she started being difficult. Because he could have any woman he wanted…of that she was certain. And he made it clear he wanted only her.

"You didn't have sex with the beautiful blonde?"

He crushed her to him, his arms winding around her in a possessive hold that shook her. "No, *porca miseria*! I would never do that to you, *mio precioso*. I promise you."

She believed him and the relief she felt was incredible. "Good, because I would never stay with a player."

He laughed, the sound strained. "I am no player. I am not even the playboy the press paints me. I thought you knew this. I thought you knew *me*."

"I did. I do, but a picture is worth a thousand words."

"Only if you are speaking the same language as the photographer. What that journalist caught on film was two strangers dancing, nothing more. But look at the picture we paint, *amante*. Look and see the difference between eyes hot to possess and a social smile that meant nothing. Look at my hands which tremble with the need to touch you, but which held the other woman with total indifference."

His words did indeed paint a picture more powerful than the one in the scandal sheet. And the feel of his body pressed against hers backed it up. He needed her and she needed him. She'd missed him so much.

"If you are not a playboy, then what are you?" she asked provocatively.

"A mere man who wants you very much."

She could feel how much he wanted her and it made her insides melt.

Her mind started short-circuiting as it always did when he touched her, but she could still think straight enough to say, "Maybe we need to go public with our relationship. I don't like seeing pictures like that, Marcello. They hurt."

He kissed the corner of her mouth, the bridge of her nose, her forehead and then her lips with aching tenderness. "You are too sweet, *cara*. The press would pulverize you and I could not bear to watch, but I will do all that I can to make sure you are not hurt this way again."

That was something, she supposed, but she wanted to argue that she could handle the press. She was strong. She'd had to be her whole life. But her mouth was too busy kissing his to utter the words that needed saying.

The next morning, Marcello was gone when she woke up and so was the scandal rag, she noticed.

However, there was a red rose on his pillow and a note beside it. It read:

Cara,
Thank you for last night. I treasure our times together and the generosity of your affection for me.
M

He'd never left her a note before. His paranoia about privacy extended to not leaving any evidence of their relationship for others to find. This was a huge departure for him. It had to be significant. Maybe he was thinking about her desire to go public…maybe he was beginning to see that she was right.

The one thing she knew for certain was that his desire for her was not feigned. If he'd found relief with a convenient body while he was away from her, she was a monkey's uncle.

He'd been way too hungry. They'd made love into the early hours of morning and he had told her repeatedly how much he missed her, how beautiful she was to him, how special. All the words her vulnerable heart longed for.

Except the three that really mattered, but then she'd never said them to him, either.

She'd always worried they would spell the end to their relationship. She'd assumed he would reject that sort of emotional tie. He'd been so clear at the beginning of their affair that it could only ever be just that. An affair with a beginning and an end and no happily ever after. She'd wanted him so much and had been so impressed with his honesty after Ray's lies that she'd said yes.

And until she'd seen that picture in the tabloid, she'd never once regretted her choice. Marcello was an incredible lover and the time they spent together out of bed was equally fulfilling. He'd made their first time together very special and every time after.

His desire to keep their relationship underwraps had suited her down to the ground at first. She was too private a person to want to share their intimacy with the world at large. In that, too, she and Marcello were really alike. She'd seen what the gutter press could do with her friend Tara. At first, Danette had been only too happy to avoid the possibility of experiencing anything ugly and intrusive like that herself.

But beyond that, she had feared that if word of her relationship with Marcello got out, she would have to deal with interference from her well-meaning but overprotective parents. She'd also been concerned that her job might be affected, no matter how much Marcello did not want that to happen. She wanted to earn her advancement and did not want others speculating what her time between the sheets with the president of the company meant for her career.

She'd spent her whole life up to now under the watchful and overly intrusive eye of her family. It was important to her to prove that the strength it had taken to beat the scoliosis that had threatened her ability to walk, and even her life, spilled over into the rest of her existence as well.

Which was one of the reasons she hadn't wanted love or a long-term commitment in the beginning, either. She'd spent years in a sort of self-imposed isolation because of the brace she'd worn until she was nineteen to correct the deforming curve in her spine. And she'd wanted to feel what it was to be a woman. She'd wanted to date, to kiss, to heavy pet and ultimately to make love.

She'd wanted Marcello beyond reason and independently of finer feelings...or at least that was what she'd thought.

When she'd arrived in Italy, the farthest thing from her mind had been a desire to get into another relationship. She'd been bent on proving she wasn't as stupid as Ray's betrayal had made her feel. The first time they met, Marcello had unwittingly given her the means to do so.

She'd been feeling frustrated with herself because Angelo had arranged for her job, wondering if she could ever make it entirely on her own. She didn't know if everyone was so nice because they liked her, or because they wanted to do Angelo a favor...or at least please their boss who had extended the favor to his good friend.

She'd been in the middle of a royal bout of insecurity when Marcello made his first appearance at her desk. "You are the friend of Angelo Gordon's wife, are you not?" he'd asked without bothering to introduce himself.

She'd known who he was of course and even how he preferred to be addressed within Scorsolini Shipping. "Yes, Signor Scorsolini. I'm Danette Michaels."

"Angelo speaks highly of you."

"I'm glad. I loved my job with his company."

"But you wanted a change of venue, to see some of the world?" he asked with a blue gaze that could probe into the very depths of her soul.

"Yes."

He nodded. "You realize that my good friend's reputation in my eyes depends a great deal on your performance here." He didn't say it unkindly, or as if in warning, more like he was confirming something she already knew.

But it was news to her...welcome news. It gave her a target to aim for and said that, far from awarding her special treatment, he would expect more from her than his other employees. The words were like honey to her ears and she lapped them up. "I won't let either of you down."

"I do not doubt this. I am sure that because you came to work for me on his recommendation, you will work twice as hard to prove that he was smart to recommend you."

"You're right, I will." And it was a vow.

He smiled then, giving her her first taste of mind numbing physical awareness. "Don't work *too* hard. But I do not believe you will let either of us down."

And in proving him right, she made the job *her* personal triumph. Every success she achieved was a gift she consciously gave to both men who had chosen to believe in her and subconsciously gave to herself. When she had been promoted and given her own office after only four months because of her diligence, Marcello had called to personally congratulate her and Angelo had sent her an e-mail thanking her for making him look so good to his friend.

It had all been very feel good and laid a strong foundation for her growing confidence as an independent woman. Marcello asking her out had added to that confidence though she'd definitely been leery of him to begin with.

Danette worked on her sales projection report, determined to make her boss glad he'd promoted her and given her a private office. If there was a part of her that wanted to impress the president of the company, too, well, that was to be expected.

After all, he'd arranged for her to get her current job on the recommendation of his friend and she didn't want him to regret that choice, either. It had nothing to do with the fact that every time she saw him, her breathing and pulse rate went wacko.

She wasn't interested in risking her heart again and for sure not with a man of Prince Marcello Scorsolini's playboy reputation.

"Do you realize the time, Danette?"

Her head snapped up at the sound of the company president's voice coming from her open doorway.

"Signor Scorsolini!" She jumped up from her chair, looking around her, trying to focus on the now while her mind was still stuck on sales figures.

The hall outside her office was on dimmed lighting for after hours and the silence surrounding them told her that she was one of the few people left in the building. The small clock on her desk said it was eight o'clock.

Her mouth rounded in an, "Oh…" and then she gave him a rueful grimace. "No wonder my legs feel like they've petrified in one position."

"You work too hard."

She laughed as she stretched, realizing as she did so that her entire body was seriously cramped from sitting at her desk for so long. "That's a bit like the pot calling the kettle black, don't you think? Your workaholic hours are legendary around here."

"I do not expect my employees to give up all life outside of work in order to serve Scorsolini Shipping." He watched her stretch with disturbing intensity. "It is not the same for me. I have more reasons than most company presidents to make sure my business is a success."

"What do you mean?" she asked curiously as she smoothed her hair with a nervous hand.

The flirtatious facade she had created to deal with men deserted her in his company. She was lucky to string two syllables together that made sense when he spoke to her.

"The people of my country rely on the income from Scorsolini Shipping worldwide to maintain a standard of living in line with the other industrialized nations."

"You mean Isole dei Re?"

"Yes, naturally."

She didn't want to sit down again, but she felt exposed standing there behind her desk. She compromised by busying herself stacking the papers related to the sales projection report. It was the way he was looking at her...not at all like a boss looks at his employee.

More like a predator sizing up its prey.

She searched her mind for something to say. "I don't understand how Isole dei Re can be so reliant on this division of Scorsolini Shipping. There are only a handful of your countrymen and women employed here."

"You know this how?"

"I asked."

"It is interesting that you care." His still predatory gaze probed her speculatively.

"Everything about the company I work for interests me."

Marcello moved further into the room. "And the man you work for, does he interest you, I wonder?"

"You didn't just say that." She stared at him, shock coursing through her.

He smiled, his blue eyes full of knowing amusement. "I did, but we will leave it for the moment and I will answer your other question. While I do not employ many of my country's subjects, half of the net profits of all Scorsolini companies are paid into the national treasury and used to maintain and improve the country's infrastructure."

"You mean things like hospitals?" she asked fascinated. It had never occurred to her that the royal family gave back to their country on such an overwhelming scale.

"That and roads, schools, police and fire departments…the many things citizens of larger countries take for granted as being paid for by tax dollars."

"Wow."

"The money must come from somewhere."

"And Scorsolini Shipping is it?"

"Along with what tax dollars we do receive in revenue and the other enterprises of our country. My older brother, Tomasso, has recently supervised the discovery of lithium mines on Rubino. He has taken Scorsolini Mining and Jewels to an unprecedented level." His voice rang with pride in his brother's achievement.

"Funny, that's what Angelo Gordon told me you had done with the Italian arm of Scorsolini Shipping."

"My father and older brother are pleased with my efforts."

"They should be." And then she blushed at the vehemence of her words.

But he smiled, apparently pleased by her words. "My older brother, Claudio, has recently informed me that when he ascends to the throne, he and Tomasso have agreed that I will take over the entire shipping company while Tomasso maintains his position as head of Scorsolini Mining and Jewels."

"Did that surprise you?"

He nodded, coming closer, his presence filling her senses. "Normally the second son would take that position and I would either continue as I am or take Tomasso's position, but because he has taken that side of our family's holdings so far and my brothers and father are content with my performance here, I will be given the honor."

"That's wonderful! I suppose you celebrated by working a few extra twenty-hour days," she teased, knowing from the company grapevine that was exactly what he'd been doing lately.

He came around the desk and leaned against it, not six inches from where she stood. "Just as you have done?"

"Touché." She stopped in the act of reaching for the papers she'd stacked so she could file them. Doing so would require leaning into him and her senses were headed toward overload as it was. "I just don't want my boss to regret his decision to promote me," she said a trifle breathlessly.

"I also feel this need…in relation to the confidence my family has put in me."

His scent was teasing at her olfactory senses and she wanted to get closer, which was insane under the circumstances. "I guess…um…that we have something in common."

He reached out and touched her. Just a light brush against her cheek, but she felt paralyzed by it.

"Perhaps more than this single thing," he suggested.

Her face tingled where he had brushed it. "I can't imagine that we could have much else. Our lives are very different."

"Perhaps, but I think you are wrong. Will you have dinner with me tonight to find out?"

"What?" She shook her head, trying to clear it. The president of Scorsolini Shipping had asked her out on a date?

"I would like you to have dinner with me."

"But…"

"I like you, Danette, and I hope you like me, too." But his confident smile said he already knew she did, that he knew exactly the effect his nearness was having on her body.

"Of course I like you, but you asked me out on a date. I'm not your type."

"And you base this assumption on what?"

"Everybody knows you date really gorgeous women."

"You are beautiful."

She snorted at that. "I have a mirror. I'm nothing like the women you normally have your picture taken with."

"That is window dressing…a facade I present to the world to keep my private life private." He looked so sincere, but he couldn't be serious.

"But—"

"Come to dinner with me and see what kind of man I am when the paparazzi are not present with their insidious cameras."

"My job…" she said uncertainly.

"I make you this promise, Danette. Your job will not be influenced for good or for ill regardless of what happens or does not happen between us."

"So, if I say no to your dinner invitation?" she asked.

"I will be disappointed, but that will have no impact on your employment, advancement or type of opportunities given here at Scorsolini Shipping. To be fair, I must also tell you that even if you were to become my lover, that would not impact those same things in a positive way, either."

"I never for a moment would have expected them to."

"You are very naive."

"There's nothing naive about believing that a person should earn their job advancement."

He smiled, but his eyes were serious. "I like that about you and I agree."

"Good."

"So, will you allow me to take you to dinner?"

Every logical impulse in her body screamed at her to tell him no. She didn't want to get into a relationship, but dinner wasn't exactly a promise for the future. Maybe he was only interested in friendship. But he'd mentioned being her lover. That implied a lot more than chatting over coffee.

Oddly enough, it was the prospect of the *more* that had her so horribly tempted. She'd dated so little in her life and she'd never spent so much as half an hour with a man as intriguing as Marcello. Not unless you counted

Angelo Gordon, but he belonged to her friend and even he didn't stir her latent sexuality the way that Marcello did.

Ray certainly never had, the lying sneak.

This wasn't about love and happily ever after, she told herself, it was about experiencing feelings she'd denied herself far too long.

"Okay. I'll have dinner with you."

CHAPTER THREE

HE TOOK her to a small, family run restaurant outside of Palermo. It was a quarter to nine by the time they reached it. She'd learned Europeans often ate late. The owner was more than happy to give them a table.

As a dinner companion, Marcello lived up to every concept she had of him. He was charming, attentive and so sexy that her body thrummed with an awareness she'd never experienced with another man.

He poured her a second glass of the rich red wine he'd ordered with dinner. "So, Angelo said you were ready for a change and that is why you came to Sicily."

She'd noticed since coming to Palermo that Sicilians made a distinction between themselves and other Italians, as if they were their own separate country. Marcello did the same thing even though technically, he was from another country altogether. She had heard that his mother was Sicilian. Perhaps that accounted for it.

"Yes, I needed a change."

"Was there a man involved?"

Strangely she did not find his question intrusive. In an inexplicable way, she felt she could tell him almost anything. "Yes."

"What happened?" he asked with an expression that compelled her to share her deepest secrets with him.

"How do you do that?"

"What?"

"Make me feel like I should tell you everything in my head."

"Ah…there is a lot more to being the head of an international business than being able to count money."

She laughed. "I know that, but I wasn't aware that playing the role of father confessor was part of it."

"You would be surprised. Now tell me about the boyfriend."

"I thought he loved me, but he used me to get pictures of Tara and Angelo so he could break into tabloid journalism."

"He was the one responsible for those stories about them in the scandal rags last year?"

"Yes. They hurt Tara, a lot. She'd been savaged by the press once before and Ray's antics got her fired before Angelo found out what had happened."

"I hate the tabloids."

"But you're in them so often."

"Like I told you, I create a facade for them to latch on to so they leave my real life alone."

She'd done the very same thing as a small child. She'd created an image of an outgoing, confident girl that hid her private thoughts and feelings. No matter how intrusively doctors, or even her own parents, played their roles in her life, there was an interior Danette who remained sacrosanct to her alone.

Knowing they shared such a coping mechanism made her feel close to him in a way she would not have thought possible.

"Tell me more about Ray," Marcello said.

"There isn't much to tell. He was looking for the main chance and took it, not caring who he hurt or how much he hurt them. I think that's what devastated me the most. He couldn't have known my best friend was going to get involved with a media interest like Angelo Gordon, or that her notoriety would be so easily revived."

At least that's what she'd thought. "Our relationship started out for the usual reasons…I think. My family is wealthy and maybe he figured all along that I might take him into circles he could use to advance his career goals, but I really think that he saw the main chance and just went for it."

"And this hurt you?"

"Very much, but I'm over him now." And she was. It had happened faster than she'd thought it could.

The move to Italy had been the right choice.

"The betrayal by a lover is the most devastating."

"He wasn't my lover, thank goodness."

"So, the relationship wasn't very old?"

"That depends on how you define old. We were together for a few months."

"And he did not take you to bed?"

"It wasn't for lack of trying on his part," she said, stung that Marcello should think that she wasn't fanciable.

"No doubt. Why did you hold back from him?"

"It never felt right. It made him angry, but I didn't realize how much. He said some very cutting things when we broke up."

"I see."

"Do you? What do you see, Signor Scorsolini?"

"First that you must call me Marcello when we are away from the company."

She smiled despite the heavy feelings in her heart from her trip down memory lane. "All right."

"Second, that the man was a fool and obviously not very good in the seduction stakes."

"Or I'm not easily seduced."

"Be assured, I love a challenge."

She gasped at his blatant claim and the implication of it. "I'm not looking for that right now."

"But you have found it, as I will delight in showing you. I want you and I intend to have you."

But he didn't push for even a good-night kiss when he took her home that night. And it was the same on the three dates they had after that over the next two weeks. No matter what he had said, he seemed perfectly happy with a platonic friendship, while her physical awareness of him grew with every moment spent in his company.

She even started having sexy dreams about him. She would wake up feeling embarrassed by her obvious desire and disturbed by the strength of it...not to mention how easily he'd infiltrated her subconscious as well as her conscious life.

He'd asked her to maintain their status quo at work and to keep their time together strictly confidential. She'd agreed without pause. No one was going to accuse her of trading on a relationship with a man to get ahead in her career. Besides, there was something really alluring about clandestine meetings with the super sexy Marcello.

She loved talking to him on the phone and knowing that they were carrying on a conversation on a whole level that the people around them knew nothing about. Then he had to go away on a business trip and she missed him like crazy. He only called once and it was a short conversation. It had to be...she'd been at work.

They had plans to eat out the night after he got back, but when he came to pick her up, she had made dinner. She wanted time with him, to be completely natural together and the only way for that to happen was behind closed doors.

He sniffed appreciatively when she ushered him inside. "It smells so good, I almost want to beg to stay in and have leftovers."

"We are staying in, only they aren't leftovers. I made dinner."

"Is it a special occasion?"

"I thought I could teach you how to play Golf."

His brow drew together in puzzlement as he looked around the cottage's small living room. "I am already a competent golfer."

She laughed at his incomprehension. "It's a card game and one of the few that is as much fun with two people as four."

"Oh. *Cards*?"

"I thought you might be happier eating in and relaxing than going out to a restaurant, but if you'd rather…I can just wrap dinner up and get my coat."

"Not at all. I have never had a woman cook for me."

"Not even your wife?"

He rarely mentioned Bianca, but she knew he'd married young and his wife had died in a tragic accident.

"To my knowledge, Bianca did not know how to cook."

"Was she a princess?"

"To me? Yes, but she was not born to royalty. She was from a very wealthy Sicilian family. Her mother was my mother's best friend."

"It sounds like a match made in heaven."

"It was, but I lived in hell on earth when she died."

Why that should hurt so much to hear, she didn't know, but she did realize it wasn't all pain on his behalf. "I'm sorry."

"Thank you. They say time heals all wounds."

"I don't know about healing, but it does dull the pain…or makes it easier to cope with."

"Are you talking about Ray here?"

"No."

"Then what?"

Funny, how she'd told him so much about herself, but never about her corrected spinal deformity. It was too painful to talk about even now. The wounds it had visited on her life were too deep to expose to him or anyone else, for that matter.

She'd never told anyone about her decision not to have children because of it, or how alienated she'd felt from the world around her and even from her own body. Her brace had acted as a barrier between her and the sensation of touch for thirteen years. It had also distorted her view of her body. How could she explain what it was like to look into the mirror and see a figure that was defined by an expensive plastic encasement? She could not even be sure whether the curves were hers, or the result of the brace.

When she'd finally stopped wearing it, she had been afraid her body would change back, that her spine would curve once again and that the female curves she saw in the mirror would disappear now that their plastic encasement was gone. She'd been twenty-one before she'd finally decided her body really was hers again.

And even then, she often saw the brace when she looked in the mirror, rather than the actual woman looking back at her.

She shrugged. "Everyone has pain in their lives, Marcello. I'm no different, but it doesn't matter. I didn't ask you about Bianca to hurt you."

He touched her hand—nothing sexy, just a small brushing of their fingers—but her entire body felt like it had been electrified. "You did not. You never dig for juicy details or push me to bare my emotions. I appreciate that."

She laughed. "You would. The only person I know who is more private about their feelings than myself, is you."

"I would not have guessed you were such a private person at first."

"Protective persona. Most of us have them."

"Not my brothers. What you see is what you get with them."

"Are you sure about that? I bet even your father has an image he allows the rest of the world to see that protects the man behind his skin...the man who isn't a king."

"There, I know you are wrong. King Vincente is exactly as he appears to be. A sovereign to the marrow of his bones."

"Or he's just very adept at hiding any weakness, even from the people he loves the most."

"Trust me, his weaknesses are in no way hidden."

She had a hard time believing the son could be so very different from the father, but she didn't know either well enough to argue the point. "Whatever you say."

"I say that I am very appreciative that you chose to cook for me."

She smiled and led him to the small dining room, where she'd set the table with candles and her best dishes.

"It looks like a scene set for seduction."

"Maybe it is," she joked.

He turned to face her and put his hand on her face, the warm fingers sending more tingles of sensation zinging through her body. "I would not mind."

"I was only kidding."

"I am not."

"Um…maybe you had better sit down."

He sat and he said nothing more, but he kept giving her looks throughout dinner that were as effective as any caress.

Afterward, they took dessert, a homemade lemon sorbet, into the living room.

He pulled her to the sofa beside him, their hips touching. "Dinner was fantastic. Thank you, *cara*."

"You…you're welcome."

"I'm going to kiss you now."

"I…"

"Do you mind?"

"No." This was what she had wanted when she invited him to stay in for dinner, but when it came to the sticking point, she was nervous.

What if he found her as big a dud as Ray had done?

Marcello followed through on his promise to kiss her with a thoroughness that had her clinging to his shoulders while desire pooled low in her belly. He tasted like the lemon sorbet and sexy, delectable male. It was so different than when Ray had kissed her. With Marcello, she just wanted more and more and more. And he gave it to her, exploring her mouth with his tongue and letting her return the favor.

Finally he ended the kiss with a series of gentle pecks on her swollen lips. He lifted his head. "That went well, *cara*. I think we should do it again."

She nodded, incapable of speech.

Then he put his hands on her waist and brushed his thumbs up and down over her rib cage. "But this time, I want you sitting on my lap."

He couldn't know it, but that kind of touch was incredibly foreign to her. She'd developed habits as a child that kept people at a distance physically. Unconsciously she'd avoided Ray's touch as well. And when they did neck, he'd had a tendency to go straight for certain body parts. She hadn't enjoyed his caresses all that much and had assumed it was because she just wasn't very sexual. She now realized she'd been absolutely, terribly…no, *wonderfully* wrong.

Because she was reacting to Marcello's touch like a woman who had been in a desert her whole life and was just now stumbling on the Lake Erie of sensation. And in many ways, it was true.

Ray had not had the water she needed, but she felt drenched by emotions from Marcello's touch.

She scooted into his lap, loving the feel of his hard thighs below her. His hands moved around to caress her back with an erotic sweeping motion that made her tremble.

"You're very good at this."

He laughed and pressed his lips to hers again.

His hands moved all over her body in gentle, brushing strokes that made her feel like he was trying to see her with his hands. It was amazing and she grew scorching hot as her breasts swelled inside her lacy bra cups and the place between her legs grew damp and achingly swollen.

He stopped kissing her. "Don't you want to touch me?"

"Huh…what?" she asked, dazed by the deep, dark cravings rolling through her.

"Your hands are clenched at your sides."

"Oh, I don't mean them to be." And to prove she meant what she said, she splayed her fingers across his chest.

Heat emanated from him to her fingertips, even through his clothes. "I want to feel your skin."

"Then do it. I am not going to turn down any way you want to touch me, Danette."

There was something important in that reassurance, but she couldn't work it out in her head right now.

She unbuttoned his shirt with shaking hands and touched him with those same trembling fingers. She'd never felt this way touching Ray, like she was on a very important journey of discovery. One that would kill her if she didn't take it.

She explored Marcello's chest with total concentration given to every nuance of feeling, every detail of his masculine build her fingertips encountered. His muscles made ridges under his bronzed skin. The dark, curling hair that covered his chest and disappeared in an enticing V into his pants was surprisingly soft to the touch. Shouldn't male hair be coarse and, well…*manly*? But it felt so sexy, so incredible…and the skin beneath it was so warm. It was like touching heated satin.

She traced each ridge and she pressed her fingertip into his belly button while her thumb brushed the hair-roughened skin below it.

He groaned. "*Cara*, you are playing with fire there."

He *was* fire…all elemental heat. Everything a man should be for a woman.

Her hands swept up his torso, stopping at his rigid male nipples. "You are so different from me," she breathed.

He choked out a laugh. "You talk like you've never touched a man before."

"I haven't. Not like this."

His hands froze in the act of pushing her top up to expose her skin to his heated gaze.

"What are you saying? *Tesoro*, you cannot be a virgin. I do not believe it."

She stared at him, and then blinked, trying to make sense of his shock. "Why not? I told you that Ray was not my lover."

"But surely there have been other men."

"No."

"But American girls date in high school and college. Everyone knows this to be true."

"This one didn't." The passion clouding her brain began to fade. "I never had a boyfriend."

"Why not? Were your parents too protective?"

"You could say that." And she hadn't wanted to date, either. She didn't like explaining about the brace and no way would she have let a boy touch her and touch it. She couldn't stand being so exposed.

Marcello moved back from her, gently removing her hands from his body. "This is not right. I thought you were a woman of experience. I cannot take your innocence."

No, he couldn't mean it. This wasn't some Victorian tragedy. She was a modern woman, and perhaps waiting for marriage was something she'd thought at one time she would do, but she didn't feel that way right now. She didn't want any other man to be her first.

Only this one.

"But I can *give* it to you."

"I am not looking for marriage here. I do not want a long-term relationship."

"I'm not looking for marriage, either." She'd missed out on so much, the dating, the furtive moments of passion teenagers share, the love affairs in college. "I want to experience it all with you, Marcello. I trust you."

"But you are a virgin. You should wait until you get married."

"I want you to be my first man. I've never felt this kind of desire before and I'm afraid I'll never feel this way again. I sure didn't with Ray."

"He was a creep."

"Yes, but you're not. I know you won't hurt me...I know you can make it special my first time."

"You know this, huh?"

"You may not be the playboy the media paints you, but you're experienced enough to know what you're doing. You make me crazy just being with you." She didn't want to beg, but she was close. "If you want me, too...at least a little...I want you to be my first lover."

"I want you a great deal more than a little," he growled, his eyes shooting blue flame at her. The hottest kind of flame and she felt singed to the depths of her soul.

"I'm glad, Marcello, because I want you a lot, too."

"Our relationship remains strictly private. I will not allow the media into my personal life, which means others cannot know about us, either."

"I don't have a problem with that."

Danette abruptly returned to the present. She *hadn't* had a problem with the secrecy then....but this was now and she did have a problem with it. A big problem. She just wasn't sure what she could do about it.

If anything.

She loved him and that love demanded a role in his life that stretched beyond a secret affair. Maybe if she told him her feelings he would acknowledge his own and they could move to the next step in their relationship.

It wasn't that she thought he lacked confidence. If he knew he loved her, he would say so, but his heart was locked up tight behind the wall he'd built after Bianca's death. Danette had managed to knock out chinks here and there, evidenced by the fact that their relationship had lasted so long and how much time they spent together doing stuff besides making love.

While he refused to tell her how many women had come before her, he had let slip that none of them had lasted beyond a very brief liaison. He had been with her for six months and made no indications he was even thinking about moving on.

There was also the fact that he frequently made love to her without protection. He'd done so again the night before.

The first time it had happened, she'd been shocked by her response. Since she had decided as a teenager not to have children and risk passing on her spinal deformity, she should have been really upset by his lapse. But her first reaction to the realization he'd forgotten the condom had not been dismay. Far from it: she'd had a piercingly sweet image of a little boy with her eyes and Marcello's smile.

She had experienced a craving for that child that was so great, it had been a physical pain in her chest.

Nevertheless, she'd brought up the option of her going on the pill, but Marcello had been adamant it was not necessary. He knew from one of the many discussions they had on every topic under the sun that she had some family history of breast cancer, and therefore concerned about the possible increased risk from long-term use of the pill.

She'd agreed to allow him to continue to be responsible for the birth control and had not raised the issue again the next time he forgot. Instead she'd researched the probability of passing her severe idiomatic juvenile scoliosis onto her children. She'd discovered that, far from what she'd feared, there was actually no known genetic predisposition for what had happened to her.

She couldn't dismiss the very real fact that her mother had been afflicted with a less severe case. Even so, she'd all but convinced herself it was a risk worth taking. She refused to allow her childhood disease and what it represented to stand between her and Marcello.

Right now, she had to weigh the fact that he talked like the future was uncertain for them against the fact that he forgot to use birth control almost as often as he remembered. No man took that many risks with pregnancy when he hated the idea of spending his future with the woman involved.

Marcello wasn't the irresponsible kind. If she got pregnant, she knew he'd want to marry her. He had a strong sense of moral and family responsibility. Both of which would require that his child not be born illegitimate. In turn, that *must* mean he was considering a future with her, even if he was leery about admitting it to her, or even to himself.

It might be a subconscious thing on his part, but his actions spoke loud and clear about where he was at with her emotionally. At least she hoped they did. No amount of wishful surmising on her part could replace hearing the words from his lips.

His wife's death had devastated him. She'd quickly realized that he didn't want to risk that kind of pain again, but she could have told him that love did not respect the fear of being hurt.

Just look at her. She had come to Italy licking her wounds. She'd been grateful for the job that Angelo had gotten her so that she could get away from her memories. And she'd been convinced that the last thing she would allow herself to do was to get embroiled in another relationship. Only, that was exactly what she had done and she'd gotten in deeper with Marcello after two weeks than she had in months with Ray.

She'd come to Marcello a virgin and she knew that was as important to him as it was to her.

Part of her, deep down, wished she would just get pregnant and then neither of them would have a choice about secrecy or the rest of it anymore. But part of her was frightened by the prospect of pregnancy, and a much bigger part needed him to come to terms with his feelings for her on his own. She wanted him to acknowledge he cared about her and she needed to know that for sure, too. Not just hope and guess at it.

Maybe telling him that she loved him would open another chink in the wall around his heart…the most important one.

She hoped so, because if it didn't, she'd didn't know what she would do.

Later that day when he came into her office to ask for her report on the Cordoba project, when he could have requested the information through his assistant, that hope blossomed.

CHAPTER FOUR

MARCELLO walked into Danette's office and felt like he'd been hit in the chest with a polo mallet when she gave him that smile she reserved especially for him.

Her amber eyes glowed golden with welcome and his body reacted as if it had been months, not hours, since he had last buried himself inside her. He became instantly hard—to the point of pain. He found himself pushing the door shut behind him, though that was probably the last thing he should do.

"I have the report for you right here." She tucked her light brown hair behind her ear with a flirtatious wink. "That is what you came for, isn't it?"

The significant look she gave the shut door belied the innocence of her words and he grinned in response. He couldn't help it. Like all of his reactions to her from the moment he had first seen her, it was beyond his usually formidable control. He had never looked to one of his employees for friendship, much less an affair and he had fought his feelings for her for four months. But in the end…he had lost.

He hadn't been able to dismiss the cravings for her body and that particular sweet smile he'd never seen her give anyone else. It was a craving that grew when fed, he'd discovered, rather than diminishing. Which put it in the realm of an addiction he could not kick. As much as he hated the vulnerability such an addiction spawned, he had learned that to give into it brought its own reward. The more time he spent with her, the more at peace he felt, and after making love was the best of all.

Even though he knew he should be opening that door and getting down to business, not putting the anonymity of their affair at risk, he was powerless to do so. His gaze skimmed her slight figure as his libido heated to volcanic levels and he acknowledged there was a big difference between knowing what he should do and being able to do it.

"That is the excuse I gave my assistant, yes."

"Perhaps there was something else you wanted from me?" she asked in a come-hither voice that went straight to his already throbbing groin.

That overtly flirtatious manner and her American frankness had fooled him into believing she was a much more experienced woman than she was for the first months of their association. Right up until he'd touched her with intent for the first time and found out she was a virgin, and an incredibly innocent one at that. She'd known almost nothing of passion.

He'd seen too late that for all her appearance of outgoing friendliness, she was actually rather shy. She knew even less of men than she did of physical desire. And he had shamelessly taken advantage of her willingness to learn with him.

He'd been careful to spell out the parameters of their affair, though. She'd deserved to know where they were headed—to bed—and where they were not going—

down the aisle toward matrimony. He'd been very clear. No commitments. No permanent ties. Absolute secrecy.

And she had still welcomed him with an innocent but generous passion that left him shaking.

She'd never brought up the other parameters of their affair and he had to assume she understood their relationship was not a permanent one, but she had become unhappy with the need for secrecy. She'd been hurt by that picture in the tabloid and he hated knowing that, but if the media became aware of her existence in his life, she would be at risk of a lot more hurt and continuous harassment.

Although he understood her current feelings, he could not give into them. It was imperative he remain strong for both of their sakes. He hated having his real private life the focus of public cynosure. He'd had enough of that with his marriage. The press had hounded him and Bianca from the very first. No doubt contributing to what came later. They'd married young and that alone had been newsworthy…to some. Many had assumed she was pregnant, but she hadn't been.

Then, when two years went by and no pregnancy showed on the horizon, speculation started. It was a mere reflection of the concerns he and Bianca shared in the privacy of their bedroom. Because they'd done nothing to prevent pregnancy from their wedding night onward. She had been the first one to undergo tests, but her reproductive system was functioning normally.

He'd offered to have the tests taken as well, never dreaming the doctor would discover a really low sperm count. He would never forget the chilling humiliation when one of the scandal rags had gotten wind of his near sterility. They had run the story and others had picked it up until he and his wife could not go out in public without being asked if they planned to adopt, try IVF or worse.

Bianca had said it didn't matter, but Marcello had seen her pain when her friends fell pregnant and she did not. He had seen the longing in her eyes when she held her cousins' babies, and he'd listened to her cry at night in their bathroom when she thought he was sleeping.

He felt like his manhood had been stripped away from him. Having it happen in the public eye had been ten times worse. He would never willingly go through that again.

"Marcello?" Danette asked, her expression concerned.

He forced the bleak thoughts from his mind and focused on the situation at hand. "There is definitely something else you can give me." It was more than her body and her desire that he was talking about. Making love to Danette banished the ghosts of the past...for a little while.

"Something more important than the report?" she asked with a vulnerability he wished he couldn't see.

She wanted confirmation that she was more important to him than the work she did for him, but if he gave it to her, then he would be implying a depth to their relationship he had been careful to refrain from establishing. He couldn't do that. It wouldn't be fair. But from the look in her lovely amber eyes, he knew not to do so wasn't being fair to her, either.

She deserved better than what he could give her. She deserved a man who could and would date her openly, one who could give her a future with a complete family. Not a playboy prince who could offer her great sex and companionship only when it was out of the public eye— and no future.

Knowing what she deserved didn't change his need for her, though. Marcello was not about to give her up. Not yet.

She added too much to his life.

One day, she would move on, but until then, he would give her all that he could and take all she was willing to offer.

"It certainly feels more urgent," he compromised.

It appeased her and she smiled again, this time her eyes going dark with a familiar fire. "What could it be then?"

He leaned back against the door, his legs spread slightly, his body telling her he wasn't going anywhere. "Come here and I'll show you."

"I don't think so." She cocked her head to one side and looked at him. "You look dangerous."

"And you feel safe with the desk between us?"

She shrugged, but the look she gave him from between her lashes was pure provocation. "Maybe. I guess that all depends on how much energy you're willing to expend."

He pushed away from the door and stalked over to her, his body thrumming with the incredible sexual excitement only she generated in him. When he reached her, she scooted back in her chair, but the primal man inside him was not about to let his prize retreat.

Marcello reached out with lightning quick movements to grab Danette's shoulders and prevent her withdrawal. Suddenly their playful banter was overshadowed by a dark, perilous desire he had never unleashed in the office before.

She gasped. "Marcello, what are you *doing*?"

She'd been playing. Flirting in a way she knew drove him crazy, but never in a million years had she expected him to take her up on it within the hallowed walls of Scorsolini Shipping.

He pulled her from the chair. "I want you, Danette. Now."

"Wh—"

His mouth slammed down on hers with primitive passion, his intent unmistakable.

The urbane and sophisticated playboy everyone else saw when they looked at him was gone. In his place was a man of earthy passion and raw masculinity that only she ever saw and she found totally irresistible.

The kiss went incendiary immediately. His lips sucked on hers, his tongue demanded entrance into her mouth, and his teeth nipped at her bottom lip. She gave back as good as she got, her tongue tangling with his in delicious, erotic abandon. She couldn't get enough. Her brain was barely functioning when he moved his mouth along her jaw to wreak havoc on the sensitive areas he knew so well.

"*Here*?" she whispered with her last grasp at rational thought. "You want to make love here?"

His answer was to growl like some primitive animal, slide his hand possessively down over the curve of her breast and squeeze. She moaned.

"Shh…*amante*, you must be silent."

"I can't…"

"You can and you will," he promised in a shadowy drawl and then challenged that assumption with sensual caresses that made her body swell with pleasure.

She tugged at his tie, undoing it and the buttons of his shirt with impatient fingers. She peeled the fabric away to reveal the hair-roughened contours of his chest and abdomen. She curled her fingers in it reflexively and the breath stilled in her chest at the sight of her fingers on his skin.

He was such a beautiful, beautiful man.

He made a harsh sound and then whispered, "Yes, just like that, Danette *mia*. Give me your passion, *amante*."

She leaned forward and took his small, rigid nipple between her teeth and nipped, then licked it to soothe the sting before sucking it into her mouth as she knew he liked.

His body jerked and he made a muted sound of passion before yanking her blouse up to expose her bra clad breasts. One flick of his fingers and the front clasp came apart and then his hands were on her, tormenting her with the kind of caresses that would bring her to the brink of climax before he ever touched her most intimate flesh.

His hands went everywhere, rubbing her back, kneading her bottom and sliding under her skirt with a lack of finesse that said better than anything else could have how out of control he really was. His big frame shuddered when she attacked his belt buckle and then the zipper on his slacks.

She slid it down with agonizing slowness, not wanting to hurt the flesh straining against it and reveling in the anticipation of what she would reveal. She pushed his waistband down, carefully pulling the elastic of his shorts over his pulsing, erect flesh. His rigid length sprang out to greet her. Curling her fingers around his satin hardness, she squeezed possessively.

"Yes, yours," he said, showing he knew exactly what she was thinking.

Then he picked her up by the waist and sat her on the edge of her desk, moving between her legs boldly so that her thighs were parted wide and left open to him.

She'd worn stockings like she always did and the fragile silk of her panties proved no barrier to his touch. He tore them from her body with primitive violence that sent a burst of humid warmth through her secret place.

He cupped her, one long finger sliding inside. "Mine."

"Yesss…" she hissed.

Then he was there, exactly where she most needed him to be, and she whimpered with the exquisite pleasure of it. He was big and she spread her legs wider to accommodate him, wrapping her calves around his lean waist. He grabbed her hips and pressed inexorably forward, his hardness stretching her almost unbearably, but feeling so right and so good that tears of intense desire burned her eyes.

"You fit me so perfectly," he whispered roughly into her hair, and thrust in to the hilt.

She couldn't reply. Her throat was too tight with the need to cry out her pleasure and the effort it took to suppress those cries.

She buried her face in his neck, biting her lips together to hold back the sounds as he thrust against her with powerful movements that shook her whole body. The pleasure spun tight and high inside of her instantly and she exploded in rapturous bliss after only a few body-racking thrusts. Her flesh convulsed around him, her entire being shuddering with her culmination.

His grip on her hips tightened bruisingly and he bit back a growl as his body went stiff against hers and he released his pleasure inside of her. They remained locked in primal ecstasy for what could have been mere seconds or much longer. Time meant nothing on that plane of existence. Only sensation mattered and it was so overwhelming, her head spun in a dizzy black void.

Even when the pleasure waned, he did not move and neither did she. She was in too much shock. She couldn't believe they had made love *in her office*. Her door didn't even have a lock, for goodness' sake. It went against everything he preached about keeping their private association private. The risk of exposure was huge and yet, he had not even hesitated.

The fact that his need for her was so great made her feel warm deep down inside. That *had* to mean something.

"I cannot believe we just did that," he said mirroring her thoughts.

"You started it."

He laughed against her temple before turning her face up for a tender kiss of soul-stirring proportions. "You provoked me, *amante,* do not try to deny it. You know I find you irresistible."

"I didn't mean to provoke *this*." And she hadn't. It would never have occurred to her to try to tease him into making love in the office.

She felt shattered by having fallen into it so completely herself. Was she a complete wanton, that the thought of her office door's inability to lock hadn't even entered her mind until afterward? Or depraved even?

"No doubt," he mused against her face as he pressed another small kiss to her temple. "You are too innocent to take such an encounter in your stride."

"And you are not?" she asked, the sensation of his body still locked to hers suddenly making her feel incredibly vulnerable.

"I left my rose-colored glasses of innocence behind me long ago, but if you are wondering if sex in the office is a norm for me, let me assure you that it is not."

For some reason, that made her feel better than it

should. His past shouldn't matter, but knowing he broke his own rules for her did.

He pulled out of her, but did not move so she could close her legs. Instead he used tissues from the dispenser on her desk to clean her up and she found that act every bit as intimate as the one they had just performed and a lot more embarrassing.

"Marcello…"

"This will make it more comfortable for you."

She didn't know what else to say, so she choked out an uncomfortable, "Thank you."

His blue gaze flicked to her face and he shook his head. "How can you blush now, when seconds ago you were receiving me into your body with a passion that could burn the sun?"

The heat of her blush intensified and she bit her lip. When he continued to look at her inquiringly, she admitted, "When you touch me, you make me forget everything else."

He continued to care for her, his attention thorough. "I am touching you now."

"It's not the same."

"No, it is not, but my body does not seem to know that."

She looked down and realized that his arousal was growing again.

"You can't want…not again!"

"I want. Do not mistake it…but I will not take again. Not here. I should not have kissed you that first time. I cannot believe we did this in your office. It was not my brightest moment."

"You make it sound like you regret making love to me." And while she agreed that their venue had not been as private as she would have liked, that implication still hurt.

After all, nothing bad had happened.

"I could never regret the kind of pleasure I find in your body."

"Good. Because I don't regret it, either."

He finished what he was doing and finally stepped back so she could bring her legs together.

He buttoned his shirt and tucked it into his slacks with quick, efficient movements. "You said that the first time we made love. Do you remember?"

"How could I forget?" she asked as she redid her bra and blouse, impatient to be put back together now that the passion no longer fogged her brain and she was all too aware of the risk of someone knocking on her office door.

"I was your first lover and you did not regret that, even though I could not make the promises that a virgin should expect her first lover to make." He spoke while retying his tie and did not look at her.

"Are we going to get into that again?" Once had been plenty for her.

He sighed, the sound odd considering what they'd just been doing. "There is no need."

"Right." Besides, promises or no promises, he'd shown her in many ways that she was special to him. She finished dressing, ruefully tossing her panties in the trash when she saw they could never be worn again. "Will I see you tonight?"

He tugged his tie into place and finger combed his hair, leaving his appearance as pristine and businesslike as before. "I have plans this evening."

"Business plans?" she asked.

"Does it matter?"

She frowned. "After our discussion last night, do you have to ask?"

He shook his head with impatience. "I am not going out with another woman."

"So, it *is* business."

He merely shrugged, which was not an answer. She was preparing to press for one when he picked her panties up out of the trash.

"What are you doing? Don't tell me you want a souvenir."

"Do not be crude."

"Um…I'm not the one who just grabbed torn underwear from the circular file." But she was the one blushing about it. Aargh! She really wasn't in his league.

"I do not wish to leave them here for the cleaning crew to find. It could cause speculation."

"And you don't think the closed door will do that?"

"There are many reasons besides having wild, urgent sex on a desk to close an office door when I am meeting with an employee, but there are no reasons *but* sex to explain ripped lingerie in the waste bin."

"I see. And of course it would be an absolute tragedy if someone were to guess that you'd been making love with me."

It was his turn to frown. "We have been over this."

"Yes."

He pulled her to him, but she didn't melt against him like she normally did.

He sighed again. "Believe it, or not, but I am protecting you as much as I am protecting myself. You do not know how vicious the scandal rags can be."

Remembering the stories her former boyfriend had

helped to dish up on her friend Tara and Angelo Gordon, she shook her head. "You're wrong. I do know. I'm just not as scared of it as you are."

She also remembered the way that Angelo had responded to the ugly stories. He had stood beside Tara, proud to be her lover. But then Angelo had wanted to marry Tara.

Marcello looked supremely offended. "I am not afraid."

"Whatever you say."

"Are you trying to pick an argument?" he asked in a tone that implied he couldn't believe she'd want to after what they had just done.

And she didn't. Not really. "No."

He picked up the report from the corner of her desk. "I must go."

"Yes."

"I do not like to see you like this."

"Like what?" Like she'd just been made love to and was still reeling from the aftereffects?

"Your sparkle is missing."

She didn't know what he was talking about. "I'm in work mode. I don't sparkle at work."

"This is not true. It was the life blazing from your golden eyes that first caught my interest."

"Well, we both know it wasn't my body," she said in a poor attempt at a joke. Her curves were slight and her face was average…it still shocked her Marcello had chosen her for his lover, secret or not.

"Your body is perfect, or is it not obvious I think this?"

It *was* obvious. The one thing she knew with total certainty was that he found her irresistibly sexually attractive. She didn't understand it and she wasn't sure that was enough anymore.

If she couldn't convince herself that he cared, at least a little, she'd fall into complete despair.

"If you don't leave, there is going to be speculation about my job performance or lack thereof because of that shut door."

He nodded, his eyes probing hers as if looking for answers. She had none for him. At least not right now…not here.

He stopped at the door. "I could come by later tonight."

His offer shouldn't have made her spirits lift, but even though it was such a small concession, it did.

"If you like."

"I do like. I enjoy sleeping with you in my arms."

"Even when we don't make love?" But she knew the answer to that. He spent as many nights during her monthly as he did when she was available sexually.

"Even then, but tonight, there will be no barriers," he said, showing that once again his mind was traveling the same path as hers.

Didn't that kind of intimacy of thought mean something?

She could only pray it did because if she really was just a body in his bed, she didn't think she'd survive the pain of that kind of reality.

CHAPTER FIVE

LIZZY came by Danette's office later that afternoon to ask if she wanted to go out to dinner to celebrate finishing the Cordoba project.

Danette accepted without hesitation. "That sounds terrific."

And much better than spending another evening alone wondering what Marcello was doing that he couldn't be with her.

"Where do you want to eat?"

"You choose."

"No way. This is your celebration."

She named a restaurant that was one of her favorites. Marcello had introduced it to her. It was a small eatery run by a local family and the food was superb. Its ambience was hardly what a prince was used to and she'd often wondered if he took her more for the relative privacy it offered than even the excellent food. It definitely wasn't the type of place where the paparazzi hung out to catch glimpses of the newsworthy.

If they tried, she had no doubt that Giuseppe, the owner, would have tossed them out with a few choice words.

When she arrived, she asked Giuseppe if Lizzy had already arrived.

"You are not eating with Principe Tomasso tonight?" he asked instead of answering.

"No."

He frowned, his expression an odd one she could not decipher. If she didn't know better, she'd think the older Sicilian man looked worried about something, but what there was to worry about in her eating dinner with Lizzy, she couldn't imagine.

But all he said was, "Your friends, they are this way."

He led her to a table in the back and it was only as they reached it that the import of Giuseppe's words hit her. Because Lizzy was not the only person at the table. Her current boyfriend and Ramon from the sales department at Scorsolini Shipping were both sitting there, too.

Ramon had worked with her on several aspects of the Cordoba project. Maybe that was why he was there, maybe he wanted to celebrate too, but more likely Lizzy was playing matchmaker. If that were the case, Danette was going to cheerfully strangle her friend.

However, she pasted a smile on her face when Ramon hopped up to help her into her chair. "Thank you."

"It is my pleasure. I am glad you finally agreed to see me outside of work."

Lizzy flushed guiltily and Danette almost said she hadn't agreed to any such thing, but refused to deal that kind of blow to the man's ego. It wasn't his fault Lizzy was playing games Danette did not want to engage in. Ramon had never been anything but kind to her, even if he was a hopeless flirt and had a reputation for dating more women than most. And really, she couldn't be too angry with Lizzy, either. The other woman didn't know Danette was already in a relationship, but she did know Danette didn't want to date Ramon.

She shrugged. "Blame Lizzy." She knew she did, and the look she gave the other American woman said so.

Lizzy just grinned back, all evidence of guilt gone, her expression now full of satisfaction in a plan well executed.

They were eating their salad and bread, Ramon at his charming best, which Danette had to admit was likable, when she felt a tingling sensation in the back of her neck. Still smiling from something Ramon had said, she looked around, trying to account for it. Her breath stilled in shock when she saw Marcello with three other people.

Danette recognized all of them from photos she'd seen in the media. The older woman, with hair the same golden-brown as Marcello's and a face that was almost painfully beautiful, was his mother. The man next to Marcello was his older brother, Principe Tomasso Scorsolini, and the woman glowing with happiness at his side was Tomasso's new fiancée, Maggie Thomson.

So, *not* business. Family. And he had clearly not wanted to introduce her to them. She understood keeping their relationship hidden from the public eye, she really did. She might not like it, but she could not fault his reasoning for it. However, why did she have to be kept a secret from his family as well? Surely none of them would leak anything to the press.

He must have felt her eyes on him because he turned and their gazes met across the small but crowded restaurant. His eyes widened fractionally and then narrowed before his mother said something to him and he turned away to speak to her, giving no indication of acknowledgment to Danette.

It sliced through her heart like a jagged blade and she touched her chest, feeling like there should be an open wound there.

"Isn't that the big boss?" Lizzy demanded in an awed whisper. "The prince himself?"

Ramon turned and he studied the newcomers. "Yes, it is."

Giuseppe was now leading the foursome to a table that would take Marcello's party right by where Danette sat.

She felt like she couldn't breathe. She didn't know what she would do if he walked right by without even acknowledging her. At least at work, he always extended the courtesy of recognizing her presence…just as he did all the employees he knew by name.

She was saved from finding out when Ramon stood up with a smile, his hand extended to Marcello. The men greeted one another. Then Marcello introduced all of them to his family…as employees of Scorsolini Shipping.

He did not linger over his introduction of her, not even by a millisecond, and there could be no indication to his family that she was special to him in any way. Which was exactly what she should have expected, but she still felt horribly slighted. It hurt, and it didn't matter that he had not really betrayed her or that he was acting only as he had always said he would.

Her heart was tight with pain and the rest of her felt numb.

She said something in response to the introductions,

though she had no idea what. Her brain wasn't functioning all that well. Marcello's eyes narrowed, and she
wondered if she'd said something wrong, but no one
else reacted strangely. So, it must have been okay.

Conversation flowed back and forth, but none of it
penetrated the pain imploding inside her.

Lizzy made a comment and they laughed, but they
were looking at Danette and she realized she'd missed
something.

Lizzy grinned. "Her head's in the clouds. She just
finished an important project and she put so much into
it, I think she frazzled her brain."

"And here I had hoped it was that she was overawed
because she finally agreed to go out with me," Ramon
said with such blatant humor that even Danette's lips
curved in a tiny smile.

Everyone else laughed out loud…except Marcello.

For the space of a single heartbeat his glare could
have singed concrete, but then a mask of imperturbabil-
ity settled over his face.

"You see, Marcello? This is what you should be
doing, my son."

"And what is that, Mama?"

"Like these young men, you should be dating some
nice girl, but it is always work, work, work with you.
The hours he puts in." She shook her head. "*Ai, ai, ai.*
He thinks of nothing but business. And here we see
there are plenty of lovely young women who work for
you that you could socialize with."

"I do not make it a habit to date employees," he said
with a perfectly straight face.

Danette gasped, her face stinging with heat as if it
had been struck.

His look of concern lasted longer than the glare, but she ignored it. So, he didn't date employees? What was their relationship then, a series of clandestine *meetings*? Even as she asked herself the question, her heart knew the answer.

That was exactly what they had. A series of secret trysts that meant nothing more to him than a one-night stand. They couldn't and have him deny her to his family so completely.

"I am glad you do not expect your employees to adhere to that principle," Ramon said with a smile for Danette.

Lizzy and her date chimed in and Marcello merely shrugged, but there was something feral in the cobalt-blue gaze he fixed on Ramon.

Danette could not leave it there. Would not do so…it wasn't right. "So, you *never* date employees?" she asked with a voice that sounded to her like shattered glass.

"I keep my private life private," he said by way of a nonanswer.

"There aren't any women at Scorsolini Shipping glamorous enough for the prince," Lizzy said cheekily. "I've seen pictures of the women he dates. They're cover model types for sure. I mean if they ended up married, she'd be a princess wouldn't she? Someone like Miss Thompson here fits the bill." She indicated Prince Tomasso's perfectly groomed and thoroughly lovely fiancée with a nod of her head. "But I can't see any of the women at Scorsolini shipping being that kind of glamour material."

Maggie Thompson made a strange sound.

Prince Tomasso smiled at her. "I told you that you are my perfect mate."

Lizzy's eyes went all dreamy. "Isn't that romantic?" she asked the table in general.

"Very," Danette said, feeling as far from romantic herself as it was possible to get. "No doubt if Marcello was dating a cover model or someone as lovely as the soon-to-be princess, he wouldn't be such a stickler for privacy."

Her words held a message for him that no one else would get, but it was only after speaking that she realized she'd used his first name. While he encouraged a less formal address amongst his employees than "Your Highness", she still should have called him Signor Scorsolini.

She didn't know if the anger tightening his jaw was for her slip or her implication.

"Are you kidding?" Lizzy demanded, filling the awkward silence. "There wasn't anything private about the picture of Signor Scorsolini dancing with that gorgeous blonde at his father's birthday party. Oooh, la, la. What a couple." She waggled her eyebrows dramatically, making everyone laugh again.

"She was only one of many gorgeous creatures he danced with that night," Maggie Thomson said, her smile wide. "I don't mind telling you, I was glad he was there to draw some of the attention away from Tomasso."

"I live to serve," Marcello said with a forced face-tiousness she doubted anyone else noticed was not entirely natural.

Danette wasn't feeling humorous, either. She cocked her head to one side and examined his brother. In many ways the two men looked alike. They were both tall and shared the same cobalt-blue eyes, though Marcello's skin was darker. His hair was lighter, but both men wore it a little long and had matching widow's peaks. The expression of supreme male confidence they wore was identical, too.

"Tell me something, Prince Tomasso, if you don't mind."

Sliding an arm around his fiancée's waist, he smiled at Danette. "What would you like to know?"

"How do you manage to balance your princely duty to socialize with your personal life? For example, could you dance with one woman as your brother did, while wooing your fiancée, persuading her you cared about her?"

"Ah, you must remember, my brother is smart enough not to have told any woman such a thing, so the question doesn't arise in his case. He's very adept at juggling excess amounts of female attention. But in answer to your question, Maggie would brain me if I danced with another woman the way my brother danced at our father's party. And rightly so. I prefer to keep my head in one piece and therefore would not risk it, no."

Everyone laughed while Danette felt the blood draining from her face. *The way that Marcello had danced with the other women...*he hadn't just been putting on a front. He'd been enjoying himself, playing the field. Maybe even looking for her replacement. Okay, so it was probable he hadn't slept with any of them, but she still felt a holocaust of pain where her heart should be.

Her eyes met Marcello's and she knew that right that second, all the pain she was feeling was there for him to see.

He cursed, shocking everyone around them and Prince Tomasso said, "What's the matter?"

"I did not dance like a damned gigolo."

"I never said you did. You merely acted like the single man you are and had a lot of fun doing it. I, however, am content to be attached." And the look he gave Maggie left no one at the table, or standing beside it, in any doubt how very sincerely he felt those words.

Tears burned the back of Danette's eyes and she blinked furiously to get rid of them. Marcello looked livid. She couldn't imagine why. His brother only spoke the truth after all.

Lizzy sighed, the dreamy look back. "That's just so sweet."

Her date grinned. "I can be just as sweet, do you doubt it?"

She laughed. "Of course not. I wouldn't be here with you otherwise."

"We shouldn't keep you from your table any longer," Danette said to Marcello through stiff lips, not meeting his eyes.

She wanted them gone and did not care if she wasn't at her subtle best in achieving that goal. As it was, she had no idea how she was going to hold it together for the remainder of dinner. But she would somehow. She wasn't making an idiot of herself in public over a relationship that no one but her and Marcello even knew about.

"And we should not keep you from your dinner any longer," Flavia Scorsolini said.

Marcello and the others followed the now moving Giuseppe, but the former queen stopped beside Danette and put her elegant hand on her shoulder, then squeezed gently. "It was a pleasure meeting you. All of you."

Danette looked at the older woman and willed the pain inside of her to stay hidden. "Thank you," she forced out. "It was a pleasure meeting you, too."

Her companions chipped in with more of the same.

Flavia shook her head as if her thoughts troubled her. "Perhaps I will see you again."

"That is very unlikely."

Flavia cocked her head to one side and studied Danette for a nerve-racking moment. "I wonder." And then without another word, she moved on.

"Wow, that was odd. Did you think the boss was acting strangely?" Lizzy asked when Flavia was gone.

"I would say he was acting true to form," Danette replied.

"I thought I was going to die when you called him *Marcello*, and in front of his family, no less." Lizzy shivered. "I'm just glad he's not as hung up on protocol as some Italian men."

"He would never fire an employee for that kind of thing, but other men might," Ramon agreed.

Then he and Lizzy's date spent ten minutes rhapsodizing over what a great guy Marcello was and how much they admired the way he didn't trade on his royal status to run the company.

Danette let the conversation flow around her for the rest of dinner, replying only when she was asked a direct question.

Marcello's table turned out to be right in her line of sight and he had taken a seat facing her. She tried to keep her gaze from straying to him, but at one point she simply had to look and found his eyes directed at her. Their gazes locked, but she broke eye contact before he had the chance to. She'd suffered enough rejection at his hands tonight.

She was careful not to look that way again, though she felt his eyes on her more than once.

When it was time to go, Ramon offered to see her to

her door and she gratefully accepted. She had no desire to ride with Lizzy as planned earlier, not knowing then as she did now that Lizzy's boyfriend would be in the car, too. She had no desire to play fifth wheel.

Ramon stopped in front of her cottage and got out to let her out of the car. He walked her to the door and waited while she unlocked it. "Thank you for an enjoyable evening."

She didn't think she'd added much to it. It had taken all her self-control not to break down and cry. "Thank you, Ramon."

He grasped her shoulders and went to kiss her goodnight, but she pulled her head back. "I'm sorry. I don't…"

He changed the direction of his lips and kissed her cheek before stepping back and smiling. "You know, I think it is just as well. The boss kept watching you during dinner and he gave me a couple of looks that wished me to Outer Mongolia. I like my job. I think I will keep it."

"I'm sure he would never fire you for dating me."

"Perhaps not, but I do not mind not putting it to the test." Then he stood straighter. "I would date you regardless if you had offered encouragement, you understand?"

"I do understand. You're not the kind of man to be cowed." She said it for the benefit of his ego, but she thought really that she might very well be speaking the truth.

After all, he had tried to kiss her *after* deciding that Marcello was interested in her. But she hadn't encouraged him and he had decided to cut his losses.

"Watch out for him, though. He is in a league far beyond us normal mortals."

"I believe you."

She was sitting rigid in a chair by the window when Marcello arrived an hour later. She'd known he would come, but she hadn't expected him for another hour, or more. He must have cut his evening short with his family.

She wondered why. Surely he wasn't worried. His supreme male confidence would not allow him to expect anything to have changed between them from something as simple as an unexpected meeting at dinner. But it had. She couldn't stand being his secret mistress any longer.

She had the door open when he got out of his car.

He walked toward her, his expression grim. "It is a good thing Ramon is not here. The entire way over, I played one scenario after another in my head of what I would do if you were entertaining him for after dinner coffee."

"I can only imagine one scenario myself," she said quietly and without rancor. She hurt so much, there was no room for anger. "You would have turned around and driven away if you saw his car. Any other option would have risked exposing the fact that you were here to see me."

"Your imagination is sadly lacking then. My fantasies centered on a very satisfying letting of blood and definitely required me getting out of my car."

"How primitive." But she didn't believe a word of it.

"I am primitive where you are concerned."

"In bed maybe, but not out of it. Fantasies is the right word. You would never have gotten out of your car to stake a claim. Admit it."

He was inside the house now and she shut the door behind him, her movements jerky and awkward. She felt like her arms and legs did not belong to her, as if she was outside of her body looking at the carnage within and wondering at it.

"You are wrong, Danette. I *would* have gotten out of my car. Never doubt it. It is a good thing for all involved it did not come to that, but you have made your point."

"What point is that?"

"You did not like seeing the picture of me dancing with another woman. I did not like seeing you out to dinner with another man."

"You believe I went out with Ramon to teach you a lesson?"

"Yes. Why else would you go out with him?"

She could have told him for the simple reason that she'd been tricked into it, but she held her tongue. She had no desire to set his mind at ease like that. "Maybe I wanted to go out on a date with a man not ashamed to be seen with me." Maybe it was as simple as that.

"It has never been a matter of shame," he practically yelled, the false front of calm blowing sky high, just that fast.

And she realized only then that it *had* been a false front. Marcello's entire being was vibrating with dark fury.

A week ago, that would have upset her unbearably. Now she didn't even care. Let him be angry. She would be angry, too…if she didn't hurt too much. "Then why not introduce me to your family? They aren't the press and you can't tell me that they would have leaked the story, either."

"If my mother thought it would push me into marriage, do not bet yourself she would not do it."

"You don't mean that."

"You do not know her. She can be ruthless. Give her the least scent of possible romance and she will be planning the wedding and compiling the guest list, which is why I have not introduced you to my family."

"Because you never plan to marry me?"

"Because I do not want my family interfering with my private life."

She had thought she'd learned all there was to know of pain growing up with the physical deformity it had taken more than a decade to correct, but there were different kinds of pain in life. She was realizing that the pain from loving unwisely was the most intense.

But her heart, that organ which was stronger than she could ever have imagined, persisted in holding onto a tendril of hope. "You said you didn't like seeing me with Ramon."

Anger glittered in his eyes. "I did not."

"What are you going to do about it?"

"More to the point," he asked, "what are *you* going to do about it?"

"What do you mean?"

"I have admitted you made your point. There is no need for you to play the farce of dating another man again."

"That's it?" she asked incredulously, her disbelief pushing her pain aside for the moment. "You tell me you don't like something and you expect me not to do it again."

"Why not? You care about me. Our relationship is important to you. You do not wish to undermine it."

"If that is true, then shouldn't the converse be true? You know it hurt me to see that picture, but I don't see you offering to change your public image."

"But I will do so."

The tendril of hope grew stronger. "You're ready to go public with our relationship?"

"No. I told you—"

"I don't care what you told me. I can't stand it anymore, Marcello. I need our relationship to be open and honest. No more hiding."

CHAPTER SIX

"I WILL be careful not to put you in the position of seeing such a hurtful picture again."

"And will you stop behaving like you are single around other women?"

"I will not dance with them."

"That's not an answer!"

He let out an impatient breath. "I am sorry."

"Are you? Do you really care how much it hurt me to hear your brother talking about you like you don't have a relationship? Does it bother you that it rips at my heart to be dismissed by you like you did at the restaurant tonight?"

"I did not dismiss you."

"You didn't introduce me as the woman in your life, either."

"You know why."

"But the reasoning isn't enough for me anymore. I'm sorry you hate to have your private life made public, but I hate being your dirty little secret. I can't do it anymore. It hurts too much, don't you get it?" she begged, her voice cracking.

He pulled her into his arms and hugged her. "I do not wish to hurt you, *amante*. Please believe me."

The tears she'd fought all night would no longer be denied and began to flow hotly down her cheeks. "I love you, Marcello. So much. I need to know you care for me, too."

He went stiff and pulled away, his expression concerned, but no reciprocal love evident. "I do not want you to love me."

"What?"

"I told you in the beginning that our affair is temporary, that I was not looking for love and had none to give."

"We've been together six months. How do you define temporary?"

"I do not define it. We do not have a limit on our time together."

"Except that it can't be a lifetime?" she asked painfully.

"I cannot give you love and marriage."

"You can't, or you won't?"

"I loved my wife, Danette. I will never love another woman. It is the destiny of the men in my family to love only once in such a way."

She heard the words, but she could not believe them. He thought he would never love again? "Please, Marcello, I know there is always some guilt involved in falling in love again after a spouse dies, but don't throw away what we have because of it. I cannot believe Bianca would have wanted that for you."

"This is not about what Bianca would have wanted. It is about my ability to give you what you say you want."

"A public acknowledgment of my place in your life?"

"My love."

"I did not ask for that."

"You did. You love me, you said."

"I do love you."

"You want me to give you my heart as well."

"I want you to acknowledge you care for me."

"I do care."

"Enough to make our relationship public?"

"And when it ends, do you truly believe that having gone public, having made you the target of media attention is going to make that situation better for you?"

"Why does it have to end?"

He just stared at her.

She desperately searched for the right words to convince him that they had something bigger than an affair that he was determined to walk away from one day. "When we first began our relationship, you tried to keep your distance, but now we're practically living together. I'm important to your life."

She needed that to be true. Please let that be true.

"I do not deny it. We have incredible sex and I enjoy your company, but you should not be constructing castles in the sky around such things." He pulled her back into his arms, his touch gentle and comforting. "I do not wish to hurt you, but it is only fair for me to be honest. I am not looking at marriage with you."

Maybe not consciously, but she had to make him see that subconsciously she played a bigger role in his life than he gave her credit for.

"If you don't see me as part of your future then why are you so cavalier about birth control, Marcello? Half the time when we make love, you forget the condom."

If he'd gone stiff when she told him she loved him, he went positively rigid now. "That is not an indication that I see a future with you."

"What is it, then?" She leaned back to look into his face. "You aren't an irresponsible man. You wouldn't risk pregnancy if somewhere deep in your heart, you didn't think you could stand being married to me."

He grimaced, looking uncomfortable. Was she getting through to him?

"I do not risk pregnancy. Since you were a virgin and I have always practiced safe sex, I risk nothing at all."

"Don't be ridiculous. I'm not on the pill and you know it."

He sighed. "This is not something I enjoy talking about, but I see I have no choice. I am sterile, Danette. Or as good as."

"What are you talking about?" This vibrant man incapable of fathering children? She couldn't believe it.

"I was diagnosed with a very low sperm count the second year of my marriage. Bianca and I tried for children until she died, but we never conceived."

"A low sperm count is not a *no* sperm count."

"What would you know about it?"

"I spent more time in hospital waiting rooms during my childhood and teenage years than most kids spend on the playground or in the mall. I read a lot of magazines. You'd be surprised what you can pick up in *Cosmo*."

"As a child?"

"I didn't finish treatment until I was nineteen."

"What kind of treatment? Why did you never tell me about this?"

She shoved herself out of his arms. "Why didn't *you* tell *me* about your supposed sterility?"

"It was not something you needed to know."

"You're wrong. I had a right to know why you've been playing Russian roulette with my body. You assumed that if you couldn't get the woman you loved pregnant, you couldn't impregnate anyone else, either. Right?"

"It is not Russian roulette. I *cannot* get you pregnant."

"I've been such a fool. I thought you were beginning to care for me but in reality the very actions I took as proof show how very little you really do feel for me." That knowledge hurt more than anything else had tonight: how thoroughly she had duped herself into believing she mattered to him. "You think me so unimportant, so incompatible with your life that you aren't even afraid of getting me pregnant because you assume you can't. I really am nothing more than a body in your bed...an expendable secret mistress." The last words came out in a choked whisper.

"That is not true."

"The facts speak for themselves, Marcello. I only wish I'd known all of them earlier." Oh, how she wished it.

She stumbled back from him, needing more distance than her small cottage could give her. "Get out."

He put his hand out appealingly. "Danette..."

"I mean it, Marcello. Get out of my home. I don't ever want you to come here again."

"But what has changed between us? Nothing. I am the same man you received with joy into your body this afternoon."

"Again without a condom."

"I told you, pregnancy is not a risk with me."

"You're wrong, Marcello. About that and a lot of other things as well. Everything has changed. I have finally realized how little I matter to you."

"That is not true. I have already said I would change my public image."

"And you think that's some great concession?"

"It is more than I have offered another woman since my wife's death."

"How big of you."

"Damn it, *amante*—!"

"Don't call me your lover. There's no love in what you feel for me. You said so yourself."

"Do you not think I would love you if I could? I will not do to you what my father did to my mother."

"Divorce me?"

"He did not divorce her. She divorced him." He sighed. "They married because she was pregnant with me, but he had already had the love of his life and his feelings for my mother were not enough to keep him from other women. She discovered he had had an affair and she left him."

"Smart woman."

"Yes, and I am smart enough to know my own limitations."

He didn't love her. He never would. He didn't even want her enough to think he would remain faithful if they were to marry. Not that he had ever considered that kind of future with her, no matter what delusions her mind had dished up.

"I wish *I* were smart, but I was stupid enough to get involved with you and to stay in a relationship that you insisted on keeping secret because I convinced myself you cared. Ramon was right. I'm *so* not in your league, and I never will be. I was a world class idiot to think you could genuinely care for me—but then, looking at my track record, I'm not exactly Einstein where men are concerned."

"Do not compare me to that little worm you left behind in the States."

"Don't worry. You two aren't even in the same stratosphere."

"No, we are not."

"He only bruised my heart, you've decimated it. He used me to get ahead in his career, but you've just used me, period. You're leagues beyond him in the 'smarmy male who doesn't care how much he hurts a woman and uses her' stakes."

"I do care if I hurt you. Have I not said it? I was honest with you from the beginning. I risked your rejection to tell you the truth. I have been honest with you tonight, sharing a painful part of my history to show you the truth of our relationship. I am damn well not a smarmy male!"

"All that proves is that I let you use me, not that you didn't do it. But I'm not going to let you use me anymore."

"I do not use you. What we have is mutual."

"We don't have anything. Not anymore."

"That is not true, *cara*. We have something very special."

"So special you don't want anyone else to know about it. So special that not only will you never love me, but you don't want my love. That's not special, that's sex at its most basic. Worse…it's pathetic."

She could tell he was frustrated, that he didn't know what to say. She wanted to tell him, "Welcome to the club." Because she hadn't known what to say to change his mind and there was nothing he could say to change hers.

His big hands clenched into fists. "I do not want to lose you."

She shook her head, the pain of the truth crushing in its intensity. "You already have."

"I will not beg."

"I would never expect you to. What I do expect is

for you to respect me enough to leave my home when I ask you to."

He drew himself up, stiff and erect. "So be it. We can talk after you have had a chance to calm down."

"There isn't anything left to say between us."

He pulled her to him and kissed her with a tenderness that she could not combat. When he was done, she was clinging to him. "I think you are wrong. I think we still have a great deal between us."

"Sex? It isn't enough, Marcello. It never could be."

But he didn't answer. He merely put her from him gently and left.

She crumbled to the floor and sobbed her heart out as the enormity of her loss washed over her. She cried so long and so hard that she lost her voice, and the next morning she called in sick to work. He called her midmorning and once she recognized his voice, she hung up the phone and then unplugged it. Her cell phone chirped and she turned it off, too.

She plugged the phone back in later that afternoon and called Tara. She told her everything and her friend was threatening bodily harm to Marcello ten minutes into the phone call.

"I just wish it didn't hurt so much."

"I understand, believe me, but Marcello was right about one thing…it hurts less when you don't have to share the pain and humiliation of a breakup in the public eye."

"It's a good thing we kept everything secret, then, because if it hurt any more, I think I'd die from it."

"Oh, honey." Tara sighed. "It will get better, but not right away. You just have to live one day at a time. I'm here for you if you need me. Remember that."

"I'll remember."

Marcello called again and this time she stayed on the line long enough to tell him not to call back. Amazingly he listened, and she got no more phone calls for the rest of the night. She spent those hours trying to decide if she would quit her job, or stick it out.

She couldn't imagine what running into Marcello in the office would do to her. However, in reality, except for when he contrived to see her, there was no reason for her path to cross with that of the president of the company. She'd tried running from heartache once and look where it had landed her—in far worse pain than what she'd tried to leave behind.

She went to work the next morning, still unsure what she was going to do with her future and so upset that she was nauseous with it despite the calm front she put on for her co-workers' benefit.

She was making copies of her presentation on the Cordoba project in the copy room when she felt a presence behind her.

"Good morning, *cara*."

She spun around to find Marcello standing less than a foot away. She backed up but bumped into the big machine making swishing noises as her copies spit efficiently out of its mechanism. "Marcello. What are you doing here?"

"Have we not had this conversation before?" he asked with one side of his mouth tilted in a small smile.

She sidled sideways, needing to get some distance between them. "It's highly unusual for the president of the company to find himself in the copy room."

"Not so unlikely if that is where his lover is to be found." The body she craved more than sustenance or life stood between her and freedom through the tantalizingly open doorway.

"Ex-lover," she snapped.

He stepped backward and pushed the door shut. "I am not ready for you to be my ex."

Memories of another shut door sent her heart rate into an erratic dance in her chest. She eyed the closed portal with nothing short of deep suspicion.

He smiled at her. "Do not worry. I am not planning to repeat the scene in your office…unless it becomes absolutely necessary. I simply want privacy for our discussion."

"Here is not the place."

"You threw me out of your home, hung up on me or ignored my calls altogether and have spent the morning avoiding your office. In essence, you chose this venue."

"So don't complain about it?"

"Right."

"Look, I'm sorry you aren't ready to break up, but I have no intention of waiting around for you to dump me."

He sighed with exasperation. "I do not want to dump you. Surely I have made that obvious?"

"You will, though…someday."

He shrugged, but the casual movement did not mask the ferocious tension she sensed in him. "Perhaps one day we will both decide we are better off apart, but why hasten that day if we do not have to?"

"Because I've already decided that I'm better off without you." Though her heart screamed at her that she was a liar.

"I want you to give me a chance to change your mind—"

"No," she slotted in before the seductive offer had a chance to take hold of her heart.

"This weekend at my brother's wedding celebration on Diamante," he continued as if she hadn't spoken.

"You want me to attend your brother's wedding with you?" He had to be joking. He couldn't mean it the way it sounded…like he was ready to go public with their relationship. "As what?"

"As my date."

"No way." But she said it more out of reflex than intent and her voice was weak from shock.

"You said you wanted to go public with our relationship. I am prepared to do so rather than lose you." He was rigid with tension and she knew this was hard for him.

"I didn't break it off with you in an attempt to twist your arm." She hated emotional blackmail.

"Whatever your intention, I have thought about it and realized I would rather deal with the unwanted media attention than to end our affair."

If only he had said that yesterday…before he told her he did not and would not ever love her. She would have jumped at the chance to meet his family before he made it clear how little he wanted a family with her.

"No." It was the hardest word she'd ever had to say and her wounded heart bled some more because of it.

He looked shocked, his dark complexion going pale. "What do you mean *no*?"

"Y-you were right…the p-pain of breaking up would only be increased if it…" She pause, taking a deep breath and trying to get the emotions making her stutter under control. She tried again. "If it happened in the public eye. And since there is no chance we *wouldn't* break up, you've made that clear, I don't want to set myself up for more pain and humiliation on top of it down the road."

"I do not want you humiliated. I do not want you hurt and I do not wish to break up."

"You should have thought of that before throwing my love back in my face," she said helplessly. "I don't mean to sound bitter. You told me from the beginning that you didn't love me, but I convinced myself that you cared. I deceived myself and hurt myself as much as you did."

"It was not a deception. I do care."

"Not enough."

"How can you say that? I have refused to have a liaison in the public eye since Bianca's death, but I'm willing to do so for the sake of keeping you."

"Because all it is is a liaison. I love you. I'm sorry it happened. I know it's inconvenient for you, but I can't handle being in the kind of uncommitted relationship you established anymore. It was killing me by inches and the last couple of days have hurt more than I ever want to hurt again."

"And I am doing all that I can to rectify that hurt."

"It isn't enough."

"I loved Bianca."

"I know," she said painfully, thinking she did not need the reminder.

He stalked her until she was flat against the wall and his body was less than an inch from hers. "I know what it is to hurt. And I can tell you this. If I had a chance to spend more time with Bianca, I would have taken it...no matter what the cost down the road. You say you love me. If your words were true, then you would crave the same thing."

With that, he backed up and spun on his heel and left.

She stared after him long minutes after he was gone...her mind and heart in a turmoil. How had he made her feel guilty? He was the one who spurned her love and yet he'd managed to make her feel like she didn't love him enough. And darned if his reasoning wasn't playing an insidious refrain inside of her head.

She *did* love him. Okay, so chances were that if she got back together with him, they would end up breaking up somewhere down the road. It was inevitable really because he didn't want marriage and he didn't want to love her.

But as he'd pointed out, life was uncertain. Bianca had died so young, but she wasn't unique in this world. No one knew what tomorrow might bring…no one could guarantee how many tomorrows they might have. Not her and not Marcello.

The question that preyed on her mind for the rest of that day and the next morning as she once again battled nausea was whether or not it would hurt more to continue her relationship with Marcello and risk a breakup down the road, or to force herself to go on living without him, knowing in her heart of hearts that she could have him?

He was offering her far more than a place in his bed…he was offering her a place in his life. A public place.

CHAPTER SEVEN

DANETTE battled her pain-filled thoughts and the continued on again, off again nausea as she presented her report on the Cordoba project to a room full of top sales and marketing staff.

She was halfway through the presentation and going over the PowerPoint presentation that accompanied the reports she'd handed out when someone opened the coffee carafe near her and she got a strong whiff of the aromatic beverage.

Her stomach roiled, and she slapped her hand over her mouth and sprinted for the washroom.

When her stomach finally settled, she rinsed her mouth and walked out to the lounge area of the ladies' room. The director of marketing, a chic woman in her fifties with kind brown eyes, was waiting for her.

"You should sit down for a while before trying to go back to your desk."

"The presentation…"

"I instructed Ramon to finish it for you. Your notes were clear and he'd worked on the project with you enough that he should have no trouble."

"But you're missing it."

"I'll skim through the PowerPoint slides when I go back to my desk, but I wanted to make sure you were all right. I remember feeling the same way, and you looked like it had taken you by surprise."

"You've had the flu recently, too?"

The woman laughed. "Not this kind of flu…not for more than twenty-five years."

"This kind of flu?"

"You don't know?" the director asked with a gentle smile.

But suddenly, Danette did. She hadn't had her period in six weeks, but she'd never been terribly regular, so that fact had not impinged on her consciousness. Especially not for the last few days. First she'd been missing Marcello and then she'd been fighting with him…the condition hadn't been one that left her thinking too clearly.

"It's not possible," she said, but knew it was.

"Are you sure about that?"

"He didn't think he could get me pregnant," she said, dazed and then realized what she'd said and slapped her hand over her mouth for the second time in fifteen minutes.

"And you took the risk anyway?" The director shook her head. "Young women these days…you can be so naïve."

"I wasn't being naïve." Well, maybe she had been. "Not about that. I didn't *mind* the risk."

"Here's hoping your young man feels the same way."

She doubted it. Marcello didn't want children with her. He would put a brave front on it, of that she had no doubt. No matter how angry he made her, he was still a really responsible guy, but he couldn't have made it more obvious that he didn't want a family with her if he had put it in skywriting.

She smiled weakly for the other woman's benefit. "Thank you for checking on me."

"Think nothing of it, but if I were you, I would stay away from open coffeepots."

Danette shuddered feelingly. "I intend to."

Marcello stopped in the doorway between his office and that of his assistant when he heard Danette's name.

"She ran out of the room so fast, I thought she was going to rush right into the door instead of going through it," one of the marketing people was saying.

"And the director followed her?"

"After telling Ramon di Esperanza to finish the presentation. Yes."

"I hope she's okay. Danette is a sweetheart and she's good at her job."

"Oh, I'm sure she's all right, but I don't think it's an illness that will end quickly for her, if you take my drift."

"What do you mean?" his assistant asked.

"Well, I remember being very sensitive to the scent of coffee when I was pregnant with my first child. She acted just that way. She had been fine before that."

"You think Danette is pregnant? But she's not dating anyone."

"It only takes one night."

"I don't think she is the type for a one-night stand."

The woman from marketing shrugged. "Perhaps you're right, but she is back in her office right as rain now. If that's not the pattern of morning sickness, then I don't know what is."

Marcello stumbled back into his office, his head

spinning with the ramifications of Danette being pregnant. Was the baby his?

It had to be.

But how could it be possible?

Danette's words from the night before last ran through his mind—*Low sperm count is not a no sperm count* and *Playing Russian roulette with my body.*

He had been, but he had not meant to. He could not believe he had gotten her pregnant after the years of trying with Bianca. He'd assumed he could never get a woman pregnant and had decided never to marry again because of it. He'd had enough of feeling like less than a man in his marriage with Bianca because of his inability to get her pregnant.

He'd been determined never to put himself in that situation again. His inability to plant his child in her womb had hurt them both and tainted what would have otherwise been a perfect marriage.

He could not have gotten Danette pregnant. It just wasn't possible. No. The woman from marketing had to be mistaken.

He picked up his phone.

His assistant answered, "Yes, Signor Scorsolini?"

"Please ask the director of marketing to come up to my office."

"Yes, *signor.*"

An hour later he had some answers and he was still reeling from the shock of them. Danette believed she was pregnant and she believed he was the father.

Not that she'd said so, but she'd told his marketing director that the father thought he could not get her pregnant. That meant it had to be him. Not that he could seriously doubt her fidelity.

She was his, and had been from their first date. She could not have had the pregnancy medically confirmed yet because she hadn't realized she was carrying his child until the director pointed it out. However, *he* was willing to believe.

He was desperate to believe.

The director of marketing had been hesitant at first to share the conversation she'd had in the bathroom with Danette, but being president of the company came with some privileges. Evincing concern for any one of his employees was one of them.

He'd assured the older woman he had no desire to fire Danette, merely make sure she was all right. She was a valued employee and he had hired her on the suggestion of his good friend Angelo Gordon. He was responsible for her. Which was an understatement he wasn't willing to get into. The director had understood the very Sicilian outlook.

After the woman left, a desire to celebrate fizzed through his insides as he asked his assistant to call Danette up to his office. She looked at him with a certain amount of speculation, but he let none of the emotions rioting through him show on his face. He was good at that. He'd learned early with the press hounding his every footstep not to show his feelings, not to express his vulnerability.

He'd come closer than he had in years that morning when he'd asked Danette to join him on Diamante Island for his brother's wedding. Her refusal had hurt and surprised him and it had taken the extent of his formidable control not to show how much.

After a couple of hours thinking and very little work getting done, he'd come to terms with it and even understood her point of view. She loved him, but he could make no promises for the future. However, part of him questioned how strong and real that love was if she found it so easy to walk away from him. Not that that was an option any longer.

Everything had changed and soon she would know how much.

"Miss Michaels left early today, Signor Scorsolini," his assistant said from the doorway pricking the bubble of elation surrounding him.

"I see. Do you know why?"

"I believe she was ill earlier today. She must have gone home to rest."

Marcello nodded. "Please cancel everything on my schedule through noon tomorrow."

"But Signor Scorsolini, you have—"

"Pass anything urgent on to my second in command." He had something of paramount importance to take care of and nothing else even approached it at the moment.

Danette read the pregnancy test results for something like the hundredth time and still had a hard time believing them. She carried Marcello's child. Her hand settled over her queasy stomach and she thought of the life she cradled there. She remembered reading once that morning sickness was the sign of a healthy pregnancy, and hers must be really healthy because she felt absolutely awful.

If she had the energy, she'd go looking online for suggested remedies, but she just wanted to curl up in her bed and sleep.

She was headed to do just that when a powerful pounding on her front door stopped her.

She peeked out, but didn't need her eyes to confirm what her instincts already knew. Marcello had come.

He couldn't know about the baby. Not yet. *She* barely knew about it. Maybe he'd heard she left work early for illness. Maybe he was checking on her. It wasn't such a far fetched notion. He'd always been solicitous of her health, babying her during that time of month and providing her with lots of chocolate…

Oh, man. She swallowed an urge to puke. Even the thought of chocolate was upsetting to her stomach. *Chocolate*? Who got morning sickness from chocolate? That was just wrong.

The door pounded again. "Open up, Danette. I know you're in there!"

He didn't sound solicitous so much as impatient.

She slipped the lock and opened the door. "Hello, Marcello, what brings you here."

"What do you think?" His blue gaze went over her like seeking hands.

She shrugged. "I haven't the faintest idea."

"You were sick halfway through your presentation this morning."

It shouldn't surprise her that he'd heard about it. The company grapevine was more efficient than the world's most knowing gossip columnist. "So, you were worried about me and decided to check on me?"

He pushed into the living room, gently cupping her shoulders to steady her as he moved past her. "You could say that."

"There isn't any need. I'm fine. It was just a temporary upset."

"That is not what my director of marketing called it. In fact, it was her opinion your upset would last for several months."

"Oh, no…"

He frowned at her, clearly bothered by her reaction. "Oh, yes. And I do not appreciate being the last to hear."

"Hear what?"

"That you're pregnant."

All of the air left her immediate vicinity and she swayed as everything went black around the edges. He grabbed her and then swung her up into his arms and headed to the bedroom.

"Are you all right? Have you made an appointment with the doctor?"

"I'm fine. I just got dizzy for a second. Anyway, I only just confirmed it with an at home test. I haven't had time to make, much less keep, a doctor's appointment."

"That's what the director thought, that you did not know you were pregnant."

Remembering his accusation in the other room, she stiffened in his arms. "Then what was that malarkey about you being the last to know?"

Red scored his cheekbones. "I am not thinking straight. I am sorry. Only, I wish I had heard the news from your lips first. It did not feel right the other way."

"If you ask me, nothing feels right about this situation."

He stopped in the process of laying her on the bed. "How can you say that?"

"Oh, I don't know. I'm pregnant with a child you cannot possibly want. We just broke up, and everyone's bound to think I got pregnant by a one-night stand because our relationship is top secret."

He gently settled her on the bed and then sat down beside her, his hand going possessively to her lower bell—which for some reason brought tears to her eyes.

"Naturally all that has changed. And please, do not ever say again that I do not want this baby."

"But how can you?"

"How can I not? A baby is a gift from God. A gift I thought never to have. I believed I would never be a father, now I know I will. I am not making the best of a bad situation. I am *thrilled*." And his eyes glowed with such deep inner joy, she could not doubt him. "I want this baby more than I can ever say to you."

She'd been wrong. Dead wrong. Marcello had been absolutely convinced of his sterility. That was obvious. She'd been wrong to assume he had been careless of the consequences of unprotected sex to her: he had genuinely not believed there would be any. But that didn't mean the opposite was true…that he cared about her like she cared about him.

The man really, desperately wanted the baby in her womb, but it had nothing to do with *her* being the mother. He wanted to be a father and the fact that she was the vehicle to making that happen did not automatically give her a special place in his heart…only his life.

Reminding herself of that reality could not prevent a small smile from creasing her lips. She'd never seen Marcello so happy and she liked it.

"I'm glad you're pleased about the baby."

"I am that, *tesoro mio*, supremely pleased." He grinned at her and rubbed a slow circle on her lower tummy. "I wonder if we can arrange a double wedding with my brother? He planned to keep it very low-key and it would be perfect."

"What in the world are you talking about?"

"We must marry as soon as possible."

Well, she hadn't been wrong about *that* anyway. He wanted to marry her, as she'd been sure he would if he ever got her pregnant, but the prospect did not hold nearly the appeal it once had for her, when she'd believed he cared about her. But she wasn't going to dismiss it out of hand, either.

Her reaction to the prospect of attending his brother's wedding had been enough to convince her that no matter what feelings Marcello did or did not have, for her, she loved him. Walking away from him was a path paved with pain.

"You're going too fast for me, Marcello."

"What do you mean? You cannot tell me that you don't want to marry me." His joyful acceptance of impending fatherhood gave way to ruthless resolve. "According to you, the greatest drawback to continuing a relationship with me was the prospect it would one day end. Once we are married that bogeyman is laid to rest permanently."

"It wasn't a bogeyman."

"Whatever. The fear will be groundless in marriage."

"Marriages end all the time…in divorce." He knew that better than most. Look at his own parents.

The possessive hand on her tummy was joined by one on her shoulder, as if he was holding her so she would not run away. "There will be no divorce."

"There will be if you think you're going to get away with being unfaithful like your father was." Memories of what he'd told her about his parents' marriage plagued her. "I'm no more tolerant of that sort of thing than your mother was."

He drew himself up and jumped to his feet, towering beside the bed like an enraged avenging angel. "How do you dare accuse me of such a thing? I have never been unfaithful in this relationship and I consider marriage vows sacrosanct."

"You're the one that told me you weren't planning to remarry because you didn't trust yourself to be faithful."

"That was before."

"Before what?"

"You are pregnant with my child," he said, as if that should explain everything.

"Well, your mother had your father's child, too, and that didn't stop him."

He crossed his arms and glared at her. "I am not my father. I won't behave like him."

"How can you be sure?" For that matter, how could she?

"Because I am, all right? I give you my word that I will never take another woman to my bed."

"I'm sure your father gave his word, too."

"Are you refusing to marry me?" Marcello asked, his voice laced with furious disbelief. "Think carefully before you answer because I warn you, married or not, I will not play the role of part-time father in my child's life."

Oh, man. She didn't even want to know what he was implying here. "I wouldn't want you to and I'm not refusing to marry you. I'm only saying I need time to think. This morning I was not in a relationship with you any longer—"

"By your choice, not mine."

"Yes, agreed, but if you can't see that what led up to our break-up is a cause for concern for me, I don't know what to say to help you see it. And frankly, it's thrown me for a complete loop to discover I'm pregnant."

"A good loop, I trust."

She turned her head away, old fears surfacing to plague her. How could she answer that? In most ways, she was totally thrilled to be pregnant with his child, but she couldn't forget the doubts that had led her to making the choice never to have children. She hadn't vanquished them nearly as much as she'd believed she had.

"You do not want my child?" he asked, sounding ten times angrier than he had been before.

She shook her head, but still didn't want to look at him. She couldn't think straight when she was looking at him and right now she needed to think. "It's not that."

"What is it then?"

"I hadn't planned to get pregnant."

"Now, or ever?"

"Ever."

"You did not do anything to prevent it, even though I often forgot the contraception."

"I know." Because she'd hoped and dreamed…only sometimes when dreams came true they could be terrifying.

"So, you had to have thought of pregnancy a little?"

"I did, but it was more fantasy than reality."

"And now that it is reality, you are unhappy?"

"Not unhappy…frightened," she admitted.

His weight came down on the bed beside her again and his hand touched her temple in a gentle caress. "Why frightened? Because of your career?"

"Because of my genes."

"What does what you wear have to do with having a child?"

She gave a choked laugh. "Not those kind of jeans." He deserved the truth. He had a right to know what kind of risks their child faced, but she had to scramble inside her mind for the right words. This was not a conversation, she had ever planned to have. "There's something I need to tell you, Marcello."

"You are not already married. You were a virgin the first time we made love—of course you could not be married," he said as if speaking to himself.

She turned back to face him and smiled, albeit weakly. "No. I am not already married."

"And the baby is mine. Do not try to convince me otherwise because it will not wash. You are a one-man woman and I am your man."

"Of course the baby is yours, and I have no intention of trying to convince you otherwise."

"Then nothing else could be bad enough to justify your look of unhappiness."

"That's what you think."

"So, then tell me whatever troubles you and I will fix it."

"You can't."

"You are so sure about this?" he asked as he took her hand in his and rubbed his thumb against her palm.

"Yes. In this case, there is nothing either of us can do but wait and hope."

"Tell me."

"I'm sorry." She swallowed. "I don't mean to make such a meal of it. It's just really hard for me to talk about, but I'd decided when I was fifteen, I think it was, that I would never have children."

"And why is that?" he asked with an indulgent look.

"Because I'd spent the last nine years of my life in a full torso brace to correct a genetic spinal deformity, and I knew I had more years to go, and I hated the thought of putting my own child through the same thing."

"*Che cosa?*"

"When I was six years old, I was diagnosed with a severe case of idiomatic juvenile scoliosis. It's an extremely rare form of the disease; the only form more rare is that found in an infant. My doctors hoped to avoid the major surgery required to correct the disease."

"I did not know that scoliosis required surgical treatment."

"It doesn't always, but in rare cases the risk of death from stress to the heart by the deformed rib cage or paralysis are so high that the only slightly less risky surgery is suggested. My parents and my doctors wanted to avoid that, but in order to do so, I had to wear a brace pretty much twenty-four seven until I was nineteen years old and the doctors were convinced that I had stopped growing. Even so, for two years after that, I was terrified my spine would revert to the curvature that is so disabling."

"You say this disease is hereditary?"

"No, not exactly, but my mother had it and so did I. What if our baby is born with it, too? I'm sorry. I should have told you about it sooner, but I'd convinced myself that if I did conceive that it would be meant to be and that our baby would not suffer my childhood. Only now that I'm pregnant, it's all I can think about. I'm so scared, Marcello."

He pulled her into his arms, wrapping her in his embrace. "You are fine now? There is no risk to your health with this pregnancy?"

"No. None. I had an eighty percent curvature correction. It was a miracle, really, and there are no limitations on my lifestyle left over from the scoliosis."

"So your fears are all for our child?"

She nodded against his shirtfront. "I'm sorry," she said again, her voice choked with tears.

"Stop apologizing. This baby is a gift. Believe it."

She looked up at him and the warmth in his eyes filled her with hope. "But…"

"Look at you. You are well now. Even if our children were to have this disease, it does not have to be life-altering."

She grimaced with remembered pain. "Tell that to a thirteen-year-old girl who looks in the mirror and sees only the brace, not the body beneath it."

"The brace is very unwieldy?"

"No. In fact, with the right clothes, you could barely tell I was wearing it, but my parents…especially my mother…were very protective of me. They never forgot I had it on and neither did I."

"In what way were they protective?"

"Mom encouraged me to avoid physical contact with others so they wouldn't know about my brace and I wouldn't have to try to explain it."

"And did they hug you?"

"No. I didn't encourage physical touch with *anyone*."

"That explains much."

"What do you mean?"

"Nothing important. It is only that sometimes you have an invisible wall around you."

"I never noticed that stopping you from touching me."

"It did not, and it would not stop me touching our child."

Tears spilled over her eyelids at that assurance. "I'm glad, but that isn't the only thing you have to take into account."

"What else?"

"Interaction with other children. Both my parents were concerned about me playing with other children and I spent grade school recesses inside, reading and doing schoolwork, rather than playing with other children."

"How did you get your exercise?"

"My parents had me on a very specific regime, one with no chance of me being tackled by another child, or hurt in any way."

"Was that necessary?" he asked, looking dubious.

"Actually not, but that isn't the point is it? The point is that—"

"Our child will be ours and we will do our best for her regardless of what challenges she might face in life."

"It isn't that simple."

"Yes, Danette, it is."

"Don't you think my parents did their best by me?"

"Yes, but they are not us, any more than I am my father. We will be different parents."

"But you are so worried about the press. Can you imagine what they would do if they got wind of something like that?"

"If our child were to have the disease, we would go public with it and detooth the tiger before he had a chance to strike. Understood?"

"Yes. I am sorry I didn't warn you, Marcello."

"I told you to stop saying you are sorry. All right? If you truly believe that what you have told me has impacted my joy at prospective fatherhood, or the way that I will feel about our child, then you do not know me as well as I believed that you did."

"We established that the day before yesterday when

I realized all the assumptions I'd made about you had been faulty. Now I realize the other assumptions I made were equally faulty. The truth is, I'm pretty confused about you right now and learning I'm pregnant with your baby hasn't improved that any."

CHAPTER EIGHT

HE GRIMACED. "As long as we are handing out apologies, I am sorry that I hurt you."

She winced tiredly. "I really don't want to talk about it right now." She yawned. "It's not that I don't want to talk at all, but I'm just so sleepy…I'm too tired to work anything out in my head, much less discuss it. Do you mind?"

"No. Whatever you might like to think, we have a whole lifetime to work out our differences. But I am not going to pretend I did not ask you to marry me."

"But you didn't."

"What?" he demanded in a dangerously soft voice.

"You didn't *ask*. You told me that for the sake of our unborn baby we should marry."

For the second time in as many days, red scorched the skin along his sculpted cheekbones. "I should have asked, but I got carried away with my delight."

It was such an endearing admission, she patted his chest in approval. "No matter what happens, I'm really, really glad you're happy about the baby."

"Only one thing is going to happen. We are going to marry."

"I'll think about it. That's the best I can do, right now. I mean it. My mind is in a muddle and I feel like I have the flu, and I'm so tired, I could fall asleep standing up."

"Then it is a good thing you are lying down. I will look into an effective remedy for your morning sickness, but for now I will get you some crackers and weak tea. My marketing director said that was something that used to help her."

He carefully laid her back against the pillows and then got up to leave.

He came back a few minutes later and cajoled her into eating half a dozen saltines and drinking a glass of water. Afterward, she slipped into sleep, secure in the fact that Marcello was watching over her and their baby.

When she awoke two hours later, Marcello's warmth surrounded her. It felt so good that she didn't move, not wanting the sensation of peace and safety to end.

"You are awake?" he asked from behind her.

"Yes, how did you know?"

"Your breathing pattern changed."

"Oh."

"My mother has invited us to have dinner with her tonight."

She went stiff with shock. "Your mother?"

What had he been doing while she was sleeping, calling newspapers and making announcements?

He turned her to face him. "My mother. She is ecstatic about the baby, but equally thrilled I am finally remarrying."

"You told her about the baby? You told her that we were getting *married*?" Every trace of lingering sleepiness vanished in the face of his revelations.

"We are close. She would be hurt if I did not tell her."

"But I never said I would marry you!"

"You will."

Danette took a deep breath and let it out slowly. "You are so darn arrogant."

"It runs in the family."

"No doubt."

"So, you will come to dinner and make my mother happy?"

"I don't know if I'll make her happy or not, but I would like to get to know her." She only wished it had happened before she got pregnant, that Marcello had wanted the meeting for her sake and not only that of their child.

"Did I not say that we would probably see one another again?" Flavia Scorsolini asked after kissing Danette's cheeks in greeting in the huge entry hall of the Sicilian villa.

"You said that?" Marcello asked. "When?"

"You had left for our table already. The looks you were giving the girl and the man with her at the restaurant that night…they spoke very eloquently to one who knows you as well as I do. But I did wonder what my son's girlfriend was doing at a restaurant with another man." She smiled at Danette. "It all became clear when Marcello explained the reason for not yet introducing us, though you had been together for six long months."

"It did?" Danette asked.

"Yes. He kept you a secret, and any man foolish enough to play that kind of game with his woman deserves to see her out with another man on occasion, though I trust it would only have taken one time for him to mend his ways."

Marcello laughed. "As always, you are too wise,

Mama. I had promised never to be caught dancing with another woman already."

"Ah, the pictures." Flavia gave Danette a sad smile. "Seeing them must have hurt a great deal."

"Yes."

"I am surprised you agreed to marry Marcello afterward."

He sucked in a tight breath. "Mama…" he said warningly.

But Danette smiled. "I haven't. Not yet. I promised to think about it."

"For the sake of the baby?" the older woman pressed as she led them into the sitting room.

Danette sat in the red velvet armchair Flavia indicated, before taking a matching one opposite the small table. Marcello sat down on the end of the long white sofa nearest Danette.

The startling red-and-white color combination with gold accents in the sitting room was very impacting and Danette said so.

"Thank you. I designed it myself. A hobby of mine," Flavia admitted. "Now, tell me…do you plan to marry my son for the sake of the baby?"

The look that Flavia gave her was so vulnerable that Danette had no desire to prevaricate in any way. Whatever Marcello's feelings for her, she would not pretend hers were other than what they were.

"If I marry Marcello, it will also be for my sake. I love your son."

Flavia nodded as if pleased. "Yes. I can see that you do. The way you looked at him the other night was very telling as well…or should I say, the way you avoided looking at him?"

"You must be a very adept people-watcher. My friends at the table had no idea anything was up between Marcello and me."

"None at all?"

"Well, my date, Ramon, noticed that Marcello kept looking at me. He thought Marcello might be interested in me and he warned me off of him."

"Smart man. Marcello is a dear son, but his reputation as a playboy...*ai, ai, ai.*"

"Mama!" Marcello protested.

"As if your young woman did not know?" She rolled her eyes. "Danette strikes me as an astute young lady. Too smart not to realize what a bad risk you are. She's shown tremendous courage in falling in love with you."

Danette didn't know whether to laugh, or to cry. The former queen had zero tact where her son was concerned, but Danette had the distinct impression it was on purpose.

"I loved his father, you know," Flavia said to Danette. "Love is no deterrent to pain. I should know."

Marcello paled, his blue gaze filling with real anger. "Mama, she has enough reservations about marrying me. She does not need you adding to them."

"Good. I went into marriage with your father blind and lived to regret it, but she will not be so foolish."

"Do you think Marcello would have an affair?" Danette asked with an honest need to know.

Marcello cursed angrily under his breath, but Flavia's militant stance relaxed and she smiled with warm affection at her son before turning her gaze back to Danette. "No. I do not. If you want to know the truth, I think that if I had stayed married to his father, he would not have strayed again, either. He was still feeling guilty for sleeping with me so soon after the death of his beloved first wife. His behavior was entirely self-destructive."

"If you believed that, why did you leave him?" Marcello asked in a driven tone.

"I did *not* believe it at first. I was hurting desperately. It took me several years to realize that he was driven by guilt and a need to punish himself for his supposed crime. I believe that in the same way, he has spent over twenty years punishing himself for the crime of infidelity to me."

Marcello looked quite stunned. "But…"

"I know he gave you boys that song and dance about Scorsolini men only loving once, but really, can you not see how he has protected his heart all these years by never letting another woman get as close as his first wife and I did?"

"I wonder if you are right."

"You yourself said I am a wise woman, but I am worried about him. If he does not stop the self-punishment, he is going to go into his old age a lonely man."

Personally Danette could never see King Vincente as lonely, but she wondered if Flavia was right.

"If you believe all this, why in the world are you trying to talk Danette out of marrying me?" Marcello asked with angry exasperation.

"Because she must count the cost. You, too, have decided to protect your heart and refuse to love her."

"How can you know that?" Marcello demanded belligerently.

"Because if you had told her you loved her, she would have agreed to marry you already. Is that not true?"

Danette nodded. "If he meant it, yes."

"You see?"

"Mama, I love you dearly, but this is not something I wish to discuss with you, or in front of you."

"No doubt. It is embarrassing to parade your mistakes in front of your beloved mother, is it not?"

"Whether Danette and I marry is strictly between us."

"If you believe that, then you shouldn't have told your mother that it was a done deal," Danette said, humor at the situation making her lips twitch.

Marcello made the sound of a frustrated lion at bay. "Shall we go into dinner?" he asked from between clenched teeth.

Flavia smiled a knowing smile. "By all means, my son. Let us eat. It is not good to make a pregnant woman wait."

Danette didn't know how it happened, but the subject of her scoliosis came up over dinner and Flavia asked numerous questions. "So, really, there is no reason to believe your children would be so afflicted at all, is there?"

"But my mother had it and then I had it…"

"And you were both diagnosed as *idiomatic* which implies that there is no known reason for the condition. Genetics would be a *known* reason, yes?"

"Yes."

"Then you are worrying for nothing. If your children were to be similarly afflicted, then you would deal with it the same as you would deal with any issue. Your love for them would cover everything you do—and of course, you would have my expert advice for help."

Danette burst out laughing as did Marcello.

"When you told me arrogance ran in your family, I

assumed you meant from your father's side, but I see now that you got a double dose. No wonder you have the bearing of the oldest son and heir to the throne."

Flavia shook her head, humor gleaming in her dark eyes. "Marcello would hate to be king…the role is much too much in the public eye."

"This is true," Marcello said dismissively. "Besides which, Claudio is forced to endure matters of state that would bore me to death."

"But there is no denying my son did inherit more than his share of masculine confidence and a certain amount of family arrogance," Flavia said with a small laugh.

Marcello just shrugged.

"So, you will be coming to Tomasso and Maggie's wedding, will you not?" Flavia asked.

"I invited her," Marcello said.

"Your most recent invitation was given in the guise of a suggestion we make it a double wedding, if I recall correctly." And Danette would be the first to admit that her thoughts from earlier were still a little muddled.

"*Idiota*," his mother said affectionately. "If Danette agrees to marry you, there will be no hole-in-the-corner affair to raise eyebrows and prod the paparazzi into speculation. We will have a proper Sicilian wedding."

"Have you forgotten she is pregnant?" Marcello demanded. "I would prefer to have the deed done before our child makes its advent into the world."

His mother simply shook her head. "With your money and your family's influence, you can have a wedding with all the trimmings in a month's time, though that is pushing the bounds of propriety where invitations to the event are concerned."

"I do not care who comes to the wedding," he growled.

"I do," Danette said. "My mom would be devastated if she couldn't invite all of her friends and our family to my wedding. If I agree to marry you, you'll have to be okay with that."

Marcello's blue gaze burned with impatience. "So what you are saying to me is that if you finally deign to marry me, I will have to content myself with a big, Sicilian wedding that could take months to organize?"

"I did not say that. Like your mom pointed out, when you're as rich as Croesus and royal in the bargain, you can get a lot done in a short amount of time."

"So, you are saying you will marry me?"

"I didn't say that," she replied with a fair amount of her own impatience. "Stop trying to bulldoze me. It won't work."

"I told you that I loved Vincente when I married him," Flavia said.

Thankful for the change in conversation, Danette smiled gratefully. "Yes."

"Had I not been pregnant, I would not have agreed to marriage, because I knew the risk was great that he would not let himself love me. Ever."

"So you married for my sake," Marcello said.

Flavia sighed, her memories not all pleasant by the look in her lovely brown eyes. "Yes. It is hard enough to be born of royal blood in today's world full of vultures and the paparazzi without being born illegitimate. I paid a price for my folly, but I cannot say that I regret that price. For had I not paid it, you would have until the day you died."

Danette got the point and her heart contracted at the

thought of her child being hurt by a decision she made. "I see what you are getting at."

Flavia smiled, oh so gently. "I knew you would, but still you must make up your own mind. Only keep the thought that life for royalty is not like life for everyone else. You can be dirt-poor and have nothing in your life of interest in the way of accomplishments and still be the target of media attention simply because you carry a title with your name."

After that, Flavia made a determined effort to keep the conversation on less volatile topics and Danette enthusiastically aided her in that endeavor.

Marcello downshifted the powerful Ferrari and took the turn with neat precision. He and Danette had left his mother's villa five minutes before. He did not know what mood she was in; he'd learned in the last few days to take nothing for granted. That included what he would term peaceful silence coming from the other side of the car.

"You enjoyed meeting my mother," he fished, wanting to know what she was thinking.

Danette shifted perceptibly in her seat, as if she'd only now remembered he was there.

His muscles tensed. He was unused to not being the center of her thoughts when they were together. He did not like it.

"What?" she asked, clearly struggling to remember what he'd said. "Oh, yes. I like her very much. Wasn't that wild, what she said about your dad?"

"It actually makes a strange kind of sense."

"Yes, but it sure blows holes in the Scorsolini men only ever loving once theory, doesn't it?"

"Does it? Mama did not say she believed Papa loved her, only that he was punishing himself for betraying her." But his father's love life, or lack thereof, was not what interested Marcello at the moment.

"Mama made a good point about giving our child legitimacy for the sake of its future."

"Yes, she did."

"So, now will you consent to marry me?"

"Are you saying that a paper marriage for the sake of our child legally holding your name is all that you want?"

Where did she get her ideas? "No. I want you to be my wife, not merely a wife on paper."

"You didn't want that yesterday."

"Today is different."

"Yes, today, you have discovered that you are going to be a father. That's got to be very emotional for you." She said it musingly, like she was trying to work something out in her head.

"Considering the fact I thought I would never father a child, yes." He did not want to dwell on those feelings however. They were best forgotten. "I should have introduced you to my mother earlier."

"That would have undermined the secrecy of our association. You heard her. She knew there was something up between us when she met me in the restaurant and you were pretending you didn't know me. If you had introduced us before that and tried to pass me off as a mere employee, it wouldn't have been any more successful."

"I did not mean that. I meant I should have introduced you as my girlfriend to her earlier."

Danette didn't reply, her attention fixed on the darkness beyond the window.

"And I did not pretend I did not know you the other night," he said for good measure.

"It felt like it."

"I treated you the same as I treated everyone else at the table." Which he could now see had been a monumental mistake.

Because she'd taken that to mean she wasn't special to him and she was. He wanted her in a way he wanted no one else.

She looked at him. "It hurt, because I *wasn't* everyone else."

"I did not mean to hurt you. You must know this."

"Part of me does know it, but the hurting part doesn't care much what your intentions were."

How was he supposed to answer that? He could not fix it, which was his natural inclination. All he could do was try once again to explain. "I did not know you had grown completely intolerant of the need to protect our relationship with discretion. When we discussed it the night I came home from Isole dei Re, I thought you were angry about the picture in the tabloid, not the secrecy surrounding our time together."

"The picture destroyed my sense of peace about our relationship."

"For which I have apologized."

"But it could not have been taken if our relationship had not been a secret."

"You have a point, but even you must admit that in the beginning, you got quite a charge out of that secrecy. How was I to know your reaction to it had changed so drastically?"

Surely she had to see that.

"It *was* romantic in the beginning." She sighed. "We

were sneaking around and that added the seductive element of the forbidden to our intimacy. Yet we weren't doing anything wrong. Not really."

"Not at all."

"I'm pregnant and we're not married. Trust me, my mom would say we'd done something wrong. There's a reason why sex outside of marriage is a bad idea."

"I am not ashamed that you are pregnant by me."

"I know. You're actually pretty proud of the fact."

An unfamiliar sense of embarrassment assailed him. He *was* proud in a wholly uncool way that he'd managed to plant his seed in her body. "Are you ashamed to be pregnant with my child?"

"I can't be blasé about being a single pregnant woman, I'm not that sophisticated. But no, I'm not ashamed."

"You do not have to be single and pregnant. You could be married and pregnant. You could be a princess. Does that carry no weight with you?"

"I think every little girl dreams of growing up and becoming a princess, but I'm not a little girl anymore. For me, marriage has to be about a whole lot more than living out a fairy tale."

"But it is about more. You carry my child in your body."

She sighed again. He was starting to hate that sound.

"Are we back to the paper marriage for the sake of the baby then?"

"I told you, I do not want a paper marriage. I want a real marriage."

"I don't like feeling like I'm the extra baggage that comes along with the baby."

He zoomed through a yellow light, pressing the accelerator just slightly. "I don't see you that way."

"It feels like it."

"I did not want to break up before I knew you were pregnant." Surely that should count for something. "And I invited you to my brother's wedding before that as well."

"You like sex with me. I've always known it."

Anger coursed through him. She was determined to see things in the most unflattering light possible. "And *you* like sex with *me*, but you do not see me accusing you of wanting me only because of it, or for the wealth I can give you."

"Why in the world would you?"

"Because most women in my life have wanted me for my title and my money…it would be all too easy to put you in the same camp."

"Do you?"

"No."

"Then the comparison isn't valid."

"It is. You accuse me of wanting you for sex and the baby you carry, but I have never once said that was all I wanted from you. Nor has our relationship in the past exhibited such a thing."

"You kept me a secret."

"Because I hate the intrusiveness of the paparazzi in my life, not because I was ashamed of you, or did not value you. In the beginning you understood this and while I comprehend how the photo hurt you, I don't think you can dismiss the fact that up until very recently, you were perfectly content with our status quo. Holding me accountable for a change of heart I did not know about is unreasonable."

She had to see that. She was a smart, logical woman and she had always been fair-minded in the past.

"But you didn't just keep me a secret from the press.

You didn't tell your family about me, because you *didn't want to marry me.* How can you say that your sudden volte-face regarding marriage isn't the result of my pregnancy? Of course it is, and that makes me the extra baggage that comes along with a baby, not a woman desired for her own sake."

"No, it does not. I do want you for your own sake. Your pregnancy has precipitated my proposal happening *now*, but I would have gotten around to introducing you to my family and sought marriage eventually regardless." It had taken a lot of thinking after she kicked him out of her house, but he'd ultimately reached that conclusion.

Not that he would have admitted it to her. He had still been fighting the eventual outcome, but he wasn't fighting it anymore.

CHAPTER NINE

SHE gasped, her attention firmly welded to him. "Now, you are rewriting history. Don't say stuff like that. It isn't fair."

"I am not rewriting history. I want you in my life. To keep you, I was willing to go public with our relationship. You are an addiction I cannot break, one I have no *desire* to give up. If the alternative was losing you, I would have married you. I am sure of it."

"Do you hear what you're *saying*?" She sounded very upset and she was practically shouting.

He didn't know what had bothered her so much about what he had said, but it was not good for her to get so worked up in her condition. "Calm down, *amante*."

"Don't tell me to calm down! You just got through saying that if I'd blackmailed you into marriage by withholding my body, it would have worked. Even in your arrogant brain, that can't be seen as a compliment."

"It certainly was not an insult and I did not use the word blackmail."

"But that's exactly what you were talking about. Emotional blackmail—and it is something I abhor."

"Why so adamant?"

"My mother excelled at it. My parents were overprotective and there were times I rebelled…like the year I joined a soccer team in grade school. My doctors said it should be fine, but Mom was scared I'd be hurt. She pulled out the guilt guns to get me to drop the team. It was always about how much she and my dad sacrificed for me, how much she would worry and how unfair that would be to her. Never mind that her fears strangled my childhood."

"You would not do that to our child."

"No, I wouldn't, but I wouldn't do it to you, either."

"I did not say that you would."

"You implied it."

"No, I did not." Were all pregnant women so irrational? "I said that, given the choice between watching you walk out of my life and marriage, I would have married you."

"Gee, thanks. A begrudging marriage is every girl's dream for life."

He grimaced at her sarcasm. "I can say nothing right with you, can I?" he asked in a driven tone.

"I'm sorry. It's just that I'm having a hard time believing you."

"That is obvious."

"Before, you said marriage was never on the cards, and now you say that it would have been even without a baby. Don't you think that's a little inconsistent?"

"I also said I would *never* go public with a private relationship, but I was prepared to do it for you. Listen, *cara*," he said through teeth gritted with the frustration of trying to explain something she was determined not to get, "I know you did not break up with me with the intention of forcing my hand."

He reached over and squeezed her thigh and then left his hand on her leg, needing the physical connection. "Had you done so, you would not be the woman you are, and therefore such a compelling addiction for me. Most likely, in that scenario, it would not have worked, but the net result was the same. If the way I have expressed myself is clumsy, I am sorry. I only meant to say that marriage was no more a certain dead loss between us than me claiming you as my lover in a public way."

"I don't know what to believe."

"We have established that. But I do not lie to you. I never have," he said, his own temper fraying around the edges.

"You can't know you would have wanted to marry me if I wasn't pregnant. You're only guessing at that… saying it because you think it's what I need to hear."

"And do you need to hear it?"

"No. Yes… I don't know!"

"If it is not, what *do* you need to hear, *tesoro*? Tell me what the big obstacle is in your mind to our marriage."

She laughed, but it was not a humor-filled sound. "I need to know you love me."

"Like you love me?" he asked, his anger growing.

Words were all that held her back? A simple declaration of love to match her own?

"Yes," she said defiantly.

He took his hand from her thigh, fury that he did not understand roiling through him. "You were willing to walk away from me, to cut me completely from your life. As far as I know, you still are. You refuse to marry me, even for the sake of our unborn child. *That* is the kind of love you want me to feel for you?"

"I—"

"You want me. You enjoy my company. But love? I doubt it. Love is not that easily dismissed."

"I didn't dismiss you."

"What would you call your refusal to get back together, to accept the olive branch I offered to keep you in my life?"

"I do love you."

"They are just words, Danette, and they mean nothing in the face of actions that prove otherwise. But if saying them will make you more amenable to marriage…then I love you. Now, will you marry me?"

"No!"

"Why not? I've given you the words you said you wanted."

"There has to be feeling behind them."

"Like your so-called feelings for me?" he asked scathingly. "Trust me, there is more than enough feeling behind them. The feeling of wanting to go into the future with you at my side."

"Stop it! You're twisting everything I'm saying."

"Perhaps I learned that skill from you."

"Please, Marcello. I don't want to argue anymore."

He pulled into the driveway of her small cottage, stopping close to the front steps, his movements jerky. Anger pulsed through him, but he knew he had to get it under control. "I'm coming inside."

"Not to argue more," she said pleadingly and with an expression that would have moved a rock to compassion.

Even a very angry Sicilian rock.

"I do not want to argue with you."

Her eyes filled with tears. "I don't want to argue with you, either."

"Then let us go inside, *cara*."

* * *

Hours later, he held Danette curled close into his body, but he was nowhere near sleep. How was he going to convince her to marry him…and soon? He did not want her to walk down the aisle on the verge of giving birth.

He'd thought for sure that his mom's lecture on the pains of being royal and illegitimate would carry enough weight to sway her. She was a compassionate woman after all, but she had still refused to commit to the marriage.

She said she wanted love, but he had to acknowledge that saying the words in the way he had done in the car wasn't going to help his case. He wasn't sure he could give them to her otherwise, though. He had loved Bianca, and the feelings he had for Danette were entirely different.

Other than their inability to have children, his life with Bianca had been near perfect. They'd been friends since childhood and hardly ever fought. Things hadn't been perfect, and he would always carry that burden of guilt. However, he knew he had loved her and Bianca had loved him, though, like Danette, that love had had limits he had not recognized until too late.

Even before the debacle of the photo spread on his father's party, his relationship with Danette had been more volatile. She challenged him in ways his Sicilian wife never had.

And their sexual relationship was very different than what he'd known with Bianca, too. He wanted Danette with a consuming passion that broke through his control in a way his desire for Bianca had never done. He wouldn't have had sex with her on a desk under any circumstances. For him, *obsession* best described his feelings for Danette, but she wanted the hearts and flowers.

He'd prefer the actions that backed up the sentiments. If she loved him, she would agree to marry him…she would not have walked away from him without a backward glance. No, he had to think her real hang-up was because he had denied wanting to marry her before she'd gotten pregnant. Her feminine pride was smarting and he couldn't fix it.

He couldn't alter the past. Not even a prince had that power. He had tried to tell her that he would have wanted to marry her eventually anyway, that his saying the contrary was only so much hot air when weighed against losing her. That had offended her, too.

But the truth was, only his knowledge of his supposed sterility had held him back before. He hadn't realized it, hadn't wanted to face the unpalatable truth. What man wanted to acknowledge such a deficiency? Certainly no prince of the Scorsolini family.

Because of that, he'd convinced himself and her that he had balked at a long-term commitment because he had been unsure of his ability to be faithful. However, lying there in the dark next to a body he knew he would crave until the day he died, he had no choice but to admit the truth.

He, Marcello Scorsolini, Prince of Isole dei Re, had hidden like a craven boy behind that excuse rather than face being less of a man than he wanted to be. He hadn't wanted to go through the demoralizing attempts at trying to make a baby and failing as he had in his marriage to Bianca. He had not wanted to ever face losing another woman the way he had lost her. But cowardice was its own punishment and he had played the coward. Now he faced the punishment—a lack of trust from his woman that should not be there.

He had wanted to protect Danette, too. It hadn't all

been about him. He had not wanted to put another woman through the pain his sterility had brought to Bianca. Only one thing had hurt more than knowing he was a failure as a man in that department: knowing that his inability to give Bianca a baby had become a festering wound in her heart.

And in the end, it had killed her. In denying himself a future with Danette, he had also been protecting her.

She wouldn't see it that way, though. She could have no idea what it did to a woman to crave children and not be able to have them. She was standing safely on the other side of an abyss that had haunted him for close to a decade and Bianca for every year of their short marriage. Danette would never feel the dark cold that wafted up from its depths to chill a man or woman's soul.

And he was glad of that, but because she was innocent of that kind of pain, she could not comprehend what a miracle her pregnancy was. Nor could she give full credence to how very much their child deserved everything they could give…including a stable and settled home life with married parents.

She was too busy being offended he hadn't wanted to marry her before, and trying to decide if he was a good risk or not.

She'd believed him when he said he was uncertain of his faithfulness factor. She wasn't about to dismiss that issue now, even if he was ready to.

He was not proud of his stupidity in hiding behind that excuse, but once again, he had no power to alter the past.

However, that did not mean he would give up. He *would* convince her to marry him. Other than his inability to get Bianca pregnant, he was not a man who failed. He had doubled Scorsolini Shipping's income in Italy through tenacity and his ability to fix problems and find solutions.

Danette would not know what hit her if she thought she was walking out of his life with his child in her womb.

He wasn't walking away from her, either. From this point on, they would be together, married or not. If she refused to move into his home, then he would move in with her. And he would sleep on the bloody sofa if she denied him her bed. He was in it now because she'd fallen asleep before she could tell him not to share it, though he had no doubt that in the mood she'd been in…had she been awake when he came to bed, she would have.

She would probably call his actions sneaky. He called them desperate.

Marcello took Danette to the doctor's office the next morning to confirm her pregnancy. He asked loads of pertinent questions, but for every one he asked, Danette had two.

The one area of medicine she had avoided reading about while she hung out in doctor's waiting rooms as a teenager was pregnancy. It had hurt too much to read about something she planned to deny herself, but now she wanted to know *everything*.

The doctor was really forthcoming, but Marcello still thought they should stop at a bookstore and get some printed material on it. They walked out of the store an hour later with two shopping bags full of books and magazines on pregnancy, parenting and early childhood development.

"You aren't seriously going to read all of those books, are you?" she demanded as he tucked her into the back of the limousine with as much care as if she were made of Dresden china.

He'd been seriously nice to her all morning despite their ugly argument in the car the night before and the fact that she'd been less than pleasant when she woke up beside him that morning. He didn't argue with her. He didn't bring up marriage. He simply took care of her and it felt very, very strange and very, very good.

"*Sì.*" He smiled indulgently at her as he slid into the seat beside her. "And do not try to tell me that you will not read them all, too. You picked half of them out."

"Yes, but somehow I just don't think we need advice on what to do for a color-blind child." She'd laughed out loud when she'd seen the clerk ring that title up, but it was only marginally more comical than him buying the book on how to teach an infant to swim. "The baby isn't even born yet! Besides, there's no reason to believe she'll be color-blind."

"Or that he won't be. You can't be too prepared."

Danette laughed. "You are a real case, you know that?"

"I am going to be a father. I think I'm entitled."

"You're so proud of yourself for knocking me up that I'm surprised your head fit through the car door."

"And yet, it did fit," he said with a smile.

She gave into the irresistible urge to return his smile. Underlying his super-patient attitude had been a glowing sense of pride in his accomplishment that a blind woman could not miss. It was sweet and she'd found it impossible to stay angry in the face of his obvious pleasure in her condition. Not that she was really angry anyway.

She was still hurting *and* feeling guilty because she hated the thought that in his mind her love wasn't real.

As reluctant as she was to give his view credence, she could see where he justified his belief.

She sighed.

"That is a sound I have come to dislike intensely."

Turning startled eyes to meet his now serious blue gaze, she asked, "What?" He hated her sighing? "Why?"

"It indicates an unhappiness in you I do not wish to be there." There was no evidence of his earlier light-hearted mood as he cupped her face in his hands. "We know how pleased I am about your pregnancy, but are *you* happy about the baby, *tesoro mio*?"

It was always so hard to concentrate when he touched her, but she made herself answer as prosaically as possible. "Yes, how can you doubt it?"

"You were frightened yesterday."

"I still am a little, but my head knows I shouldn't be and the thought of having your baby is a very sweet one, if you want the truth."

His hands dropped away and he sat back against the seat, his expression disbelieving. "So sweet, you do not wish to marry me."

"Can we not talk about that right now?" They'd been getting along so well and she didn't want to mar the pleasure of that rapport. She didn't like being at odds with him...she was used to her time with him being a source of pleasure, not pain. Even when they disagreed.

"Just accept that I am happy about the baby." Before he could say something cutting, she went on. "By all rights, you shouldn't be pleased that your secret lover is pregnant with your child, but you are and I accept that. I don't care if it makes sense in your brain that I'm content to be pregnant with your baby, or not. I am, all right?"

"I am glad."

She nodded. "Good."

"If you do not wish to discuss marriage…"

"I don't."

"Let us discuss you moving in with me."

"*What?*" The expression "jumping from the frying pan into the fire" sprang to mind.

"You are pregnant with my child."

"That's been well and truly established."

"Even if you do not wish to have a relationship with me, I want to look after you. Will you allow me that privilege?" He looked so serious…so determined.

But he'd picked her up wrong.

"You believe I don't want to have a relationship with you?"

"You said so. As you have pointed out repeatedly, you broke up with me."

Guilt flayed her and she didn't think he meant it to. He was right…but darn it, it wasn't because she hadn't wanted a relationship with him. It was because she'd wanted something more than he'd been prepared to give…because she'd wanted one for the right reasons.

He's prepared to give you what you want now, an insidious voice inside her head told her.

"I didn't break up with you because I didn't want you." She remembered what he'd said the night before about how he thought her willingness to do so meant she didn't really love him. "And it wasn't because I don't love you, either. It just hurt too much to be with you."

"As my *secret* lover?"

"Yes," she whispered painfully.

"But when I offered to remove the secret aspect, you still refused to be with me."

"Because I didn't want to hurt more down the road when you left."

"Not to be too repetitive, but that is no longer an issue. I want marriage. That is a permanent relationship."

"I want to believe that, but…"

"But you do not?"

"I want to," she said again.

He sighed. "But you do not trust me to remain faithful."

"I didn't say that."

"You do not have to. I have convinced you that I am not the faithful type."

"Well, actually, that summation of your character never rang true."

"But you do not believe our marriage will last a lifetime."

"How can it, with nothing but an unexpected pregnancy and your stubbornness to hold it together?"

"We have much more than that."

"Like what?"

"Like *your* stubbornness, for starters, and a whitehot passion that has not ebbed in six months, and a commitment to family and a desire for the same kind of future. We even work for the same company."

"Correction…you own the company I work for."

"But that is something in common, something that holds us together. We are both content to live in Sicily. That matters. Our marriage will last. We are both too strong and determined to allow anything else."

Was he right? She just didn't know, but one thing he said made a lot of sense. They were both very determined people.

She sighed.

He frowned. "You were not happy to wake up with me beside you in bed this morning."

But she had been when he insisted on her staying there while he got her toast and tea so her tummy would settle. She'd liked being looked after, especially by him.

"You surprised me." It sounded lame in the face of his certainty she didn't want to be with him, which was not the problem. "Everything is just happening so fast. I feel like my life has been changing with the regularity of a metronome and swinging just as drastically from one extreme to another too."

"But they are extremes you have instigated."

"I didn't get myself pregnant," she gasped, and glared at him.

He grinned, not in the least offended now that she had assured him she was happy about the baby. He looked supremely satisfied. "No, *amante*. *I* did that."

She couldn't help it. She burst out laughing.

For some reason her laughter triggered something in Marcello and before she knew what was happening, she was being kissed to within an inch of her life. He tasted so good and it felt so right to have his arms around her that she didn't even think to try to deny him. When he lifted his head, she was sitting securely on his lap and tingling in places she'd prefer not to talk about.

As if he could not help himself, he kissed her once more, hard and on the lips. "You taste good, *cara*."

"So do you." But she might respect herself a little more if she had at least minimal defenses against him.

"So, you will move in with me?"

She went to sigh and stopped herself. She wasn't unhappy, not really. And didn't want him thinking otherwise. She just knew when she was beaten. The truth was she was pregnant and feeling vulnerable and she'd rather live with him than fight the good fight by herself. Especially when she wasn't sure it was the *good* fight anymore.

"Well?" he demanded when she didn't answer right away.

"And what will you do if I refuse, move in with me?"

His expression gave him away.

"That was exactly what you had planned, wasn't it?"

"If you want separate beds," he said with what she thought was total overkill considering the fact that she was on his lap and making no moves to go anywhere, "then my place is the most logical. I have spare bedrooms."

She snuggled into him, laying her head on his chest. "That's good to know," she said punitively.

She could play cool, too.

CHAPTER TEN

"ARE you ready to go?"

Danette looked up from her computer. Marcello stood in her doorway looking so gorgeous her heart rolled. "I would have thought you had too much to do to leave on time tonight. We spent the morning in the doctor's office and the bookstore. Then you insisted on stopping for lunch before we came into work. I'm surprised your secretary isn't climbing the walls from canceling all the meetings you've missed."

He shrugged. "She is paid well to do what she does and my meetings can wait. The most pressing issues can be attended to from my study at home. I do no want to keep you in the office."

"Don't think you have to leave on my account. To tell you the truth, I've still got a ton of catching up to do myself."

He stepped into the room and shut the door. "I do not think working extra hours is a good idea. You need your rest."

"I'm pregnant, not sick, Marcello."

"Funny, I was sure you were sick when you went rushing for the restroom at the doctor's office this morning."

"Don't remind me. But I'm not feeling like that now and I'd rather work when I've got the energy for it."

"How much longer do you need?"

"Two or three hours."

He rolled his eyes and shook his head. "Do not push it, *cara*. Even prior to your pregnancy I did not approve of you working long into the evening. I will be back in ninety minutes, be prepared to go."

She might love him to death, but she wasn't about to let him start running every minute of her life. "I'm not going to be ready to leave in under two hours. You are of course welcome to go home without me."

"That is not going to happen."

"Then I will see you in two hours."

"Yes, you will."

"Your bossy nature is showing again," she informed him with interest.

He shrugged, a smile tugging at his lips as he turned to go. "And your stubborn streak is in full evidence, but I can deal with it, just as you will learn to deal with my so-called bossy tendencies."

"So long as you realize I reserve the right to return the favor, I'm sure you are right."

He stopped with his hand on the doorknob. "In what way?"

Clearly the idea of a woman getting bossy with him was a completely foreign concept. However, she had no doubts that Flavia had asserted her will with her son on more than one occasion, even if she'd been more subtle about it than Danette had the finesse or desire to be.

"If I think you are working too many hours, I will demand you go home," she warned him.

"I will remember that," he said, looking strangely pleased and not at all put out by the prospect, and then he left.

Ten minutes later, a young woman who worked in the company cafeteria arrived at Danette's desk with a tray of nutritious snacks and some bottled water, per Marcello's instructions.

"Did he order himself anything?" Danette asked.

"No, *signorina*," the young woman said, her eyes alight with curiosity about the employee the president of the company had taken precious time from his busy schedule to order food for.

"I see." She dug in her purse and pulled out some money and then handed it to the cafeteria worker. "Then please take him a bottle of fruit juice and a plate of snacks like the one you brought me."

"I do not know…"

"It's all right. Trust me." In the end, Danette was pretty positive it was the woman's curiosity that convinced her to do it rather than her assurances.

"Oh, and put this on it." She scribbled a quick note, folded it and handed it to the bemused cafeteria worker.

Ten minutes later the phone on her desk rang.

She picked it up. "Danette Michaels here."

"Thank you, *tesoro*."

She smiled and twisted the phone cord around her finger as she leaned back in her chair. "You're welcome. I appreciate your thinking of it to begin with."

Her tummy stayed more settled when she kept small amounts of food in it at all times. She'd learned that pretty quickly.

"I liked the note, too."

She'd written:

> Tit-for-tat.
> Love,
> Danette

"Did you?" She wondered which bit he'd appreciated the most, her subtle one-upmanship, or her avowal of love.

Probably the former, she conceded. He didn't believe she loved him, but she aimed to convince him otherwise. Even if he didn't love her, she realized she couldn't marry him with him believing her feelings for him were no more than physical lust and friendship. Which come to think of it was not a terrible definition of love, but it didn't stretch to explain a depth of feeling that made her certain she'd give her life for him, too.

"Yes. Be ready to go at seven."

"What will you do if I'm not?"

"Carry you out of your office."

She didn't doubt he meant it. "That might look a little odd to the other employees."

"I am not worried about it—are you?"

She knew what he was asking. They'd arrived at the building together that afternoon and he'd made no effort to hide the fact that they were very much together. Considering the rumors already rife because of her bout in the bathroom the day before, the company grapevine had no doubt drawn all the right conclusions plus some. She'd been getting odd looks all afternoon, but the truth was…she *didn't* care.

"I thought it would bother me more to have my co-workers know that you're my lover, but it doesn't. I

know I'm good at my job and don't trade on our relationship. That's all that really matters."

"So, I *am* your lover?"

"Um…I don't understand the question."

"It is a matter of how many beds will be occupied in
my home this night."

Crunch time. She hadn't expected to have to share
her decision over the phone. "You seemed pretty intent
on getting some use out of one of your spare bedrooms."

"If that is what you need to feel comfortable moving
into my home, then so be it."

She didn't know what she needed. She wished she
did, but realizing she was pregnant had muddled everything up in her brain and her heart was already a hopeless
mess. "I like sleeping in your arms," she admitted.

"I, too, like this."

"I know, but…"

"But?" he asked, a tremendous amount of tension
conveyed in that single word.

"I don't know if I'm ready to make love to you. If
I did, you'd see it as capitulation. You'd start planning
the wedding."

"You know me well."

"I suppose. In some ways."

"So, you would allow me to sleep next to you, but
do not wish me to touch you intimately?"

"Yes, but…"

"Another but?"

"It isn't fair to you. I know you'd want to make love."

"I will take what I can get right now." He didn't
sound happy, only resigned. But then he didn't sound
super disappointed, either.

"Do you find my pregnancy a turn-off?"

"How can you ask me such a question?"

"Well, you're taking this better than I thought you would."

"Do I have a choice?"

"Only in the way you react, I guess."

"You guess?"

"I mean, I know what I need right now…"

"And that is?"

"Space."

"I cannot give you that."

"If you don't try to make love to me, that will be more space than I expected from you in your current territorial mood."

"You believe that my *territorial mood* as you put it is a result of your pregnancy?"

"Yes."

"Even though I did not want our relationship to end, prior to me finding out about it?"

He was right, that didn't make any sense, but… "It's all muddled in my head and sex will only make it worse. I'm sure of it."

"Maybe it would make it better. I know it would for me."

"No pressure. You promised."

"When did I promise?"

"Just now?" she asked, rather than stated, because she wasn't sure that's what he had done.

"I promised to sleep with you without touching you intimately."

"Yes."

"I did not promise to pretend I no longer want you. Indeed if I did, your active imagination would no doubt have you thinking all sorts of wrongheaded scenarios."

"It wouldn't!"

"You can say this after asking me if I no longer found you sexually irresistible because of your pregnancy, merely because I had not reacted with enough disappointment to your no sex edict?"

"Oh…well, I suppose. Do you think it's pregnancy or finally accepting I love you that has me so muddled?" she asked.

"Pregnancy." There was no doubt in his voice.

"I do love you," she said with a catch in her voice. "I wish you would believe me."

"Give me something to believe."

"Like what?"

"Like marriage."

She should have seen that coming. "Anything else?"

"What else is there? You refuse me the succor of your body and the comfort of giving you and our child my name. I do not mean to hurt you, Danette, but that is not a love I can recognize."

Her eyes began to burn. He didn't mean to hurt her, but his lack of belief hurt all the same. "I need to get back to work."

"Yes, I also."

"I…um…are you sure you're going to be okay with sleeping with me and not doing anything else? It's just not what you're used to," she babbled, not even sure what she was trying to say. "Even when it was that time of month for me, we never slept completely platonically."

And she was afraid that even the lightest caresses on his part would crumble her defenses against making love.

An explosion of air sounded at the other end of the line. "If you are that worried about sharing my bed, then it would be best if you stayed in the guest room. I do not wish to importune you in any way."

"I didn't mean—"

"Your meaning was clear. Do not let it concern you. I must go now. *Ciao, bella.*"

"*Ciao.*"

But she didn't work after hanging up the phone, not for several minutes, as she blinked back tears and mulled over what he had said. Obviously it was important to him that she sleep with him. Why couldn't she give him that much?

But she knew why. She couldn't trust her own shaky defenses where he was concerned. If they made love, for her it would be comfort…for him a commitment she was not yet ready to make.

CHAPTER ELEVEN

DANETTE woke after a less than satisfactory night in the guest room bed. Not that the bed was unsatisfactory in any way. Just like everything else in Marcello's four-bedroom apartment, it was top-notch. The mattress was comfortable, the decor in the bedroom peaceful and eye catching, but she missed Marcello.

They had eaten in relative silence the night before, their conversation, what there was of it, centered around the baby. Marcello had excused himself directly after dinner to catch up on work in his study and she had tried watching television for a while. He still hadn't come out of his study when she went to bed two hours later.

She ached from the distance she felt between them. It was worse than right after the breakup because her heart kept telling her that they *should* be together, they *could* be together, if not for her refusal.

She'd woken several times in the night, reaching for him only to find an empty bed. Had she been a fool to demand space that only seemed to hurt and add to her turmoil instead of making it easier to think, like it was supposed to? Was he right in thinking that making love would actually clarify their situation, not make it worse?

Talking was supposed to help, but it felt like all they did was talk in circles.

She wanted him to accept that she loved him *before* they got married. But from what she could tell, it was going to take her risking marriage to him for him to believe her feelings were real.

If he had demanded it as proof of her love, she would rebel. That kind of emotional blackmail left her cold.

But that wasn't what was happening. He was genuinely confused by her actions. Everything he did and said showed just how little he understood what motivated her. And how little he believed that motivation was anything resembling true love. Maybe Bianca had been better at showing her love than Danette was, but then the other woman had known she was loved in return. That made a huge difference and Danette was only beginning to see how stingy unrequited love could be.

But love shouldn't be selfish and it shouldn't hold back out of self-protection, either. In one respect, Marcello was very right. Love that was spoken, but not acted upon wasn't much of a love at all.

Love shouldn't make a woman a doormat, but it should make her strong enough to take risks she wouldn't otherwise take. Shouldn't it? Loving Marcello definitely shouldn't make her act in a way that hurt him, but that was exactly what had happened.

Her rejection had hurt him every bit as much as his desire to keep her a secret and never to marry her had hurt her. She had absolutely no doubts on that score and it made her feel terrible. She didn't want to hurt him.

Her thoughts were cut off by a vise squeezing tight

around her stomach and an urge to throw up that had her leaping from the bed and running to the en suite. She was retching, her face clammy and her whole body aching, when a warm hand settled on the small of her back.

"Why did you not wait for me? I was bringing you tea and toast."

"I didn't have a choice," she breathed, feeling shaky and light headed, but her stomach finally settled.

He made a noise that was part protest, part remorse and she turned her head to rest against his body kneeling so close to hers.

He cupped her cheek. "*Amante*, what am I going to do with you?"

"Help me stand up?" she asked in a voice that was shockingly weak.

He said nothing more until he had not only done that, but helped her rinse her mouth with water and then washed her face and neck with a cool cloth.

When he was done, he lifted her in his arms and carried her back into the bedroom. "If I had been here, I would have known the moment you woke and been able to take care of you. This sleeping in separate beds is foolish!"

She nibbled on a piece of dry toast and sipped at weak, but very sweet tea while he vented his frustration in a mixture of Italian, English and a couple of other languages she could only guess at.

He finally wound down and sat beside her on the bed, his usually immaculate appearance having taken a decided turn for the worse. His hair was mussed from running impatient fingers through it and he'd even loosened his tie and the top button on his dress shirt as if he'd needed more air.

He took her hand in his big tanned one, his fingers playing softly over the back of hers. "I apologize. I am going on like a madman and you are feeling ill. Forgive me."

"Wow. For a guy who doesn't say he's sorry very often, you're really good at it."

He grimaced. "Thank you. I think."

She smiled, feeling much better than she had been five minutes ago. "I think you're right though."

"*You think I am right*?" He sounded stunned. "About us not sleeping in separate beds?"

She nodded, making no sudden movements that might bring back the nausea. "I slept very poorly last night."

"You missed me?" Satisfaction gleamed in his blue gaze.

She had to stifle her own humor at his reaction. She didn't think he would understand it, but humility simply was not his thing. "Yes."

"I missed you, too, *tesoro*."

"So…um…no more separate beds."

"You are sure?"

"Positive."

"And your concern I will try to seduce you?"

"I trust you."

"That is something."

Yes, it was. But was it enough?

She got her first personal taste of the intrusiveness of the press an hour later when she answered the phone in her office to discover a reporter who wanted a quote on her relationship with Marcello at the other end of the line. She hung up after a firm, "No comment," and

stopped answering the outside line on her phone altogether after the third such call.

Voice mail was a wonderful thing.

She really appreciated the fact that Marcello lived in
a high security building with underground parking, and
that Scorsolini Shipping also had underground parking
and a crack security force. Somehow, word of her relationship with Marcello had gotten out and she had no
desire to run a gauntlet of reporters to and from their
car.

She wondered how he was handling the media attention. It was the one thing he'd made it very clear he did
not want to deal with. And now they were smack in the
middle of it. She shuddered to think what would happen
when the press learned about the baby.

A light rap sounded on her open office door and
she looked up.

Lizzy came in, a grin on her face and her eyes lit with
curiosity. "So, what is this I hear about you and the big
boss having a thing?"

"Um…what did you hear?"

"Come on, Danette. It's all over the place. You
moved in with him and everything. I can't believe I
didn't guess. Did it happen that night at the restaurant?
But then how would you have gotten pregnant so fast?"

"Pregnant?" she asked faintly.

Lizzy just looked at her. Danette had known word
would spread around the company, so she needed to just
bite the bullet and come clean with her friend. "We've
been going out for a while."

"In secret?" Lizzy asked with awe.

"Yes. Neither one of us wanted our relationship to
become public knowledge." Now was not the time to

explain that the relationship, such that it was, wasn't actually on anymore.

After agreeing to share his bed, even platonically, she wasn't sure that was true anyway.

"I understand." Lizzy leaned on the other side of Danette's desk. "It's going to make it a bit awkward for you around here, but you're fab at your job and everybody knows it, and you're definitely strong enough to handle what little flack may come your way."

"Thanks for the vote of confidence." Danette smiled.

"So, are you really pregnant?" Lizzy whispered.

Danette nodded.

Lizzy squealed and came around the desk to hug her. "Congratulations, *chica*! That's wonderful news! I'm so happy for you!"

Danette laughed and hugged her friend back. "Thanks. I'm pretty happy about it."

"Not when you're puking, I bet you're not."

"It comes with the territory."

"I won't ask when the wedding is because I don't want to accidentally let it slip and be responsible for the news cameras showing up, but I just want you to know I'm really, really, really happy for you."

Lizzy's visit left Danette in high spirits and she was powering through her to-do list and doing a fair job of ignoring the messages left by reporters on her voice mail when a representative for an exclusive boutique arrived in her office. The woman looked more like a cover model than a boutique employee and explained she was there to show Danette a selection of clothing for her upcoming trip to Isole dei Re.

"I have several outfits per the prince's instructions

here," she said, indicating a portable clothes rack she'd rolled into Danette's office.

"Marcello sent you?" Danette asked.

The other woman nodded even as Danette was picking up her phone to dial Marcello's private line.

He picked up on the second ring. "What is it, Danette?"

"There's some kind of personal shopper woman here—in my *office*. She wants me to look at clothes, Marcello. Why is she here?"

"I want to fly directly to Scorsolini Island after work today. Our takeoff slot is for four-thirty."

"What? You want to fly out early? Why?"

"My father wants to spend some time getting to know you before my brother's wedding."

Remembering what he had told her about Maggie Thomson's first meeting with the king, Danette did not smile at the prospect. "Oh."

"It is important to me, *amante*."

"Then we will go of course."

"Good. We can fly to the States in order for me to meet your parents after the wedding."

"All right." She hadn't even told them she was dating, much less that she was pregnant. She'd have to do it from Isole dei Re because they wouldn't even be out of bed before she and Marcello flew out. "But that still doesn't explain the personal shopper with her rack of elegant clothes."

She gave the boutique employee an apologetic smile for talking about her as if she wasn't there.

"I knew you would not want to take time off from work to pack, and assumed you would refuse to leave with me if you did not have some clothes and an appropriate outfit to wear for the wedding."

"And this is your idea of a preemptive strike to gain my compliance?"

"Yes. Does that bother you?"

She looked at the three outfits the woman had turned to hang face out, and had to shake her head. "How can it? She's got impeccable taste."

"Both my mother and Therese favor that boutique."

"Then I guess I'm in good company, but what about my toothbrush?" she asked facetiously.

"All personal toiletries have been taken care of."

"Thank you. I guess I'd better take care of the clothes thing so I can get back to work."

"You do not sound overly excited about it."

"It beats shopping by regular means, that's for sure."

Marcello laughed. "We will leave for the airport at three. Be ready."

"Yes, sir."

"Tease me at your peril, *tesoro*."

"What will you do about it?"

"That is for me to know and you to worry about."

"Note, I'm not worried."

"You are relying on the pregnancy card here?"

"Maybe…"

His laughter lifted her spirits as high as Lizzy's visit had.

"I'll see you later, *caro*."

There was silence for a few seconds and she thought they'd somehow been disconnected, but then he said, "Until then, *cara*," in a voice that sent tingles clear to her toes.

The man was definitely lethal. She'd be doing the sanity of women everywhere a favor by taking him off the market.

With that tantalizing thought playing over in her mind, she selected four outfits and answered a list of personal preference questions for the boutique. Then the personal shopper left after promising to have everything packed in a set of luggage and transported to Marcello's jet at the airport.

Danette wasn't entirely sure why four outfits required an entire set of luggage, but she had too much to do for a sales report due later that afternoon to spend any time thinking about it.

Marcello hung up the phone with a smile on his face. No way could she know about the stories in the tabloid press. She sounded too natural. Too relaxed. He did not think she would respond so carelessly to some of the ugly innuendo and downright provocative assertions being made.

His decision to leave early for Isole dei Re had been the right one. She needed to be protected and he would protect her. Always.

He glared down at the offending tabloids spread across his desk. They had been waiting for him when he arrived at work that morning. Some would not hit the newsstands until the next day, but they all had something in common…they implied things that would hurt Danette. And she had been hurt enough.

It had never been his intention to cause her pain, but he had. It made him angry that he hadn't seen the toll the secrecy of their relationship would take on her eventually. Because other women did not interest him, he assumed pictures of him with them would not bother her. He had been wrong.

And he understood how wrong after seeing her that

night with Ramon. He had to admit to himself that if she had been dancing with the other man, blood probably would have been shed.

It was a good thing that hadn't happened. There was enough ugly speculation surrounding their relationship. His fury at the press was barely containable, but mixed with it was a surprise.

He felt no personal embarrassment at the headlines proclaiming him everything from a cuckolded boyfriend to a emotionless seducer who had taken advantage of his role as president of the company. He simply didn't care, but the knowledge those same headlines would hurt Danette ripped at his gut.

He would not allow her to see them, and if it took an extended stay behind the walls of their palace in Isole dei Re to protect her, that was what they would do.

Danette assumed Marcello didn't want to discuss the fact that the press were obviously on to their relationship because he didn't bring the matter up during the drive to the airport or their flight to Isole dei Re. It was a long flight and they both spent the first couple of hours working. Then they had dinner and Marcello went back to work, but suggested she relax and watch a movie on the personal DVD player.

What she really wanted was a nap, and she fell asleep halfway through her movie.

Danette was sleeping when they touched down and only woke up when Marcello gently shook her shoulder. "We are arrived, *amante*."

She blinked her eyes, trying to focus. "Okay. Um…what time is it?"

"Close to 3:00 a.m. in our time zone and about nine in the evening in Paradiso."

"Okay." She was so tired, she just wanted to go back to sleep.

He smiled. "You are really out of it, aren't you?"

She nodded. He laughed, and the next thing she knew she was being lifted from her seat, high into his arms, and being carried off the plane. When he ignored her sleepy protest that she could walk on her own, she laid her head against his shoulder and dozed. She was vaguely aware of being placed in a car and of a short ride before the car stopped.

Once again Marcello carried her. This time, she didn't even make a token protest, but wrapped her arms around his neck and snuggled into him. He said something to someone else as his arms tightened their hold on her.

Suddenly lights blazed against her eyelids and she blinked her eyes open to look around her. There was Italian marble everywhere, and large Roman-style columns as well as statuary that rivaled anything she'd seen on her trip to Florence the first month she started working at Scorsolini Shipping.

"Looks like a museum."

A deep, masculine laugh sounded from behind her. "Yes, perhaps it does."

She turned her head and beheld the king of Isole dei Re. She was too sleepy to be overwhelmed. She simply stared at him.

"Hello, Danette Michaels. I hear you are pregnant with the next Scorsolini grandchild."

She glared up at Marcello. "You told him, too?"

"You expected him not to? I assure you, after reading today's papers I would have been aware anyway."

"*Papa.*"

Something passed between the men that she was too rummy to get, but the king shook his head. "She will learn eventually."

"The only thing I want to learn right now is where I'm supposed to sleep," she mumbled and then realizing how horribly rude that sounded, she blushed to the roots of her hair. "I'm sorry. I didn't mean…"

"Do not worry, child. Marcello's mother was the same way when she was pregnant with him."

"What way is that?"

"Cranky and easily tired."

"I'm not cranky." She looked at Marcello, her eyes going misty for no apparent reason. "Am I cranky?"

"No, *tesoro*. You are fine." The glare he gave his father could have singed brick.

"Flavia was very emotional, too. I did not mean to offend you, little one. Please forgive an old man his less than tactful tongue."

"Not old," she mumbled against Marcello's chest. "But definitely tactless."

She thought she'd said it too low for him to hear, but the sound of the older man's laughter followed them up the stairs. At least he hadn't been offended.

She awoke the next morning to gentle prodding from Marcello. He had a delicate china cup of steaming tea in his hand. "I hoped if you had your tea and toast right on waking, you would not get sick."

"It's worth a try." And surprisingly, it worked. Her nausea never made it past the point of discomfort and by the time she was done with her toast, it was gone completely.

She was feeling quite decent when she followed

Marcello down the marble staircase and along several long corridors that made her feel like Alice in Wonderland. "It really is a palace, isn't it?"

"Naturally. What else would a royal family live in?"

"But you're all so normal."

"In some ways, of course, we are like anyone else. But there is a responsibility to our birth that changes us and the way we must live our lives."

Was he trying to explain the secrecy thing again? He shouldn't have to, she was finally ready to admit. After all, she had been more than okay with it at first. It was just that as her love grew her ability to keep it hidden diminished. And the need to do so started to hurt.

Well, okay, and dancing with blondes was out. Forever.

Only, surrounded by the trappings of Marcello's royal birth, she thought maybe she was beginning to understand what motivated him a little better. Both in regards to their relationship and the baby.

They found his father in a large room that was imposing not only for its size but the opulence of its decor.

"I feel like we're in the Vatican," she whispered to Marcello. "I'm afraid to sit down and be thought disrespectful."

A deep laugh she remembered from the night before sounded from the other side of the room. "Maggie told Tomasso the same thing, he said."

"You heard me?" Oh, great. It wasn't like she hadn't been outspoken enough the night before.

King Vincente sat on a throne. A real live throne. It was huge, like thrones should be, she supposed. Made of dark, ornately carved mahogany and the royal crest above his head gilded in gold. Oh, goodness. The throne and the man were both incredibly impressive.

His eyes were the same blue as Marcello's and though there was silver in his hair, he was drop-dead gorgeous. Just like his son.

He smiled, showing even, white teeth. "The acoustics in this room were designed so that when my ancestors entertained they could easily keep track of conversations from every direction, but you will note that in order for you to hear me, I must project my voice."

"This is the formal receiving room," Marcello added.

"But it has a throne…I thought that made it the throne room."

"No." Marcello led her to a seat on a pristine white Queen Anne style chair near his father's throne. Three dozen or so of them lined the walls in the immediate vicinity of the throne. "The official throne room is much more ostentatious, to impress visiting dignitaries. This room has a more prosaic purpose."

"More ostentatious?" She wasn't sure she was ready to see the other room.

This one was impressing her to death…and intimidating her a little, too. She was really glad Marcello was the third son and not the first.

King Vincente laughed and Marcello nodded. "Yes, very much so. I will show you later. Tradition dictates that my father meet with his subjects in this room every Friday, all day long."

"The first visitors will be admitted in one hour's time," King Vincente added.

"Every Friday? That makes you a pretty accessible king, doesn't it?" Danette asked.

"That was the intent of my forefathers. They did not want the unrest often encountered in the City States that then comprised Italy, nor the deep distrust that developed between the monarchy and the parliament in England."

"That was smart of them."

"Yes, but then there is no doubting my ancestors were brilliant men."

She laughed out loud and turned to face Marcello who had taken a seat beside her after greeting his father with the customary kiss on both cheeks. "It definitely comes from both sides of your family."

"What does?" King Vincente asked.

Marcello's smile was warm and sent a sense of well-being spreading through her. "Danette considers me arrogant."

"And you believe he gets this trait from both his mother and myself?" King Vincente asked her.

"I'm sure of it."

"You find Flavia arrogant?"

"Had she been a shy retiring little thing, I'm sure she would never have interested you," Danette replied by way of compromise. She didn't know if he would find her assessment of his former wife flattering, or not.

Something told her he was not tolerant of any criticism directed at his family and that included the woman who had had the temerity to divorce him.

"This is true," he mused, his expression giving nothing away regarding what he thought of her comment. "And was it *your* arrogance that drew my son's interest?"

She stared at him, not sure what to say. She'd never considered herself arrogant, but wouldn't it sound self-serving to say so? Especially after teasing both Marcello and his father about the fact that they were?

She hadn't meant to give offense, but neither did she think either man could even begin to deny the claim.

"She is not arrogant, Papa. Stubborn, yes. Proud as well, but she is far too compassionate with others to be arrogant."

"You say she is compassionate?" King Vincente asked with a wholly unexpected scathing disbelief and Danette flinched.

What had she done to give him such a low opinion of her?

"Yes, she is."

"And you," he asked, meeting Danette's gaze. "Do you consider yourself compassionate?"

"Yes, but why are you asking me that?"

"You refuse to marry my son."

"I didn't…I don't—"

"Papa, do not get into this right now," Marcello said in a voice that could have flash-frozen lava.

But King Vincente ignored him, his attention fixed wholly on Danette, his eyes raking her with disapproval. "You are willing to bring a child of Scorsolini blood into the world without the benefit of matrimony. The newspapers are slaying Marcello, making him out to be a fool and worse."

Marcello jumped to his feet, yelling at his father to shut up, but King Vincente went on remorselessly.

"You allow this vilification by the press of my son and know it will be no better for your child—yet you continue to deny Marcello his right to give you his name. How do you call that compassionate?" he demanded, his scorn withering her.

"I brought her here to be protected, not browbeaten," Marcello gritted out between clenched teeth as he grabbed her upper arms and lifted her from the chair. "You will not speak to my woman this way. Come, Danette, we will leave."

"Is she yours?" King Vincente demanded mockingly and she felt Marcello flinch, even though she knew he didn't want her to.

"It appears I have arrived just in time."

Another voice intruded, that of Flavia Scorsolini, and the effect it had on the king was electric.

CHAPTER TWELVE

THAT vaunted arrogance drained away along with the color in his face. His head snapped sideways. "*Flavia?*"

"As you see." She came forward and hugged both Marcello's rigidly furious form and Danette.

She patted Marcello's cheek. "Relax, my son. Do not be so angry with your papa. He wants only to protect you as you wish to protect Danette."

"I am no child to be protected!"

"You will always be our child. Accept it." She smiled at Danette, her eyes filled with warm understanding. "Do you wish to leave, *cara*?"

"No." The king had made some comments that she wanted explained and she wasn't going anywhere until they were.

"You see, Marcello? She is not ready to go."

"I will not allow her to be hurt."

"Some things cannot be hidden from her," was his mother's enigmatic reply.

Marcello looked entirely unconvinced and Danette pressed her hand over his heart. "Please, Marcello."

"I do not want you upset."

"Thank you, but I want to stay."

He stared at her, his eyes filled with some unnameable emotion. Finally he nodded and then turned his gaze to Flavia. "Mama, we did not expect you."

"I learned yesterday evening from the owner of my favorite boutique that you planned to fly over early. I guessed your reasoning, what your father's reaction to it would be, and changed my own plans accordingly."

"You think Miss Michaels needs your championship?" King Vincente asked in a voice that sounded strained.

Danette looked at him and sucked in a breath. He was watching Flavia with an expression so akin to agonized need that Danette's heart squeezed on his behalf.

Flavia appeared oblivious. "I think that you will browbeat the poor child out of that arrogance that up until now she has found rather amusing."

"Do you deny that her refusal to marry our son is detrimental to the welfare of everyone involved?"

"And did your son tell you that Danette refused to marry him?"

Anger replaced the strange expression on the king's face. "I read the papers. Nowhere was there a mention of an upcoming marriage. I know my son. He would never allow his child to enter the world without the benefit of his name. If there is no marriage planned, it is because she has refused him."

Flavia shook her head. "There is no fool like an old fool."

"I am not old," he said, sounding thoroughly outraged.

"But you are a fool."

King Vincente looked ready to spit nails, but he didn't yell. Danette found that fascinating.

"What newspapers?" she asked.

"The ones my son hoped to hide from you by coming here," Flavia replied.

"And it damn well would have worked if Papa had kept his big mouth shut."

"Marcello! I did not raise you to speak with such language or so disrespectfully to your father."

Marcello's glare gave no quarter, but Danette wasn't interested in family dynamics at the moment. "I repeat…what newspapers? Do you have copies?"

"Yes," King Vincente said at the same time Marcello growled, "No!"

Danette ignored the man she loved in favor of giving his father a gimlet stare. "I want to know what is being said. I want to see the papers, and I want to see them right now."

Marcello pulled her around to face him, his blue gaze more than a little troubled. "Danette, seeing the stories will serve no purpose but to hurt you. I do not want that."

"I know, but I can't hide from it. Your mom is right."

"No, she is wrong."

"I'm no wimp, Marcello. Either you trust me to handle the tough stuff, or you don't."

"And if I don't?"

"You do," she said with bone-deep certainty.

He didn't want her to see the stories, but he didn't doubt her ability to deal with them. She could see it in his eyes.

"I do."

Just then a young man in a business suit appeared beside King Vincente. "You buzzed me, Your Highness?"

"Bring me the papers with my son's picture plastered all over the front of them."

"This is foolish," Marcello ground out, but without much heat.

King Vincente frowned at him. "She has a right to know what is being said and if she is not strong enough to deal with it, she is not strong enough to be your princess."

"I'm not weak," Danette insisted, her own voice as heated as Marcello's had been earlier.

She'd spent her childhood being forced to submit to a bodily infirmity. She had fought, and won that fight. She would never submit willingly to any weakness again.

Flavia shook her head, making a clucking sound. "Vincente, I swear you grow only more stubborn and opinionated with age."

"Do you disagree with me?" he demanded with an edge that said her opinion really mattered.

"No, but if you had an ounce of sensitivity, you could have put it differently. Nor do I doubt this woman's strength."

"So, I am not a diplomat with my family," the older man grumbled. "A man should have some people in his life with whom he can be honest without fear of reprisal. Even a king."

"Yes, but some honesty is better left unspoken."

The aide returned with the papers and Danette looked through them while Marcello smoldered beside her. The headlines were vicious and the story copy wasn't much better.

"Prince's Secret Mistress Pregnant, But Is It Really His Baby?" read one. She winced when she read the next: "Sterile Prince To Be Father At Last… Or Is He?" Then there was, "Playboy Prince Has No Plans To Marry Pregnant Lover."

"I didn't realize they knew about the baby."

"Our trip to the bookstore was not the smartest move I have ever made," Marcello admitted in a roughened undertone.

But it wasn't just their reading material that had tipped off the press. Someone at Scorsolini Shipping had heard about her trip to the ladies' room during her presentation and about the employees from the warehouse who were commissioned to move her things from her little cottage to his big apartment.

Whoever it was had put the facts together correctly and tipped off the press. A sense of betrayal washed over her. It was hard to believe a co-worker would sell her and Marcello out like that.

She skimmed the articles and felt bile rise in her throat. The speculation ran all the way from the baby being someone else's to her refusing to marry because he'd already moved onto another woman before she discovered her pregnancy. The picture of him dancing with the blonde played prominently. So did old pictures of him with Bianca, and new ones of Danette and Marcello together coming out of the bookstore.

Unflattering comparisons were made between the two women and Danette's unsuitability for being the mother of a prince's baby was touted by more than one reporter. Her mother was going to have a fit for more reason than one when she read the article…if she read it. Danette sincerely hoped her mom didn't.

But the worst by far were the innuendos that implied she'd gotten pregnant by someone else and was trying to trap Marcello into marriage or bilk him for money.

She dropped the paper and said, "I think I'm going to be sick."

Marcello went to pick her up, but Flavia was faster, pushing Danette onto a short white sofa that matched the chairs in the reception hall. "Lie back. Yes, just like that. Now breathe deeply and concentrate on something else."

Danette did the breathing, but she couldn't think of anything but the horrible things said in those articles. She turned stricken eyes to Marcello. "I'm sorry. I didn't mean—"

"None of this was your fault," he said fiercely, dropping to his knees beside her.

But it was. She'd worried what would happen when the press knew about the baby and now she knew. It was awful. "You hate this…this is what you wanted to avoid more than anything. I'm so sorry," she said again, knowing the words were inadequate for the way his pride had to have been savaged by those stories. "You don't doubt you are the father, do you?"

"How can you ask me that? I have already said I had no worries on that score."

"But now that all this has come out…"

"Make no mistake, I hate those stories and the attention is unpleasant, but my thought since reading the first one yesterday morning has been to protect you. I do not care what they say about me. I know that baby inside you is mine."

"It is, Marcello."

"Of course he knows it is." Flavia shook her head and patted Danette's hand. "My son is no fool…usually."

"And what is that supposed to mean?" King Vincente asked with umbrage.

Flavia spun to face him. "You can take full credit for his idiocy, too. Because he was already married and loved once before, he convinced Danette that he is no more capable of fidelity than you are."

The king had looked pale before, but he looked positively gray now. "I—"

"You have to stop punishing yourself. Do you hear me? You have planted this stupid idea into the heads of our sons, and the good God above alone knows how much damage it has done with the older boys."

"Your Highness, the people are awaiting entry outside the doors." The aide had come back.

"I must do my duty," King Vincente said, his expression of a man who was going through hell and saw no way out.

Flavia nodded, her expression unreadable. "Of course. Marcello, bring Danette. We will retire to the private apartments." She yawned delicately. "I could use a nap. I flew through the night and got very little sleep."

"You could have flown with us," Marcello said as he helped Danette to her feet and led both women from the big reception room through a door in the back.

"I did not learn of your departure until after the fact."

Marcello put his arm around Danette's waist, guiding her toward the door behind the throne his mother had come in through.

Danette stopped at the door and turned to look back at the king. "I didn't know about the articles."

He grimaced. "So I saw. I am sorry for my earlier accusations."

"I don't want to hurt Marcello."

"And he does not want to hurt you, but as Flavia and I learned, good intentions are not always enough."

Danette impulsively ran back into the room and put

her hand on the king's arm. She wanted to hug him, but didn't have the nerve. "It's going to be all right."

His gorgeous blue eyes were filled with an old sadness. "I hope you are right."

"Trust me and trust your son. He's a good man."

"Yes, he is. A better man than his father."

"I don't know. I think you must be pretty special to have raised Marcello the way he is."

"Flavia had more to do with that than I did."

Danette smiled and gave into the urge to hug the intimidating older man. King or not, he was hurting. She spoke near his ear. "It was a joint effort and you may as well accept it. Ditch the humble bit, it doesn't suit you."

He laughed and she stepped back.

"I believe you will make a very good princess, Danette Michaels."

Danette smiled, warmed by the vote of confidence. "Thank you."

He pulled her into an embrace, kissing both her cheeks, and tears stung her eyes for no apparent reason. She stepped back and turned to go, but then stopped and leaned toward him to whisper.

"A small piece of advice? When a woman stands up for you like Flavia just did—she doesn't hate your guts."

King Vincente's jaw dropped and Danette rushed to catch up with Marcello.

"Come," Flavia said and Marcello pulled Danette through the door, closing it firmly behind them.

"Come for a walk with me on the grounds," Marcello said after they left Flavia at her rooms so she could take the nap she said she wanted.

"I'd like that."

He took her out into a formal garden that looked like

it had come right out of a Renaissance painting. "It's gorgeous out here."

"I have always enjoyed it."

"But you chose to live in Sicily rather than here on Scorsolini Island when you came of age."

"Yes."

"Why?"

"I wanted to be near Mama, and I wanted to make my own mark on the world. Besides, Papa wanted me in Sicily looking after Mama."

Danette nodded. She had no problem believing that.

"Why did you want to hide the stories from me?" she asked, cutting to the heart of what they needed to deal with.

"I knew they would upset you and I was right."

"But they upset you, too."

"You are my woman. It is my job to protect you."

"It's my job to protect you, too."

"Is it?" He smiled down at her winsomely. "There are other things I would prefer you spent your time doing."

Remembering the entire set of luggage loaded onto the plane for her benefit she said, "You didn't plan on going back to Sicily right away, did you?"

"No. I thought a long visit here would protect you from the brunt of the media frenzy, but my parents thought differently."

"Please don't be angry with either of them. They are only doing what they think is right."

"And what do you think is right?"

"Knowing, no matter how much it hurts, is better than being ignorant." She bit her lip and then asked, "Would there be as much of a story if we were getting married?"

He shrugged. "The lack of a marriage is gossip fodder,

to be sure, but it would be no guarantee against more stories. I learned that to my detriment with Bianca."

"Even so, I'm surprised you haven't used the stories to press your advantage in getting me to marry you. You had to know I would feel badly about them. Instead you tried to hide them from me."

"I did not want you hurt."

And maybe part of him didn't want her to see all the vicious things being written about him, either. She certainly hated knowing he'd read the stuff speculating that she'd been unfaithful to him and that the baby belonged to someone else.

"And to use the articles as leverage with you would be using emotional blackmail and I refuse to do that to you. Ever. It is a promise I made to you."

"I don't remember that promise," she said.

"That is because I did not make it out loud."

Oh, gosh…she was going to cry and really that shouldn't be happening. "That's really sweet," she choked out.

He sighed. "Tomasso warned me, and so did Papa actually."

"Warned you?" She swiped surreptitiously at her eyes. "About what?"

"Pregnant women have a tendency to cry over very small things."

"It's not a small th-thing t-to me that y-you are s-so honorable," she said, trying to breathe between words and not make her tears any more obvious than they needed to be.

He stopped and pulled her around to face him with gentle hands. "Shh…*tesoro*. It is all right. That I am an honorable man, this is a good thing, no?"

"Yes," she said in a wobbly voice.

"And you are an honorable woman."

"Y-yes…I think so."

"I know so."

"But maybe your dad is right. My refusal to marry you is selfish when I th-think of wh-what our child could face with the media."

"You are not selfish. Merely frightened and confused by too many changes coming at once."

"I'm not stupid."

"I never said you were. You were smart enough to date me—that shows a better than average IQ, does it not?"

She laughed as she was meant to, but her mind was spinning with the knowledge that she *had* to marry him. It was the right thing to do, and royalty were not the only people in the world who knew something about duty. Besides, marrying the man she loved was not exactly a hardship.

She'd told him she wasn't stupid. And waiting around for a romantic proposal from a guy whose whole reason for wanting to marry her was to secure his child's future and his role as a full-time papa would indeed be idiotic.

He wasn't going to all of a sudden realize he loved her, and she finally admitted that was what she'd been waiting for. Not just for him to accept her love, but for him to return it, and that wasn't fair. He gave her every-thing he could and demanding more wasn't going to make life for their baby or themselves any better.

She gripped his arms, her mouth going dry as she prepared to say what needed saying. "I'm smart enough to know that marriage between us makes a lot of sense and that the sooner we start making plans for it, the better off we all are. I suppose a small wedding like Tomasso and Maggie's makes the most sense, too."

Marcello stilled. "You are agreeing to marry me?"

"Yes."

He kissed her, his mouth devouring hers with a desperate passion that found a response in her own heart.

When she was trembling and plastered against him, he lifted his head. "There will be no small wedding. My mother and you have convinced me that only a traditional Sicilian ceremony will do."

"But the sooner we get married, the better."

"The delay of one month or even two will not harm anything."

Danette's mother would be very happy to hear that, and so she thought would Flavia. Perhaps the announcement of an upcoming wedding would be enough to declaw some of the nastier paparazzi predators. "If you're sure."

He frowned, his arms tightening around her. "You are being much too diffident…I do not recognize this side of you."

"Those stories in the tabloids were so awful, Marcello."

"But they mean nothing to us, because we know the truth. I do not care what they say so long as you agree to be mine."

She felt more emotion welling and buried her face in his chest so he wouldn't see it. "Your father's right, you know?"

"My father is lucky. I would have stayed angry with him for a good year over his stunt this morning, but I am too happy at your agreement to be my wife to remain angry. He should thank his lucky stars and his newest daughter-to-be."

"He was still right. I am arrogant." She sighed and nuzzled Marcello's warm, muscular chest. "I was so sure that keeping our relationship a secret wasn't necessary, but I realize now that it would have been awful if the press had gotten wind of it before."

"No worse than now."

"Not a lot could be worse than what they are saying now, but *before* you didn't know you wanted to marry me, and I think you would have felt obliged once ugly stories started to circulate."

"This is true. I would have felt the need to protect you, as I do now."

"I admire that, Marcello, I really do."

"And I admire your strength, both in refusing me until you were sure and in accepting me for the sake of our child's future." He kissed the top of her head, his hands warm on her back. "You are a very special woman, Danette."

"Thank you."

"I have a deep need to make love to my fiancée. Is that permissible?"

"More than permissible. It is desired."

They saw no one on the way to their royal apartments and he closed the door firmly behind them after they got inside. Then he locked it. "No interruptions."

She smiled, desire coiling tight in her belly. It had been too long. "Exactly what I had in mind."

"Which should tell you something."

"What?"

"That we are a good match."

"Because we both want privacy for making love? I hate to tell you this, but lots of men and women have the same requirement."

He smiled. "You can be a real smart mouth, you know that?"

She laughed. "It's part of my charm."

"Yes, it is. I meant because we so often think along the same paths. We belong together, *amante*. Do not doubt it."

"If I did, do you think I would have agreed to the marriage?"

"Yes." He went very serious. "For the sake of our child you would, but you have nothing to fear in accepting my proposal. Our marriage will be a good one. I promise you."

It didn't bother him that she was marrying him for the sake of the baby. None of the feelings of turmoil she was experiencing showed on his face. He looked supremely happy by her acquiescence. She wished she was so sanguine and she was going to try to be.

He might be marrying her for the sake of the baby, too, but that didn't mean he wouldn't be a good husband. "No more dancing with gorgeous blondes?" she asked just for good measure.

"I have already promised this, but make no mistake—no woman is as beautiful to me as you are."

"Not even Bianca?" She wanted to cut her tongue out the minute the words left her mouth.

As mood killers went, that had to be a classic. Worse, it made her sound like an insecure weakling, and she wasn't. She didn't need to be his first and best love to have a good relationship with him. As long as he stayed away from other live women, she could leave the dead one alone.

Couldn't she?

Surprisingly Marcello didn't look in the least annoyed. His expression was filled with an emotion she didn't understand when he cupped her face with his big, masculine hands. "Bianca has been gone for four years. You are very much alive. Your beauty to me is incomparable in *every* way."

"That's so sweet," she said, as those stupid pregnancy hormones made her eyes smart again.

He shook his head and then lowered it so their mouths were almost touching. "Not sweet. Truth. Accept now that I will never lie to you, or even exaggerate for a good cause. You can trust me completely."

"I want to. I'm marrying you," she reminded both of them.

"And you will never regret that choice. I guarantee it." His mouth sealed the words to her lips in a kiss unlike anything they had shared before.

She could taste his desire, but there was something else there, too. A tenderness she thought was probably because she was pregnant with his baby. She was no longer his illicit lover in a passionate affair, but the mother of his child who had just consented to marry him.

That made her special.

She responded with all the pent-up love in her soul, giving him back tenderness for tenderness and passion for passion. Everything else faded from her consciousness except for the feel of his lips on hers and his hands holding her face with such poignant possessiveness.

He licked along the seam of her lips and she opened her mouth, wanting his entry.

Their tongues teased one another and something that had been tight inside her heart since the break-up began to loosen. This man belonged to her on a fundamental level that denied the importance of declared love and emotions that could not be measured.

He was hers.

She was his.

They belonged to each other in an intimacy that no one else could share. The knowledge had been there in the back of her mind since the beginning. It was why she had not kicked him out the night she'd seen the picture of him with the blonde. Because the picture had shown a woman enjoying herself and a man smiling, but that man had been holding himself apart from the other woman. Danette had not realized it at first, not consciously. But she did now, in this moment of odd clarity.

He had denied her in the restaurant, but he could not deny her on an instinctive level. Ramon had seen Marcello's claim on her and so had Flavia. Danette had been too hurt to recognize it, but she knew it had been there. Just as the pain of seeing her with another man had been there.

"I didn't go out with Ramon to prove a point," she said against his lips.

Marcello reared back as if she'd struck him, his hands dropping from her face, his eyes for once perfect reflections of the maelstrom of emotion going through him. "What?"

"I wasn't trying to teach you an object lesson. How could I be? I didn't even know you would come to the restaurant that night."

"You *wanted* to go out with him?" Marcello asked in a hoarse voice that hurt her to hear.

"No."

"What are you saying then?"

"Lizzy tricked me into meeting them. I thought it was just going to be her and me, but she'd invited her boyfriend and Ramon along. She thought I needed to get out more. She didn't know about you. She thought I was lonely and she cared enough about me to try to fix that, but she knew I would have said no if she'd asked."

"She knew that because you'd said no before," he guessed.

"Yes."

"Our secrecy hurt you more than I knew."

"Yes." She couldn't deny it.

"I did not know that it hurt you at all. Please believe that."

"I do." She sighed. "You're not a sadist."

"It goes far deeper than that, if you could but see it. I never wanted you to be hurt by your association with me, but I could not walk away from you. I tried. It did not work."

"Rampant lust gone mad."

"It is more than lust."

She smiled, agreeing. Much more than lust now. "Yes, I am pregnant with your child."

"It was more than lust before you told me of your pregnancy."

She turned away, suddenly hurting in a way she didn't want him to see. She loved him. She would always love him and whatever he felt for her, no matter how much more it was than simple physical passion, it was not love. It never could be. She was not Bianca.

His hands curled around her waist and his mouth pressed against the sensitive skin of her nape. "I love you, Danette."

She tore from his arms, stepping back and turning on him, her heart slamming in her chest. "Don't say that! You don't mean it!"

His expression was fierce. "I do mean it."

"You can't. You just think you have to love the mother of your child. That's all it is, misplaced chivalry, but I don't want it. I can handle honesty between us. I can't handle that."

He glared and crossed the room with the speed of a predator, grabbing her wrists and pulling her body close to his. "You say you can handle honesty, then let us be honest. No woman has shared my bed for longer than two nights since Bianca's death and there were very few that made it that far, but you have had my heart and my body at your feet for six months, you faithless little termagant."

"I'm not…"

"You are. You take everything I do and say and interpret it with the worse possible connotations. You do not trust me. You even reject my declaration of love. You have no faith in me at all!"

"I…" She couldn't think of what to say in her own defense, which was an awful admission that she didn't have one.

He glared down at her. "I thought I could not get a woman pregnant. You cannot know what that did to me, but I believed I had nothing to offer a relationship of longevity."

"Babies aren't the only thing that matters in marriage."

"That is easy for you to say. You don't know the pain of wanting and never having. Bianca knew and it tore her apart." He stopped speaking and swallowed as if the pain was too much for him to bear. "She killed herself rather than face a future without children. I was not enough for her. I could not give her what she wanted most."

"No…if she'd killed herself…" It would have been

all over the press. "You're wrong. You blame yourself, but—"

"She did a pregnancy test that morning. It was negative...they were all negative." He took a deep breath, his big body taut with pain. "She went walking along the cliffs."

"And the ground gave way beneath her. That isn't suicide, Marcello."

"She could have thrown herself to safety...if she had wanted to."

Horror gripped Danette's heart. "You don't really believe that. It's not true."

"You were not there."

"Neither were you. She fell, Marcello. She didn't jump. She wouldn't have jumped. She had too much to live for."

"What had she to live for? Her dreams were in ashes in the waste bin of our en suite. One more pregnancy test. One more disappointment."

"If she wanted to be a mother that badly, she would have tried in vitro, or adoption."

"She said we were young, that we had time."

"And she meant it."

"You did not hear her crying at night when she thought I was asleep."

"I'm sorry if this hurts you, but those tears were probably for you. She knew how proud you are, how much not being able to make her pregnant hurt you. She loved you, of course she cried. She shed the tears you would not shed for yourself." She groped for corroboration. "If she'd been as deeply unhappy as you think she was, don't you think the press would have picked up on it? They would have had a field day with that kind of grief."

"They printed plenty of pictures of her looking unhappy."

"And you believed the pictures?"

"They do not lie."

"The camera lies all the time. If you get a picture of me first waking up in the morning, I look unhappy. I don't wake up for at least an hour and two cups of coffee. You scowl when you read the stock reports, but that doesn't mean you are unhappy."

"You don't know what it was like."

"No. But I can guess. Bianca loved you, like I love you. It hurt her to see you hurting."

He snorted at that. "You cannot say you share that affliction."

"Oh, yes, I can. I would have walked away from you rather than trap you in a relationship you didn't want. I finally agreed to marry you when I understood it would hurt you more for me to say no than to live in a marriage thrust on you by my pregnancy."

"But you said—"

"Some face-saving stuff, some stuff that was true, but wasn't the whole picture. Marcello, you aren't at fault for Bianca's death."

The ferocious tension in him arced higher rather than depleting. "Maybe you are right."

And she understood the increased tension. Marcello needed a catharsis for his pain, but he would not let himself cry. He was too strong, too macho for that outlet.

She brought his face down to hers and pressed her open mouth to his, taking the kiss to a level of hungry desire that could only be satisfied by two naked bodies writhing together on a bed. They made love in a firestorm of need and she screamed her love for him when she reached orgasm, only to have the words repeated fiercely back to her as he shattered.

He collapsed on top of her. "That was amazing."

"Yes, it was."

"You do not think we hurt the baby?"

"No, but he's probably going to be born with a love for storms after that."

Marcello laughed softly, but then he met her gaze, his own so serious, she ached for him. "I've carried that burden of guilt for four years."

"But it was a false burden."

"She was too young to die. I thought it had to be someone's fault."

"And you were already busy feeling like you'd let her down in the marriage stakes. It was easy to take the blame."

"Yes."

"But it wasn't your fault and you didn't let her down. Marcello, she was still young. She was probably glad in some ways she hadn't conceived yet."

He carefully disengaged and rolled off of Danette and then propped himself on his elbow at her side and laid his other hand possessively over her womb. "She refused to try in vitro."

"Maybe she felt guilty about that, too."

"Maybe."

"Do you feel better?"

"When I am with you, I always feel better."

"I'm glad."

"There was a lot of miscommunication in my marriage with Bianca, or maybe lack of communication is the better term, and it hurt us both. I don't want that with you."

"I don't, either."

"I refused to believe you loved me when you told me the first few times."

"I remember. Are you saying you believe me now?"

"Yes. I have to. You were willing to marry me believing I still loved a dead woman."

"It's okay that you still love her."

"But that love is in my past. You refuse to believe my vow of love today."

"I—"

"I do love you, more than life itself. I am sorry I was so messed up about marriage, but I want our marriage to be based on honesty and true understanding."

"Yes…"

He nodded, took a deep breath and then said, "I want to wait to get married until I have convinced you of the reality of my feelings."

"What?" She couldn't believe what she was hearing. "What if that took a long time? What if I didn't believe you until after the baby was born? This is crazy."

"Then so be it. I will marry you, Danette, make no mistake, but I will not build the foundations of the rest of our lives on mistrust."

His words went through her heart like a blazing sword. He had to love her to be willing to risk the illegitimacy of his child. He was telling her in an unmistakable way that there was nothing more important in life than she was to him.

Her eyes filled with tears as a glorious smile spread across her face. "I do believe you. I do."

He gave her a narrow-eyed look. "You are sure?"

"I've never been so sure of anything."

He breathed in a sigh of relief as if the weight of the

world had finally been lifted from his shoulders. "*Te amo, amante*. I love you with all my heart."

"And I love you."

They made love again, this time finishing the tender beginning they had had when they first came into the room. He took a long time arousing her and reveled in every touch she directed at him. When he penetrated her softness, he set a slow, love-filled rhythm that brought them to a mutual climax that shattered them both.

Tomasso and Maggie's wedding went off without a hitch and Danette finally got to meet the other sister-in-law, Therese. She'd been staying with Maggie, helping her with the wedding preparations.

Danette stood beside Marcello while Tomasso and Maggie spoke their vows under the pavilion on their private beach. It was a beautiful ceremony and Danette found herself wiping her eyes several times as the couple spoke their vows with obvious love and devotion.

Marcello's arm came around her and he whispered in her ear. "Soon, that will be us, *amante mia*."

She nodded, swallowing back more tears of poignant emotion.

He kissed her temple. "I love you."

She turned her head and kissed his shoulder, giving him her love silently.

Afterward, the family teased her about being emotional because she was pregnant, but Therese smiled and laid a gentle hand on her arm. "I think it is very sweet."

She smiled back at the sister-in-law she knew she would love despite the fact she barely knew her and the other woman's background was so different than her own. Therese Scorsolini was far too kind and friendly to intimidate Danette.

"It's just so neat to see Tomasso and Maggie so happy together. It's the way marriage should be, you know?"

Therese's beautiful brown eyes filled with a sadness that Danette did not understand. "Yes, that is how it should be," was all she said, however.

Flavia sighed and the look she gave King Vincente accused without giving a clue as to what she was holding him accountable for.

"What?" he asked, sounding bewildered and very much like a man and not a king.

Flavia shook her head. "I can see I should have taken things into hand years ago, but pride is a hard barrier to overcome."

After that incomprehensible speech, she asked Tomasso's children if they wanted to go for a walk on the beach. Upon receiving enthusiastic agreement, all three removed their shoes, left them under the pavilion and headed toward the waterline.

She stopped just as she was leaving the pavilion and turned her head back to catch King Vincente's eye. "Are you coming?"

"I am invited?" he asked, sounding as stunned as his three sons looked by the comment.

"But of course. Didn't I just say so?"

The king went, his expression one of a man totally bewildered by life.

Danette couldn't help laughing. "I wonder if she's decided to take a personal interest in him not growing into a lonely old man."

"You cannot be serious. For years, she wouldn't even allow his name to be spoken."

"Well, she's speaking it now, isn't she?" Danette asked and then added, "She loved him once."

"She stopped loving him years ago," Claudio, Marcello's oldest brother, said.

"True love does not die that easily," Therese said with an edge in her voice.

Marcello agreed. "No, it doesn't." He looked down at Danette, his eyes filled with fierce emotion. "I will love you forever."

She stared at him, her heart squeezing so tight, she could barely breathe. "And I will always love you."

He kissed her, and the sound of his brothers' laughter faded as the man she knew would be part of her heart for eternity showed her she would also be part of his.

The Scorsolini Marriage Bargain

LUCY MONROE

For Marilyn Shoemaker, a dear friend and valued reader. Your support and encouragement means the world! And thank you for helping me to name the secondary islands, Diamante, Rubino and Zaffiro, of Isole dei Re for this trilogy.
Hugs, Lucy

CHAPTER ONE

"SOME days, being a princess is right up there with long-term incarceration on Alcatraz." Therese muttered the words as she pulled up the zip on her favorite mint-green sheath dress while preparing for yet another formal dinner in the Palazzo di Scorsolini.

It wasn't the prospect of one more dinner eaten with King Vincente and the dignitaries who had come to visit him that made her cranky, though. It was frustration with a day spent in her own version of purgatory. She loved the king of Isole dei Re and was closer to him than her own father.

But there were still times she wished she and Claudio had their own home, not just a set of apartments in the royal palace of Lo Paradiso. No matter how beautiful, the suite afforded little privacy when she and Claudio were expected to eat most meals in the formal dining room. The fact that her duties as princess ruled even her personal time could be a major drawback. Especially tonight, when she was jittery with the need to share the news she'd received from her doctor in Miami. She'd gone to the States for this particular examination in order to guarantee absolute discretion.

She almost wished she hadn't now. Because if the press

had gotten hold of the story, at least she would be saved from having to impart the news to Claudio.

It was a craven thought and she was no coward.

But even she, with years of training as a diplomat's daughter, could not look on the end of her marriage with equanimity. Unlike her parents, she did not see life as a series of political and social moves and countermoves. For her…real life hurt.

Claudio finished putting on his second cuff link and pulled both sleeves straight with precise, familiar movements that made her heart ache at the prospect of losing that familiarity. His lips twisted, giving his gorgeous face a cynical cast. "I will be sure and tell your mother you think so."

Therese stopped on her way to the table where she had left the jewelry she planned to wear tonight. "Don't you dare."

Claudio found her mother's social climbing tendencies a source of amusement, but Therese was not so sanguine. She, after all, was the ladder her mother expected to climb up on.

"I have no desire to listen to Lecture 101 from Mother on how lucky I am to be a princess, or how privileged my life is." Not to mention the bit about how amazing it was that Claudio had chosen Therese from amongst all of the eligible women in the world. She really didn't want to hear that particular treatise, right now.

"Perhaps she will be able to understand your apparent disenchantment with your lot in life better than I can." The edge in Claudio's voice said he was only partially kidding and his dark gaze was serious and probing.

"I'm not disenchanted with my lot." Merely devastated by it, but now was not the time to tell him so.

And she couldn't help feeling her charmed life had been cursed…probably from the beginning, but she'd been too blind to see it. She'd bought into the fairy tale only to discover that love on one side brought pain, not pleasure. The happily-ever-after was only for princesses in storybook land…or those who were loved for themselves, like the two women married to the other Scorsolini princes.

"Then what is this comparing being my wife to that of a convict incarcerated in prison?" Claudio towered over her with his six-foot-four-inch frame, his scent surrounding her and reminding her just how much she would miss the physical reality of his presence when it was gone.

He was every woman's dream, the kind of prince that fairy tales really were made of. She had woven enough fantasies around him to know. He had black hair, rich brown eyes and the dark skin tone of his Sicilian forefathers, but the height of a professional athlete. His body was muscular, without an ounce of fat anywhere and his face could have been that of an American film star…perhaps of a different era, though. No pretty boy looks, but rugged angles and a cleft chin that bespoke a strength of character that she had come to rely on completely.

She had to swallow twice before speaking. "I did not say being *your wife* was like that."

"You said *the life of a princess,* which you would not be if you were not married to me."

"True." She sighed. "But I didn't mean to offend you."

He cupped her cheek in a move guaranteed to send her nerve endings rioting. He so rarely touched her when they were not in bed that when he did so, she didn't know how to handle it.

"I am not offended, merely concerned." She could hear that concern in his voice and it made her feel guilty.

He had done nothing wrong…except choose the incorrect woman to be his princess. "It has been a rough day, that's all."

His second hand joined the first and he tilted her face up so she could not hope to avoid his discerning gaze. "Why?"

She licked her lips, wishing again they were not going downstairs for dinner with his father. She wished even more that the twinges of pain in her pelvis were just the regular preperiod cramps she had believed them to be when she first went off the pill so they could try for a baby. "I spent the whole morning with representatives of Isole dei Re's foremost women's organization discussing the need for day care services and preschools on the islands."

He frowned as if he couldn't understand what bothered her about that. She'd had many such meetings and they had all gone rather well. However, all he said was, "I thought Tomasso's wife was spearheading that."

"The helicopter flight between the islands exacerbates Maggie's morning sickness, but she didn't want to put the meeting off. I convinced her to let me take her place. Looking back, I should have had the delegates flown to Diamante to meet with her instead."

His hands dropped from her face and she felt an immediate chill from the withdrawal, though she was sure he hadn't meant it that way. "Why? You and Maggie share views on this subject. You have certainly discussed it enough to cover all the points adequately."

"Not according to the delegates." She grimaced. "They felt that a woman without children, moreover one who had never been forced to work for her living, could not comprehend the challenges faced by working mothers. They believe that Maggie is ideal for this endeavor and that I should keep right out of it."

"They said this to you?" He didn't sound offended on her behalf, merely curious. He could have no idea how much the other women's disapproval had hurt.

She felt both exhausted and savaged, especially after the phone call from her doctor in Miami. "Yes."

"It is a good thing that you grew up learning political diplomacy then."

"Meaning it might have upset you if I had told them all to take a flying leap?"

Claudio gave a masculine chuckle as if he could not imagine such a thing. "As if you would."

"Maybe I did."

But he just shook his head. "I know you. No chance."

"Maybe you don't know me as well as you think you do." In fact, she knew he didn't. After all, he'd never once latched on to the fact that she'd married him because she loved him. The marriage of convenience aspect had been a plan hatched in his and her mother's more mercenary brains.

"Did you?" he asked with a sardonic brow raised.

She wanted to say yes just to prove him wrong, but told the truth instead. "No, but *I wanted to*."

"What we want and what we allow ourselves to do are rarely the same thing. And it is a testament to your suitability to your position that you live by this stricture."

She turned away from him and started putting on her jewelry. "And you wonder why I compared being a princess to being a prisoner?"

"Are you unhappy, Therese?"

"No more than most people," she admitted. She'd been raised from the time she was a tiny child to hide her true emotion, but she was so tired of pretending.

"You are unhappy?" Claudio demanded in a voice laced with unmistakable shock.

The man so well-known in diplomatic circles for his perspicacity was thick as a brick where she was concerned.

"Two of the delegates were less than subtle in expressing their belief it was past time I gave you an heir," she said instead of answering.

"And this upset you?" Again the shocked surprise.

"A little."

"But it should not. Soon you will be able to share happy news on that score."

She winced as his words sprinkled salt into wounds left open and bleeding by the doctor's phone call.

"And if I can't?" she asked, testing waters she was not ready to tread into.

His big, warm hands landed on her shoulders and he turned her to face him with inexorable movements. "You are bothered that you have not yet conceived? You should not be. We have only been trying for a few months. The doctor said that women who have been on the pill for a prolonged time can take longer to get pregnant, but it will happen soon enough. After all, we know everything is in working order."

Worse than salt on wounds, those words were like the lashing of a cruelly wielded whip. Prior to marrying three years ago, he had required they go through several tests including blood type and the compatibility of his sperm with the mucus on her cervix. He had also requested she have her fertility cycles tested, just to be sure.

Knowing that a big part of why he was marrying her was so that she could provide heirs for the Scorsolini throne, she had agreed without argument. Everything had come back normal. They were compatible for pregnancy and she was as fertile as any other woman her age.

The biggest surprise for her had been his desire to wait to have children for a while. She hadn't understood it, still wasn't sure why he had requested they wait, but now she knew that whatever chance they had of making babies together was over.

Unable to stand any level of intimacy in the face of what she knew was to come, even such a simple touch, she turned away from him.

Helpless anger filled Claudio as Therese moved from him, her womanly curves taunting a libido that ached for her night and day. He wanted to grab her back and demand to know why after three years his touch was no longer acceptable, but that would be the act of a primitive man and the crown prince of Isole dei Re was in no way primitive.

Besides, physical rejection from her was not a new thing. It had been happening for months now, but each time she turned away from a physical connection, it still shocked him. After two years of receiving an incredibly passionate response on every occasion when he touched her, he could be forgiven for finding it nearly impossible to reconcile to her sudden change of heart.

Prior to the last few months, he would have sworn that Therese loved him. She'd never said so, but for the first two years of their marriage, she had shown in many subtle and not so subtle ways that she felt more for him than the mercenary satisfaction of a woman for a marriage well contracted. Her love had not been one of his requirements, so he had not dwelt on it too much…until it was gone.

It was not that he needed the emotion from her, but he could not help wondering where it had gone and why she no longer seemed to want him with the latent passion that had drawn him to her in the first place.

Her physical rejections had started a month or so after she went off the pill so they could try for a baby. At first, he had thought that maybe her hormones had been at fault. After all, he'd read about that sort of thing happening, but in the intervening months it had gotten worse, not better.

Then sometimes she would make love with him the way she used to and all his concerns on that score would disappear. Only to reappear when she turned him down again. He was not a man who had suffered much rejection in his life, particularly from a woman he desired physically. For it to come from his own wife was totally unacceptable.

And it had been happening more and more lately.

He'd begun to wonder if deep down, she did not want to get pregnant. "Do you not want my baby? Are you frightened of what will happen?"

She flinched as if he'd slapped her, her face going unnaturally pale. "Yes, I want your baby. *More than anything*. I don't know how you could believe anything else."

She was so fervent he could not doubt her. "Then there is nothing about this situation that should upset you."

The look she gave him from her green eyes was not encouraging, but he forged on, certain of his own conclusions. "Soon enough you will be able to silence busybodies with the reality of a pregnancy. As for today, you will simply play the scenario differently next time and send the delegates to meet with Maggie."

She spun to face the mirror and pulled her silky, long brown hair up into a twist on the back of her head with deft fingers, securing it with a clip. "And that makes it all okay, does it?"

"It should," he said with some exasperation. "I do not understand why you are reacting so strongly to this. You have dealt with far more annoying people than these women."

Therese shrugged her delicate shoulders and headed toward the door. She was so beautiful, almost ethereal in her appearance despite curves that proclaimed her one hundred percent woman. And times like this he felt as if she was as untouchable as a spirit. But she was his wife, it was his right to touch her.

He did it, taking her arm as she walked by.

She stopped and looked up at him, her beautiful green gaze filled with a vulnerability he did not understand and liked even less. It implied an unhappiness he did not want her to feel.

"What?" she demanded.

"I do not like to see you like this."

"I know. You expect everything in your life to go smoothly, every person to fulfill their role without question. Your schedule is regimented to the nth degree and surprises are few and far between."

"I take great pains to make it so."

"Even to the point of marrying a woman with all the proper qualifications. You had me investigated, tested and then tested me yourself to be sure of my fit as your *principessa* and future queen. I am certain you never expected me to be a source of frustration for you."

She was right, but he didn't understand the bitter undertone in her voice. She had not seemed to mind his endeavors to make sure of her suitability at the time. "You are everything I wanted in a wife. Naturally in my position, I would make every effort to make certain our future was assured, but you were and are perfect for me, *cara*."

She flinched at the endearment, much as she frequently flinched from his touch anymore. As if any allusion to intimacy between the two of them hurt her. But they were intimate. They were husband and wife. There was no relationship more intimate than that.

So why did he feel like they existed in completely different hemispheres at the moment?

He pulled her close, ignoring the subtle stiffening of her body. "We do not have to go down to dinner, you know."

Her eyes widened in surprise. "Your father is entertaining dignitaries from Venezuela."

"They are his fishing buddies."

"They are official diplomats."

"He will not care if we send word we are not coming. And there are far more interesting ways for us to spend the evening than listening to fishing stories."

"Talking?"

"That is not what I had in mind."

Her face set, she pulled away, her rejection as obvious as it was final. "That would be rude."

Had Therese found someone else who engaged her affectionate nature? Perhaps she had even taken a lover. Rage poured through him at the thought, but in his arrogance he could think of nothing else that would explain the way she rejected him physically. Add that to the fact that at times she acted like her mind was definitely not in the here and now, and he had a compelling argument for believing she had found someone else.

So compelling he was not sure he could control the fury his reasoning evoked. He hated feeling like that. He had married her in order to avoid this kind of emotional upheaval in his life.

Which was the primary reason he had never voiced his suspicion. He knew Therese better than most men knew their wives. He's made sure of it and everything he knew of her character said she would never, under any circumstances act so dishonorably as to have an affair. That was one of the reasons he had married her. She was a woman of fierce integrity, but she had also used to be a woman of intense passions.

If the one could change…could the other? Did some unknown man have claim on her secret sensuality that used to delight Claudio so much? He could not believe it of her, but as unlikely as it might seem, he had to know the truth.

He would call the detective agency Tomasso had used to trace and investigate Maggie and order an investigation of Therese's present activities and past movements for the last year. Hawke, the owner of the international detective agency, was wholly discreet and the very best at what he did.

One way, or another, Claudio was going to get to the bottom of the mystery of his wife's behavior. If another man was involved, he would find out and deal with the situation accordingly.

The thought brought a surge of primitive anger he had no intention of giving in to.

Therese regretted rejecting Claudio's invitation throughout dinner. So what if all he wanted was sex? She could have made him listen. The problem was, she didn't want to. As long as she kept the news to herself, part of her could go on pretending her marriage had a chance. But even if they had talked…even if they'd made love and it had hurt a little, she would have one more memory stored up for a future without him. Instead she was sitting with a smile pasted on her face while conversation she had no interest in flowed around her. Claudio had been right. King Vincente and his fishing buddies from Venezuela were too busy swapping stories to even notice her and Claudio's presence at the table.

Claudio had gotten a phone call halfway through dinner and disappeared to answer it, leaving her entirely to her own devices. Not that he'd been all that communicative beforehand. He was too much the crown prince to make his displeasure with her obvious to the others at the table, but she had felt it.

Just as she had known he would not come back once he had left to take the phone call. He had often chosen work over her company. Tonight would certainly be no different. So, when it came time to take their coffee in the other room, she excused herself.

She'd been feeling twinges of pain in her pelvic area all day even though her menses were not due for a few days. Every month the pain got worse and it no longer limited itself to the days of her monthly. According to her doctor, that was typical for her condition, but it certainly wasn't pleasant.

It was getting harder and harder to hide the truth from Claudio as well, but soon…she wouldn't have to. She would tell him the results of the laparoscopy she'd had performed in secret on a trip to Miami. Then she would tell him what the doctor had said her condition meant for the future and he would tell her that their marriage was over.

The thought was far worse than the pain in her lower abdomen and she forced her mind to deal with the present, not the probable future.

Maybe a long, hot soak coupled with a couple of over the counter pain meds would suffice and she wouldn't be forced to take one of the pain-killing bombs the doctor had prescribed.

They always left her feeling so loopy and she hated it. There were days she couldn't even remember what she'd done because she'd spent so much of her time in a fog. The shock was that Claudio had never noticed. If she needed proof that she was nothing more to him than a convenience, that was it.

How could a man, even a man as oblivious to the normal issues of life as Claudio, not notice his wife had the behavior pattern of a drug addict? But he never said anything when she was zoned out on pain meds. To give him credit, she did her best to hide her condition from him…in every way. But there was a big part of her that resented the fact it was so easy.

If he cared at all, it wouldn't be. She was sure of it.

Her heart heavy, she started a bath. No woman should have to live with the constant knowledge that she loved where there was no reciprocating emotion to be had. It hurt too much.

Once the bath was full, she dimmed the lights in the en suite and poured soothing aromatherapy oil into the steaming water. Then, while the whirlpool jets mixed the water, sending forth a soft fragrance, she took her pain meds. She shed her robe, letting the silk fall to the floor and not caring that she should have hung it up. Refusing to even think about how the responsible Therese would have taken care of it so someone else would not have to, the in-pain-and-tired-of-hiding-it Therese slid into bathtub.

She'd been soaking for thirty minutes when she heard sounds in the bedroom. She'd let her mind float, so it only registered on the periphery of her consciousnesses what those sounds meant.

"If you've fallen asleep in there, I'm going to be more than mildly annoyed with you."

Her eyes slid open and the impact of his presence slammed into her like it always did. No man should be this beautiful. "Not sleeping. No need to be irritated."

"You certainly looked asleep," he said accusingly, but his dark eyes were eating her up in a way that said bathtub safety was not the only thing on his mind.

His obvious interest found an answering hunger in her body. The effectiveness of the hot bath and painkillers meant she could act on it if she wanted to and she did. Once she told him the truth and he accepted there was only one practical solution for their future, she would have to live the rest of her life without feeling the things his touch invoked.

"I don't suppose you would consider being my bathtub buddy?" she asked, giving his magnificent body a once-over. "Purely for safety's sake, you understand."

His eyes narrowed. "Is that an invitation?"

"What do you think?"

"I think I don't understand why you forced me to sit through an hour of fishing stories if you were feeling like this." He made a sound that was suspiciously like a growl of frustration, while his lower body reacted in a basic and obvious way to her suggestion.

She hid her smile of satisfaction at the evidence that if nothing else, the man wanted her. Then she looked up at him from between her lashes. "Are you saying you're not interested?" she asked in a tone that said she didn't believe it. "Your body says otherwise."

"Maybe my body isn't the one in control here."

She arched her back, relief coursing through her when the

shift in her pelvis the movement caused didn't so much as result in a tiny twinge of discomfort. "Maybe it should be."

"Damn it, Therese, what is going on?"

He never swore in front of her. It shocked her so much that she relaxed back into the water. What if he *didn't* want her? A man might not be able to control the physical responses of his body, but he didn't have to give in to them. Not if his mind was turned off in spite of his body's cravings.

He was upset with her for turning him down earlier. She should have realized he would be, but normally he acted as if her diminished desire didn't impact him at all. After all, he was a busy man. He had about as much time for sex as he did for meaningful conversations with her, which meant he had almost no time at all.

Saying nothing because she was afraid she'd beg if she did, she stood to get out of the tub.

"What are you doing?" he asked in a low growl.

"What does it look like? I'm getting out." He could turn her down, but he didn't need to rub her nose in it.

He made a sound that sent a shiver down her spine. "Stay where you are, you provoking little witch."

CHAPTER TWO

"I WASN'T trying to provoke you," she denied.

He yanked his tie off and started on the buttons of his shirt. "Then I don't want to see what you are like when you do try."

It suddenly occurred to her that he *wasn't* turning her down, but intended to get into the oversize tub with her. She smiled in pure relief. "Are you sure about that?"

He jerked his pants down, pulling his shorts with them and revealing the impressive length of his angrily throbbing erection. He *really* wanted her, but from the expression on his face, he wasn't happy about it.

He stepped into the tub and pulled her to him all in one movement, rubbing his rigid length against her in a blatantly sexual gesture. "I'm not sure about much of anything with you anymore."

She wrapped her arms around his neck, reveling in the feel of his hard muscles and heated skin against her. "I thought you were always sure of me…about everything."

"I wish." His mouth slammed down onto hers and there was none of the seductive finesse she'd come to expect from him.

Something had really upset him and he was barely in control. Her ultraurbane husband was showing a basic side to his nature he'd always kept carefully hidden. She doubted he even knew it was there. She had always suspected, though. She saw glimpses sometimes when they were making love, but this was the first time she sensed his control was really at risk. She didn't mind. In fact, she loved it.

Uncomplicated passion was exactly what she needed right now to get her mind off things she could not stand to think about. She kissed him back, letting the desperation she felt translate into a physical need that more than matched his. A growl rumbled low in his chest and he deepened the kiss with a thrust of his tongue that took total possession of her mouth.

She let her fingers run down the hard contours of his chest, tangling in his black, curling hair and tugging gently.

His mouth broke from hers. "*Sì, cara.* You know how much I like that. Do it again."

She did and then bent forward to taste the salt of his skin with the tip of her tongue. If only he could love her and not merely what she could do to him. But thinking along those lines would bring pain, not pleasure and she slammed the door shut on that part of her mind with a ferocious clang.

She nuzzled him, loving his scent and the feel of his warmth against her face. He was so perfect for her physically.

His big hands cupped her bottom and he lifted, rubbing his erection against the juncture of her thighs bringing forth a damp throb of response that she wallowed in. She made a mewling sound, her need so intense she dug her fingers like claws into his hot skin.

She loved him so much and in this—for right now, he was absolutely and totally hers.

She pressed her breasts against his chest and rubbed side

to side, the stimulation to her aching peaks along with the way he was bringing their bodies together intimately almost enough to send her over the edge.

Suddenly he dropped into the water with her on top of him, sending hot, scented waves sloshing over the sides of the tub and onto the marble floor. He spread her legs so she straddled him and thrust upward pulling her down with a near-bruising grip on her hips. His aim was perfect and his rigid length speared into her, filling her completely in one powerful thrust.

Her body jerked at the shocking intrusion, but it didn't even sort of hurt.

It felt so good, so right…so tight. They fit each other so absolutely perfectly in this way…how could her body make her imperfect for him in the one way that mattered most?

His mouth tore from hers. "What is it? What's the matter?"

She stared at him, her eyes burning with tears she would never let him see. "Nothing. You feel so incredible inside me," she panted.

"You went stiff."

"It's always a little tight at first."

He smiled, masculine ego glowing from his dark eyes. "Yes, but you like it, no?"

"I love it." *I love you,* she whispered deep in her heart. *Forever.*

"Then let me take you again."

"Yes."

And she did, thrilled by the lack of pain and hoping it would last the entire lovemaking session. She was careful not to take him too deep and he let her control things. She'd often teased him this way in the past and it was highly pleasurable for both of them.

Putting his head back and breathing harshly, his face contorted with pleasure, he said, "You are so good at this."

"And you are incredible."

He went stiff beneath her, his body filled with a tension that had nothing to do with sensual delight. "Then why do you turn me down so often lately?" he asked, his voice edged with dark emotion.

She didn't have an answer...at least not one she was prepared to discuss right now when the pleasure was on the verge of letting her forget everything. So, instead of saying something that might mess that up, she kissed him.

He kissed her back, his mouth quickly taking control and then claiming her lips as if intent on punishment. Only she didn't feel punished. She responded with ferocity of her own and increased the pace of their lovemaking until she felt the pleasure spiral tight inside her and she went through the stratosphere, all rational thought flying from her mind as her body convulsed with the ultimate satisfaction.

He grabbed her hips and thrust upward, once, twice... three times and sent her into a second climax, so close to the first that her lungs seized along with everything else.

He shouted and she felt his warmth inside of her as she took a long shuddering breath into her oxygen-starved lungs before collapsing on top of him.

She kissed his chest. "That was wonderful."

"Yes," he said, his breathing still heavy. "It always is."

"Yes."

"So, why—"

She put her hand over his mouth. "No talking. Just enjoy. Okay?"

He frowned.

"Please," she pleaded.

He nodded, one quick jerk of his head.

She smiled and let her head settle against his chest again. "I wish we could stay like this forever."

"You said no talking."

"So I did." She kissed him again because she couldn't help herself and then relaxed there.

His hands moved from her hips to her back and she cuddled in the circle of his arms, their bodies still connected in the most intimate way possible.

Eventually he carried her to the oversize glass shower stall and they made love again under the cascading spray before washing and then going to bed where she fell asleep as soon as her head hit the pillow.

She woke up alone and buried her face in his pillow, wallowing in Claudio's lingering scent.

The night before had been incredible. He'd woken her sometime in the early hours of the morning and made love to her with such tender gentleness, she had cried when she climaxed. He'd held her afterward, rubbing her back and whispering how much he enjoyed her body and how beautiful she was in Italian.

But after three years, she realized being beautiful to him was not enough. It was not love and could not last forever because outer beauty did not last forever. And outstanding sexual satisfaction could not make up for her inability to give him the one thing he expected from her.

Heirs for the Scorsolini throne.

It was time to tell him the truth.

But when she went downstairs, it was to discover he'd flown out for a meeting in New York. She'd forgotten all about his trip and didn't know if she could wait the three days until his return to settle things between them.

She didn't miss the fact that he'd left without bothering to wake her and kiss her goodbye, either. Somehow, that made everything worse. Maybe because it was a huge indication of the lack of true intimacy in their relationship and any real reliance he had on her.

There wasn't any. They were married, but she was no more necessary to his life than any of his other many employees. If it wasn't for the sex, their relationship would not be any more personal than it was with any of the others, either. And when the sex wasn't on, neither was their relationship. How many business trips had he scheduled during her monthly? Had he ever once asked her to accompany him? No.

She was a convenience to him and she might as well admit it.

But damn it, it hurt.

She needed to be more to him. The only hope for their future was for her to mean something more to him. Which meant there was no hope at all.

Her mobile phone chirped and she scooted up in bed to answer it. When she saw that it was Claudio, her breath caught. She flipped it open. "Hello?"

"Good morning, *bella*."

For some reason that endearment hurt this morning. Wasn't she more than a face and a body to him? Was her value truly determined by her outer looks and her poise as her mother had always insisted it was?

"Good morning, Claudio." She waited expectantly for him to get to the purpose of his phone call.

"I'm on my way to my hotel and wishing you were with me."

Her heart stopped. "Are you really?"

"*Sì*. I do not like when our schedules separate us."

"Then why didn't you ask me to come with you?" she asked, hope uncurling like a slow bud inside her heart.

"You have your obligations. I have mine."

"And do the obligations always come first?"

"They must. It is our duty."

"They don't always for Tomasso and Maggie or Marcello and Danette." But then his brothers were in love with their wives.

One of the things that had hurt the most this past few months was seeing what a Scorsolini prince in love acted like and acknowledging it was nothing like Claudio's behavior toward her.

"My brothers are not in line to be the next ruler of Isole dei Re. They can afford to put duty second on occasion. The country does not depend so heavily on them. And their wives do not have the same requirements put upon you as my wife." He spoke like a teacher reciting a lesson to a student that he had recited many times before.

The practiced patience in his voice was worse than if he'd snapped at her.

"I miss you," she said baldly.

"I have been gone less than a day."

"Are you saying you don't miss me?" she asked, wishing the question did not feel like a razor shredding her insides. So much for him wishing she was there.

"I will miss you tonight."

If he had planned it, he could not have said anything more wounding. "In bed," she said flatly.

"We are good there."

"But nowhere else?" she asked, for once making no effort to hide how much that displeased her.

"Do not be ridiculous. You are my wife, not my concubine. Why would you even ask such a question?"

"Perhaps because that is the only place you deign to miss me."

"I did not say that."

"Excuse me, but you did."

"I did not call you to get into an argument." The frozen tone of his voice came across the phone line loud and clear. "But for the record, if you took what I said to mean such a thing, it did not."

Maybe he didn't know he meant it that way, but he had. The facts spoke for themselves.

"Why *did* you call? We both know it was not merely to say hello. I don't rate those kinds of phone calls from you."

"What is the matter with you? Perhaps that is *exactly* why I called."

She wasn't even remotely convinced. "Not likely."

"I was thinking of you and wanted to hear your voice, all right?" he asked, sounding thoroughly annoyed with her.

Oh. Man. Did he mean it?

Of course he meant it. Claudio never consciously lied, but still she had to ask, "Is that true?"

"I do not make it a habit of lying to you."

"I know you don't. It's one of the things I appreciate most about you."

Her father had lied to her, to her mother, to anyone at all…all for the sake of convenience and had called it diplomacy. But she didn't think that that kind of diplomacy belonged in a family. It was best saved for other politicians, all of whom were expecting it.

"Can you say the same thing?"

Shock coursed through her that he would ask such a thing. "Of course I can. You know I don't lie to you."

"Only perhaps you do not feel withholding information from me is the same as lying?" he asked.

Could he know about her condition? Impossible…she'd been far too careful to keep it a secret. "I don't know what you mean." That at least was no lie, but it was also not the full truth. Perhaps there was more of her father in her than she wanted to admit.

"Are you sure about that?"

"No one tells everything, but that doesn't mean I lie to you," she said, defending a position he did not know why she'd taken. But there was no way she could tell him the news of her infertility over the phone.

"I hope that is true, Therese." He sighed. "I have another call coming in. I have to go."

"All right. Goodbye, Claudio."

"Goodbye, *bella*."

She hung up the phone, but as she got ready for the day and then left her apartments to traverse the grand marbled hallways of the palace, she couldn't stop thinking about what he had said, what she had said and what she hadn't been able to say. She owed him the truth—both about her condition and what she planned to do because of it.

He would be relieved. He had to be.

But a tiny part of her heart hoped against all logic that he wouldn't be. That he might even refuse to let her do the right thing…the only logical thing to do in the circumstances.

Walk away.

"Your Highness…"

Therese looked up from her musings to find her personal

secretary standing in front of her. At one time Ida had worked for her mother, but the year Therese had married, her mom had sacked Ida in order to hire someone else. The other woman was younger and had connections high in the social set Therese's parents were now moving in. Ida had been only too happy to accept Therese's offer of a job.

Ida's loyalty was unwavering, her discretion without equal and her finesse with a schedule second to none. She was the only other person besides Therese's Miami doctor and his assistant who knew about the laparoscopy and the results.

"Your morning appointment is waiting."

"Ida…I have to go to New York."

The older woman barely blinked. "I believe I can clear your schedule. If you could take care of your current appointment, I will have a maid pack for you while I begin clearing your schedule."

"Just like that?"

"There are things you and the prince need to talk about," Ida said kindly. "I'm assuming those things did not get said last night."

Therese shook her head.

"That gives a trip to New York precedence over anything else in your schedule."

"I hope Claudio feels that way."

"Men, even brilliant men, are not always the brightest spark when it comes to relationships."

"Even brilliant men, hmm?"

"Yes." Ida sighed, the sound filled with exasperation. "Sometimes I think it's the really bright ones that are dumbest when it comes to women."

Therese laughed. She thought maybe Ida was right. Look at how stupid King Vincente was about Flavia.

"Just you remember, young lady…a marriage is not all about having children."

Therese smiled disappeared. "My marriage is."

"Don't you believe it."

She wished she shared the older woman's assurance, but she couldn't.

She landed in New York later that evening, her nerves stretched to screaming point. She'd spent the entire flight going over in her head what she was going to say to Claudio, but she couldn't get past the first sally because every time she thought about him agreeing that their marriage should be dissolved, her throat clogged with tears.

She had asked security not to alert her husband to her intention to join him. For some reason, she felt the element of surprise might be on her side. She was informed he was at the hotel preparing for a dinner meeting when her plane landed. It seemed fortuitous and she hoped it boded well for the meeting to come.

Her eyes barely registered the opulence of the oversize suite when security let her inside. She was too busy trying to control her tortured emotions.

Claudio was tying his tie when she walked into the bedroom.

"Hello, *caro*."

His big body jerked, blatant testament to how shocked he was by her presence. Then his head snapped up, his dark eyes zeroing in on her with physical intensity. "*Therese*, what are you doing here?"

"You said you'd like it if I was."

"You are not here because of my phone call this morning." His expression dared her to contradict him…to lie.

"No, I'm not. We need to talk."

"Do we?"

"Yes," she said, trying to ignore the fact that his expression was about as welcoming as an accountant faced with a tax auditor.

"I suppose you have something you have to confess that has weighed on your conscience long enough," he said in a voice that dripped in ice.

She didn't know what triggered his hostility, except maybe that she'd changed her schedule. Claudio didn't like surprises and he had a worse one coming.

"You could put it that way." She couldn't even assure him it was nothing bad because it was.

In a marriage like theirs, it was a death knell and nothing less.

Claudio went back to what he was doing with cold precision. "It will have to wait. I have a dinner meeting."

"Can you cancel it?"

"You mean like you obviously canceled all of your obligations so you could fly up here and have a conversation that surely could have waited the three days it would take me to get home?"

"Yes." She didn't care how he made it sound. That was exactly what she wanted.

"That's not going to happen."

"Would it really be so terrible?"

"Obviously you do not consider it so, but I do not appreciate my wife letting down her obligations and therefore me."

"And are our duties the only thing that matter in our life together?"

"Duty must come first. At one time, I believe you understood this."

"Is that why you married me?"

"You already know it was one of the primary reasons I decided you would suit me well as a wife. Your parents could not have raised you more suitably for the life of a princess if they had been royalty themselves."

That reminder was as unwelcome as it was painful. For she better than anyone knew how carefully her parents had raised her. Her father with the hopes she would pursue a political career and her mother with the desire to live her life's ambitions through her daughter. Neither had ever cared what dreams beat in Therese's heart.

"My appreciation for duty was my main attraction to you...and of course the fact that I was physically compatible with you," she said, long denied hurt coming out as bitterness.

"Would you have expected me to marry a woman who did not understand or fit the role of princess and future queen?"

"Your brothers weren't so worried about suitability when they chose their wives," she reminded him.

"As I said last night, I am not my brothers."

"No, you are the crown prince, which means duty must come first, last and always with you."

"You knew this when we married. It is not something I expect to be raised as an issue of contention now."

"You don't expect anything to be raised as an issue of contention."

"How perceptive of you to realize that." He pulled on his black dinner jacket. "As scintillating as this conversation is, I must go or I will be late."

"Just like that? I fly all the way from Isole dei Re and you walk out on an important conversation because your damn schedule demands it?" How was she going to tell this cold-faced stranger anything, much less the intimate details of her latest doctor's visit?

"Do not swear at me," he said, contriving to sound shocked.

She said a truly foul word. "You mean like that?"

"I do not know what your problem is, but I suggest you get over it. I will be back quite late. If you still feel the need to discuss whatever it is you think is so important, we can talk then."

"And if I don't feel like waiting?"

"You have no choice."

"When have I ever?"

"You made a choice to marry me. No one forced you to speak your vows. If they are chafing now, please remember, you have no one but yourself to blame for your circumstances and I will not tolerate you dismissing your promises or your duty as my wife as easily as you did your duties as a princess this morning."

"They're pretty much the same thing, aren't they?" she asked in a voice filled with angry pain.

"*No*." His gaze seared her. "You have personal obligations to me that have nothing to do with your responsibility to the crown."

He meant sex, she was sure…but he was wrong. That aspect of their marriage was as wrapped up in her role as princess as everything else. Because it was supposed to result in an heir to the throne and it wasn't going to.

"Maybe I'm feeling unsure about all of my obligations right now."

Fury filled Claudio's gaze, but his voice was controlled and even when he spoke. "I suggest you get sure of them by the time I return to the suite tonight."

"And if I don't?" she dared to taunt.

"Then it will be a very unpleasant night for us both, but I warn you…my weapons are and will always be superior to yours."

"You are so damm arrogant, Claudio." She sighed, her anger draining away. "Anyway, don't be so sure my weapons can't best yours because I have an awful feeling they can."

Her condition and infertility because of it was pretty much nuclear bomb strength when it came to the power necessary to destroy their marriage.

He paled.

"I do not have time for this."

He left.

CHAPTER THREE

THERESE heard the outer door to the suite close with a sense of unreality and then sank onto the edge of the bed, her legs feeling like jelly.

He'd never spelled out for her how little she really meant to him before, but his parting shot pretty much summed up their relationship. He didn't have time for her unless she was playing her role of princess wife to perfection or concubine in his bed.

They'd been married three years and not once had she put her feelings ahead of her duty. The one time she did, he let her know in no uncertain terms that he would not tolerate such behavior from her.

Tears burned a slow path down her cheeks.

She didn't have a marriage. She had a business partnership where she was the junior partner all the way. And the primary partner had no interest in or desire to renegotiate terms. She would fulfill her duties, or else. Only the *or else* in this instance was both permanent and painful. And the thing that hurt the most was that she didn't think it was going to bother him at all.

He would just move on to another businesslike marriage after shattering her heart and not even knowing he'd done it.

"Your Highness, would you like me to order you some dinner?" one of the security men asked from the open doorway.

She averted her face so he could not see the tears, then took a breath to steady her voice. "No, thank you."

"If you are not hungry now, I can order later delivery."

Oh, gosh…she could not handle this. She just wanted to be alone. She forced her convulsing throat to speak. "I do not want any dinner, thank you. And, Roberto, could you…" She had to swallow back a sob.

"Your Highness?"

"Could you please shut the door?"

Her answer was the quiet snick of the door latch catching.

She felt her control slip another notch as the nominal privacy of the shut door registered with her emotions. She'd been holding herself in check for so long; forcing herself to bite back the words of love she'd wanted to utter, to hide her distress at the frequent separations from Claudio brought about by their schedules, and for the past several months pretending that the horrific pain of endometriosis did not exist.

At first, she'd convinced herself it was just the period pain made more intense by going off the pill. But then, one night when Claudio had been gone on yet another business trip, she had fainted from the cramps and when she woke up on the bathroom floor in a pool of blood, she'd known she had to find out what was wrong.

She'd gone to see her doctor in the States, a habit she'd developed early in her marriage to protect her privacy. Trips abroad were easy enough to justify in her schedule that she found it quite easy to hide the purpose of her stopovers in Miami.

Her doctor's initial prognosis had been utterly disturbing. He'd thought she was probably suffering from endometriosis, but the only way to tell for sure was to perform a laparoscopy. She thought she could handle it and accepted a prescription for painkillers, only to give in the following month and schedule the outpatient surgery.

She'd gotten the results the day before along with a big bucket of ice water to dash her hopes that she would be one of the lucky ones who wasn't impacted too heavily by the disease. Apparently she'd had it for quite a while, but being on the pill had mitigated its effects. There was major tissue build up on both of her ovaries and even with the surgery to remove it all, her chances of getting pregnant without IVF were less than ten percent. Even with IVF, there were no guarantees.

Those were not the kind of odds Crown Prince Claudio had been counting on when he had her take fertility tests before announcing their engagement. A future king had responsibilities to the throne and one of the most important ones was providing an heir to carry on his lineage. He expected her to be able to do that with one hundred percent success and for all intents and purposes, she was infertile.

After seeing the way the press and the Scorsolini family had reacted to Marcello's supposed sterility, Therese knew there was no chance her proud husband would willingly suffer similar vilification for her sake. And she wouldn't expect him to.

If he loved her, it would be different, but then so much would be. Love was not an emotion that could be faked, nor could it be replaced with a sense of duty.

Claudio might offer to remain married, but his heart wouldn't be in it and she could not live with the knowledge that she was a burden around his neck…a source of humiliation to his royal pride.

A sob snaked up from deep inside her to explode out of her mouth and she had to clamp her hand over her lips to keep the sound from traveling to the other room. Feeling like an old woman, she pushed herself to her feet.

She would take a shower…she could at least have privacy for her tears in there.

Once she'd shut the door, then the door on the shower and turned the water on full blast, she cried herself hoarse. She grieved the loss of her marriage, the loss of her hopes of motherhood and stopped fighting the pain that came from loving a man who did not and never would love her.

She ruthlessly quashed any hope that everything would be okay. Deep in her heart, she knew it would not be. After Claudio's reaction to her unexpected departure from her schedule, she didn't even have the tiniest hope that her marriage could or *should* survive this setback.

And that was destroying her. All along, she had harbored the foolish hope that she was wrong, that somehow they could weather the treatment for her condition and the problems it would bring. She hadn't admitted it to herself because it would have hurt too much, but now that she was faced with the final end to her marriage, she had no choice but to acknowledge the living flicker of hope as it died a painful death.

Claudio could not have made it more obvious he did not love her if he had tried. His every action pointed to the carefully defined roles she played in his life, none of them connected to his emotional needs. Unless she counted sex and even if he did…she didn't.

She'd had such hopes when they married. They would make a family and she would know the love she had never known with her parents at least with the children that would come. She had also hoped that eventually Claudio would come to love her. She had wanted it all and now there was nothing but the dead ashes of a fire that had consumed her for almost three years.

She had wanted to be a mother. She'd wanted it so much. Why had he wanted to wait? Why? It wasn't fair. If she had gotten pregnant right away, the endometriosis might never have even shown up. But "if onlys" were as futile as wishing on the moon, an exercise for small children who still believed the possibilities of life were endless.

She had learned they were far too limited. She'd wanted to give birth to the Scorsolini heir and raise him knowing that love lit his path, not duty, that there was more to life than his position. She'd wanted to rectify the mistakes her parents had made with her. She'd wanted a chance at love, knowing that her children would love her, even if their father could never bring himself to do so.

Hadn't she loved her parents, no matter how much they hurt her? And she would have been a good mother, a truly loving mother. She would never have made her children feel they were nothing more than the sum of what they could do for her.

Falling to her knees, she cried, "God in Heaven, it isn't fair!" The words echoed around her in the shower stall, no one there to answer…or if He did, she did not hear the Heavenly voice.

She covered her face and sobbed, but eventually her

tears had to abate. She'd cried herself dry. She turned off the shower, her throat sore and her eyes almost too puffy to see out of. No way would anyone looking at her now and not know how she'd spent the last hour, but it didn't matter. Claudio wouldn't be back for ages and when he did arrive, she planned to be asleep. She was beyond tired, her emotional reserves used up completely.

She hadn't realized how exhausting her pretense of contentment had become until she gave herself permission to let it go. With aching limbs, she pulled on a nightdress and climbed into the bed, not caring that it was just going on seven o'clock.

Without thought, her hand automatically searched out his side of the bed, but of course it was empty. As it had been on so many nights of their marriage and would be every night once she left New York. A dry sob caught in her throat and she bit it back, but she'd soaked her pillow with silent tears before she managed to slip into a fitful sleep. Her last thought that tears were never ending…

She woke sometime later to the sound of the shower going in the bathroom and light spilling from the cracked door into the bedroom. The digital clock beside the bed read nine o'clock. She blinked, trying to think what that meant. It was earlier than she had expected him, but not so early that she could trick herself into thinking he'd rearranged his time for her.

The shower cut off and a minute later, Claudio strolled into the room, completely naked and drying his hair with a white towel. He leaned over to flick his bedside lamp on the lowest setting, casting his bronzed body in a golden glow.

Her mouth went dry as desire and emotional need spiraled low in her belly. It had no place in the devastation inside her and yet it continued to bloom as if her heart had not been decimated in her chest.

He tossed the towel to the side and looked over at her. He paused when her eyes caught his dark gaze. "You are awake."

"You're back."

"Obviously."

She winced at his sarcasm. "How did your meeting go?"

She didn't really care, but nothing else came to mind and total silence simply did not work right then. Nevertheless, she had no doubts that the meeting had gone exactly as he had wanted it to. He was that kind of man. It took a will of iron with the intelligence of Socrates and Einstein combined to defeat Claudio's plans.

Or a woman's rebellious reproductive system, a voice in her head mocked. *He couldn't battle that, no matter how smart and stubborn he was, could he?* And in all likelihood, he wouldn't want to. It would require her having treatments that may or may not be successful for pregnancy that the press was bound to get wind of.

She couldn't bear the thought of what that would mean and knew he wouldn't tolerate such an intrusion into his life.

"It went much as I expected it to."

"I'm not surprised."

"What do you mean by that?"

"Only that you are very good at getting your own way."

"I am not selfish."

"I didn't say you were."

"What *are* you saying?"

"Nothing."

"Roberto said you did not eat dinner."

"I ate on the plane."

Claudio frowned. "A cup of coffee and two cookies is not dinner."

"It was all I wanted."

"Skipping meals is not healthy."

"One missed dinner is not going to kill me."

"Are you sick?" He asked it so baldly, without the slightest trace of compassionate concern that she winced again. "If you are, you should not be traveling."

"Don't worry, I'm not going to give you the flu, or something. I'm not sick." Not with anything he could catch anyway.

He did not look appreciably cheered by that assurance. "I expected you to be awake when I got back, but you were not."

"I had no way of knowing when that would be."

"It is barely nine o'clock." He said it like he couldn't imagine going to bed this early. And probably, he couldn't. The man needed less sleep than anyone she knew.

If he knew she'd gone to bed as early as seven, he'd be convinced she was ill. She saw no reason to enlighten him. "I was tired."

"But you are not sick?"

"No."

"You are certain?"

"Yes."

"Are you pregnant?" He asked the question with the same lack of emotion he'd asked if she was sick to begin with.

The words skewered her. And there was no sense of anticipation in his features, no warming at the prospect, which hurt just like everything else did right then.

"No. Not pregnant," she forced out of stiff lips.

"You are sure?"

She hadn't started, but she was sure. "I'm positive."

"Then this strange behavior is the result of period hormones?"

No doubt a good portion of what she was feeling and her willingness to act on those feelings *was* caused by hormonal imbalances. "If it pleases you to think so, then yes."

Hormone driven, or not, the knowledge her marriage was over was real. His lack of love for her was fact. Her unpredictable reproductive system was not the stuff fantasies were made of and the pain inside her was a physical ache that made it hard to breathe.

He made an impatient movement. "Nothing about this situation pleases me."

"I am sorry."

"I do not want an apology. I want an explanation. You said you had things you wanted to talk about but I come back to the suite only to find you sleeping."

"Is that a crime?"

"No, but you are making no sense to me right now."

"Heaven forbid I should stop fitting in the slot you've assigned me to in your life."

"I have done nothing to deserve your sarcasm."

"Except refuse to listen to me."

"On your timetable. I am here now. Ready to listen." He spread his hands in an expansive gesture that also served to draw her attention back to his beautiful naked body.

Tears burned the back of her eyes, but maybe they were not as never ending as she had thought because no moisture glazed her vision. She was going to miss him so much and it did not even shame her to admit that part of that missing would be pure physical need going unmet. Because for her, the desire was part and parcel to the love and both would be starved of his presence soon enough.

She sighed, trying to breathe through a very different kind of hurt than what had been consuming her body for months now. "I realized that I was foolish to fly up here to talk to you. Waiting three days won't change anything. I'm not even sure there is a point in having the discussion I wanted to have at all."

Really, she just needed to tell him about her condition and then let him work out the details of the separation and divorce. But after her emotional holocaust in the shower, she didn't have the wherewithal to discuss that with him. Her inner reserves were all gone and she simply couldn't face telling him of her failure as a woman, as a wife, especially in the face of his obvious hostility.

"Why is that?" he asked in a dangerously soft undertone she was too drained to understand. Shouldn't he be relieved she didn't want to get all emotional with him?

"Some things cannot be changed." No matter how much she wanted them to be.

"And what are those things?"

"I'd rather not talk about it right now," she admitted in a voice that sounded dodgy to her own ears.

In a move she did not expect, he came around to her side of the bed at supersonic speed and lifted her right out of it. "That is unfortunate because I do."

She gasped and wrapped her arms around his neck to stop herself from falling. "You can't always have your way."

"That is not a concept I recognize."

"Then it's time you did."

He tightened his hold on her. "Stop playing games and tell me what the hell has you acting so far out of character."

The furious undertone in his voice said his patience was about used up. And the iron-hard glint in his brown eyes said he wasn't giving up until she spilled, either. No matter what she wanted, no matter how hard it might be for her, he would settle for nothing less than full disclosure.

She knew it and finally accepted it. She'd started this thing and she had to finish it, no matter how much she might want to put it off. No matter how deeply she might regret her impulsive decision to come to New York. Tears choked her throat and she knew she couldn't begin tell him about her body's deficiency with even a semblance of emotional detachment. There was only one thing she could say.

And she wasn't even sure how to say it.

Feeling pressured beyond endurance in her current overly emotional state and overwhelmed by the simple sensation of being held in his arms for what she was sure was the last time, she ended up just blurting it out, "We have to divorce."

Eyes filling with inimical rage, he dropped her in an act of such utter repudiation her stomach knotted with pain to add on top of all the other hurt she was feeling. If she hadn't grabbed him for support, she would have fallen flat on her bottom.

But he shook her touch off with disdainful rejection. "*You bitch.*"

She'd never seen him so angry and it scared her silly. "I...I h-have to tell you—"

"You will divorce me over my dead body," he interrupted in a deadly voice.

Her mouth opened, but she couldn't make anything come out. She tried, but no words would issue forth. It all hurt too much. She'd never believed she would have to say those fatal words to him. She would have done anything, given any amount of money...even years from her life not to have had to do so. And yet as horrific as his response was to her demand for divorce, she could not make herself speak the truth that labeled her a total failure as a woman.

He had hurt her too much and there was nothing left inside her of trust for his willingness to spare her emotions.

And the harshness of his reaction confused her…made it harder for her to think, to cope with what needed to be said. She simply had not expected him to respond with such fury. After all, they were in effect discussing the dissolution of what he considered a business contract. Nothing more.

For him. For her, it was the end of everything beautiful in her life.

Unless…maybe their marriage was more important to him than she had thought. Could it be true? Could his reaction mean he cared after all? Inside her, her heart leaped…*could she have misread him from the beginning?* All of the evidence she had compiled in her own mind pointed to the fact that she did not matter to him on a personal level, not for who she was—the person inside who craved his love so ardently.

But had she misread it all? She didn't see how she could have. No. She shook her head. It simply wasn't possible. Maybe she could have misread a misspoken phrase here and there, but not an entire lifestyle that continuously pointed out how small a role she played in his life. And nothing could be more convincing than her knowledge of how a Scorsolini male acted in love, because she'd seen it in his younger brothers.

Yet, he was behaving as if the end of their marriage really mattered to him. "Why are you so angry?" she asked in an almost whisper, trying not to let hope build again.

He looked at her in incredulous fury. "You have just told me you want a divorce and you ask me this?"

"Yes." His answer meant so much, she was trembling with fear and anticipation of what it might be.

"I had certain requirements when looking for a wife, you knew this," he gritted from between clenched teeth.

"Y-yes." It was not sounding promising.

"One of those requirements was a wife who understood and accepted the importance of duty and sacrificing one's personal happiness for the sake of what is best for Isole dei Re."

"Were you sacrificing your personal happiness to marry me?" she asked painfully.

She'd always wondered if he'd wanted a different woman, even a different kind of woman. One who was more vivacious and exciting. A woman who would not necessarily make the ideal princess, but who would have matched the fiery passion that bubbled beneath the solid surface of his duty.

"Happiness never came into it one way or the other."

Hurt lancing through her, she said, "It did for me. I was happy to marry you. I wanted you more than I could imagine wanting anyone else."

For some reason, her words made him flinch. "But now you *want* a divorce. Your desire for me, this happiness you mention was short-lived. It did not last even three full years. And yet what did I withhold from you that I promised to give you?"

"Nothing." He had withheld nothing except his love and that had never been on offer as part of their bargain.

"So, you will accept that I have not reneged on my side of our marriage bargain?"

"Yes, I accept it."

"You accept also that you married me with the understanding that it was for a lifetime?"

"Yes, of course."

He moved to tower over her, his fury all the more powerful because he stood there magnificently naked and not in the least bit ashamed of it. "Then you must also accept that I will not allow you to renege on the lifetime commitment you made to me."

"Sometimes things happen that make it impossible to keep a bargain." Even in his vaunted world of business.

"Not in our marriage, they do not."

"They do. They have. I have…" Her throat closed over. She had to say it, but it hurt more than she'd ever expected to say the words out loud.

"Do not say it," he barked. "I will never let you go."

She stared at him. "You don't mean that," she gasped out.

He spun away from her, his whole being vibrating with a palpable rage she still did not understand.

"You will not walk away from our marriage and make me the second sovereign in Scorsolini history to be divorced. Do you understand me?" he bit out in a voice as sharp and frozen as an icicle shard. "I will not allow you to make me a laughingstock amidst my peers and subjects."

Finally she understood. It wasn't his heart being impacted here, it was his pride. He didn't need her…only a whole marriage, because he did not want to look like a fool. Anger welled from deep in her soul. She'd agonized over the prospect of losing him, but all he cared about was how he appeared to the international community.

"Is that all that matters to you? That people might compare you to your father?"

He spun back to face her, his expression a mask of stone. "My father broke his marriage promises. I did not break mine. I will not let you divorce me simply because you want to break yours...*or have already done so.*"

The emphasis he gave on the last bit sent chills down her spine and she had to swallow before she answered. "I don't have a choice."

He said a word that made her flinch. "We all have choices, you are making bad ones. You promised me an heir to succeed me on the throne. What about that?" he asked with pure derision.

She almost choked on the pain his demand evoked. She could not give him that heir and his wording reiterated the fact that that alone was her primary requirement as his wife. "I didn't want it to be this way. Please, believe me."

But he looked like he'd rather strangle her than believe her. Even knowing he would never, ever physically hurt her, she found herself stepping backward and away from him.

If possible, his jaw went more rigid.

A knock sounded on the door and she jumped.

"Go away," Claudio barked out.

She'd never heard him use that tone and she knew if she had been the one on the other side of the door, she would have listened, but after a brief pause another knock sounded again. "Your Highness, it is *extremely urgent.*"

Claudio said something else vicious under his breath in Italian. Then he grabbed his robe and put the black garment on with jerky movements before stalking over to the door and yanking it open. *"What?"*

She could not make out what the security man said, but she heard the ugly curse that spit forth from her husband's mouth as his body jerked as if receiving a blow.

"Claudio…what is it?" she asked.

But he just shook his head and opened the door wider, obviously planning to leave the room. He stopped on the threshold and looked back over his shoulder, his expression feral. "This is not finished."

The security man gave Claudio a worried look and her a curious one before following his employer to the other room. Therese did not know what to make of either her confrontation with Claudio or what had interrupted it.

And for the second time that night, she stood stock-still in the middle of the bedroom reeling from unenviable emotions after he walked out on her. She did not wonder what could be more important than the end of their marriage because it could be just about anything, she thought sadly. However, she acknowledged that whatever it was, it had to have been singularly important for security to interrupt Claudio against his express wishes.

She walked across the room, feeling like she'd been through World War III and was not quite sure if she was a survivor or not. Yet neither she nor Claudio had actually ever raised their voices. He was incredibly good with undertones, though. No one listening could have doubted how furious he was with her, or how determined he was to keep his marriage for the sake of appearances.

She rubbed her eyes with thumb and forefinger, feeling tired despite the fact she'd woken from what amounted to a longish evening nap and that it still wasn't all that late. She'd been so stupid to think that she meant anything to Claudio on a personal level. His whole reason for wanting to stay married to her had to do with him not being the second Scorsolini sovereign in history to be divorced by his wife.

In his eyes, she had no right or reason to make a

mockery of him in that way. He'd gone to pains to marry a woman who would not do just that very thing. She remembered when he told her about his stepmother divorcing his father.

Therese had been shocked the woman had gone to such extremes. She'd grown up around couples who had stayed married in similar circumstances for the sake of political unity. She realized now why Claudio had liked that reaction so much. Although he'd been absolutely committed to fidelity, saying it was one sin he would find impossible to forgive in either himself or her, he had liked knowing she had been trained to believe that marriage vows were to last a lifetime despite personal differences. Duty came first, last and always.

Which was exactly why she'd asked for a divorce, but he didn't know that. Once he did, he would grasp for an end to their marriage grabbing a divorce with both hands.

Therese slowly sank into one of the armchairs in the corner, weariness overcoming her.

She could not have handled the confrontation with him worse if she had tried. Instead of telling him of her condition and almost certain infertility, she had told him they had to divorce. While that might well be true, it *was not* the first thing she should have said to him.

He thought she'd brought up divorce because she wanted one, which could not be farther from the truth, but duty dictated she let go of the man she loved for both his greater good and that of his country. His final words before they were interrupted had said it all. He needed heirs. She could not guarantee providing them. The odds of conceiving were not good enough for a future king.

Those facts left her dreams in shambles around her feet.

Why was life so hard? What had she done wrong to bring this kind of misery on herself? Her doctor had said it wasn't personal, that endometriosis happened to lots and lots of women, but it felt personal to her.

Especially when the results of the disease were ripping her life apart into big jagged patches of pain and more pain.

And that was her only excuse for the way she'd handled the news. She was hurting so much, her usual diplomacy had completely deserted her. Her father would be so ashamed, but then he'd never been overly impressed with her to begin with.

In his eyes, she'd always had two strikes against her… she'd been born female and she had no interest in politics. No matter how pleased Mother had been, the fact that Therese had ended up married to a crown prince meant nothing to her father. He would have been happier if she had gone to the right schools, made friends with the right people and pursued American politics. Then she would have been of benefit to *him*.

Regardless of Claudio's influence in world politics, she could not personally significantly benefit her father who had moved on to a diplomatic position in South America. He therefore considered her useless to him and let her know it in all the subtle ways he had been employing since her childhood.

Psychologists said that women often married men like their fathers and she'd been determined not to. She had always believed that she had succeeded in marrying a man very different, but now she realized she'd done exactly what she'd sworn not to. She'd married a man who was no more enamored of her person than her father was.

Looking back over almost three years of marriage, she

saw that Claudio employed a subtle means of letting her
know the insignificance of her place in his life as well. She
simply hadn't seen the road signs for what they were because she so desperately wanted them to say something
else. Because he had needed her in the most basic ways—
sexually and as an adjunct to his position—she had believed he had more feelings for her than her dad did.

She couldn't even blame him for deceiving her, the
delusion had been entirely self-perpetuating. But acknowledging that did not make the pain of realization any less.

Talk about being an idiot. She had that role down to an
art and admitting it hurt almost as much as Claudio's rejection.

And his attitude had been nothing less than that. He
wanted to keep their marriage intact, but only for the sake
of his own pride and for the baby he expected her to give
him. Not because he wanted to keep her as his wife. Not
because she meant anything to him.

She shivered, her entire body shaking violently and she
realized she was very cold. It was a chill that came from deep
inside, but nevertheless she got up and pulled the blanket
from the bed to wrap up in as if it might help. It didn't.

Feeling so torn apart standing was not an option, she sat
back down in the armchair…and waited.

Claudio had said it was not over and as much as she had
no desire to continue their confrontation, she had no doubt
that was exactly what would happen when he came back.
And no matter how much it might hurt to give, or how
angry his pride filled responses made her…she owed him
an explanation.

She didn't know how long she sat there, thoughts skit-
tering through her brain. It could have been a few minutes,

or as long as an hour, but at some point he came back into the room, his expression one she had never seen on his face before.

"Get dressed."

CHAPTER FOUR

"WHAT? Why?" Was he kicking her out of the suite because she'd asked for a divorce? No, that made no sense.

"We have to fly back to Lo Paradiso immediately."

She jumped up from the chair, holding the blanket tight around her like a shield. "Is something wrong?"

"My father had a heart attack."

"*No.*" Not King Vincente. "How bad is he?"

"He is stable, but requires a bypass surgery. He is in the hospital," Claudio gritted out, his eyes accusing. "He is alone, without any family around him because you saw fit to fly up here for no good reason."

"Where is your brother?"

"On his way now that I have called him. Papa refused to have him called and allowed me to be contacted only after he had stabilized. Had you been there, this would never have happened."

She gasped. "You cannot blame me for him having a heart attack."

"No, but had you been there, you would have contacted my brothers and myself despite my father's wishes. He could not have ordered you like a servant."

"Are you sure about that?" Perhaps the king would not

have ordered her compliance like that of an employee, but she cared for him and might well have acquiesced for the sake of his stress levels.

But then she acknowledged, she would have somehow managed to do what she thought was best...which would probably have been to call Claudio. She, and the rest of the family, were used to relying on him in a crisis. Indeed, her first reaction when she had started having pain in her lower abdomen had been to tell Claudio, to ask for his help dealing with it.

She had decided against that course of action out of a need to protect him.

"Yes, I am certain. You would have contacted me, even if Papa had not known you had done it," Claudio said, showing he knew her well in almost every way but the one that counted most to her.

He did not know of her love for him and could not care less about its existence, she painfully admitted to herself.

"You have been contacted now," she pointed out.

"What if he had died? What if it is worse than he told me that it is?"

"I could not have controlled either of those outcomes and I have no doubt you have spoken to the doctor already and know exactly the extent of your father's illness."

"I have and it is not good. You should have been there," he repeated as if that betrayal was as bad as her request for a dissolution to their marriage.

"You're not being fair. You know I felt I had to come. I needed to talk you."

"About breaking your promises to me. And yet you had already decided before I returned to the hotel suite tonight that the discussion could wait. What was so imperative was not really that important to you at all. You left on a selfish whim and my father paid because of it. I made a huge miscalculation when I asked you to marry me," he said in a final slash of derision.

However, she was too inured by her own anger at his reaction to the news of his father's illness to experience the pain his words would have caused a few short hours ago. "I can see how you might think that way," she said with a sigh. "But there are things I still have to tell you."

"I do not want to hear them."

"You need to."

The disdain in his expression said it all. He was listening to her explanations when hell froze over. "I am leaving here in ten minutes. If you wish to go with me, be dressed."

Therese spent the first two hours of the flight between New York and Lo Paradiso simmering with anger. She'd taken a seat as far away from him as possible when they boarded the plane and hadn't even cared when he showed every sign of being content with that fact. A one word description of his behavior came to mine and it was anything but complimentary.

When had she ever given Claudio cause to believe that she was flighty or selfish? She had fulfilled her duty as princess, dismissing her personal needs time and again, but apparently two years as the perfect diplomat's daughter and political ally had gone up in smoke with one act he did not approve of.

Didn't she, as his wife, deserve even a little understanding in that regard? But he'd made it clear…she was a princess, first, last and always to him. Her role of wife was always overshadowed by her primary role as his future queen. The knowledge shredded what was left of her feminine ego.

She had shown the temerity to reorganize her schedule for something she felt was important and he had gone ballistic. Not only that, he just assumed that her reasons for saying they needed to divorce had to be spurious and selfish ones. Why? She had given him everything she had to give as his wife, even if he had not realized it. When had she ever made any choice related to him out of selfishness? Even her decision to marry him had been made with the knowledge that she could be the kind of wife he wanted.

She had loved him, but she would not have married him knowing he did not love her if she had believed she would not be the right kind of wife for him. Looking back at how much she had agonized over what was best for him and how little time she had spent worrying on her own behalf, she wondered if she was some kind of masochist or a real idiot, or both.

But then she'd spent her whole life trying to please other people. First her parents, each of whom had a different agenda for her life. She'd fulfilled her mother's because it had seemed the only one she had a chance at succeeding at.

Mother had said time and again that Therese's beauty and poise were her greatest assets, that she was to play those assets carefully. That had been easy to do. The physical beauty was a gift of Providence and the poise was something that no diplomat's daughter could survive her school years without.

Those attributes had won Claudio's attention, but even her perfect manners and political savvy added in had not been enough to sway him toward the marriage vote. He'd wanted to be sure she would not disappoint him in bed and had tested her on that score.

She remembered Maggie saying Tomasso had done the same thing. Not in those exact words, of course, but she'd known what the other woman meant. After all, Therese knew these Scorsolini men. She'd been shocked by Tomasso's behavior only because it had been so obvious to her from the beginning that he really cared about Maggie.

He loved her and no one in the family could doubt that fact. Not now. Not ever, in her opinion.

But Claudio did not and had not loved Therese when he had been courting her with an eye for marriage. He'd kissed her and touched her with searing passion, evoking a response that she had learned to accept, but which had at first shocked and terrified her. To be so at mercy to her body's desires had gone against her need for control and the way she had been raised to suppress any deep emotion.

Truthfully she would probably never have allowed her love for Claudio to bloom fully if he had not evoked her latent sensuality. It had broken through her every emotional barrier and laid her heart bare to his influence.

Now she would pay the price for her weakness.

Vulnerability always came with a cost. Hadn't her father told her that time and again, and her mother…though in different words? Yet, she'd been powerless to stop herself falling in love with the prince who had a heart made of stone.

The cost of that love was her own shattered heart.

Learning of King Vincente's illness had added another level of pain to the maelstrom of hurt inside of her. She loved her father-in-law in a way she'd never been free to care for her own father. But then King Vincente had accepted her as her father had not. He admired her feminine strength and told her so. He enjoyed her company and told her that as well.

He commented on his son's dedication to duty in less than complimentary ways when he thought she was being neglected. He had been her ally for three years and if she lost him to death, it would tear her apart. It would also mean her husband's need for an heir would be even greater.

Claudio had said the older man was stable, but she knew how unpredictable a heart condition could be. And no one had even known that King Vincente had suffered from one. As unfair as she'd felt Claudio's accusations about her behavior had been, if she had known her father-in-law's health was at risk, she *would* have waited for her husband's return from New York to talk about their marriage.

Because she cared too much for King Vincente, who was a better father to her than her blood relative to have ever allowed for the possibility that he might end up alone in a hospital room worried for his life.

Her own fears in that regard were enough to make her heart quake. On top of that, she was still reeling from the way Claudio had smashed her every hope that she meant anything more to him than a body in his bed and a political sidekick of the necessary sex.

She honestly did not think she could stand an ongoing war of silent hostility with her husband in addition to everything else. Though once she explained about her endometriosis at least that would end. He might be bitterly disappointed. He might even see her as a complete feminine failure, as she did herself, but he would no longer be furious with her.

Her own anger said she should not care, but her heart was too bloody from recent wounds to withstand much more and she was smart enough to realize it. Besides, it was entirely possible she would not be able to hide her physical agony from the endometriosis when her monthly came.

At least if she told him about it now, she would not have to deal with revelations during a time she was least up to doing so. Every month got worse and until she had the surgery, it would continue to do so. While he might not like hearing the truth, it couldn't be worse than his belief that she was selfishly letting him down.

She moved to sit beside him, anger and the need for honesty between them still at war inside of her. "Claudio."

He looked at her, his dark eyes winter-cold. "What?"

Remember, diplomacy and tact, she told herself. "I don't want to add to the burden of worry you are dealing with King Vincente, but—"

"Then do not."

"What?" she asked, not having expected to be cut off like that. After all, despite the way he'd been acting earlier, he'd been trained in diplomacy since infancy, too.

"You are about to tell me why you want a divorce, are you not?"

"Yes."

"Do not."

"But I need to."

"I do not wish to hear it."

"But—"

"You can have your divorce, Therese, but not until my father's health is stable enough to withstand news that his treasured daughter-in-law has feet of clay. Until that point, we will continue the facade of our marriage. *Capice?*"

"No, not really. I don't understand at all, actually," she admitted, reeling for the third time that night at a totally unexpected reaction from him. It was as if he had become a completely different man to the one she had thought she married. "I thought you said our marriage would end over your dead body."

"I have changed my mind."

"I can see that, but why?"

"You are not the only one who has grown bored with the setup, but I would have done nothing about it which I am sure you think makes me a fool for duty."

And she had thought she had grown inured to more pain. What a joke. She felt like her heart was being ripped right out of her chest. "I never said I was bored."

"But I am." He flicked his hand in a throwaway gesture that implied their marriage meant that little to him. "The truth is, I am only too happy to give you a divorce, but as I said…it will have to wait on my father's health. You can live with that limitation, I imagine?"

"You *want* a divorce?" she asked, that portion of his words the only ones that registered with any real impact.

This was worse than any scenario she could have predicted. She'd thought it was very possible he might accept her solution with an equanimity that would hurt, but she had never envisioned he would actually welcome it. That he had grown *bored* being married to her.

"You are beautiful, Therese, but a man needs something more than a pretty face and impeccable table manners to ease the prospect of an entire lifetime together. Once you started turning me down in the bedroom, your stock in my life dropped dangerously low. As I said, I would have stuck it out because once I make a promise, I keep it. But I will not fight for a marriage I do not actually want."

"You don't want to be married to me?" she asked faintly, needing him to verify his words.

"Why so surprised? You feel the same way."

"I…do?" she asked stupidly, her brain having ceased to function on an analytical level.

"And you did not even have the strength of character to stick it out," he said, treating her words like a confirmation rather than a question. "Funny, I always thought there was more to you than that, but I will not pretend grief I do not feel."

"But earlier…"

"I allowed my pride to dictate my words. Certainly I was not reacting to what I really wanted."

Feeling sick to her stomach from some very real grief, Therese lurched up from her seat. "Then, I guess there is nothing left to say."

"Nothing that I could want to hear, no."

She nodded jerkily, amazed on one level at how much agony the human heart could withstand without ceasing to beat and simply hemorrhaging internally from that pain on another.

Claudio watched his wife stumble down the aisle back to her original seat and wanted to hit something. Damn it, why did she have to look so distraught? She was the one who had asked for a divorce. She was the one who had found someone else.

And she'd wanted to tell him about it. As if hearing the details could somehow make her infidelity all right.

She was probably going to tell him that she had fallen in love, that she couldn't help herself. He'd heard that line used before by friends and acquaintances in the world he moved within. But rarely did even the love vote move those people in positions of major political impact to divorce.

He had understood his stepmother's need to leave his

father, but he'd never understood her going so far as to get a divorce. It wasn't as if she had ever remarried…and one time early on he'd overheard her tell someone she probably never would. So, why get a divorce, why drag the royal family's name through the mud.

For a principle?

He'd been so damn sure Therese would never do anything so rash, but he had not accounted for her finding someone else.

Perhaps arrogantly, he had assumed he was enough for her both in and out of bed. He had been wrong. So why was she acting like his words devastated her?

He'd said them to save face. They'd come bursting out, totally unexpected, when he'd realized she was about to tell him all about the other man. He wasn't proud of lying. He was an honest man and that shamed him, but he would not unspeak the words if he could.

His pride had been lacerated by her request for a divorce and the subsequent realization that his every niggling fear about her lack of sexual interest and ditzy woolgathering had been justified. She had found someone else and she wanted to divorce him, Principe Claudio Scorsolini, for this other man.

There was no other explanation possible for the night's revelations.

The knowledge made him furious enough to want to kill, but it wasn't her he wanted to hurt. It was the man who had lured his gentle wife to a passion that had obviously surpassed what they found together.

Claudio could barely believe that was possible.

The biggest lie he had told Therese was that he had grown bored with her. He continued to crave her body, even with her lack of recent sexual availability. In fact, it had challenged him as much as they had frustrated him. It was the natural predator in him, but having her move away had drawn him inexorably into chasing her.

The knowledge that he had planned seductions and had put so much effort into claiming her body when she had been pining for someone else made him sick with anger. Even so, he could not believe he had said what he did to her. Not because he wasn't capable of being as ruthless as any of his ancestors who had settled Isole dei Re, but because the words had been so far from the truth. He was shocked he had come up with that line of defense.

Their marriage had never been only about the sex, though it had been a big issue for him. For what man wouldn't it be? But she'd believed him. Which said what about how she saw him? He had been nothing more to her than a body in her bed and a way to fulfill her mother's ambitious social climbing nature.

So who was the new guy? Not a nobody that was for sure. An American. That would make sense of her frequent trips to the States. It shouldn't be too hard for his private investigator Hawk to find a name. For some reason, the idea of getting details on his own did not grind in his gut like broken glass like the thought of having her tell him did. Maybe because he felt in control when he was the one garnering the information.

What Claudio would do with that data once he got hold of it, he was not sure.

The desire for revenge was a bloodlust inside him.

Would he ruin the other man? Would he do anything to prevent the chances of Therese finding happiness with him? All he had to do was refuse the divorce. It was no easy thing to end a marriage to a member of the royal family of Isole dei Re.

Flavia had only succeeded with his father because the marriage had taken place in Italy, and even in that case because he had not contested the divorce or denied her charge of infidelity. She had no physical evidence to make a case with, but Papa had felt so much guilt over letting down his own high moral standards, he had let his wife walk away.

Claudio did not know if he had the same fortitude. He had told Therese that he would not cling to a relationship he did not want. That was truth…but it was not true that he did not want his marriage. He didn't know if he could touch her again, knowing her body had belonged to another man, but he did not know if he could let her go, either.

And the knowledge galled him, making him feel even more vicious than learning of her unfaithfulness.

They arrived in Lo Paradiso sometime after one in the morning and went directly to the hospital.

Therese had tried to doze on the plane, but she'd found it impossible to sleep with her thoughts careening from the shock of Claudio's expressed desire for a divorce and King Vincente's heart attack. She had believed that nothing could be worse than learning she had endometriosis with a high chance of total infertility.

She had been wrong. Finding out she had no option but to let Claudio go had hurt, but discovering he wanted out… that he was bored with her had destroyed her. She no longer had any doubts about whether or not she was a survivor of their private war. She knew she had not survived, that her heart was dead inside her.

Only if it was dead, why did it still hurt so much?

When they arrived at the hospital, Claudio grabbed her arm to stop her from stepping out of the limousine. "Therese…"

She didn't look at him. She couldn't. "What?"

"My family is under enough stress right now."

"Yes." So was she, but he'd made it painfully clear he didn't care about that.

She'd had the audacity to ask for a divorce and that made her persona non grata where he was concerned.

"I do not want them further distressed by news of our imminent breakup."

Did he have to put it that way, as if he couldn't wait to be rid of her? "Of course."

"I expect you to behave as you always have toward me."

"I'm sure we will have no trouble maintaining the status quo." She glared at him. "It's not as if we have a marriage like your brothers. No one expects us to be affectionate."

She shook his hand off with an angry jerk and stepped out of the car, her public mask firmly in place. Then, showing that she had indeed been raised by a mother who had drilled her to the point where she had once sat out the whole second half of a girls basketball game in the sixth grade with a broken ankle rather than cry in public and let the coach know the extent of her injury, she waited for Claudio so she could walk with him into the hospital.

It was expected of her. She would do her part to display the outward appearance of solidarity. She directed her gaze straight ahead, her body only a few inches from his, but it might as well have been a mile.

How many times had she walked beside him and wished he would put his arm around her or take her hand…to show her in some way that he felt the connection between them?

But he never did. It made her furious with herself, but she wished for that physical support even more right now.

She had no idea what they would find inside that hospital and she was scared, her heart bleeding and battered from all sides.

They walked toward the building through a barrage of noisy reporters and flashing cameras.

One man broke through the security barrier and got right into her face. "What will it mean to you if King Vincente dies, Princess Therese? Are you looking forward to being queen?"

She put her hand up and averted her face, but her feet faltered and she had to force herself to keep moving. The insensitivity of the question shouldn't have surprised her. She knew how intrusive the press could be, but she was in no way up to handling that thoughtlessness right now. She did her best to hide it, but she flinched when another reporter got close with a flashing camera.

Suddenly Claudio's big body was there, shielding her from the reporters, his arm strong around her shoulders and his voice barking orders at the security team to do a better job at keeping the paparazzi away.

Despite feeling like she was leaning on the enemy, she turned into the comfort his human shield offered and let him lead her past the clamoring reporters and continuously flashing camera bulbs. She couldn't help thinking it would be like this, or worse if the press got wind of her inability to get pregnant without IVF. What kind of rotten questions and accusations would they throw at her and Claudio then?

It didn't bear thinking about. Not if she wanted to maintain her sanity in the face of her fear for King Vincente's health.

Once they were inside the hospital and the solid steel door had closed behind them, Claudio let her go as if he could not stand being close to her for another second.

They walked down the hospital hallways in silence. The head of the hospital himself came to meet them and lead them to the waiting area designated for King Vincente's family. He and Claudio talked, but when she realized he was saying nothing she hadn't heard before about her father-in-law's condition, she tuned the two men out.

Somewhere within these quiet walls, her father-in-law lay in a bed fighting for his life. Stabilized, or not, his condition was what could hardly be termed safe if a bypass surgery was necessary. She'd read of people, perfectly healthy people dying of a second heart attack before the surgery could be performed. She could only give thanks that the first one had not killed the country's ruler.

CHAPTER FIVE

MAGGIE came rushing to Therese the moment she and Claudio walked through the archway that led to the waiting room.

The other woman took one look at her and grabbed Therese, hugging her hard. "It's going to be all right. He needs a bypass as I'm sure you know, but he's a strong man. He'll be fine."

Therese let her sister-in-law hold her, pathetically grateful for the human contact that was not motivated by a need to put on a facade for the press. "I don't know what I'll do if he dies," she whispered.

She hadn't meant to say the words and shocked herself silly doing so. She was so used to protecting her feelings, it was second nature, but her emotions were too close to the surface to be completely hidden.

"He won't die, sweetie. Don't talk that way." Maggie patted Therese's back like she was comforting a child and she felt tears slide into her eyes.

She could not remember the last time someone had acknowledged she had feelings. Had touched her to comfort her. Certainly not Claudio. He acted as if her heart was made of iron ore and twice as hard as it should be.

Her parents had never even comforted her as a child. She was supposed to hide her every fear and never admit to pain. Hence the basketball game that had led to a week in traction as payment for the folly of not expressing her pain in any way.

She pulled away from Maggie, knowing that if she didn't, the other woman's compassion would be her undoing. "Can we see him?"

"Tomasso is with him now. He's sleeping, but you can look in on him." She bit her lip. "He looks pale, but he's doing fine. Really."

Therese nodded and then turned to go to King Vincente's room, not waiting to see if Claudio followed. He did, the presence of his tall frame beside her obvious to her senses even though he was not in her line of sight and was walking as silently as a Black Ops agent. There was a connection between them that she doubted divorce and the separation of an ocean and a continent could even sever…on her side anyway.

She pushed the door open to the room, quietly stepping inside.

A dim light was on behind the bed and the king lay, unmoving, his normally bronzed features the color of flour paste except for the dark, bruising circles under his eyes.

"He looks so weak." Claudio's voice from right beside her was hoarse with emotion.

"Yes, but he will be fine," Tomasso said from nearby.

And Therese found herself praying, *Please, Lord, let him be fine*.

Tomasso moved to stand beside his brother and whisper, "You must have gotten an immediate takeoff slot at the airport to get here so quickly."

Claudio shrugged. "It was necessary."

"They have scheduled the surgery for tomorrow morning."

"Marcello and Danette should be here by then."

"Yes. Flavia as well."

"She is coming?"

"Danette called her with the news as soon as she heard and Flavia wanted to fly out with them."

"Will Danette be all right on the long flight?" Claudio asked with genuine concern.

Envy that made Therese feel small and mean twinged through her.

Tomasso smiled, though it wasn't up to his usual wattage. "According to Marcello, she insists that she is pregnant, not ill. Maggie says the same."

"Maggie is certainly ill with her pregnancy. I am surprised you let her fly over."

Tomasso sighed, his expression a mix of emotions that hurt Therese to see because it was so obvious his wife's distress truly mattered to him. "There was no stopping her, but I wish to take her back to the palace for some rest soon."

"Yes." Claudio moved a step closer to his father's bed and reached out to touch the older man's arm. "It is a good thing Danette's morning sickness is not so acute."

They were so patently not the words he was thinking that Therese felt a sudden constriction in her throat.

"He is going to be fine. Believe it, Claudio," Tomasso said, showing he was not fooled by his brother's comment, either.

Claudio said nothing, his attention focused entirely on his father's still form in the bed.

Tomasso patted his brother on the shoulder and left the room.

Therese moved to stand beside Claudio and laid her

hand against King Vincente's cheek. It was warm to the touch and that gave her comfort. No matter how pale he looked, his heart was pumping life's blood through his body. They stood that way for few minutes, both of them touching the man in the bed, but not touching each other.

Then Therese dropped her hand from King Vincente's face and moved to the other side of the room to pray, her pleas that went Heavenward filled with an uncertain faith. Tomasso returned and whispered something to Claudio. Claudio nodded and said something back and the other man left again.

He caught her gaze. "Tomasso and Maggie are going back to the palace. He wants her to rest and she will not go without him."

"I'm glad he's willing to go then."

"I told him you would go as well."

"I would rather stay here."

"That is my place."

"It is mine, too."

"Not after tonight."

She felt like he'd slapped her. "I love King Vincente. You know that. I want to stay here with you."

"You need your rest," Claudio replied, about as movable as a rock wall.

"I won't sleep. I couldn't."

"Do not be a fool, child. Go home and come back in the morning." The raspy voice came from the bed and Therese's knees almost buckled when she heard it.

She crossed the floor in a rush and took the hand that did not have an IV in it in her own. "King Vincente…"

"How many times…" He paused, taking a couple of shallow breaths. "Told you to call me Papa."

"I—"

"Surely that is not too much to ask," Claudio said in a controlled voice she knew masked an anger he did not want his father to guess at.

She'd never felt comfortable calling the older man Papa, but now even more than before…it would feel wrong. Soon she would be gone from their family completely.

Yet, how could she deny him such a simple request? The answer was: she couldn't. "I'm sorry, Papa, but I want to stay with you."

"You need your rest."

"I need to stay with you."

"Do not argue with him, he is sick."

"I know that, but I also know you're only bringing it up to get your own way," she accused her stubborn husband.

King Vincente laughed weakly, his blue eyes dulled by fatigue. "That is my daughter-in-law. She is a perfect match for my son."

The words hurt because according to Claudio, she was no match at all, but Therese forced a smile. "Please, won't you let me stay with you?"

"There are things my son and I must discuss. Just in case. I will not rest afterward if I am worried about you not getting your rest."

"Don't talk like you are going to die, *please*."

"We must all face death sooner, or later, child."

"But I want it to be later. Tomasso said you will be fine. The doctors said so."

The king shrugged, the casually confident movement at odds with his frail appearance. "The surgery has a very high success rate, but there is always a risk in things like this. It will be as God wills."

"I don't believe it is your time."

"Neither do I, *cara,* but it would be remiss of me not to settle last minute issues with my heir."

Therese looked to Claudio. She did not know why. He was no longer her champion…if he ever had been. Certainly she could not expect any sort of comfort from that direction, but she'd gotten used to relying on him.

Their eyes met and his dark gaze held…nothing. She blinked and turned her head, unable to deal with that as she all at once realized that while their marriage had not been the love match of the century, there had been intimacy. She recognized it only now that it was gone.

Always before when their gazes met, she had seen a recognition of herself and her place in his life in his eyes. To see nothing of the kind now made her realize that perhaps there had been more to her marriage than she had thought, but whatever there had been—it was gone now.

"Go home and rest. I will it," King Vincente said, managing to sound arrogant and in charge even in his weakened state.

She had no trouble seeing how he had kept news of his heart attack from his sons until he desired it to reach them.

"I will leave," she said, knowing he would take the words for acquiescence. But she'd lived enough years around politicians to know how to appear to make a promise without doing anything of the kind.

She would leave…the hospital room.

"Good."

She leaned down and kissed both his cheeks. "Be well, Papa. For all our sakes."

"I will do my best."

She forced another smile. "I'm sure you will."

She could not make herself meet Claudio's gaze again. "See you later," she said in his direction and walked from the room.

She went directly to the waiting room where she knew she would find the others and she sent Tomasso and Maggie on their way. Maggie was dead on her feet and it didn't take much persuasion to get Tomasso to leave so his pregnant wife could be put to bed.

Therese took up residence in the waiting room, having the small comfort that if King Vincente took a turn for the worse, this time she would be on the spot. She curled up on the sofa and watched the television sightlessly as it created a sort of white noise to the background of her unhappy thoughts.

She woke up to the sound of voices. Claudio, his brother Marcello, his wife Danette and Flavia were talking in hushed tones as if trying not to wake her.

Therese sat up. A suit jacket that had been placed over her like a blanket fell off one shoulder. Claudio's scent and warmth from his coat surrounded her, comforting her when it should do anything but in the current situation. He must have found her here earlier and covered her.

He turned to face her, even though she'd made no sound. His face was an impenetrable mask. "You did not go back to the palace."

"I never said I would."

"You said you would leave."

"I did." She looked away from his regard, no more capable of dealing with this new remote Claudio than she had been earlier. "The hospital room."

"But not the hospital."

"No."

"Why not?"

"I wanted to be here in case something else happened."

"You knew Papa and I assumed you would leave with Tomasso."

She shrugged, dislodging the suit coat further. "I am not responsible for assumptions brought about by two men's arrogant belief that the rest of the world will fall in with their plans simply because they say so."

Flavia chuckled. "That is telling him, Therese. Do not let this bossy son of mine believe he rules you completely."

"There is no chance of that, Mamacita."

Therese was fairly certain she was the only one who heard the harsh undertone in Claudio's voice, but to her ears it was as loud as if he'd shouted out how much he disliked her.

"I am glad to hear it. You are far too much like your papa, believing you control the world around you and everyone in it. Life does not work that way, as I am sure Vincente is realizing for perhaps the first time."

"He is more than aware, I assure you," Claudio said, his voice now subdued.

"And you, my son?"

"Content yourself with knowing that he and I are both aware how little our will carries the day."

Flavia's face softened with concern. "I am sorry, Claudio. Times like this are difficult, but Vincente will be fine. Believe it."

"I hope you are right."

"I am always right, it is just the males of this family are slow catching on sometimes."

Danette laughed out loud while both Scorsolini brothers smiled wryly. Neither one would hurt the older woman by arguing with her, but both were too arrogant to believe anyone else ever knew better than they did. It was all Therese could do not to blurt out that Flavia had been wrong about one thing.

Like King Vincente, she had always believed that Therese and Claudio were the perfect match and had been vocal in saying so. Once his father's health could withstand the blow, Claudio would make sure everyone knew just how wrong both his parents had been.

Flavia said, "I would like to see Vincente."

"Yes, of course," Claudio replied. "He is sleeping now, but may waken again. He will be glad to find you by his bedside."

Marcello nodded. "I will stay as well."

"In that case, I shall see our wives to the palace. It appears that is the only way I can be assured that Therese will return to rest."

"When is the surgery scheduled for?" Therese asked, ignoring the barb and doing a fair job of avoiding his gaze while making it appear she was looking at him.

"Five hours from now."

"I want to be here."

"Then you will return with me now to the palace and get at least some semblance of rest beforehand."

If there were shares in the bossy market, he had a stranglehold on them. "I don't need you telling me what to do."

"I'd prefer to stay here with Marcello and Flavia," Danette said before Claudio could answer.

Marcello gently put his arm around her slightly thickened waist and pulled her close, kissing her temple. "You are pregnant, *cara mia,* you need to rest for both your sake and that of our unborn child. Please do me the favor of returning to the palace with my brother."

Therese wondered if Claudio would ever have been as tender with her...even if she had been pregnant. A tiny voice inside her heart said it wouldn't have mattered. She would have had her dreams with, or without he extra bit of tender care. Seeing her deepest wish living out fulfillment in another woman's body brought a poignant pain that had nothing to do with envy.

She adored Danette and wanted only the best for her, but Therese could no more stifle the urgent longing inside herself for a child than she could pretend that Claudio loved her.

Danette turned in Tomasso's arms and kissed him on the lips, right there in front of the rest of the family and he did not even sort of flinch. "If that's what you really want, all right. But are you sure you don't want me here as moral support?"

"Thank you, *mi precioso*. Your offer is appreciated, but I will feel better knowing you are taking care of yourself." Then *he* kissed *her,* putting enough enthusiasm into the effort to show that he was not in the least embarrassed by the public show of affection from his wife.

Therese could not help comparing the way Danette and Marcello interacted with the way that she and Claudio did. She would never have dared to kiss him in something as public as a hospital waiting room. She'd never even kissed him in front of any of his family members in the private apartments of the palace.

Looking back, she realized that in three years, she could probably count on one hand the number of times she had kissed him when they were not already in the process of making love. She had never felt the confidence to instigate lovemaking, but she had always responded...with more passion than she had believed possible.

He'd praised her for it, but now she wondered if she had been too enthusiastic. He'd grown bored with her... because she'd been too easy?

And even before he had told her he had grown bored with her, she'd known he hadn't felt anything tender toward her like his brothers did for their wives.

She looked at Marcello and Danette, so close they were obviously two halves of the same whole and an ache seared Therese's heart. She would never know that kind of love because she knew she would never stop loving Claudio, even if right now she disliked him almost as much as she loved him.

Her future stretched out like a bleak, lonely wasteland ahead of her.

What was wrong with her that she did not inspire love in the people who were supposed to hold affection for her? Her parents had only ever seen her as a means to an end or a sore disappointment and Claudio had given her only a marginally more important role in his life. That of lover and helpmate, but he was only too happy to snatch it away.

Danette's parents adored her, if they were a bit overprotective. Therese had seen that at the wedding. What did the other woman have that was so lacking in herself?

Envy was a sin that she had always been determined never to feel, but as she looked on at her sister-in-law so obviously loved and pregnant with the child Therese craved but would never have, she ached so badly for those things herself that her teeth hurt. She would die rather than see them taken from the sweet Danette, but was not sure her own life was worth a counterfeit dollar without them.

She surged to her feet, needing to get out of there and the suit coat fell to the floor. She bent down and grabbed it and then held it out in Claudio's general direction. "Here."

He took it, his fingers brushing her own and she yanked her hand back, stumbling against the couch as her body instinctively retreated as well.

"Therese, are you all right, child?" Flavia asked, her voice laced with concern.

"Fine. J-just tired," Therese choked out, her eyes burning with tears that were only partially linked to the man lying so fragile in a hospital bed down the corridor. "I'll wait in the car."

And dismissing etiquette for the first time in her adult life, she rushed from the room without a single farewell to any of its occupants.

Therese was like a quiet wraith sitting on the seat beside Danette during the car ride to the palace. She spoke only in response to questions from Danette. Claudio, she ignored entirely. Luckily his family had already decided she'd taken his father's ill health hard and he did not think her behavior would give rise to speculation on his sister-in-law's part.

But when Therese had gone rushing from the waiting room, he'd had to convince his stepmother not to follow her. He had suspected that her distress had not been centered solely on his father's condition and he hadn't wanted to take the risk of his family finding that out.

She'd refused to meet Claudio's gaze for the past few hours. He didn't know what she'd seen when she'd looked to him for solace in his father's hospital room. He'd been certain that his anger toward her did not show because he had not wanted to upset his father. Yet, something she had seen in his eyes had upset her to the point that she had looked away with an expression on her face that made him want to grab her and hold her, no matter how stupid that desire made him feel.

After that, she did not look at him again...not then and not later.

If the prospect of imminent divorce was so upsetting, then why the hell had she asked for one? Or was the reality of her perfidy coming home to roost?

She was beloved by both his parents and he knew they would be hurt deeply if there was to be a divorce. Particularly if they were to discover that Therese had betrayed her wedding vows. She adored both his father and his mother and would not want to see either hurt by her actions.

Was she finally starting to realize what the result of those actions would be?

Pity she hadn't considered it before becoming involved with another man. Just thinking of her with someone else made him feel murderous and he had to bite back angry questions he would rather be boiled in oil than ask in front of Danette. Was Therese regretting that involvement now? Was she counting the cost now that it was too late, wishing she had not asked for the divorce? Or was he merely engaged in wishful thinking?

Perhaps it *was* simple worry for his father that had upset her so much, but Claudio had never once seen her as lacking in control as she had been when she'd practically run from the hospital room. And he could not get past the fact she still would not look at him.

His jacket smelled of her...a soft floral scent that had the power to drive him mad with need.

His muscles were rigid with the desire to reach out and take her in his arms. Not that he would have done so in the circumstances, even if she had not asked for a divorce and confirmed his worst suspicions. He did not engage in public displays of affection. His dignity as future sovereign on the Scorsolini throne demanded he be circumspect in his dealings with his wife.

But seeing his younger brother kiss his wife, not caring who was there to watch had given Claudio a strange twinge in the region of his heart.

And he was almost positive that it had impacted Therese as well. If he had not thought it impossible in the face of the night's revelations, he would have believed she was hurt that he was not that way with her. He'd seen her giving his brothers and their wives oddly wistful looks over the past couple of months and wondered at them.

Had she gone looking for affection from a man who was more outwardly expressive? The thought flayed his ego and his sense of masculine confidence. To not be all that his woman needed was not a prospect any man wanted to contemplate. Yet, how could a man who had to hide his relationship with her give her public affection?

And the relationship *was* hidden very well. Until she'd asked for divorce, Claudio had been almost certain his suspicions in that direction were mere musings of a befuddled male brain. Because he'd never once seen even a hint of impropriety on his wife's part.

He'd spent the hours on the plane going back over the last year, trying to see where she might have strayed. What had at first glance appeared to be a casual greeting took on different significance until he forced his overactive brain to stop dissecting his memories.

This was doing him no good and driving him crazy in the bargain. Claudio would let Hawk do his job and then he would confront the truth head-on. Like a man.

Like he had faced the prospect of his father's death…with no whining, or refusing to accept what such an event would mean for his own life. He had been taught since he was a small child that life must be faced and dealt with from the perspective of one's birthright. His carried more responsibility with it than most and those responsibilities pervaded every aspect of his life—including his marriage.

He had known for as long as he could remember that one day he would rule Isole dei Re. He had accepted that duty and all that it entailed on every step of the journey through his life. He had never rebelled against what his birthright dictated. There had been no need for him to make promises to his father that he would fulfill it should the unthinkable happen and the older man not survive surgery.

Both men were fully confident in Claudio's suitability for the job. He had been born to it and raised to know what that meant. He was a crown prince, destined to be a king. Yet, they *had* talked, as his father had told Therese they must…about political issues, family circumstances and personal matters.

His father had revealed a way of thinking that had shocked Claudio, but nothing more astonishing than the fact that the older man was still very much in love with Flavia.

All of the nonsense about the Scorsolini Curse his father told him about had been just that. Every mistress after Vincente's divorce (and apparently there had been none between the one indiscretion and when the marriage's dissolution became final) had been an attempt on his father's part to forget his love for a live woman. Not a dead one.

Oh, he had loved Claudio's mother all right, but he had fallen fast and deeply for Flavia. Too fast and too deep. It had made him feel incredibly guilty, like he was being unfaithful to his first beloved wife. Particularly when Flavia had gotten pregnant with Marcello. Before that, he had at least had the comfort of knowing his relationship with Flavia was merely a sexual one.

But then he had been forced to marry her and completely replace the first wife in his life. Intense feelings of guilt mixed with a grief he had never let himself vent in a public manner plagued Vincente the first years of his marriage. He had found it impossible to utter the necessary words of love to Flavia because he could not admit those feelings even to himself.

He had known his lack of outward affection had hurt Flavia, but he had told himself he could do nothing to mitigate that.

Yet, the feelings inside him grew until he was desperate to find a way to deny them. Finally, in a state of confused grief both for what he had lost and the state of his current marriage, he had betrayed his promise of fidelity. Flavia had found out and while she had been willing to suffer a marriage with love on only one side, she had refused to tolerate infidelity.

Proving she had not been raised to put duty above all, she had taken all three boys to her parents' home in Italy and filed for divorce. Out of shame, King Vincente Scorsolini had done nothing to prevent his wife divorcing him. He'd made up the fiction of the Scorsolini Curse to soothe his aching conscience and lacerated pride shortly after the divorce.

He had even believed it until he woke up to reality at Tomasso's wedding. They'd been walking along the beach with the children afterward. Vincente had taken a long look at the woman who had given birth to his third son as she chatted away with their grandchildren.

For some reason he still did not understand, but had confided to Claudio that he thought it might have been a premonition of things to come, everything had fallen into place after more than two decades of idiocy. Or so he had labeled it.

Claudio did not know what to make of his father's revelations, or why the older man had made them to him. But he knew that his father had finally accepted his love for Flavia and was prepared to act on that love. If Claudio knew his father as well as he thought he did, his stepmother's days as a single woman were numbered.

Provided King Vincente survived surgery.

CHAPTER SIX

WHEN they reached the palace, Therese managed to get out of the car and walk side by side with Claudio all the way to their private apartments without so much as making a second's eye contact or allowing her hand to brush against his. It bothered him. He did not like being ignored by his wife and she still was his wife, no matter if she wanted to pretend otherwise.

He followed her slender form into the apartment, a sense of being ill-used riding him with the tenacity of a jockey in the last leg of the Melbourne Cup.

She looked so damn lost though and it infuriated him that even amidst his own turmoil, he cared. "You should have come back to the palace with Tomasso and Maggie."

"I didn't want to," she said in that soft voice that even now impacted his libido. Damn it, she was everything he had ever wanted in a woman…except faithful.

But had she been unfaithful? Was she only thinking about it? Was her request for a divorce in preparation to entering another relationship? The questions blindsided him with the possibility that while her heart might have strayed, her body might yet remain his alone.

"I noticed," he ground out, frustrated by her on more than one level and several he did not want to examine too closely.

"I wanted to be there if anything else happened," she said with a sigh as she slipped her shoes off and padded across the sitting room in stocking feet.

The longer she went without looking at him, the more irritated he became. The fact that he found himself following her like a puppy dog did not improve his temper any, either. "You being there could have made no difference."

"That isn't what you said when we were in New York."

"I was angry."

"And taking it out on me. I noticed."

And who did she think he should have taken his anger, spawned by her request for a divorce, out on? Rather than ask a question for which he did not want an answer, he said, "I do not like the idea of you sleeping on a sofa in the waiting room. You were so out of it, you did not even notice me coming into the room."

She'd cuddled into his suit jacket, though, whispering his name as she did so and he'd felt like someone had kicked him in the gut. How could she still seek his comfort in the night when she wanted someone else?

They were in the bedroom now and she went to the cupboard to pull out a nightgown. "Security was on duty the entire time."

His tie was already long gone, but he shrugged out of the suit jacket that carried her scent mingled with his own. Like their bodies did after making love. He did not like remembering that. For reasons he could not fathom, he wanted her now more than ever.

He should be disgusted by the thought of touching her. But far from it, since considering the alternative that she was still his alone in a physical sense, the need to stamp that possession on her body once again grew with every breath he drew in. "That is not the point."

"There is no point…not to arguing about it now." She headed for the bathroom, clearly intent on finishing her changing in there when only days ago, she would have undressed in front of him quite naturally. "What is done is done."

He supposed that was how she saw the demise of their relationship, but he was not so accepting. "We agreed that we would present a united front for the time being."

"A united front does not mean I am going to start taking orders like your pet dog."

"Look at me, damn it!" he exploded, having had his fill of talking to the back or top of her head.

She did, her body turning rigidly to face him, her head coming up and her exotic green gaze glaring defiantly at him.

He glared right back, his patience completely gone. "I have never treated you in such a demeaning fashion."

"Let's not get into how you treated me at all," she said scathingly. "It doesn't matter anymore."

"Are you saying that your request for a divorce is because you are unhappy with your treatment in this marriage?" The thought had never occurred to him. The weak sense of hope that coursed through him at the possibility made him angry and yet elated at the same time.

But wouldn't a woman complain about things that bothered her before doing something as drastic as ask for a divorce? Particularly a woman as conscious of her duty as Therese?

"I did not ask for a divorce because I wanted out of our marriage over the way you treated me. If you will recall, I did not ask for a divorce at all."

"Do no argue semantics with me," he growled. "You said we had to divorce."

"We do."

"But not over my treatment of you?"

"No."

Only one circumstance could have prompted a woman as responsible and loyal as Therese to dismiss those considerations and ask for divorce. She *had* to be in love with another man. Love made fools of even the wisest and most strong minded people. Look at his own father. His love for Flavia, coming as it did when he was still in love with his dead wife, had tormented him and ultimately because of it, he had betrayed himself and her.

The thought of Therese loving another man like that evoked a feeling of jealous rage so strong it almost overcame him. He forced it down however, unwilling to give way to such weakness. "I would appreciate you having a formal pregnancy test done."

"That won't be necessary."

"Having a period is no guarantee you are not pregnant."

"And if I was pregnant…would you be bored with me? Would you still be so content to give me a divorce?" she asked with a scathing sarcasm that was entirely unlike her.

Pride forbade him give her an honest answer, so he said nothing at all.

She sighed, deflating like a pricked balloon. "That is what I thought. I'm sure I am not pregnant. Let's just leave it at that."

"You have been doing something to prevent conception?" he asked suspiciously.

How deeply had her subterfuge gone?

"*No.*"

"Then the risk is there. You will have a formal test done."

She shrugged tiredly, giving in with her body language before saying the words. "If that is what you want."

"What I want has little to do with this conversation."

"Well, it certainly isn't about what *I* want."

Claudio's expression said he thought their conversation was about exactly that. He grabbed Therese's shoulders, his grip not hurting her physically but causing mental anguish he would not begin to understand. "If you carry my child, there will be no divorce."

Which was exactly what she had thought. She didn't understand how she could feel more pain on top of everything else inside her, but she did. He'd spelled it out with words that could have no other interpretation. She mattered to him only in her capacity as potential incubator for the Scorsolini heir. For his child, he would remain married to a woman who bored him.

"Whatever you say." She was so tired and disheartened, she didn't have the energy or the desire to argue.

Besides, it didn't matter. She knew she wasn't pregnant. Having the test would not change anything.

His big body vibrated with a tension she did not understand. "You must be very certain it is not a possibility because the prospect of losing your possible freedom does not appear to upset you."

Beyond caring what she revealed, she sighed. "Perhaps because I am not overly concerned about it."

"Yet you just now told me that you are taking nothing to prevent it."

"I'm not."

"If that is true, how can you be so certain?"

"I don't lie and I am certain."

"The only evidence you have that you are not is that you have started your period. That is hardly full proof."

"I haven't started."

"But you said—"

"That I'm sure I'm not pregnant," she interrupted, just wanting the conversation over so she could take a hot shower. "I know my own body and my period is coming. All the signs are there." Including the pain of the endometriosis. Though, thankfully, so far only the twinges she had had the other night.

"As I said, your period is no guarantee."

"I told you I would have the tests. I don't understand why we have to argue about it. Can't we drop this conversation now? I want to change and go to bed."

"Yes, you agreed to have the tests, but you also told me that you wanted to have my baby *very much*. I do not know what to believe. I do not understand."

And he could not let it drop until he did.

Tears that should have been impossible considering how much she had cried already, burned the back of her eyes. "I did want to have your baby."

She still did, which made her stupid as well as a complete failure in the love stakes.

"*Did*…past tense."

"What do you expect? No woman wants to learn she is pregnant by a man who is bored with her and their marriage."

At least she shouldn't, but the thought that he would not let her go if she was pregnant taunted her, making her wish for the impossible and angry at herself for doing so. Bored or not, he would never allow the mother of his child to walk away.

"I do not know what to expect from you at all any longer,

Therese. I do not understand you," he said again, his undertone one of angry bewilderment. "I thought I knew you well, but discovered I was very wrong in that assumption."

"What difference does it make? You're bored with what you do know. You said so." She spun away and rushed into the bathroom, shutting the door behind her, unwilling to let him see how much those words hurt.

She stripped and stepped into the oversize shower stall. Not because she wanted another shower after the long one she'd taken in the hotel, but because it was the one place she could safely vent her emotions. She turned on the taps and icy cold jets of water hit her from five directions.

Her mind was in such a state of turmoil, that the frigid temperatures barely registered before the water started to warm to her preset selection on the control panel by the door. Pleasantly hot water was cascading down her body when she felt another presence in the cubicle.

She turned around, her mind telling her instincts they had to be wrong, but they were not. Claudio was there just as she had known he would be.

He stood magnificently naked, the water running in rivulets down his bronze chest. "I decided not to wait on my shower."

"Get out," she gasped.

"But why should I? We've done this together many times before."

"But everything is different now."

"You are still my wife." And there was a message there she did not quite get.

"Only temporarily," she said to punish herself as much as him.

"So you have said."

"And you agreed. You said you wanted it…the divorce," she said, unable to hide her pain at that truth.

"Perhaps I spoke hastily. I am not bored with every aspect of our relationship, *cara*. Not yet."

Was that supposed to make her feel better? It didn't and neither did the look of desire hardening his features.

"You want sex?" she asked in total shock, having just worked that out.

"Why so surprised? It is something we are very good at together."

"But you said…" He'd said that her value as a partner had gone down when she started turning him down, not that he didn't want her anymore.

"I said?"

"Things that hurt me."

"And your demand for a divorce did not hurt me?" he asked.

Had it? Probably. But then why would he want sex now? Nothing made sense anymore. "I don't understand," she said, echoing his sentiments earlier.

His dark eyes narrowed. "Welcome to the club."

"You can't want me."

"Now that is where you are wrong, Therese. Very much wrong." He leaned down and kissed her with blatant seductive intent, his lips molding hers, his big hands sliding around her waist to pull her closer to his naked maleness.

She was so stunned by this turn of events that she did nothing, neither fighting him nor acquiescing.

He lifted his head, the slumberous passion in his eyes much hotter than the water pelting their bodies. "What is the matter? You were quick enough to respond only a night ago."

How could he ask something so stupid? "That was before…"

"Before you told me we had to divorce?"

"Yes. I don't think—"

His wet hand covered her mouth. "I do not want you to think. For then I must think and I do not wish to. About anything."

And she understood…or thought she did. Had she not been so tired, she would probably have anticipated this. Claudio needed comfort. His father lay in a hospital bed, his future uncertain and her strong husband would never willingly admit fear on that score. Or any other if it came to that.

The question was what was she going to do about it?

But even as she asked herself that, a realization came to her. She needed comfort, too.

He did not love her and that hurt. King Vincente's health was at risk and that hurt as well. Even if he survived his surgery, which there was every chance he would do…she would lose him along with the other Scorsolinis from her life when her marriage ended. That knowledge added pain on top of pain.

The careful little world she had built around herself in which she had people she loved, if not those who loved her in return, was crumbling.

Soon, she would be living a life entirely separate, one in which she would have to stand on the sidelines. She would have to watch from afar while the things and people she cared about existed and thrived apart from her.

Her pet projects would be taken over by someone else, the issues she thought were so important would find another spokeswoman. Her role in the political infrastructure of Isole dei Re would be filled in by someone else, doing things differently…prioritizing differently and wanting to accomplish different things.

More painful to her heart was the knowledge that her sisters-in-law would blossom in their new roles, have their babies, and more children besides. All without her around to experience, if only vicariously, the reality of a family love.

Flavia and Vincente would finally find their way back to each other…it was obvious to anyone with eyes in her head that they were head over heels in love and always had been. But she would not be around to rejoice with them. She would once again be on the outside looking in.

She would try to fill her life with meaningful endeavors, but the cold winds of loneliness were already blowing across her soul. Because most devastating of all, Claudio would one day remarry and have his own children and they would not be hers.

Pain so intense it was physical shook her frame as Claudio stared down into her eyes, his own expression unreadable except for the physical need that burned in his dark gaze. "I want you, *cara.* If you are honest with yourself…you will admit you want me, too."

She looked down where his gaze had traveled. Her breasts were flushed a soft pink with desire, her nipples as hard and crimson as frozen berries. They ached under his hot scrutiny, the skin tight and throbbing with the blood pulsing below it and the engorged tips crying out for the relief of his touch.

A million memories of how it felt to have his mouth and his hands on her erogenous zones tormented her mind. And what he could not see, but she could feel, was the way her most intimate flesh had swollen as well and throbbed with a need to be filled by him, connected to him.

Both her emotional pain and the physical need surging through her sprang from the deep well of love she had for him. It did not matter that he did not return that love. It was too much a part of her being to dismiss and each set of emotions caused by her love warred for supremacy.

One promised empty loneliness that tears would not assuage and the other oblivion. She chose the oblivion. "Yes, I want you," she said with some despair.

He took no further urging, but swooped down on her mouth with the speed and power of an invading armada as he yanked her into full-body contact. His lips devoured hers and his hard, masculine body imprinted a message of sexual need on her own.

It was one that found an answering craving in her and she did not remain passive against him, but touched him as if it would be the last time. She reveled in the contrast her fingertips found between the silky tautness of his skin and the whorls of dark curling hair that marked his body so different from her own. A man's body, the epitome of masculine perfection to her senses.

She traced the outlines of ridges created by honed muscle, memorizing anew the way his body felt. She did not know how she was going to live the rest of her life without this. It was too special...so perfect, she often cried afterward at the sheer beauty of the feelings he evoked in her.

Tears burned her eyes and she blinked them away as the hot water masked any signs of her inner turmoil. Her hand hovered above his hardness, her nails scoring through the nest of dark hair from which it sprang. His big body trembled and sounds of need rumbled from deep in his chest.

Incredible how much she loved those sounds. She was addicted to them and she had spent hours in bed with him listening, watching, paying oh so very close attention to his reactions so she could have more…and more…and more.

His hands were busy, too, molding her breasts and caressing sensitive areas he knew so well. It was as if he knew this was a special moment in time, a unique opportunity that might not come again because he touched her so carefully, arousing her to a fever pitch of sensation. And she made her own sounds of desire, moans and whimpers that mixed with the beat of the pouring water.

Her control slipped moment by moment until she was a living, breathing, quivering mass of feminine sexual need. She cried out against his lips from his touch even as she demanded more with the movement of her body and hungrily caressed his body with all the fire burning inside her.

The sound of Therese's sexy whimpers drove Claudio crazy as she went wild for him. She had always been incredibly responsive…when she let him touch her, but there was a quality to her response right now that had never been there before. Her body shook and trembled and her hands were all over him, so hot against his skin that he felt singed.

She touched him with a furious desperation. As if she had never touched him before…*or would never touch him again*.

But he dismissed that last thought as ludicrous in the face of how much she so obviously wanted him. This kind of desire did not get assuaged in one attempt at lovemaking… or even a hundred. He should know. He wanted her that much.

Would always want her.

And his shy and proper wife was practically climbing his body in an attempt to join her body with his. She was completely out of control and he refused to believe she could give even a fraction of this reaction to another man.

She might think she wanted someone else for reasons he had yet to discover, but it was he who could touch the very core of her soul with a simple hand to her breast.

It had been that way since the very first time he touched her with the intent to seduce.

Their sexual connection was too strong to be tampered with, too primitive to be explained or even understood on an intellectual level. She might have withheld herself from him more in the past few months than she had at first, but when she did allow him close…she went to pieces. Perhaps not as spectacularly as this time, but definitely too strongly for him to seriously believe she could want another man.

No way could she be this way with anyone else and still respond in such a primal fashion to him…not his wife, a woman who had spent her whole life tamping down her emotional reactions and hiding them. It went against everything he knew her to be.

Unless she was thinking of the other man when Claudio touched her…unless she was using him to assuage a need she could not have met another way.

Where the thought came from, he did not know, but it detonated with the power of a nuclear blast in his head. *No, damn it. He would not believe that.* And yet, it made sense of a woman who asked for a divorce and then made love like she would die if she could not have his touch.

He broke his mouth from hers as he lifted her up his body to position his hardness at the entrance to her slickened flesh. He had to have her…even the disturbing thoughts could not dampen his need, but he couldn't allow her to use him like that. He would not let that scenario be reality for them. *"Say my name…ask me to take you."*

Her eyes opened, revealing beautiful green and very dazed depths. "Wh-what?"

"Who am I?" he ground out in harsh demand.

"*Amore mio*."

The words slammed through him like a sledgehammer…was that her pet name for the other man or was she calling Claudio her love? He could count on one hand the number of times she had used that expression with him during their marriage and none of them in the last six months. "My *name*, say it."

Her lips curved softly, her expression an odd mixture he could not decipher. It seemed as if both exultation and sadness resided in her green gaze, but that made no sense. "Claudio…my prince."

Then she leaned forward to reconnect their lips and kissed him with desperate passion, devouring his mouth before kissing along his jaw until she was right at his ear. She whispered, "Love me, Claudio. Please. Be one with me…if only for a little while."

Her voice had a strange quality to it, as if it was not merely sex she was asking for, but he did not know what else she wanted. He could give her the sex, though. Was in fact dying to do so. He levered her body onto his shaft at the same time as surging upward so that he was impaled in one urgent thrust.

She cried out, her head falling back on her shoulders, her expression one of agonized bliss.

He grunted, a sound that was entirely primitive and would have at any other time embarrassed his sophisticated sense of self. "You feel so good around me, *amante*."

"You feel…perfect…inside…me…" she gasped out as he withdrew and thrust again.

Therese thought maybe she would die from pleasure. If she did, it would be the way to go…so much better than the pain inflicted by the endometriosis every month.

The feel of him inside of her was so incredible. She and Claudio had made love many times in many ways, but never anything as primal and basic as this. There was no bed to support them. He was not even using the wall to support her as he had other times they had made love in the shower, just sheer animal strength.

It was as if they were in a world entirely apart from anything normal, anything they had known before. Steam surrounded them like a heated fog as hot water cascaded down their bodies locked in ecstatic intimacy.

She cried out as he thrust upward and hit that special pleasure zone inside her.

"That is right, *mi moglie*. Come apart for me. Show me this side to you that no one else ever sees." His mouth landed on her neck, sucking, nibbling, licking and sending shivers of sensation to the most sensitive areas of her body.

She locked her ankles behind his back and rode him… he surged into her…she squeezed his hardness into her… he guided her body with a bruising grip on her hips and buttocks.

She opened her eyes to look at him and saw that his head was thrown back in abandon like hers had been, his face etched with sexual pleasure. She leaned forward and bit his chest in an act so primitive, even in her advanced state of passion…it shocked her.

He was not shocked, though, but merely growled and increased the rhythm, slamming into her with pounding force with every thrust. It was so intense, she felt like she was on the verge of shattering into a million over-pleasured bits.

Tension spiraled inside her, a feeling of leaping from one experience to the next up a circular incline, traveling toward a precipice and then going over as her body convulsed around him and she cried out his name. She was falling too fast and she cried out in fright.

He gripped her tighter and she wrapped her arms around him, pressing to his body, the only sense of reality in a universe exploding from pleasure. He was silent when he climaxed, his teeth bared in a feral grimace that said more eloquently than any words could have how intensely he was feeling.

CHAPTER SEVEN

AFTERWARD, he wrapped her up against him, soothing her with gentle words and tender caresses against her back until the sobs she had not realized she was crying ebbed. Her body relaxed slowly, until she dangled in his arms, a boneless heap.

He held her for several long and silent moments, while her legs dangled and the connection between their bodies remained, reminding her that once was rarely enough for this man...even when their lovemaking culminated in a mind-blowing pleasure that left her completely spent.

Finally he lifted her off of him and began washing her with gentle hands that touched every inch of her as if to say, "Mine. Mine. And this is mine, too."

She tried to return the favor, but her hands were clumsy, her movements jerky with a special kind of fatigue only he could induce. Eventually he turned off the water and stepped out of the shower, his arm still supporting her.

She forced herself to move away so they could dry off, but even in that he ended up helping her. Then he pulled her into his body and walked her from the bathroom, her nightgown forgotten on the floor of the en suite.

They climbed into bed together and she went willingly

into his arms, closing her eyes, so tired that she fell asleep immediately.

She woke scant hours later to a kiss on her temple. "Wake up, *cara*. We must hurry and dress or we will not make it to the hospital before they take Papa down to surgery."

She sat up, feeling out of sorts. Despite the pleasure of lovemaking beforehand, she had had disturbing dreams and her sleep had not been restful. Pain was dragging at her lower abdomen and she wished she could have kept on sleeping. Because restful, or not, it was at least a respite from the reality she was loathe to face.

Her period was due soon, not that it was super regular now that she wasn't on the pill. But she knew the pain would only get worse every day until it started and unbearable during the flow of blood from her body.

Claudio was already half dressed and looked over his shoulder as he did his tie. "Get a move on, Therese."

She nodded, wincing as her head ached from the movement. She climbed gingerly from bed, her eyes glued to his figure. That at least gave pleasure. She could not imagine life without this man and said so before she thought better of the admission.

He stopped in the act of pulling on his suit coat. "But you do not have to. After last night, it is obvious we can forget this talk of divorce."

"Are you saying you aren't bored with me anymore?"

"You need to ask after our sojourn in the shower?" he asked with the devil's own smile.

But she did not smile in return. Their time in the shower had been incredible, but they had spent what remained of the night wrapped in each other's arms. Only he didn't mention that, did he?

Sex. That was all he wanted from her and when it was on offer, she was the perfect wife. He'd said that when he told her he was bored with her…that her value had dropped significantly when she began turning him down. The fact that the night before and his reaction to it only supported that truth was not a particularly pleasant reality.

She turned her head away. "Last night did not change anything important."

He said a truly foul word and her gaze flew back to him.

He finished shrugging into his coat, his dark brown eyes hard as granite. "You are *not* telling me you still think a divorce is necessary. I refuse to accept you are saying that."

"But that is what I am saying," she admitted wearily, her head now pounding.

The look he gave her would have brought about her demise if looks truly could have been lethal. He looked like he hated her and he didn't say another single, solitary word. He simply finished dressing and left their room.

Moving as quickly as she could with the cramps now reaching toward debilitating levels, she dressed as well and followed him. She found him downstairs, giving instructions to his father's assistant as well as his own.

"The others are waiting for us in the car," he said when he saw her. Then he dismissed the employees and headed toward the back of the palace where the car would be parked.

"Claudio."

"Do not speak to me, Therese." The venom in his voice silenced her as effectively as a gag.

He did hate her.

He was like that for the rest of the morning, only managing to maintain a thin veil of civility in front of his family. It slipped to blatant hostility when they were not within earshot.

The one bright spot was that King Vincente came through the surgery with flying colors and was mostly lucid for visits with his family afterward. When Flavia offered to stay at the hospital with him, he gratefully accepted and sent the rest of them home with a good dose of his trademark arrogance.

Despite her father-in-law's continuing improvement in health, the next few days were a torment for Therese. Both in mind and body. Claudio stayed in their suite for appearance's sake, but the width of the Great Divide ran down the middle of their bed…that was when he was in it. He also refused to speak to her when they were alone, except to discuss their respective duties.

If she even looked like she was going to get personal, he made an excuse to leave…or walked away without an excuse. When he was there to begin with. Which wasn't often. She saw him more frequently in the company of others than she did in the privacy of their suite and that was rare enough.

He had always had a backbreaking schedule, but now it was even worse. He had to cover both his own responsibilities and those of his father. As a world leader, those duties were such that he could not leave any of them undone. He'd always functioned on less sleep than she did, but now she wondered sometimes if he slept at all.

His brothers pitched in where they could, but Claudio's role in the family dictated that the majority of the decisions, responsibility and stress fell squarely on his broad shoulders.

No matter how much his angry rejection hurt, she felt badly for him, worried about him and wished about ten times a day that she had waited to ask for a divorce until after the crisis had passed. He refused to accept comfort or help from her in any form and she didn't blame him, but she longed to help him somehow.

Her request for a divorce had stung his pride and shattered his ego when he could least afford that kind of wounding. He needed a full store of inner strength in his current circumstance, but he was handicapped by his anger over her defection. She wanted to explain that it wasn't defection, but the physical pain from her endometriosis and the haziness resultant from the drugs she took to control it depleted her ability to pursue anything.

It was all she could do to make it through each day, much less fight with her husband to put their marriage to rights…only to convince him that it had to end anyway.

In every way she looked, she couldn't help but see that it would have been so much easier on both her and Claudio if she had waited to tell him of their need to divorce until after he got back from his trip to New York. At least then, all of this hostility and energy draining anger during such a critical time could have been avoided.

The guilt of hindsight weighed her down, making it harder than usual to deal with her physical pain and there were some nights she simply laid in her lonely bed and cried. As the doctor had predicted, this month's pain was worse than the one before once her period arrived and some days she didn't know how she was going to survive it.

Her own duties did not magically disappear because of the family crisis, but in fact increased. And she had to spend at least part of every day at the hospital, where she put on her best front. She visited King Vincente and made sure Flavia was not wearing herself out playing nursemaid and then would go home only to worry about Claudio.

She was leaving King Vincente's room one evening when she ran into Claudio.

He looked almost haggard with tiredness, but when he saw her, the mask of invincibility fell into place.

"You need to rest," she said instead of a greeting, laying her hand on his arm.

He shrugged off her touch with a frown. "I am fine."

"No, you aren't. Everyone says you're pushing yourself too hard, but no one knows what to do about it."

"There is nothing to do. It is my duty to care for my country while my father is ill."

"Your brothers—"

"Have their own responsibilities."

"They're worried about you."

He glared down at her. "Did one of them ask you to speak to me?"

"Yes," she said with a sigh. "Both of them actually."

"I should have known you would not evince concern on your own."

"I care about you, Claudio."

"Of a certainty…you do not."

She winced at the surety of his tone and the cynicism in his dark gaze. "I'm sorry."

"So am I. Now if you will excuse me, I have only twenty-five minutes to spend with my father."

"Are you coming home afterward?"

"No."

"You have to sleep sometime."

"Is that an invitation to your bed?"

Without volition, her expression twisted in revulsion at the thought of sharing her body intimately with him while pain racked her so incessantly.

He paled, his gaze hardening. "Well, that says it all, does it not?"

"No." She reached out to grab him before he could walk away. "Please, Claudio, listen to me."

He glared down at her. "You have nothing to say that I would want to hear."

A cramp so severe sliced through her she slumped against the wall the moment it hit her. She couldn't do this right now. Casualties were all around her and she could do nothing to help any of them. Her own self included.

"All right. I'll see you later…whenever." Forcing limbs to walk that just wanted to crumble, she left.

Claudio watched Therese leave with a mixture of rage and incomprehension. She behaved as if his cold attitude really hurt her, but she was the one who wanted a divorce. When she'd told him she still wanted it even after their incredible lovemaking, he'd been gutted.

She had just been using him.

The knowledge had hurt more than anything he had ever known, which in turn had filled him with fury. She wasn't supposed to hurt him. She was his woman, flesh of his flesh…bone of his bone. The quintessential helpmate and lover…only she'd turned out to be a betrayer instead.

The fury brought about by that realization had not abated in six days. He walked around feeling like a bomb ready to explode. He was grateful for the extra workload of his father's responsibilities because it gave him an outlet for the energy generated by his suppressed emotions.

He did not want his brothers to worry, but he had no intention of slowing down.

His father and his country needed him even if his wife did not.

* * *

Therese woke late that night to horrific pain and the sensation of sticky wetness on her thighs.

She'd bled through.

It wasn't anything new since the endometriosis had begun, but usually if she got up and changed frequently in the night, she didn't have to worry about it. She'd been so exhausted when she went to bed that she slept four hours straight.

She'd also forgotten to take her pain meds, she now remembered.

She tried to get up to take care of both problems, but fell back to the bed, a cry of pain tearing from her throat. The tiniest movement brought about sheer agony.

But remaining still hurt, too. So much she could barely breathe because of it.

She looked across the empty expanse of the bed. Claudio was not there of course. He often did not come to bed until the wee hours of the morning, if he came to bed at all. He'd slept in his office on a couple of nights and no one but she was the wiser. After their altercation at the hospital, he would no doubt be planning to do that again tonight.

Pain tore through her and she moaned, tears drenching her eyes and wetting her cheeks hotly as her body contorted in misery. If she could just get to the pain meds, but she couldn't even reach the bedside table.

How could she have forgotten to take them?

She inched toward the edge of the bed, but the progress was slow going. How far away was the table? Pain made everything around her hazy. Maybe if she rolled. She pushed from one side to her stomach and almost blacked out from the pain. It would have been welcome if she had, she thought muzzily.

Still feeling dizzy, she pushed to her back to complete

the roll, but instead of coming down on the mattress, she felt nothing but air and then landed on the floor with a thump. She could hear someone whimpering and she wanted to help them, but she couldn't move. She tried to focus in the near darkness, but could barely make out the shape of her nightstand. It looked further away than it had from the bed.

She reached for it, sobs wrenching from her throat and doing nothing to lessen the pain racking her body.

"Therese? What the hell is going on?" The overhead light came on, turning everything from black and white to glaring Technicolor.

It hurt her eyes and she closed them, collapsing against the floor in a shivering heap as Claudio cursed in voluble Italian.

"What happened?" He dropped to her side, his hand on her shoulder. "You are bleeding. I will call an ambulance."

"No!" She looked up at her tall, gorgeous husband, her eyes awash with tears she was trying to blink back now that he was here to see them. "I need my pain pills. In… the…drawer," she gasped out around another wave of cramping.

"Pain meds are not going to stop this bleeding."

"Don't need to…it's my period."

"Like hell. You are hemorrhaging."

He picked up the phone and she cried out. "No! *Please, Claudio*…" she gasped and then moaned as pain snaked through her. "Just get me…" She panted, trying to get enough breath to go on. "The bed. Please. Hurts…" She curled into a fetal position.

He dropped the phone and then she felt a blanket settling over her. He tucked it around her as he picked her up, but he did not lay her on the bed. He headed for the door.

"Where…going?" she asked weakly.

"The hospital and you can save your arguments. I won't call an ambulance if that's what you want, but you need a doctor."

"I've seen a doctor. Told you…my pills…*need them*."

"You need a hell of a lot more than pain pills," he ground out without breaking his stride.

"Yes. Surgery. Not today."

"Yes, today. If that is what you need, you get it now."

"Can't."

"Why not?" he asked as he stopped in front of the intercom by their door.

"Not safe." She looked at him, her face contorting with another spasm of pain. "Please. I need the pills."

He looked down at her, his eyes narrowed. "You need a doctor."

"Please," she begged, in so much pain she would have given anything for those pills.

His jaw looked hewn from rock. "All right, but you had better be right about the blood. I will not let you die on me. Do you hear?"

He jogged back into the bedroom, careful not to jar her and then he gently laid her onto the bed before opening the bedside drawer. He pulled out a prescription bottle, looked at it and then opened it, shaking two tablets into his hand. There was a glass of water beside the bed.

She'd poured it from the carafe and put it there to take her pills with and then spaced it, she now remembered. One of the negative side effects of taking them to begin with was her spotty memory. She lived in fear of taking too many and overdosing, which might explain the number of times she ended up in severe pain wishing she'd kept to her schedule.

He put his arm behind her shoulder and lifted her into a semisitting position and helped her take the pills as if she could not do it herself. And the truth was, she couldn't. It was taking everything she had not to scream at the agony ripping through her insides.

After she swallowed the pills, he carefully laid her back on the bed.

"How long?"

"Twenty to thirty minutes."

"Can I do anything else?"

She was in far too much pain to refine on the fact that the man asking had been treating her like a leper for the last few days. "Hot water helps."

"To drink or to soak in?"

"Soaking...shower, too."

He nodded and disappeared into the bathroom. She heard water running and then he was back and he was naked. She couldn't make sense of that and didn't even try.

She simply tried to control the pain as he picked up the phone beside the bed and spoke some instructions into it about having the bed cleaned and remade. She was just glad he wasn't calling a doctor in after all.

She had gone through too much to keep her secret from the media...she didn't want to risk it with a doctor. Even a Scorsolini Royals approved one.

"I am going to undress you."

"Okay," she said woozily, the drugs taking effect quickly because she'd taken them without food.

He removed the blanket and her clothes with careful hands. He cursed when he saw how much blood was on her legs. He surveyed her grimly. "You are certain this is only period blood?"

"Yes."

He shook his head, but didn't say anything. He simply bent and lifted her from the bed. As gentle as he was, the movement still jarred her and brought on a wave of dizziness as pain overcame her again.

She moaned.

He cursed. "This cannot be normal, *cara*."

"Didn't say it was normal," she muttered, her eyes shut, her head lolling against his shoulder.

Strangely he didn't ask what it was.

"I'm surprised," she said.

"About?"

"You aren't demanding answers."

"You do not have any idea how terrible you look, do you?"

"I look terrible?" she asked, a fresh spate of tears rolling down her cheeks. "Ugly?"

"Ill, you foolish woman. You are as white as paper and you look like even a weak wind would blow you over."

"I hurt."

"I know." And he sounded like the knowledge was tearing him apart, but that had to be a trick of her hearing.

Why would he care if she hurt when he hated her?

Only the way he held her was not the cruel grip of hatred or even the impersonal grip of a stranger. He held her to him like she was precious in some way and even if it was a delusion, she clung to him, needing the comfort and too weak to pretend otherwise.

She didn't realize where they were headed until he stepped into the already steaming shower with her and then she understood why he'd gotten naked, too. He planned to hold her while she bathed. Tears of relief seeped from beneath her closed eyelids as the hot water cascaded over her skin.

He hadn't left her alone to face her pain and she felt pathetically grateful. She kept her eyes closed, not caring that some sprayed her face. He directed water over her legs, balancing her on his knee so he could wash the blood away.

"There's so much," he repeated in a subdued undertone.

"It gets worse every month," she said, wondering at her lack of embarrassment to have him caring for her like this.

But then how many times had she wished he was there to take care of her, that he cared enough to notice how hard her monthly had become and comforted her because of it? Such thoughts had always been in the realm of fantasy before, but now it was a reality and she had a hard time taking it in.

He took care of her with an efficiency and instinctual understanding she couldn't help but admire.

She didn't know how long they showered, but at some point he said, "I think you're safe for the whirlpool now. The bleeding has either stopped or slowed down considerably."

"It comes in fits and starts," she said tiredly as she let him carry her dripping wet to the whirlpool bath.

He didn't drop her into it like she expected, but climbed the steps and stepped down into it with her still in his arms. She made a sound of protest.

"You cannot bathe by yourself in this condition."

"I only plan to lie here."

"And so you will…in my arms."

She didn't argue any further as he settled her between his legs with his arms around her torso so that she did not have to worry about staying afloat or staying put. He took care of it all for her. She sighed contentedly, the meds be-

ginning to take effect and leaned back against him peace-
fully.

She should probably feel guilty for letting him take care
of her like he was taking care of everyone else right now,
but it felt too good…too right for guilt. *And resting in a
whirlpool was not a bad thing for him, either,* a voice inside
her head told her convincingly.

As the pain receded and her sense of well being increased, she let herself relax totally. "This is nice."

"Are you feeling better?"

"Yes." She sighed. "But we'll have to get out soon."

"Why?"

"I may start bleeding again."

He sighed. "We have established that this is not a normal period."

"No, it's not."

"What is going on?"

"I tried to tell you on the plane from New York, but you
didn't want to hear." Which was an accusation, not an
answer, but it still hurt he'd been so ready to dismiss their
marriage that he hadn't even cared what her reasons were
for believing it had to end.

"No. I would remember."

"Yes, I did."

"When did you try to tell me about this awful bleeding
and pain?" he asked, still sounding as if he doubted her.

"When I wanted to tell you why we have to end our marriage, but then you told me you wanted it over anyway and
it didn't seem to matter." Try as she might, she could not
make herself treat it lightly.

It had devastated her and that remembered devastation
was in her voice.

Tension filled the muscular body cradling hers so close. "This is why you asked for a divorce? Because of this pain and bleeding?"

CHAPTER EIGHT

"In a way, yes."

"Explain what way."

"I don't look terrible anymore?" she asked with some of her old sense of humor.

"You sound so tired you can barely stay awake and I should leave this until tomorrow, but I cannot."

"Neither can I," she admitted. She wanted the truth out. She wanted him to stop looking at her as if she'd sold him out to the enemy.

"I have endometriosis."

"What is that?"

She tried to wrap her muddled mind around the clinical description the doctor had given her. "It is a condition linked to my menstrual cycle."

"I had figured that much out myself."

"Yes, well…I'm not a doctor. Explaining diseases doesn't come easily to me."

"I apologize. I should not have been sarcastic."

"It's all right." She was glad he wasn't looking in her face, that their position precluded eye contact because she didn't think she could get through this if she had to see his reaction to her news.

"I…um…"

"Begin at the beginning. What causes the pain?"

"In clinical terms, it's where tissue similar to that in my uterus finds its way into other parts of my pelvic area… well, it can go other places, but isn't as likely to."

"Che cosa?" he asked, sounding shocked.

"Did you have sex education in school?"

"Isole dei Re requires a certain amount of information imparted in its public school system during the final years before university."

"And you went to public school?" she asked with interest, never having actually wondered on that point before.

She knew that his brother's children attended a public school, but Diamante was a small island. She'd never asked if the princes had done the same thing in Lo Paradiso growing up.

"Sì. Of course. If it is good enough for our people, it is good enough for us."

"That's not the attitude of most of the world's royalty."

"We are unique," he said, his voice loaded with arrogance.

"Definitely."

"Enough of the school system, explain this tissue you mentioned."

"Well, I was going to say, can you remember the pictures in sex ed or health class of the female reproductive system?"

"Sì. I am not so old my school days are a blur."

"Good. Picture little dots of tissue on the outside of the fallopian tubes, or the ovaries…or lining the vaginal walls."

The muscular thighs beneath her were rigid with tension. "You are saying you have growths in all these places?"

"Yes."

He cursed.

She sighed. "It could be worse. I'm actually lucky." But not as lucky as the women who did not have the added complication of infertility.

"You do not sound lucky. So these lesions cause pain?"

"They aren't cuts...they're growths, but they fill with blood during the menstrual cycle. There's nowhere for it to go and that causes pain. Lots of pain," she added for good measure.

"This pain...it makes it difficult to make love, no?"

She bit her lip and nodded.

"This is why you have been turning me down so much these past months?" he asked, his voice curiously neutral.

"Yes," she said on a sigh.

"I do not understand why divorce. Surely you know that if you had told me about the pain, I would not have asked for sex."

If only it were that simple. "Yes, I knew that." But knowing it did not change the fact that without the sex she had little value to him.

He might have stayed married to her without the infertility issue, but he would not have been happy about it. She wondered if she had not blundered in her telling, though, if she would ever have known that. She had the sneaking suspicion that his anger had made him more honest than he ever would have been otherwise.

"So, why divorce?"

"My doctor said that between thirty and forty percent of the women who have endometriosis become infertile."

He sucked in a charged breath and then let it out. "Which means that sixty to seventy percent do not."

"I am not one of them."

"What are you saying?"

"The doctor told me that there was almost no chance I could conceive without IVF and even then, there could be no guarantees."

"But you were tested for infertility before our marriage."

"Endometriosis isn't something you can predict. They aren't even sure of what causes it. There are no markers that would show up on tests before it begins happening, so the doctors had no way of knowing that I would have it, much less the impact it would have on my ability to conceive."

"And your doctor, he is certain of the impact it has had on your reproductive capabilities?"

"Yes."

He was silent and she could not stand that silence, so she said, "There are some researchers who estimate it is the cause of up to fifty percent of female infertility."

Which said nothing about the emotional devastation that all too significant statistic wrought. Cold numbers were only that until applied to a flesh and blood woman whose life was forever altered by the disease.

"Obviously many women have this condition then."

"Yes." She could have given him numbers, but they didn't matter. The fact that millions of other women suffered from it did not alter her circumstances.

She was defective and as much as she wished it otherwise, that could not be changed.

"When did it start?"

"I'm not sure. My doctor said that birth control pills are one of the prescribed therapies. It could have started any time since our marriage…even before, but I didn't know because I didn't think the monthly cramps I had were all that unusual."

"The tests…"

"I told you, there is no test for it that gives a marker. Routine fertility tests would only have told us whether my system had been affected prior to our marriage and it wasn't."

"So, you could have had it all along?"

"Yes, but it doesn't usually hit until a woman is in her mid-twenties."

"I see."

"Do you?" She wished she did.

"How did you discover you were suffering from it now?"

"The pain."

"I am sorry."

"Me, too. After I went off the pill, I started bleeding more and hurting way more than I used to during my monthly."

"You never said anything."

"It wasn't your burden to carry."

"How can you say that? I am your husband."

"But I am responsible for myself."

"So you took it upon yourself to find out what was wrong?"

"Not at first, but…" She sighed and told him about the time she woke from a faint with blood beneath her on the bathroom floor. "After that, I knew I had to find out what was wrong."

"Even then, you kept it to yourself."

"It's the way I was raised."

"I cannot believe your parents would have expected you to deal with something of this magnitude on your own."

"Then you do not know them as well as you think you do." Suddenly overcome with tiredness, she slumped back against him.

The pain bombs were having their predictable effect and

her brain was turning to mush. Thankfully she had said pretty much everything that needed saying.

"Perhaps," he admitted, surprising her. Normally he was too arrogant to admit the possibility he was wrong. "You have had the diagnosis confirmed absolutely?"

"Yes." She turned her head against him and closed her eyes, her body so relaxed, she was close to sleep.

He said something, but she didn't quite comprehend it.

"Therese…"

"Hmm…"

"You are not tracking."

"The pills make me loopy. I want to go to sleep now."

She didn't have to tell him twice. He lifted her out of the tub and took care of her as if she were a small child. He dried her and dressed her, making sure she was prepared for more nocturnal bleeding.

Then he carried her through to the bedroom and laid her down on a miraculously clean bed. "The blankets don't have blood anymore."

"I instructed the staff to change it while we were in the bath."

"Oh."

"You did not hear me?"

"Don't know…I miss a lot of stuff when I'm on the pain pills." But vaguely she remembered that phone call. She opened her mouth to tell him so, but then closed it again when she forgot what she was going to say.

"I see."

"What?" she asked muzzily, wondering what he could see that he thought he needed to make note of.

Strange man, her husband.

He said something that she didn't answer. She was too

busy snuggling into her pillow and falling asleep. She vaguely registered being taken into his arms before slipping into total oblivion.

Claudio stared down at the detective's report on his desk with unseeing eyes. It held no great revelations. Not after last night. He now knew...everything. There was no other man. Therese had not been unfaithful, nor did she want to divorce him because she wanted to move on to something better.

She had a medical condition that apparently affected at least one in ten women between the ages of twenty-five and forty. He could not imagine it, had never heard of it and in some respects that made him angry. One day he would be sovereign of his country...did he not need to know about things like this?

Perhaps he and the minister of health should discuss the compilation of a report of women's health issues. He was a twenty-first century prince...not a patriarch from an outmoded era. He was sure his father would agree.

So would Therese...or she would have before. In fact, she would have insisted on taking the project over...before. Now she was intent on leaving him. Filing for divorce and ending their marriage—all because this strange disease had left her virtually infertile.

She saw no hope for their future, but his entire being rebelled at such a solution to her predicament.

He would not let her go.

Only he had this awful suspicion that it wasn't going to be about what *he* wanted. Therese could be incredibly stubborn and she had decided that their marriage was no longer viable because she could not guarantee giving him children—an heir to his throne. Even if he could convince her that he did not see things that way, that he wanted her to stay, she might insist on leaving for the good of Isole dei Re.

She took her duty to her adopted country seriously. She had spent several months hiding debilitating pain and excessive bleeding in order to protect its inhabitants and the rest of the royal family from turmoil and speculation over her health. He could not believe he had been stupid enough now to believe that she would have an affair.

Even if she fell in love, she was too intensely aware of her duty to ever do anything to compromise her position. Which knowledge did not make him feel better, though it should have.

Not when she had refused to discuss anything further that morning. She had insisted she had no time if she was going to visit his father before her other duties began for the day. And she had laughed sarcastically when he had suggested that perhaps she should stay in bed and rest.

She'd curled her lip at him with a most un-Therese-like expression. "I've been dealing with this for months now and I'm not in the habit of abandoning my responsibilities because of it."

"But you are ill." And he had not known it, damn it.

"I was ill last month, too, but I did not take to my bed."

"Perhaps you should have."

"This from the man who read me the riot act for canceling my appointments to fly to New York to see him?"

His reaction to that event was going to haunt him for a long time, he just knew it. "I did not realize what was at stake at the time."

"*Nothing* was at stake."

"You can say that when you asked for a divorce?"

"I can say that when I know it to be true. The timing of

my telling you was unfortunate. I should have waited to tell you about my condition until you got back."

"No, you should have told me about your condition as you call it as soon as it began happening." And definitely before she had asked for a divorce, but he wasn't about to say that.

Blaming his vicious reaction to what he thought was news of an affair on her would not help the situation at all. He had to pay for his sins with humility…though it would not be easy to do. It was not a natural state of mind for him.

"You weren't around to tell," she said with unexpected anger, her green eyes snapping at him with derision. "Not during that time of month. You were always careful to plan your out of town business trips for when I wasn't available sexually."

She made it sound like she'd been nothing more than a sexual convenience. "It was not like that."

"It was and is exactly like that. You've been doing it since practically the beginning of our marriage."

"But it is not because I saw you as only a sexual convenience." He'd begun scheduling his trips that way when he realized it embarrassed Therese for him to make sexual overtures during her menses. He always wanted her, so the best solution was to get out of temptation's path.

"You could have fooled me."

"Apparently, I did."

She shrugged. "I have to go."

But he could not leave it there. "I was not *always* gone during your periods. You could have told me, but you chose to hide it from me instead."

"You didn't make it very hard, did you?"

"What the hell is that supposed to mean?"

"You've been swearing a lot lately," she said with what he thought was total irrelevance.

"And you have been lying to me for months."

"Covering…it's not the same thing. Ask any politician."

"But you are not a politician. You are my wife."

She pulled on a short pink-and-brown tweed jacket that matched her stylish skirt and flipped her hair out from her collar. "I am a princess…in today's age, that makes me a politician."

"It is because you are my wife that you are a princess. Our relationship comes first."

"Like it did in New York?" she asked as she headed for the door.

"You took me by surprise."

She opened the door, her expression one of cool challenge. "Hindsight is always twenty-twenty, or so they say, but your eyesight has been purely myopic where I'm concerned from the very beginning, Claudio. You see what you want to see, perceive only what is convenient and totally disregard everything else. Trying to rewrite our short history for the sake of my feelings or your pride will not change that reality."

"I thought you were happy being my wife." At least he had until the last few months.

"I was, but that doesn't alter the fact that you made it so easy to hide my illness from you. Why was it so easy, Claudio? Why didn't you care enough to notice that some months it was all I could do to hold it together?"

He had no answer, his gut tightening at the question and something in the region of his heart squeezing in a painful vise. She had turned and walked away then. No more questions. No histrionics, just a dignified exit…something she excelled at.

He had made it a point to be at the palace for lunch, but she had treated him like he was a stranger. Tomasso, Maggie and Flavia had been there as well and he had received a few odd looks from each of them, but no one pried. Flavia had looked at Therese several times, her brown gaze darkened with worry…but still no questions were asked.

And Claudio wondered why it was that an obvious problem could exist and yet no one remark upon it, but he could never remember it being any different. They were a royal family and they did not air their concerns in public, but when had that stretched to meaning he should not ask his wife why the heck she was acting so loopy?

He'd made assumptions about what that had meant and could not have been more off target if he had tried. He had believed she was having an affair and it had gutted him. But never once had he simply asked why she did not want to make love as frequently, why she zoned off when they were talking sometimes and why she had started pulling away from him.

Why hadn't he?

The easy answer was that he had not wanted to hear what he thought was the answer, but it was more complicated than that. It had to do with an unspoken rule in his family that one did not discuss unpleasantness. A rule he had been completely unaware of on a conscious level until now.

The Scorsolinis were men of action, but talking about something as esoterical as feelings was an anathema to most of them. And admitting weakness was even worse. To have admitted he was worried, that he missed her formerly generous passion in bed would have been beyond his ability.

Which meant what? That he was willing to pretend nothing had changed when things patently had changed for the sake of his pride.

While all along, his wife had been battling this horrible, painful disease and telling no one. Because no one had asked. *He had not asked.* Guilt consumed him. He should have known something was wrong, even without asking. She was right…he'd made it too easy for her to hide her illness, but not because he had not cared.

Would he be able to convince her of that?

He got the impression she did not think he cared at all and nothing could be further from the truth. He had thought she was growing bored with his lovemaking when in fact she had simply been protecting herself. Did she not realize that a man needed to know these things?

Looking down at the report he had to acknowledge that there apparently was a great deal she had kept from him during their three-year marriage. Things she had obviously not realized he needed to know.

He found it incomprehensible that she had a secret doctor in Miami who had diagnosed her. She'd said that she had been going to this doctor for anything of a delicate nature since the very beginning of their marriage. How many appointments had she kept in secret, how many trips had she made and worked the visit in?

And how had she managed to do it while traveling with a security detail? He did not like the feeling there was a whole side to his wife he had not known existed. He did not like much of anything about this situation.

She said the doctor was discreet and that was why she had gone to him. She'd wanted to keep gossip out of the tabloids, but that did not explain her reticence in telling

Claudio the truth. He was her husband, but she treated him like an adversary to be warily regarded and gotten around. She did not trust him at all.

There might not be another man in her life, but Claudio did not hold the place he should rightfully hold in it, either. And if her comments over the past few days were any indication, she did not believe she held the right place in his priorities, either. Their marriage was in trouble on a wholly different level than he had suspected, but it was in trouble nonetheless.

Things were not supposed to come to this pass. He had married Therese for the express purpose of preventing that eventuality. He had chosen her not based on emotion, but because she appealed to every need he had identified in having a wife meet.

She was not meeting those needs now and had some harebrained idea of ceasing doing so altogether. She wanted to end their marriage because her body would not cooperate in her role of providing him an heir. She seemed to think he would understand and approve this so-called solution. But there was no honor in abandoning a wife because she could not have children. And he was a man who had been raised to have honor.

She would learn that a Scorsolini did not give up at the first sign of adversity.

CHAPTER NINE

THERESE was dressing when Claudio walked into their bedroom. She flicked him a quick glance and then looked away again. There was an air about him she did not want to contend with at the moment. Creases around his eyes spoke of tiredness, but the look in them spoke even more eloquently of determination.

He had made some kind of decision. And why was she so sure she was going to argue with him about it? She didn't know, but her instincts were warning her with clamoring bells to be on her guard.

His hand settled on her shoulder and she had to fight a rearguard action against her body's natural response to his touch. She wanted to lean into him, to draw on his strength, but she'd learned the only strength she could rely on was her own.

His thumb brushed up the curve of her neck. "How are you feeling, *cara?*"

Stepping away from the insidious touch, she grimaced at the question she had heard numerous times already that day. "Fine."

He sighed and then moved to the other side of the room. "Why do I not believe you?" he asked as he started stripping out of his business suit.

"You have a suspicious mind?" she mocked without looking at him. Visual contact with his spectacular form was bad for her self-control. Even when the prospect of making love was absolutely off-limits.

"Perhaps my suspicious mind is justified," he said with an undertone she did not like.

Her gaze swung to him, but he was facing away, pulling off his shirt. Her heart accelerated as his tawny, muscular body came into view. A fierce wave of possessiveness poured through her and it was all she could do not to cross the room, touch that bare skin and declare it hers.

The primitive part of her did not recognize the practical need to end their marriage.

"What do you mean?" she asked, her voice a little high as she slid her feet into a pair of Vera Wangs.

They perfectly complemented the green sheath dress she'd chosen to wear for dinner, but their pointy toes weren't quite as comfortable. The dress was formfitting but did not rub against her abdomen and the hem stopped right above her ankles, making modest sitting easier without having to stay perfectly erect with her knees right together.

The less stress on *all* of her muscles the better.

Claudio turned around to face her, catching her ogling his body, but he didn't seem to notice.

He buttoned his shirt with deft fingers while his eyes challenged her. "You have kept a lot hidden from me in the past months. Pain you should have told me about. Excessive bleeding that could have been dangerous. I can be forgiven for not taking your word for how fine you feel at the moment."

His complacent judgment made her angry. She had been protecting him, darn it. "You want the truth?" she asked shortly and glared at him. "I'm cramping so badly I just want to lie down and die, but I'm not going to and telling you about the pain won't make it go away."

He paled at her words, but made no signs of backing down. "I cannot fix what I do not know about."

Typically arrogant Scorsolini male, thinking he had control of everything in his known universe.

She turned away from him to put on her jewelry. "You can't fix this at all."

He said nothing and she worked at putting her earrings on with trembling fingers. When she finished, she surveyed her image in the mirror critically. Her hair was down because she simply hadn't wanted to deal with putting it up, but she didn't look messy…or like she was in pain.

And for that she was grateful. She turned to leave and almost ran into him.

He steadied her with his hands on her shoulders, his expression grim. "Perhaps I cannot rid you of this condition, but I can arrange for you to lie down and have a tray brought up for your dinner."

It was so tempting, but she couldn't start giving into the endometriosis now. She'd fought too hard not to. "No."

He frowned, his eyes narrowing in disapproval. "Why not?"

"I don't want your family speculating about my health. They are under enough stress as it is."

"So are you."

"It is my choice, Claudio."

"And if I take that choice from you?"

It wasn't an idle comment. She could see it in his eyes. He would follow through with the least provocation.

"Don't threaten me."

He made a sound of disgust. "I am not threatening you. I am trying to take care of you as I should have been doing for these past several months."

Oh, no…a Scorsolini male in guilt mode was a terrifying thing. "That has never been your job, Claudio. I don't need you to take care of me. I'm not a child."

"How can you say it is not my job? You are my wife. My responsibility."

"A prince cannot look at life that way."

"This prince does."

He could have no idea how much she'd wanted to hear that sentiment months ago, but she'd already learned by then that a princess could not rely on coddling or tender loving care when she was sick. At least not from her husband. And not from anyone if she had duties to perform in the face of it.

"That's something new."

"Perhaps," he acknowledged without apology, "but it is still the right thing."

"No, it is not. It is you being stressed by everything else and adding me to your list of burdens, but I won't be added. Do you hear me? You've got enough to worry about right now without worrying about me."

"I will not dismiss you because I have other things that require my attention as well."

"Why not? You've done it before."

His mouth settled in a grim line. "That is not true."

She stepped out from under his hands. "You're welcome to your perception."

"There have been times I have had to put you second, yes, but that was because I was forced to do so by circumstance. I have never forgotten about you, or dismissed you from my thoughts or consideration."

He sounded like her believing him really mattered, but she wasn't up to an all out discussion on their marriage right now. She hadn't been exaggerating when she told him she was in pain and arguing with him wasn't making her feel loads better.

"We need to hurry, or we'll be late for dinner."

"I prefer that you stay up here and rest."

"I don't."

He sighed again. "You do not wish my family to worry about you, but it is all right for me to worry because you will not take better care of yourself?"

"I'm not doing anything that is putting my health further at risk," she said with exasperation.

"You are in pain, you should not be pushing yourself like this."

"Eating dinner with your family is hardly what I term pushing myself."

"Because you are so used to putting duty first."

"That isn't what you said in New York."

"It is exactly what I said, if you would remember. That is why your behavior shocked and worried me so much."

"You did not act worried. You acted angry." Furious, in fact.

"I *was* angry. I believed you had other reasons than your health for doing as you did."

She stopped with her hand on the doorknob, her attention arrested. What motivations could he have attributed to her behavior that would have made him as full of rage as he had been in New York? "What other reasons?"

"Nothing I wish to discuss now."

Somehow, she just knew he was hiding something…
maybe even something important. "But I wish to discuss it."
Then the dinner gong sounded over the intercom and she
frowned. "We'll return to this after dinner."

"There is no need. It does not matter."

"It does to me." But maybe she would take her painkillers first.

He put his arm out to her, "Shall we go?"

She took his arm, unable to stifle the zing of electricity
that arced between them at the touch. "No more arguing
that I am better off in bed?"

"I am conserving my energy." He opened the door and
led her out into the hall.

"For what?"

"Our discussion after dinner."

"But you said you didn't want to discuss what you believed." She couldn't believe he was giving in so easily
about her going to dinner or about having the conversation
he was so set against.

It was so unlike him. She'd fully intended to persuade
him to come clean, but she'd thought it would take a lot
more effort.

"I do not, but we have other things on the agenda."

"Like what?"

"Like the fact that there will be no divorce."

There was no chance to respond as they met up with
Tomasso and Maggie in the corridor and walked down together. Marcello and Danette were waiting in the drawing
room when they arrived.

He smiled when he saw that Claudio was with Therese.
"I am glad to see you have decided to eat a decent meal
for a change."

"I have been eating," Claudio said with a frown.

"In high stress, business environments or at your desk. Time with your family is more relaxing."

Claudio smiled, making Therese's heart twist in her chest. "Are you so sure about that?"

His affection for his brothers was so strong. All she had ever wanted was for a little of that to rub off on her, but it never had and now he had some harebrained idea they had to stay married. But she knew it would be for all the wrong reasons...reasons she could not give in to.

The Scorsolini guilt gene at work, but that was not enough to carry a marriage facing the challenges theirs would. Not for long anyway.

"But of course," Marcello said drolly. "Would you deny it?"

"No," Claudio said quite seriously. "It has been a hectic week all told."

Marcello and Tomasso both nodded, frowning. Tomasso said, "I wish there was more I could do to carry Papa's burden."

"But there is not." Claudio smiled, but it was rough around the edges and Therese wondered if his brothers saw that. "I am his heir. I alone must fill many of the gaps left by his absence while in hospital."

"You are doing an amazing job," Maggie said softly, her sweet smile warming Therese despite the dragging pains in her lower pelvis.

"I forget what kind of pressure you all live under when Marcello and I are in Italy. The world seems so normal there. I can almost forget I'm married to a prince...being a tycoon is enough, I guess. But the minute we arrive here, the burden you all carry becomes apparent." Danette shook her head. "I pray it will be easier for our children." She rubbed her tummy as if comforting the baby within.

When Marcello reached over to do the same thing, something painful twisted inside Therese.

"I think it will be," Tomasso said.

"Yes," Marcello added. "You must remember, *amante,* that our baby has only a prince, not a king for a father."

"This is true," Tomasso said, "but even the children Claudio will have one day will have the benefit of more extended family to help carry the burden of office. Our father had no brothers to help carry his burden. I see a marked difference already in Gianni and Anna's childhood to our own."

"But Claudio's children will still have a harder time of it than ours will."

Tomasso agreed with a sigh. "I feel selfish in my gratitude, but I am glad that my son will not grow up to one day rule Isole dei Re."

"It's strange to think that our children will get to choose their own paths, while their cousins will have most of their future determined by their birth," Maggie said with a thoughtful frown.

"Did it bother you to know growing up that you had no choice but to be king?" Danette asked Claudio as the men led their wives into dinner.

Claudio waited until after he had seated Therese to answer. Then he looked at Danette. "I never rebelled against my future. I remember only knowing from the earliest age that one day I would be king and that that role carried with it grave responsibilities. It has meant at times that I had to put my life as an individual man aside."

Therese felt there was a message for her in his words.

"I don't envy Therese her position," Maggie said with a smile for Therese. "It's got to be hard to share your husband in such a big way with the people of his country."

Therese could not deny the words, but something was not right about them either. If Claudio loved her, she did not think sharing him with the people and problems of Isole dei Re would bother her at all.

"It is a difficult role, but my wife has always been more than equal to the task," Claudio said, approval for her lacing his voice.

She turned to face him and for several seconds the other occupants of the room seemed to fade away. There was just her and Claudio and some message was being spoken between them without words.

For no reason she could discern, tears burned the back of her eyes. "I cannot regret marrying you."

"It is not my intention that you ever shall." Then he leaned forward and did something he had never done before.

He kissed her softly and full on the lips right there in front of his family. Afterward, he straightened and began talking to his brothers as if nothing out of the ordinary had happened.

But Therese felt like her world had rocked on its axis.

Dinner was a convivial meal, but as time wore on, it became more and more difficult for her to mask her pain. She stopped eating more than a bite or two from each course after the soup. The cramping was getting very bad again, almost debilitating. Probably because she had taken non-prescription pain meds all day, not wanting to be so loopy she could not fulfill her obligations.

Perhaps she should have taken some before dinner, but she hated zoning off in the middle of conversations. And her sisters-in-law were very astute women. They would have noticed something was wrong…unlike Claudio.

Trying to find a more comfortable position, she shifted in her chair for the third time in ten minutes. Rather than make the pain more tolerable, the shift made it more acute and she had to stifle a gasp. She couldn't quite mask her wince though.

Claudio stood suddenly. "I believe Therese and I will retire early."

Tomasso frowned. "But dessert has not been served."

"We are both tired and need our rest."

He reached for Therese's arm, the expression in his eyes one of a hawk ready to swoop down on its prey. "Come. It is time you were in bed."

She knew she had no chance and therefore did not argue.

"That is not a bad idea," Tomasso said, but the look he was giving Maggie indicated sleep was the furthest thing from his mind. She blushed, but smiled back with obvious delight at his words.

Claudio waited until they were out of the room before swooping. He reached down and lifted her high against his chest with a gentle hold that made her feel secure and coddled as she had told him she did not need to be.

Liar. For it was exactly what she wanted.

"Put me down," she protested nonetheless. "I can walk." But it was so nice not to have to. "What if one of your brothers comes out and sees you carrying me like this, or one of the servants? There will be speculation."

"I never realized you were so afraid of gossip."

"I'm not."

"Then explain why all of your doctor appointments have been secret and in the States."

"I was avoiding a media frenzy."

"Gossip."

"Are you saying you aren't worried about it? You wouldn't care if the papers got word of my infertility tomorrow? I remember how upset you were with me for going to the hotel's hot tub rather than staying in my room when I took Maggie shopping in Nassau."

"You were inviting gossip then over something quite innocent. It is different to feel the need to hide a very real health problem for the sake of appearances."

"I wasn't hiding it for the sake of appearances."

"Were you not?"

"No. I just…I didn't want it to come out before we divorced. It would have made you look badly in the eyes of the public. The average person just doesn't understand what it means to be royalty."

"Since there will be no divorce, your concern was not justified."

"You're being foolishly stubborn and I don't care what you say. I don't want your family getting all worried over nothing."

"Your condition is far from nothing, but as for your current agitation. Calm yourself. Any servant who saw me carrying you like this, or my brothers for that matter, would assume I was in a hurry to have my wicked way with you."

"That's not on." Not that she didn't want him…she always did, but pain was a strong deterrent from making love.

He stopped halfway up the marble staircase and glared down at her. "Do you really believe I would try to seduce you in your current condition?"

He looked thoroughly put out with her.

She grimaced. "No, of course not. I don't know why I said it."

She really didn't. She knew in the very depths of her being that he would never willingly hurt her physically. She remembered the pains he'd taken with her virginity and felt a familiar lump of emotion form. He was such a good man and the last thing she wanted to do was let him go.

She'd spent months shoring up her defenses against him, enumerating his faults in her mind so that she would not be tempted to fight for her marriage, but all those defenses were crumbling. It was going to hurt so much to walk away from this man that she loved.

"Good, because only a selfish bastard would ignore both your period discomfort and pain to try something like that."

"I never said you were those things."

"Perhaps not in so many words…" he allowed, but the implication was clear that she had convinced him she thought that.

She stared in shock at his granitelike features as he resumed his climb up the stairs. "I have never implied I believe that about you."

"What do you call assuming divorce was the only option when you discovered you had endometriosis?"

"Practical. I call it practical." The only solution that made sense. Particularly now that she knew he had grown bored of her. Had come face-to-face with the reality that her only value to him was a sexual one. Only, even knowing that to be true, part of her heart rebelled at it.

Part of her…the very foolish part…simply refused to believe.

He said nothing, but his expression was not pretty.

Once they reached their apartments, he carried her straight through to the bedroom. "I will get your pain pills."

He laid her on the bed and then turned to get her meds. He shook two out into his hand and gave them to her. Then, like the night before, he helped her swallow them, sitting beside her and putting one arm around her shoulders for support.

She took the pills.

"Is this your version of coddling?"

"Do you feel coddled?"

Regardless of her pain, she smiled. "Yes."

"Then, yes."

"Thank you."

"Do not thank me. This should be your right."

"So, you're being so careful with me out of duty?"

"Tell me something, *cara*."

"Yes?"

"Until recent months, your response to me in bed and generosity with your body were all that a man could wish for."

"So you've said." He had valued her for them.

"Were they the result of doing your duty?"

"No, of course not. How could you ask me that?"

"As easily as you now ask if what I do for you is from duty alone."

"You don't love me, Claudio."

"I care for you. I have always cared."

"I thought so, too…in the beginning."

"What changed?"

"I don't know. Maybe nothing."

"But still you became convinced I do not care."

"You said you were bored with me."

"I was angry. It was a lie."

She didn't believe him, but bent over in an acute attack of pain before she could say so.

He lowered her to the bed. "Therese?"

The tightening in her lower abdomen relaxed some and she straightened, breathing shallowly to manage the pain.

"Is it very bad?" he asked.

"Yes."

"The hospital?"

"No."

"You are not reasonable."

"Arguing does not help me control the pain."

His jaw clenched. "We should not have gone down to dinner."

"Is that the royal we? If I recall, you were proposing I stay here to eat off a tray, not you."

"But naturally, I would have stayed with you."

There was nothing natural about it. In fact, this whole coddling thing was unnatural in their relationship. "Why?"

"You are ill."

"And you have obligations to your family."

"Which I was content to dismiss in favor of obligations related to my office for the past week. I was here at the palace for you."

"I don't understand why."

"You are my wife." He said it as if that should explain everything, but it didn't. Not by a long shot.

"I was your wife two years ago when I had the flu as well, but you didn't stay with me then. In fact, you had me moved to another room for convalescence so there was no risk of passing the bug on to you. I was your wife last year when I had a cold and you left me to the tender care of servants while you flew to Italy on business."

He looked at her like he did not understand the corre-
lation she was trying to draw. "Those circumstances were
different."

"In what way?"

"You were not in excruciating pain and we knew each
ailment would run its course."

"And *duty* precluded you offering anything resembling
tender loving care."

"Did you want me to become your nursemaid? I did not
see that desire in you at the time. You are a very independent person when you are ill. But then I think that for all
your quiet gentleness, you are an extremely independent,
not to mention stubborn woman all of the time."

"Thank you for not mentioning it," she said sarcastically. "And I'm not independent."

"Oh, but you are. So independent that you have taken
it upon yourself to make decisions about our marriage
without consulting the other primary partner first."

"That's why I went to New York…to consult."

"A demand for a divorce is not a consultation."

"I wasn't going to start it that way, but you put me on
the defensive the way you jumped down my throat for
coming at all."

"I leaped to a false conclusion and was cruel to you
because of it. I am sorry." He said it stiffly, like he was embarrassed, and she remembered his comment before dinner.

"What false conclusion?"

"I would prefer not to get into that."

"Too bad…just wondering what could make you look
so uncomfortable is taking my mind off my cramps."

He said something she didn't get, but there was no mistaking the irritation in his manner as he scooted to sit back on the bed with his back against the headboard.

At her questioning look, he shrugged. "If you're going to grill me, I want to be comfortable."

She hid an unexpected smile. He sounded so surly.

"Tell me about your false conclusion."

CHAPTER TEN

"It was a conclusion that made sense at the time."

"You're stalling. Tell me about it."

"I believed you had found someone else."

"What?"

A dark burn washed across his sculpted cheekbones. "I became obsessed with the idea you had fallen for another man. Your demand for a divorce clinched it."

"Why?" she asked in stunned amazement.

"I could conceive of no other reason you would ask for a divorce."

"But—"

"You had started rejecting me sexually. I did not understand it."

"It hurt."

"But you did not tell me that. I had to draw my own conclusions."

"And that was that I'd taken a lover."

"I did not go that far—I could not imagine it."

"Thank you…I think."

"You had started zoning out during conversations…like you were thinking about someone else."

"My medication."

"Yes."

"I thought you didn't even notice."

"I did. Believe me."

"But you decided the reason was because my heart had become unfaithful to you, if not my body."

"I could not be sure I ever had your heart."

"What do you mean?"

"You have never said you loved me."

"Love was not a requirement of our marriage bargain."

"No, it was not."

Inexplicably she got the impression that he had wanted it to be…for her anyway. But why would he want her love when he did not feel deeply for her? It made no sense. Any more than his newfound desire to coddle her because she was sick.

Or *did* that make sense?

"I think I understand."

"I am glad."

"Not why you believed I'd found someone else." She disabused him of that notion immediately. "But I think I understand you feeling the need to coddle me now."

"Because you are ill?"

"Because you are feeling guilty for thinking I was unfaithful."

"That is not the reason I want to take care of you now."

"But you do feel guilty."

For once it was very easy to read his thoughts. They were written all over his pained features. "Yes. I should have realized you were ill."

"At least you noticed my behavior was out of the ordinary."

"Of course I noticed."

"There really is no *of course* about it. I thought you

didn't particularly care one way or the other that I had started saying no in the bedroom."

He looked at her like she'd lost what was left of her mind. "That is absurd. Naturally I cared, but I was not going to be a petulant child about it. A woman's no is no."

"And why I said no wasn't important?"

"Of course it was important."

"But you would rather think me guilty of immorality than to ask."

"I did ask."

Then she remembered. "And I didn't want to talk about it, but it had been going on for months. Why wait so long?"

He shifted on the bed, his face a study in hard angles and stonelike passivity. "It stung my pride for you to reject me sexually. To talk about it would have made it worse. I would have felt like I was begging for your favors."

"That's absurd."

"It is not absurd. It is truth. Why do you think I was gone so many months during your period?"

"Because it was convenient."

"You do not think much of me, do you?"

"That's not true."

"I believe it is, but it is not the issue under debate, so we will leave it. I organized my travel plans to coincide with your monthly because you made it clear that even light touching during your monthly made you feel uncomfortable. I find it a real challenge to keep my hands off you and the best solution was to be gone from our bed completely. You can believe me, or not…but I organized my schedule for your sake, not my own."

"You have no problem not touching me outside the bedroom."

"If you truly think that, you are blind. I would touch you all the time, but it is not seemly for a king to be that way with his wife."

"You aren't a king yet."

"But I will be. And because of my position, I have set standards for my own behavior. Achieving those standards challenges me, especially where you are concerned. The only place I gave myself permission to be completely free with you was our bedroom. I found it very difficult to police my behavior in there as well," he said as if admitting a grave sin.

"I didn't realize…."

"In my own defense, I thought you knew."

"How could I?"

"I thought my desire for you was obvious."

"It wasn't obvious when you took no so easily and acted as if nothing was different between us. I thought it didn't matter."

"Now you know differently."

"I know that sex is a key element in our relationship, yes."

"You say that like it is a bad thing."

She bit her lip and looked away. How honest should she be? Her marriage was over even if he wasn't willing to recognize that. Was there any use in rehashing old hurts? Then again, hadn't she spent enough of her marriage hiding from him?

She turned her head so their gazes met. "I wanted you to care for me on a level that was more personal than the sexual."

"What is more intimate than sex?"

"I'm not sure how to explain it," she admitted. "It's just that I wanted to be important to you for my own sake…not only because of the pleasure you found in my body, or even how well I did my job as your wife."

"You want me to love you."

"Maybe." She shrugged. "Maybe nothing less than love would have satisfied me, but it doesn't matter anymore."

"You no longer want my love? Is that why you fight my coddling as you call it? You are content to do without me?"

"I don't mean to fight your attention," she said around a yawn as the pain meds started taking serious effect. "It's just come as such a surprise."

The truth was she liked it. Too much. If she let herself get used to it, it was going to be that much harder to walk away, but she couldn't seem to summon the necessary will-power to keep rejecting it, either.

"I'm glad you're here with me right now," she said softly. "Even if you should probably be somewhere else. I know you have too many other responsibilities right now to be worrying about me, but I can't help enjoying the attention. I suppose that makes me weak."

She was speaking to herself really, but he answered.

"No, it does not. It makes you human." He seemed pleased about something, but she couldn't imagine what.

She sighed. "I guess, but you can't afford to take the time to be calling me several times a day, or to keep playing nursemaid."

"You must stop trying to take care of everyone else in the world. I can well afford the time for phone calls and if I do not care for you, who will? You refuse to tell anyone of your condition."

He had a point, but she couldn't leave it there. He was trying to make everything sound so easy and it wasn't. Only her muddled brain was having a hard time remembering why exactly. She remembered one thing.

"You didn't have time for phone calls before."

"I did…until you stopped answering all my calls."

She stared at him, remembering through the mist trying to cloud her mind. What he said was true. He used to call her several times a day, no matter where he was in the world. There had rarely been any more discernible reason for the phone call than to connect briefly. He would ask about something on her schedule or give her a short run-down on his latest meeting. In fact, a lot of communication she took for granted had happened during those calls. It was only when he stopped making them that she realized it. She had started ignoring some of his calls and even cutting him off when she did answer…because he wasn't saying the right thing. "It felt like you were only checking on my role as your princess. The calls were too impersonal."

And that hurt, but then so had having him stop making them.

"How could I have made them more personal?"

Looking back, she saw that for him those calls had been personal, his way of being with her when duty kept them apart so frequently. Her throat tightened with emotion.

"You could have told me…just once…that you missed me."

"I am sorry I did not spell it out. I thought the calls them-selves would give you that message."

"You called me because you missed me?" she asked, even now shocked by the concept.

"*Sì*. For what other reason would I have called and dis-cussed such inconsequential matters?"

"I don't know. My brain is getting fuzzy."

He frowned and got up from the bed.

"If you follow the pattern from last night, you will not be cognizant enough to converse at all in about twenty minutes and there is something I wish to discuss before that happens."

"It was worse last night because I'd lost so much blood and gotten so little sleep," she said woozily.

"If you say so." He began pulling her shoes off. "You have said that surgery is the prescribed cure for endometriosis?"

"Not a cure exactly, but close. It's my best chance for living a fairly normal, pain-free life." She watched as he put her shoes aside and then rolled down her thigh-highs. His eyes flared with hunger as he looked at her exposed legs, but his touch was almost completely impersonal.

"What do they do? They only have to remove your reproductive system?"

At least this conversation was easy. She'd researched the alternatives so thoroughly, she thought she could recite them and their benefits or detriments in her sleep.

"No. Not anymore. They can actually usually remove the growths of tissue through laser surgery. Recovery time is minimal and I don't even have to stay overnight in the hospital afterward."

"But you will."

"I *will?*" she asked delicately, her eyes narrowing.

The look he gave her from his brown eyes said she could argue all she liked, but his mind was made up. "Even laser surgery carries risk and is traumatic to the body. I do not agree with this move in the medical community of dismissing a patient from care too early."

"I'm sure insurance companies have more to do with that than doctor preferences. If you are willing to pay for it, I have no doubt the hospital will happily keep me in residence." She wondered if doing so would help assuage his guilt.

"And this surgery…it is a guaranteed fix?"

"No, but like I said…it's my best chance. A high percentage of the women who elect to have the surgery end up having it again sometime down the road."

"It seems a small price to pay if it will alleviate the kind of pain and bleeding you have been having."

"That's how I see it."

He was taking her dress off and she was letting him. No matter what she said to the contrary it felt wonderful having him care for her like this. Especially knowing that soon he would not be there to even scrub her back in a sexy shower.

He did not offer to get her a gown, but said, "Do you need to fix things up for the night?"

She swung her legs over the side of the bed. "Yes."

But before she could stand up on her own, he was once again lifting her and carrying her into the en suite. He left her to take care of things and was undressed and in bed, his laptop and papers scattered around him when she returned to the bedroom.

"You don't have to go to bed just because I am."

"It is no hardship after the week I had, I assure you."

She nodded, too sluggish from the pain meds to argue further. "Will you at least try to go to sleep before midnight?"

"Do you want me to?" he asked as if the idea pleased him.

"Yes. I don't want you having a heart attack like your dad."

"That would be unfortunate, would it not? After all, who would run our country if we were both convalescing?"

"The mind boggles, but I wasn't thinking about the good of Isole dei Re," she said more candidly than she would have if she wasn't slightly loopy from the pills. "I worry about you. I l—um…I'm going to sleep."

She climbed into the bed, unable to believe she had almost blurted out her love for him.

* * *

Claudio worked beside the sleeping Therese, his mind split between his duties and his wife. If she but knew it, that was not such an uncommon state of affairs. But to hear her tell it, she mattered to him only in a very peripheral way.

And he had allowed her to believe so. It had been a conscious decision, but he had not foreseen the consequences. He had been protecting himself from taking his father's path. He'd never wanted a love that could turn a strong man into a cheat. After the talk with his father in the hospital, perhaps he understood what had driven Vincente so many years ago, but with understanding did not come peace.

The result was the same. Love made fools of men.

But had denying the tender emotion in his relationship with Therese been any big improvement over the vulnerability love caused? He still felt vulnerable…he still felt fear at the prospect of losing her. That was no improvement…and after his erroneous conclusion drawn from her behavior, he felt a fool.

Worse than a fool, he felt like a cruel monster. It had never been his intention that Therese should be hurt by marriage to him. He had believed he was offering her a good life and had thought he would make a good husband. Not a normal husband—a king in the making could not be that—but a good one regardless.

He had not anticipated the current events, but even so…to have failed so miserably at his first real test in the husband department was galling. He did not take failure well. He never had, which was why he worked so hard to avoid it. But there was no denying that he had misjudged his wife and in misjudging her, he had added to her suffering.

He had also destroyed fragile bonds that if he did not repair were going to result in the end of his marriage. He would not accept that, but he was not sure what to do to fix the problem. He felt helpless and that was not a pleasant feeling.

A prince in line to the throne should not be helpless.

He would not be if she cared for him…her love would be a tie that could bind them together, even if he'd made a few rather ugly errors of judgment. But she did not love him. Though, for a second there…just before she had gone to sleep, he had thought she was going to say she loved him. And he had wanted to hear the words. Very much.

She had not said them, though, and he could not help wondering if it had all been a figment of his imagination. Even if she had loved him once, and he thought that was possible, she loved him no longer.

Why did that knowledge hurt so much?

As she had pointed out. Love was not part of their marriage bargain.

But he wanted her love. He…needed it. Somehow, he would convince her to stay married…and perhaps in doing so, give himself another chance at the love that had warmed his very soul before he realized it was ever there. She had married him loving him and only now, looking back, could he recognize that.

She probably thought he did not care, but she was wrong. He cared very much. She was wrong, too, about divorce being the only solution to their dilemma. Just as she had been wrong that his phone calls hadn't meant he missed her. Only now did he recognize how many things she had taken the wrong way and he did not know how to fix that, either.

He had been trained to be a ruler among men, he had not been taught how to soothe a woman's emotions, how to convince her of his affection. He and Therese did not see the world in the same way and he had made the mistake of believing they did. Because of the way she had been raised. But she was still a woman, different from him and her thinking steeped in a logic that was no kind of logic to him.

He'd taken for granted that she knew many things that in retrospect he had to admit had not been as obvious to her as they were to him. He could not be sure if that was a man-woman thing, or something unique to their personalities, but it did not matter either way. She had made faulty assumptions just as he had. If he could admit the fault of his own reasoning, and everyone accepted he had a corner share of the market on stubborn, she could, too.

"You've got to be kidding. Having the procedure right now is impossible."

In a rare moment of solitude, Therese had been relaxing in one of her favorite spots on the manicured grounds behind the palace when Claudio had tracked her down. The sun warmed her while a gentle breeze ruffled her long hair. It was lovely and peaceful…or it had been. Now she had six feet four inches of masculine energy vibrating down at her.

Claudio sat down on the bench beside her, his vitality calling to her senses on a level that had nothing to do with logic or reasoning. "The doctor said there was no problem with you having the surgery as soon as your monthly is over and that should be within the next couple of days."

She was not used to these frank discussions they had been having when for almost three years, the only earthy talk that ever happened between them was in bed. Even then, there were things she simply would not discuss. He'd blown the lid off the taboos in their marriage when he'd taken care of her the other night and seemed to have no desire to go back to the more circumspect relationship they had once shared.

Accepting that truth with what grace she could muster, she argued, "That's not the only thing to consider. Your father is coming home from the hospital today and he will be convalescing for a while yet."

Claudio tensed, his mouth sliding into a frown. "Are you saying you prefer to wait until his health is completely restored?" he asked with disbelief.

"Well, at least until he is well enough to begin taking over some of his duties again."

"That will be six weeks from now," he said grimly.

"Yes, I know."

Claudio cupped her nape, his face set in stern lines. "I will not allow you to go through another period like this last one."

"It is my body." But the words came out breathy. His touch was doing things to her and he wasn't even meaning to, she was sure of it.

Though casual affection was another thing she was not used to from him and didn't know what to make of it now.

"*Sì*. It is your body…a beautiful, generous body that it is my privilege and responsibility to ensure you care for adequately."

"You're my husband, not my father."

"Your father would have ignored your pain. I will not."

He was right, but somehow that memory did not have the power to hurt her as it once had. "I don't want *your* father upset."

Claudio moved his touch from her nape to take her hand in his. He aligned their fingers, his long tanned ones dwarfing hers. "Your hands are so small, so delicate…so beautiful."

The breath froze in her chest for a second and then she inhaled as her heart started tripping. He had commented many times when they were making love how much he adored having her hands on him, but never had he said anything outside the bedroom. "Um…your dad…"

Claudio clasped her hand in his and smiled, disconcerting her further. "Vincente is fine. At my request, he has spent several days longer in the hospital than the doctor initially recommended. During that time, he has been on bed rest and restricted from the phone, but he has been up and about, walking the corridors and visiting other patients since two days after the surgery. He is well on his way to recovery."

"But he's still weak."

"Do not let him hear you say that."

Therese had to acknowledge the justness of that warning. "It's all Flavia can do to keep him in the hospital and resting for long periods."

"Precisely. He would not thank you for trying to protect him at your own expense. I only thank God Mamacita decided now was the time to come back into his life because I do not think the rest of us would have been so successful."

"They're a good couple."

"Yes. It is too bad they took so long to figure that truth out."

"Infidelity isn't something you can easily dismiss."

"Not my father in himself or Flavia in him, I know…but she seems to have come to terms with the past as has he."

"I'm glad." She loved both proud people and was so happy they had found each other again.

"I also, but do not think you are going to derail this conversation. I have spoken to your doctor in Miami and he has agreed to fly here in four days to perform the operation."

"You had no right to call him," she gritted. "And I do not want to have the procedure here."

Claudio glared right back at her, all affability gone, but his hold on her hand was still gentle…as if even in his anger he was cherishing her. "*You* had no right to keep your condition a secret from me. You could have had the surgery months past but for your attempts to do so."

"I told you why I did that."

"I do not agree with your reasons. You should have told me. This is the truth."

She looked out over the grounds. They were sheltered from a view of the palace by trees and shrubbery, but she could see the spires rising above the treetops. "You are too arrogant for words sometimes."

"Only sometimes?"

She laughed. She couldn't help it. He was so unapologetic, but he was being bossy for her benefit. Not to hurt her and deep in her heart she knew that. "It only makes me mad enough to spit nails *sometimes.*"

"I cannot imagine you spitting anything, my proper little wife." He spoke close to her ear, his lips settling in a gentle kiss against her temple before he pulled his head back.

It was a full three seconds before she could respond. Because she knew she had to fight the impact of that kiss, she forced herself to dwell on the unpleasant side of reality. "A proper wife could give you a child. I won't be able to and if I have the surgery here, the whole world will know about it. You'll be labeled heartless and selfish when we divorce."

In a totally unexpected move, he grabbed her by the waist and lifted her onto his lap, then cupped her face so she had no choice but to meet his eyes. "There will be no divorce and if you attempt to leave me, I will be labeled worse than that."

"What do you mean?" she asked and was embarrassed by how weak her voice sounded.

"You will not leave me, Therese."

"You're not talking kidnapping…you can't be." But by the look in his eyes, she could tell he *was* thinking about it. "That's ridiculous, Claudio. You are not one of your marauding ancestors."

"Who says my ancestors were marauders?"

"They were pirates, plain and simple. They used their ill-gotten bounty to establish a country, but they were not the pillars of society their descendants became."

"Are you saying I am a pirate beneath my layers of civility?" he asked, sounding an awful lot exactly like that.

"No…I am attempting to remind you that you are one of those rational, civilized descendants." She looked into his eyes and what she read there made her shiver.

"I would have agreed with you…before, but in the last weeks, I have discovered a heretofore unknown streak of primitive possessiveness where you are concerned that hearkens back to my ancestors quite effectively."

"So you do realize it's there…"

"Yes. And you must also, which then means you should realize how foolish it would be to attempt to leave me."

She glared at his complacent certainty. "If I decide to walk, I will walk."

She meant it, too. Maybe she didn't descend from Sicilian pirates, but she had the blood of Romans running in her veins as well as a good dose of American assertiveness.

CHAPTER ELEVEN

"Do not decide to walk." The pleading in his voice was more astonishing than the fact he'd allowed his primitive streak to show so blatantly.

"What will you do?" she asked softly, trying to read his expression, but not understanding what she saw there.

He was silent several seconds and then he sighed. "Follow you."

She laughed because it was absurd. He was more proud than his father and if Vincente had been unable to bend enough to apologize for behavior he had known was reprehensible, Claudio would never stoop to chasing after a wayward wife. Besides, he couldn't, even if he wanted to. "Your duties wouldn't allow it and you would never lower yourself to tagging after me like a lost puppy."

"Puppies are harmless. I am not. Make no mistake...I would follow you."

"But your duty—"

"My first duty is to you, my wife...and to our marriage. I will not let you go."

He would...if she really wanted to go. Primitive streak, or not...he was a modern man. But what he was saying here was that he would not make it easy. She didn't know if she had the strength to fight both him and her own desire to stay. However, she wasn't sure anymore, either, if she had the strength to stay in a marriage in which she was not loved.

It hurt, as much or more than the endometriosis. She'd learned something last night. Her pain and vulnerability that resulted from loving where the feeling was not returned had made her misinterpret his actions, thereby adding more hurt to her beleaguered heart. Without his love, wouldn't she continue to do that very thing?

No matter how much she might want to avoid it.

She laid her hand over the one against her cheek. "You have to be reasonable about this. Please, Claudio."

"I am not the one being unreasonable here. It is both foolish and dangerous for you to wait to have the surgery. And it is criminally shortsighted for you to believe we must divorce."

"I am infertile. I cannot give you an heir."

"Your doctor said that IVF had a seventy percent success rate with endometriosis patients."

"That is still not a guarantee."

"Neither is unhindered fertility."

"But there's a better chance for you to have children with a woman who does not have endometriosis."

"I do not want another woman!"

She dropped her hand and leaned back with a jerk, stunned by his vehemence. "That's just guilt talking."

He shook his head, barely banked rage glittering in his dark gaze. "It is not guilt. You are my wife. I want you to remain my wife. If there is no other man, why are you so intent on ending our marriage?"

"There is no other man," she exclaimed. "I can't believe we are back to that."

"Then why?"

"It's for the good of the country, Claudio. You would see that if you were thinking with your brain and not your pride."

"No." He glowered. "The good of the country is best served by you staying as my wife."

She couldn't believe he was being so stubborn. "Not if I can't give you children."

"If you cannot, I have brothers and a nephew who are in line to the throne."

"You heard your brothers last night. They don't want their children to have the pressures of growing up to be king."

"Tough," he said without the slightest hint of apology. "While they may not have been born first, they *were* born to a king. If I were to die before having a child, Tomasso would have to take my role and his son would then inherit the throne. It is the way of our bloodline."

She put both her hands on his chest, needing the feel of his warmth under her fingers. "Don't talk about dying."

"Do not talk about leaving me."

"It isn't the same thing."

"No. It is worse, for a man does not choose when he may die but you are talking about willfully killing our marriage and removing yourself from my life."

"For your own good. *Don't you understand that?*" she appealed in a choked voice.

"I understand you believe it is for my good, but you are wrong."

"But—"

"Stop arguing with me. You made a lifetime commitment to me, Princess Therese Scorsolini. I will not let you break it. I will not let you leave me."

"You can't stop me."

"I can. Even if you walk away, I will not remarry. There will be no other chance at heirs for me."

"Once the divorce is final, you'll change your mind," she said, hurting because she was sure it was true.

"There will be no divorce. Perhaps I am not so archaic that I will physically keep you against your will, but there will be no other marriage for either of us."

"You can't stop it."

"I may be powerless to stop some things, my intransigent little wife, but we are talking the divorce laws of Isole dei Re here, not American law. You cannot divorce a member of the royal family without their consent. I will not give it. Ever."

"*That* is archaic."

"Perhaps." He shrugged, obviously not in the least offended by that judgment. "But it is our law. And we were married here, Therese...not in the States. Remember that."

"But—"

"There are no buts." He seemed supremely pleased by that statement, as if a great weight had been lifted from his shoulders.

She didn't understand it. Surely marriage to her was the weight. "You want to be a father."

He smiled and one hand settled gently over her lower abdomen. "Yes, and I would like nothing more than for you to carry my child, but we can adopt if you cannot conceive. You will be such a good mother once you get this notion of divorce out of your head."

"We can't adopt," she gasped. "What about progenitor?"

"Of course we can. As for the ascension to the throne, I will have to name my nephew my successor, but it can be done. We are modern royalty, not one of my ancestors."

"This from the man who just told me he was sticking with an archaic law to keep me married to him?"

"I have had enough of this talk of divorce." He carefully lifted her from his lap and set her on the bench. Then he stood up and looked down at her, his eyes filled with censure. "You are one of the most compassionate people I know, but you do not seem to care when you stomp with hobnailed boots all over my feelings and my ideals. If all you wanted was a sperm donor when you married, why did you not go to a sperm bank instead?"

"What?" Had he lost his mind? "I don't think of you as a sperm donor!"

"But the moment you discover I cannot get you pregnant you are ready to divorce me."

"Not for my sake, *for yours,*" she stressed, but she was beginning to doubt the validity of her own arguments.

He patently did not want a divorce. Whether it was guilt, a sense of responsibility, pride or just plain physical desire not spent that was prompting him, he wanted to stay married...to her. She'd never anticipated this reaction.

He was still glaring down at her. "It is not for my sake if it will make me unhappy."

"*Would* divorcing me make you unhappy?"

"What the blasted hell do you think I have been saying here?"

She stared at him, totally unsure what to say.

"Say something."

"I'm in shock."

"And that makes me angry. What have I done to make you believe our marriage meant nothing to me?"

"We married for convenience. It wasn't about love. I

knew that when you asked me to be your wife. I fit your requirements. All of them."

"You are right…I married you because you were the ideal woman for me. That being the case, what made you determine I have no feelings for you? Of course I do." But he looked like the words shocked him, as if he was having some kind of major inner revelation.

She refused to speculate about what that could be. She'd hurt herself too much already believing in moonshine and manmade miracles.

"You are everything I wanted in a woman and more, *cara*," he said more quietly.

"But you don't love me."

"What is love, if it is not what we have?"

That at least, she had a definitive answer for. "It's what your brothers have with their wives. I've seen a Scorsolini male in love…first Tomasso, then Marcello and even lately your father with Flavia. *It is not the way you are with me*."

"So, what is it you think I feel for you?"

"Desire. I think you like me…or at least you used to. I think you feel guilty now…because you wish you'd noticed my condition before, and maybe even because you were so cruel about the divorce before you knew why I had suggested it."

"But you are certain I do not love you?"

"Yes."

"I suppose that makes us even," he said on a sigh. "But things are about to change around here."

With that he turned and walked away.

With King Vincente's return to the palace, things were too hectic the rest of that day for Therese to think much about

Claudio's final statement in the garden. However, that night when she was alone in their apartments while he attended a function in his father's stead, her mind chewed on it endlessly.

She had suggested she should go with him to the State dinner, but Claudio had refused and no amount of arguing on her part would change his mind. She had even had to assure him that she was feeling much better, which she was, before he had been willing to go himself. Which was a hundred and eighty degree turn around for him.

Duty came first, last and always for Claudio Scorsolini.

Or it had…maybe it still did. He said his duty to her as his wife was of primary importance, but it hadn't always been that way. She knew it hadn't. There was too much evidence to the contrary. What had changed? Or, maybe she was tipping at windmills to think anything really had. Only, was guilt really strong enough of a motivator to make someone as entrenched in his responses to life as Claudio change so much? It seemed a stretch, even for a Scorsolini.

Equally as important, what had he *meant* in the garden?

In saying they were even did he mean that he agreed with her and that *he* didn't think he loved her, either? Or was he saying that he didn't believe *she* loved him? And in either case…what did he mean that things were going to change? No matter how she looked at it, the implication was that love was entering into their marriage bargain…by Claudio's say so.

Despite her final plea to the contrary, he told his family about her condition the next day. He also told them that she would be having surgery for it, and how soon. In a move that was again totally out of character, he had gone on to tell them that while surgery would hopefully take care of her symptoms, enough damage had already been done to her female organs that without IVF, she was for all intents and purposes infertile.

His brothers and father were clearly stunned by his openness, but the other women treated the news as if it was something that the whole family should know. But just as Therese had thought it would, the news caused a minor uproar in the family with Flavia taking it hardest of all.

She and King Vincente were sitting together on the butternut-yellow suede leather sectional sofa in the family reception room.

The family reception room was the only one in the palace that was decorated with comfortable modern furniture. Therese had insisted on disposing of the formal pieces and furnishing the room in warm tones and comfortable seating arrangements. King Vincente had informed her that the two recliners she'd had installed were the only ones that had ever been allowed in the palace. A month after the room was finished, he requested a recliner for his own apartments as well.

She'd wanted a place to congregate comfortably as a family once their children came along. It had been important to her to raise her sons and daughters with a sense of normalcy pocketed into every aspect of their lives. She'd wanted warmth and togetherness to be a natural part of their lives, not an anathema. The Scorsolinis were warm and loving people and cooperated with her despite their royal heritage.

Everyone was in there now except Tomasso's children, who had gone to bed already. King Vincente should probably have been sleeping as well, but that was not an option.

While he had been willing to sit with his feet up on the chaise lounge at one end of the sectional, he had drawn the line at being sent to bed like a child as he had put it. Flavia had grumbled, but she had fussed around him to make sure he was comfortable and then taken her seat beside him.

Therese was sitting on the part of the sectional catty-corner to her mother-in-law. Claudio had pulled her down to sit beside him rather than allowing her to take an arm-chair which was her normal habit. Then he'd draped his arm over her shoulders with casual possessiveness. It felt nice, if a bit strange.

Tomasso was seated in one of the recliners with Maggie settled snugly in his lap. Which was a lot more intimate...so Therese was not embarrassed. Marcello and Danette were at the other end of the sectional, his arm around her waist and her back against his body rather than the sofa.

Flavia's beautiful dark eyes filled with stricken emotion. "I knew something was wrong, but I hesitated to say anything. I am so sorry. Many times, you must have been in pain and hiding it."

Therese couldn't deny it, but she didn't want her mother-in-law to feel guilty because of it. It was hardly Flavia's fault that the endometriosis was so painful. Or anyone else's for that matter.

She reached out to touch Flavia's hand. "It's all right. Saying something would not have made a difference."

"On the contrary, had we known sooner, your treatment could have happened sooner."

She glared sideways at Claudio. "It's hardly your mother's fault."

"I did not say it was, but had you said something earlier,

it would have been better for your own sake and much could have been avoided between us."

She couldn't believe he was saying that in front of his family. "Let's not get into that right now," she hissed.

"If that is your wish, but it is the truth."

She couldn't quite stifle her sigh of irritation.

Tomasso made a choking sound on the other side of the room and Maggie nudged him with her elbow.

"What is so amusing, *fratello mio?*"

"Therese is frowning at you."

"You find this funny?" Claudio asked, sounding far from amused himself.

"You must admit, it is not like her," Marcello said, his own eyes shimmering with amusement.

Therese looked at both brothers and wondered what had gotten into them. "You think the fact I am upset with my husband is a joke?" she asked with a puzzled frown.

They were both usually more sensitive than that. They were Scorsolini men, which meant they weren't the most intuitive when it came to emotions, but this was odd even for them.

Danette bit her lip and then smiled with a shrug. "You've got to admit, it isn't like you, hon."

"The day your father and Claudio grilled me, you were really annoyed with them, but you were so subtle about it. The classic princess." Maggie grimaced. "I was sort of awed by you, to tell the truth."

Therese didn't know what to say. They were all right… she was not hiding her emotions as well as she used to. But why should they find that *funny?*

"When you are annoyed with my brother, you do not hide that fact," Claudio said to Maggie.

"Not in front of family, no," Maggie agreed with a rueful smile.

"You can say that again," Tomasso said with a laugh and promptly received another playful elbow to his ribs.

Ignoring the byplay, Claudio turned to look down at Therese. "Our marriage is not so different from theirs."

In that moment, when he was behaving toward her very much the way his brothers were toward their wives, she wasn't sure what to say…if anything to refute that statement.

"No, I do not think your marriage is so different," Flavia said, her expression stern. "But I had wondered when *you* would wake up to that fact, my son."

"I assure you, I am very awake to it now," Claudio replied allowing his gaze to flick momentarily to his step-mother, apparently not in the least offended by her censure.

It almost seemed as if there was another level of silent communication going on between them. Like this discussion was not entirely new to them.

But Therese gasped. *Was he trying to imply he loved her?*

His focus returned to her, his eyes filled with wary vulnerability. "What? You have not noticed the similarities?"

"No…um…I hadn't."

Flavia shook her head. "That is not surprising after your upbringing, but child, you must stop looking at our Claudio through the eyes of a diplomat's daughter and begin to see him with the eyes of a woman who is willing to trust his heart and her own."

Flavia had her full attention now. "What do you mean, considering my upbringing?"

"You have not known unconditional love…I think in fact, you have known very little love at all. You are used to assuming it is not there, when in fact, it is."

For no reason she could discern, Therese's chest tightened with emotion. "I don't understand."

"We all love you, that is all I am saying." Flavia squeezed Therese's hand.

Tomasso smiled. "Yes, and while I would be honored to have my son one day sit on the Scorsolini throne, I cannot help hoping IVF works for you two."

"Because you don't want him to know the pressure of ruling a kingdom?" Therese asked, painfully uncertain of the rightness of staying married to Claudio.

"Because any child born to you and my brother will be very blessed and a beautiful addition to this world."

"That is a lovely thing to say and quite true besides." Flavia smiled her approval on Tomasso and then turned to adjust the blanket covering King Vincente's legs.

"Stop fussing, *amore*. I am fine." The king reached out and brushed a finger down Flavia's cheek. "So long as you stay with me, I am fine."

Flavia smiled, her eyes filled with obvious love, but said nothing.

"Is this where you two announce you are getting married again?" Danette asked, her hazel eyes alight with pleased speculation.

Incredibly, Flavia blushed and sent an uncertain look at each of her sons. The king just grinned. "Yes, my children that is exactly what happens next."

"That is wonderful! When is the wedding?" Marcello asked.

"In three month's time...when it is safe to have a wedding night," King Vincente replied with a roguish look at Flavia. "Though I tried to convince your mother six weeks was sufficient, she was adamant."

A real blush now staining her cheeks, she slapped his arm gently. "We have waited more than two decades to be together that way again, we can wait a few additional weeks so my worries are set at rest."

After that, hugs and kisses of congratulations ensued. The attention was firmly removed from Therese and Claudio, for which she was eternally grateful.

Later, she was lying awake in the dark, her mind spinning with what Flavia had implied and the strange way Claudio had been behaving. Even now, he slept facing her, his head above hers on the pillow, one hand on her shoulder, the other resting lightly on her hip and his calf slung over hers. She was wrapped up as if he was afraid she would get away.

"Explain to me how you believe a Scorsolini man in love behaves." His deep voice coming out of the dark startled her.

"I thought you were asleep."

"I am not."

"Apparently."

"So, tell me."

"Why?"

"Please, *tesoro mio,* do not play games with me."

"I'm not trying to, but I don't understand where this is coming from."

"You told me you were sure I did not love you because I am not the husband to you that my brothers are to the women they love. I want to know how in specific terms I have failed."

She felt like she couldn't breathe. "Why?"

"So I can fix it."

"You want me to believe you love me?" she asked softly.

"Is that not obvious?"

"Maybe it should be, but no…it's not really."

"It is as Flavia said…you are so unused to receiving love, you do not recognize it when it is around you."

"I want to be loved," she admitted with a vulnerability she would never have shown him before the watershed of events in the past two weeks.

"I do love you, Therese, and one day you will know it."

No, it wasn't possible, but why was he saying it? Guilt could prompt a lot of things, but not a false confession of love from him. She didn't think. "Are you saying you love me because you think you have to…are you trying to make up for something?"

"No." That was all. A simple no. He didn't get all offended, or cranky, or try to convince her with more words.

And there was something incredibly convincing about that simplicity.

"I…"

"You are unsure. I understand this. I did not realize I loved you when I married you. You can be forgiven for not being aware of it as well. Flavia noticed, but she also saw that I was fighting it. *Porca miseria*…I was so foolish, I did not even see your love for me, but I noticed when it was gone."

"Gone?" she asked faintly, tipping her head back so she could see his face.

Or at least the shadow of it in the darkness of the room.

She could feel his gaze burning into her even though he could not see her any better in the dark than she could see him. "Yes, gone. Did you think I would not notice? I assure you, I am not quite that unobservant. The way you used to look at me as if I was all you could ever want…the way you lit up when I came into a room. It is gone." His voice was laced with a pain she understood only too well. "I only pray that with God's help and the advice of my family, I will be able to earn it back again."

"You've asked your family…your *brothers* for advice… on winning my love?" she asked in total shock.

"Yes, though neither seems particularly smart on the subject." Claudio sounded very disgruntled by that truth.

"What did they say?"

"Tomasso suggested I woo you in bed, but that is not an option and I do not want to wait until it is to convince you."

"Oh…"

"Marcello suggested I talk honestly with you, but I have been doing that for days now and it does no good."

"Honest communication is necessary to a strong relationship." But the person you were communicating with had to believe you and not second-guess your motives… like she had been doing with his.

Could it be true? Did he love her? She'd been wrong about so many things and so had he, but he apparently wanted to fix his shortcomings. He wanted her to feel loved.

"That is what Flavia said, but Papa thinks you need proof. Again, I did not find that very useful. I do not know what proof to give you."

She actually smiled at the disgruntled tone in his voice. "Your brothers had no suggestions for that?"

"As I said, nothing I could use."

"Bed is not the only place to express love." But she saw now that it had been the place he had been most comfortable doing so.

"I know this. I reserved all my affection and the release of my emotions for the bedroom, but that only convinced you your primary use to me was as a bedmate. And it isn't, *amore.* Please believe that you have always mattered to me on every level a woman can impact a man. I could slice out my own tongue for some of the things I said after you told me you thought we needed a divorce. You believed every one of them too easily, but then you could not believe me when I told you they were prompted by temper and hurt, not truth. I had been too negligent as a husband and had convinced you too strongly of my lack of feelings for you to easily believe I have them for you now. I did not realize any of this until it was too late."

"Too late?"

"I woke up to many things too late." The sadness in his voice was too real, too deep to ignore.

He really did love her. He hadn't realized it and in typical Claudio fashion, had been intent on not being controlled by his emotions. But he realized it now and he was hurting.

Just as she had been hurting.

She felt like his agony was inside her own heart. And conversely, she thought that if she asked…he would say he could also feel the pain that had been causing more internal hemorrhaging inside her than the endometriosis. Because he loved her and her pain was his pain.

The evidence had been there all along, but she'd attributed every motive under the sun except the true one…that he loved her.

She turned on her side to face him fully and reached up to press the button above their bed that turned on dim lights. They cast a golden glow over his features, revealing glittery dark orbs and telltale wetness on his temple.

She reached out and touched it, unable to believe that he was crying for her. Men like Claudio did not cry. Not ever.

"It isn't too late," she whispered.

The big body curled so protectively around hers went rigid, his gorgeous face contorted with a hope it was painful for her to see. "It is not?"

"No."

"Wha…" He swallowed and took a deep breath and then let it out. "What exactly are you trying to say here?"

"I wondered what made Danette so special…why she could be loved by her parents, by Marcello, but I was destined not to be loved by the people that mattered most to me."

"Danette is special, but, Therese…to me you are infinitely more precious. I do love you and I will spend the rest of my life proving it. Your parents are two rather stupid people."

"They aren't. They're both very smart."

"Not when it comes to love. You are incredible and to have you in my life is my greatest blessing. That they could not recognize that very thing makes them idiots."

"You didn't recognize it as first…"

"I did, but I did not label the feelings you evoked in me love because to my mind that made me dangerously vulnerable."

"Like your father."

"*Sì.*"

"We all learn things from our parents."

"But we can unlearn them, too. I have. I love you, Therese, and that does not make me a fool or weak. It gives me strength and it fills me with pleasure when I think of one day sharing that love with you. And we will, Therese. Because even if you won't tell me what it is my brothers do, I will figure it out and I will do it and you will know you are loved."

"You want to stay married to me even if it means not having your own son inherit the throne of Isole dei Re."

"*Sì.* This is true. You finally believe me?"

"Oh, I believe you…" And the belief was making her giddy. "I love you, Claudio. Yesterday, today and forever."

The hand curled around her hip convulsed, grabbing her in an almost painful grip. "You can't."

"I can and I do." She took her own deep breath and then plunged into a pool she had never swum in before. "I believe you love me, too. I really do."

"I do love you, my precious wife. I do. Thank God you believe me…thank God." He closed his eyes as if sending those thanks on the wings of angels and then opened them again. "From this point forward you will never again have cause to doubt it. I give you my word as a prince."

"I believe you," she said again, her heart burbling with a kind of happiness she had never known.

He leaned forward and kissed her. It was the most poignant meeting of their lips they had ever known, for it affirmed in a wholly nonsexual way that they were two halves of one whole. Always.

EPILOGUE

THE surgery was a complete success and, miraculously, so was the IVF procedure performed two months later. Therese's doctor was shocked it had worked on the first try, but she wasn't. After discovering Claudio loved her as she loved him, she didn't find it all that difficult to believe in miracles anymore.

Her pregnancy was confirmed on the eve of Flavia and King Vincente's wedding. The entire family rejoiced and were still rejoicing seven and a half months later when she gave birth to triplets, one girl and two boys. Although the babies were slightly premature and tiny, they were healthy and strong.

Their daughter was the oldest and when King Vincente laid his hand on her head and confirmed the right of progenitor, Therese almost fainted.

"I thought only males could inherit the throne."

"Where did you get that archaic idea?" Claudio asked with a laugh. "Just because Scorsolini babies are almost always male, that does not mean we do not allow our daughters to inherit. We are a modern royal family…I keep telling you that."

"But…you always talked about your nephew inheriting."

"He's the oldest."

"Oh. So, she's going to be a queen?"

"Just like her mama. Yes."

Therese grinned, exhausted from the delivery, but happier than she'd ever been. "It wouldn't have mattered. I would have loved her the same anyway."

"Of course you would…our children will know nothing but love from us all the days of their lives."

She smiled, her heart so filled with joy that some days she did not know if she could hold it all in. He'd been showing her his love in ways she could never mistake. He'd started with allowing his brothers to share more of the burden of leadership while his father was convalescing so he could oversee her return to health with minute attention.

He even stayed in the hospital with her and the tabloids had a heyday with it. Some poking fun, but most saying that it was obvious this royal family did not stick with the tradition of marrying for convenience. He had made huge inroads into spending more time together all the time and now when he traveled, she went with him.

Even when she'd been pregnant.

She reached out and took his hand, loving the feel of his long, strong fingers intertwined with hers. "I happen to know you are an expert at giving love, I have no doubts our children will know nothing but an abundance of that commodity from you."

He grinned down at her.

And King Vincente smiled at them both. "The Scorsolini men are very lucky…we must raise my grandchildren to know the blessing of love the Scorsolinis are known for."

Remembering the curse the king used to believe it was, Therese felt tears fill her eyes. "We'll make sure they know the blessing of love, Papa."

And they did…all the days of their lives.

millsandboon.co.uk Community

Join Us!

The Community is the perfect place to meet and chat to kindred spirits who love books and reading as much as you do, but it's also the place to:

- **Get the inside scoop from authors about their latest books**
- **Learn how to write a romance book with advice from our editors**
- **Help us to continue publishing the best in women's fiction**
- **Share your thoughts on the books we publish**
- **Befriend other users**

Forums: Interact with each other as well as authors, editors and a whole host of other users worldwide.

Blogs: Every registered community member has their own blog to tell the world what they're up to and what's on their mind.

Book Challenge: We're aiming to read 5,000 books and have joined forces with The Reading Agency in our inaugural Book Challenge.

Profile Page: Showcase yourself and keep a record of your recent community activity.

Social Networking: We've added buttons at the end of every post to share via digg, Facebook, Google, Yahoo, Technorati and de.licio.us.

www.millsandboon.co.uk

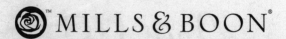